THE

END

A Novel
By

Timothy Brannan

Cover: Background photograph by Timothy Brannan

Other Works by Timothy Brannan

Shards of the Urn
Ho'okele: The Navigator
TEARS OF ALLAH
TEACH
Into the Elephant Grass
Adventures in Another Paradise
'74: A Basketball Story

Suggested Music for
THE END

1. *All Along the Watchtower*, Bob Dylan (performed by Jimi Hendrix)
2. *Star-Spangled Banner*, Francis Scott Key (performed by Jimi Hendrix)
3. *A Day in the Life*, John Lennon & Paul McCartney
4. *Devil with the Blue Dress On*, Mitch Ryder & the Detroit Wheels
5. *Give Peace a Chance*, John Lennon
6. *It's Alright Ma . . . .*, Bob Dylan
7. *Star-Spangled Banner*, Francis Scott Key (performed by Jimi Hendrix)
8. *Someday: Prologue, August 29, 1968*, Chicago
9. *I'm so Tired*, John Lennon & Paul McCartney
10. *Sympathy for the Devil*, Rolling Stones
11. *All Along the Watchtower*, Bob Dylan (performed by Bob Dylan)
12. *Can't find My Way Home*, Blind Faith
13. *A Hard Rain's A-Gonna Fall*, Bob Dylan
14. *Don't let me down*, John Lennon & Paul McCartney
15. *White Rabbit*, Jefferson Airplane
16. *Awaiting on You All*, George Harrison
17. *Hey, Jude*, John Lennon & Paul McCartney
18. *Purple Haze*, Jimi Hendrix
19. *Sounds Of Silence*, Paul Simon
20. *The End*, Jim Morrison & The Doors

BOOK I

"There must be some kinda way outta here,"
said the joker to the thief
"There's too much confusion, I can't get no relief
Businessmen, they drink my wine,
Plowmen dig my earth
None of them along the line
Know what any of it is worth"

"No reason to get excited,"
The thief, he finally spoke.
"There are many here among us
Who feel that life is but a joke
But you and I, we've been through that,
And this is not our fate
So let us not talk falsely now,
The hour is getting late.

All along the watchtower,
Princes kept the view
While all the women came and went,
Barefoot servants, too.

Outside in the cold distance
A wildcat did growl
Two riders were approaching, and
The wind began to howl.
"All Along the Watchtower," Bob Dylan

Part One

THE WAY THAT CAN BE NAMED
IS NOT THE WAY

Tao Te Ching

GOD

ZO

Matthew Parkrow started from his nap in the saddle. Sand blasted planks creaked on rusting nails in the wind blowing up from Mexico. There was the promise of rain in those clouds scattering from twin mesas in the east toward the sun. He squinted at the crumbling placard tacked to a fir framing stud driven into the sand by a workman twenty-four years before. Matthew reined in the bay quarter horse from Hickock's Livery. He patted the gelding's neck as it snorted and pranced nervously beneath him. "Easy, Rocinante. It's just the wind." Matthew dismounted and led the gelding toward the padlocked gate in front of the sign. It was the only entrance through the jagged link fence surrounding what was left of Project Manhattan.

GODZO.

The other letters sand covered. The parched stud was splintering in the center from the years of pelting sand. Staleness of rain not falling swept past on another Santa Ana gust from the southwest. From below the Rio Grande, you could almost smell the enchiladas stuffed with chunks of cilantro and cumin spiced chicken still clinging to the bone. Slamming kitchen doors, the wind whirled north toward Gallup. The bay pawed at scrub grass growing around the edges of the fence that squeaked from the years of exposure in this corrosive desert. Matthew buttoned his denim jacket over his work shirt. Inside his jeans watch pocket, his left hand found the coiled strand of leather. He pulled it out, looped it around his black curls as they flopped in the wind and tied the leather strip around his head.

GODZO.

After tethering Rocinante to his left ankle, he squatted in front of the corroding lock. He brushed graphite-like dust from around the padlock tumbler. A sunburst of gouges surrounded it like the Military Intelligence insignia, like his court martial. With the Swiss Army knife he had carried since he took his first oath as a Cub Scout, he jimmied the lock in a matter of seconds. That the lock had been forced many times before made it that much easier. In fact, he was a little surprised that the gate was locked at all after so much time had passed. He shoved the gate inward, untethered the bay and led him through. "Cheeh, boy. Come on, boy." Desert wind, dry as the sand it whirled at the wooden sign, howled. No rain left in those clouds.

GODZO.

Opie Openheimer had code named it Trinity.

"So, this is where we were born?" Matthew turned, closed the gate, and slid the open lock back into place. "We could've all been blown to hell that day. Instead, it was merely another explosion. Only this explosion was eight thousand feet up and five thousand two hundred and eighty feet out." Under the emerald mushroom, Oppenheimer, Bainbridge, Kistiskowsky, and Greisen shrieked the *Los Alamos Blues* and leaped in primordial dances to celebrate the fires of hell with which they had just vitiated the desert morning darkness.

Now I am become Death, the destroyer of worlds.

Four weeks later, eyes dribbled from sockets, singeing stunned cheeks in Hiroshima . . . then Nagasaki . . . .

"Easy, Rocinante . . . easy now." Matthew stroked the fidgeting gelding's neck as they approached the disintegrating skeleton of an outhouse sprawled on its side near the observation blockhouse. According to Hickock, Rocinante was one of a dwindling number of Spanish Mustangs that descended directly from the horses of the Conquistadors. "No dancers celebrating our birth today, huh boy?

Just you and me and that armadillo over there. Is that what spooked you? Hell, while we were waiting to go to the Nam, we used to chase them on the tank course at Fort Hood, flying across the prairie in front of a rooster trail of jeep dust. When you got real close to one, it would roll up into a ball." Nothing else to do but get ripped and play softball with the armadillos at night in the spring. Waiting.

GODZO.

The armadillo scurried through scrub brush behind the outhouse toward four eroding concrete pillars which had once held the steel tower where the throbbing prick had dangled above vagina earth. *A shudder in the loins engenders there the broken wall, the burning roof and tower and Agamemnon dead.* No armadillos rolled themselves up into impenetrable balls. No prairie dogs scurried. No rattlers rattled. The antelope fled. Matthew lashed the reins to the outhouse door hinges. The door itself was gone. All the doors were gone to the outhouse, to the ranch house, to the blockhouse, to the Skinner maze instrument bunkers.

Just like it said in *Esquire*: "*Alamogordo, Mon Amour.*" The twentieth century Gordian knot, its doors torn from their hinges for souvenirs or firewood when—surrounded by the incense of memories—the yearly pilgrims gathered on the Sunday nearest July 16 to commemorate the creation of their age, their era, their generation. The town of Gallup, New Mexico had reported tremors and windows rattling like snake tails that day. Cordoned off by Army evacuation forces in case the wind shifted during the test, Carrizozo, a town unaware of its real peril, thought Judgment Day was at hand. Thousands applied to Bomb Shelters, Inc. They would pioneer a new market. Millions flocked to the churches. The churches said: "A million American lives were saved. Praise God! From whom all blessings flow." Still confused by Hiroshima and numb from Nagasaki, the Japanese surrendered on the U.S.S. Missouri. General MacArthur's voice broke: "These proceedings are completed." The pilgrims bowed their heads: "Praise God! From whom all blessings flow . . . ."

GODZO.

Sand swirled as Matthew pulled the leather strap through the lock loops. Opening the left saddlebag was like opening a time capsule fashioned out of fresh cowhide. In the bag, his left hand felt the rough sides enclosing a six-inch iron skillet, one box of Ohio Blue Tip matches, a ballpoint pen, his journal, the most recent *Rolling Stone* he had picked up at the train station, a new Rand McNally atlas he had lifted from his father's Continental before sneaking off without eating breakfast or saying good-bye last Christmas, an aerial photo map of the missile range and adjacent areas he had salvaged from his aborted military days, a small match box holding his stash, his crisp new parchment attesting to the world his mastery over literature and the English language, six full cartridge boxes, a paperback copy of the *Tao*, and some fuzzy thick rope . . . .

"I'll need some hobbles for that horse you rented me," he had reminded the hardware salesman in Hickock's Livery & Hardware two blocks north of Don Amerika's Gun Shop. Hickock squinted at him from under scar tissue lumped over his dull green eyes like make-up putty as he stacked gallon cans of Spread Satin outside white.

"For your hoss, hoss?" His words poured down steel chutes into forms for driveways, sidewalks, patios overlooking the vast desert beauty. "Don't carry such ready-tied." He scratched his bald head as if he had a full head of hair growing on it. "Got some good, strong rope though. You can tie 'em yourself. The hobbles." While he muttered, he walked to the end of the plywood paint counter in the rear of the creaking wood store, extracted a spool of rope from the top shelf behind the counter and lugged it back to where Matthew was popping his knuckles, waiting. "I'll show you how to tie 'em, hoss. Used to be a mustanger myself . . . tied millions of 'em . . . ." As an afterthought he added. "No charge, of course, for the lesson."

As Hickock smiled, Matthew stared at his withered gums. The boxer once. Turpentine and nails and rope remained to remind him every day of that red sash once girded around his head, a sword swishing the air in his right hand. Some have been bred down in the hips so much for show that they can bear pups only through cesarean section. Dysphasia. Or bulldogs. Some dogs tenacious. Probably got his windpipe busted a few times as well as his African elephant ears. Matthew nodded again or had he nodded the first time? He paid Picasso of the hobbles for the rope and left, both of them shaking their heads.

GODZO.

Matthew hobbled the bay's front legs, fed him a few cubes of sugar fetched from his denim jacket pockets. "Be easy, fella. It's just the wind." The bay whinnied, then stood quiet, munching the sugar cubes. The wind was voices. Voices of past pilgrims: "Praise him all creatures here below . . . ."

"Be back soon, Rocinante." Matthew patted the horse's neck. His boots squeaked in the sand as he followed the armadillo's path through the scrub brush to where the twenty-five-foot vagina lay covered by billowing sand under the hundred-foot steel tower that vanished in the fireball. Bites of trinitite nestled in sand like emeralds in a thief's hand, the remaining evidence of that conflagration. At twenty-four, the crater still bore the stretch marks of the rough beast born out of its belly and of the many pilgrims, some of whom had left a generator propped against one of the pillars, a rusting sacrifice: "May the Lord bless you and keep you and make his face to shine upon you . . . ." A chill in the dry rot wind, then olfactory vacuum.

The rain clouds had passed with the shifting of the wind. Now, they were streaming across the sun, wound red and sliding toward Japan. It would soon be too dark to make camp. He knew he had to get out of White Sands before dark. According to his intel, the area was still sometimes patrolled at night. Wouldn't be a very good idea to stay anyway. Probably still a little hot even now. Should've brought a slide rule, a protractor, a calculator, a Geiger counter . . . . Excalibur.

GODZO.

Matthew could still see the sculptured hollows that were Don Amerika's cheeks, the cascading yellow hair that was his neck, the Captain America outfit that was his skin as he rode his quarter horse across the desert away from the sunset and chain link fence toward the twin buttes two miles north of imploded concrete dugouts which surrounded the perimeter. The soiled Winchester slung on the right side of his saddle bumped in two-four time in its rawhide sheath as Rocinante trotted through wild sand in their faces. When the first shock waves shot across the desert, a herd of antelope, grazing on those same buttes, had vanished in a crazed stampede into Mexico. Desert shifted to prairie, advancing toward the Sacramento Mountains.

Receding, Trinity and the wrecked rigging tower. A sculpture twisted from three hundred feet of melting steel hunched against the earth like a person worshipping or cowering. Spattered about the blackened tower, eruptions of blood brown dirt. Headless observers. Tomorrow he'd try to wangle a closer look at those silos towering to the south like tusks in an elephant grave yard, a place bulging with fruit from this withering harvest. But, they don't like us to know we've become strontium 90. Beta. Cesium 137. Cobalt 60. Europium 152. Gamma. Jade air absent of smell with a musty texture.

The pilgrim wind: "God our help in ages past, our hope for years to come, our shelter from the stormy blast."

Deceiver.

"Remember the rickety wooden guard tower at the rear of the compound on Pham Nu Lau Street. It would sway in the monsoon winds blowing the moon from Saigon toward Cambodia and Laos?" He patted the horses' flank. "Remember how we always hoped for rain during our guard?" Rain seemed to keep the F111 size mosquitoes grounded in the saw grass marshes that strangled the banks of the tributary of the Saigon River running under the Bien Hoa Highway bridge.

"It's time for you to drive Ward to the airstrip." Sergeant Smiley's frog voice echoed off of the low panel walls which divided the stone warehouse into offices. Ward Who? Ward Crampton, his best friend from childhood, flying into the Iron Triangle. Ward: chopper downed beyond our outer perimeter. Four guards saw the fireball of the crash. MIA. Presumed dead. Everything a blur . . . b.

Matthew clucked his tongue. "Of course you don't remember, Rocinante." The bay dug his rear hooves into the crumbling sandstone slope and scrambled up and over a low ledge onto the top of twin mesas. Where the antelope once played seemed to have been ravaged by rhinos, napalm, white phosphorous, aldrin. No. None of these left a fine red powder. Oxidation: only the rust of years. In the center of this southernmost of the two mesas, a semi-circle of smutty stones squatted like an altar scorched from sacrifice. Someone had camped here before, many times before.

Won't get much of a fire going, though. Not a damn thing to burn out here but sage and radioactive outhouse planks. The sage burns too fast. Be lucky if I can cook my eggs while I try to keep warm in the serape Linda gave me.

Matthew touched his right saddlebag. Hope none of the eggs have been broken. Be a mess in there if they did. He dismounted a few feet from the foot-high crescent of rocks built against the prevailing winds from below Carlsbad Caverns and hobbled the bay.

"Got to scrounge something up for a fire, boy." Reaching behind his saddlebags and bedroll lashed behind the unscrolled, oil darkened saddle, he untied the burlap feed bag.

"This is the last of your oats, fella." Matthew whispered while he fitted the bag over the gelding's mouth and behind his ears. Bet Buzz Aldrin built a great fireplace after he collected his forty-eight-and-a-half pounds of dirt and rocks from the moon. He was flying around up there just anticipating the hell out of that landing. But, there's no wood on the moon either.

"Eat 'em up, fella. We'll both be living off of sugar and water by tomorrow unless we run up on some indigenous supplies."
GODZO.

Matthew struggled under an armload of split logs. He had found a cache under a ledge at the far end of the butte. Not simply left by some previous pilgrim. "Hardwood firewood . . . ." Matthew wagged his shaggy head, the black curls falling over his denim-covered shoulders, muttering to the wind. "Out here in the middle of the desert . . . ." Had to be somebody's main camp, he inferred. Still. He reeled across the mesa top to where the bay stood munching oats. Matthew paused, then stumbled the few steps further to the rock pile, dumping the wood into the red dust.

Maybe, like Colonel Flanger had warned, THEY are trailing me. Why would THEY plant firewood for me? Could that be true? Haven't felt really free since I was kicked out of the Army. But . . . . No fresh ashes either. No fresh tracks. Don Amerika was right about that spying shit, though. THEY want you to look under your bed and in your closets every night, before you retire. For now it was look for communists, but who knows what might come later. And, I do look every night, but for bugs . . . and I don't mean bed bugs or moths or any other kind of insect. Perhaps I should check out the sage brush and cacti, too, for listening devices.

The purple sky was cloudless now as his gray eyes pierced the twilight. In the west, the shrunken site appeared to be exactly what it was: White Sands Missile Range. As Matthew constructed a teepee of three logs over sagebrush and wood chips, he shivered. Even cold as it gets at night, this pile ought to be enough. He shoved more sage underneath the teepee and struck an Ohio Blue Tip with his thumbnail. He pushed its yellow flame into the sagebrush. The brush crackled and flared toward the sky where a few stars were beginning to cluster near Mercury. The communion wafer moon was climbing from behind the eastern horizon. The dry timber caught quickly. Sparks floated into the darkness of the adjoining butte: fire flies.

He scrambled eggs with his knife as they firmed at the edges in his iron skillet. The last of the dozen he bought from a Pueblo farmer the morning before. Soured a little in the heat of the saddlebags and the plastic bag that held them in a cardboard carton cradled and cushioned in Linda's serape. The quarter horse snorted, tried to paw at the sandstone ridge with hobbled hooves.

Something upwind. Rocinante senses it. Matthew thought he heard a coyote howl. No. None left out here. We did save millions of cows from their ravenous jaws by tempting them with strychnine baits until there were none left to tempt. Now scientists study their sacred-cow children that witnessed the blast for signs of radioactivity like Ward and I studied the five-legged black Brahma bull near Kuala Lumpur. We searched for stitches, graft scars, anything. There weren't any. Only a fifth leg, its hoof flopping alongside the Brahma's velvet hump. Brown skin showed in spots where the mutation had rubbed hair from the hump as the Brahma, pulling always at his leather tether, stomped in a muddy circle below the thousand-and-one crumbling stone steps hand cut into the mountain which led to the caves of darkness and light.

The dark cave, they say, runs from Malaysia to Thailand. Many have tried it only to never be heard from again, so the legends go. In the light cave: all those gods encased in glass. Couldn't take a photo without too much glare except where the cave's ceiling ruptured into a twenty-five-foot gash of topaz sky. The only vegetation in the cave was the ferns drooping from that hole toward the sandy floor and one sapling stretching from the rupture toward the ferns and the sun.

"The girls say we have to get back to town now if we're gonna make our R&R flight to Saigon, Matthew."

Seven days. Where had they gone? "Yeah, Ward. I'm coming." Matthew had snapped one last shot of a black figurine almost directly under the hole in the cave ceiling: god of fire and pestilence. Then, he shuffled across the sandy floor toward the luminous mouth of the cave where Ward was already helping their lovers for the week down the first of the mountain's thousand steps.

Tanya, Ward's girl, was from Morocco originally, and she was saying as Matthew approached: "Ward, if you ever be in Marrakech, go see my brother there. I give you name, address before you leave. He take good care of you if you say you know Tanya."

"Okay," Ward had chuckled, "but tell him not to hold his breath until he hears from me. Okay?"

Matthew had laughed with them as he caught up with them on about step nine-hundred-and-ninety and descending. The girls seemed puzzled by these crazy GIs who laughed on their way back to war.

After the blast at Alamogordo, nothing was left for over a mile. The towering steel pelvis disintegrated like that outhouse had, only its dissolving was instantaneous when its penis rammed home. Matthew pulled the pan from the fire as the eggs bubbled and hardened, almost too much.

After the stabbings at Altamont, there had been nothing much left either. He balanced the pan on the edge of the rocks and stumbled through flickering light and shadows being weaved by the fire as if they were on a loom to where his saddle sprawled in the red dust covering the only rock ledge to the east. Suddenly, he felt chilled. In his right saddle bag he located the serape . . . silver-and-turquoise thunderbirds decorating it . . . given to him by that eighteen-year-old vamp from Memphis.

"If I can't keep you here with me," Linda had whimpered while smothering him with her olive flesh, "then at least you won't forget me when you're wearing my favorite serape from Leon."

It had only been three weeks since Atlanta jam when he gave in to her entreaties and visited her in Memphis . . . not exactly a longhair's city . . . only four weeks since his orals at Columbia. He had met Linda Tallefero in the medical tent at the jam. That was fate. That he visited her in Memphis was a mistake. Matthew wrapped the serape around his shoulders as he shuffled back to the spark spitting fire. Eggs okay. Atlanta Jam could've been Atlanta crazy glue with his Egyptian vamp from Memphis who swore that computers could write books.

"You don't have to go to that place to write about it," she said, and maybe she was right. It was all mathematics anyway. Language: metaphorical mathematics.

"You're living in a dream of individuality, Matthew. Hot vaginas and fast computers . . . that's where it's at, baby!" Her writhing body almost burned him, it was so hot as she squeezed him clean again and again with a grunt and a smile.

"Can't you stay with me, Matthew, and keep my honey pot boiling? Please?"

The artist's tools become the computer program. If we reduce everything knowable to ones and zeroes, then there's simply nothing we can't understand, now is there?

Matthew popped the fork attachment out of his knife and wolfed the eggs from the still-sizzling skillet in six steaming slurps. Hummm. Pungent eggs ala campfire. An appropriate birthday dinner. "To the day the music died!" He placed the mescaline tab from Don Amerika's stash box on the back of his tongue. He could feel it beginning to dissolve even before he was able to take a swig of tepid canteen water. He drank the water anyway, washing what was left of the tab down his throat cleanly.

Just over twenty-four years before, President Harry S. Truman had received a coded message at the Potsdam Conference:

Babies satisfactorily born.

Fat Man . . . . Little Boy . . . .
Rocinante whinnied.
Nothing moved.
GOD ZO.

Part Two

THE WAY IS AN EMPTY VESSEL

Tao Te Ching

The letter had come by special courier to the Quonset hut inside the perimeter patrolled by mounted Capitol Hill Police that Matthew and Kip Klopps called home in those days of confrontation. The Military Intelligence Mobile Van that acted as their base of operations was only a short walk from the Quonset hut and Tent City serving as temporary quarters for the military security forces deployed to protect the Pentagon.

OFFICE OF THE MAYOR
CITY HALL
ROANOKE PARK, N.C.

October 17, 1967

SSG Matthew Parkrow
Permanent Party
Fort Holabird, Maryland

Dear Son:

I hear you've been selected as part of the security forces for when them radical hippie communists march on Washington in a few days. A real switch from those other marches you made back when you were still a kid in college. You marched <u>with</u> them, then. But, that was before you put away childish things. Now we're all right proud of your service, Matthew. Proud that you didn't run off to Canada or desert to Sweden or go off to federal prison like so many of your weirdo generation did. Traitors! I'm sorry, son, but I just don't understand what's happened to your generation of young men. When I was your age, The War was in full swing, and I knew what I had to do for my country. I had to help Uncle Sam kick the shit out of Hirohito and Hitler. And, believe you me we didn't hold back on our duty. We went at that fighting with a vengeance. You haven't held back either, Matthew, like so many of the shaggy bastards have. Jail or exile's too damned good for them if you ask me.

I guess you must've read by now that Roanoke Park has another four years of "Progress with Parkrow." Thanks to you, son, and all your medals, I got re-elected by a landslide. I know we've had our differences over the years, but they've been only political, not fundamental. And God's been good to us, son. If only you would come back to your senses about that and quit seeing His practical jokes in every corner. You carry around your guilt like you used to carry around that black Duke Snider bat, you know, the one with the silver lettering that I gave you for your fifteenth birthday when you made the high school team. You used to sleep with it on nights before a big game, even when you were a big deal senior.

Damn! Before you took that step forward to join the Army, the proudest day of my life was in the state championship game when you hit that grand slam against them citified fools from Raleigh with their airs and education. Except, maybe, for the day when you and Ward Crampton signed with the State University. The best damned double play combination in the whole damned state. Damn!

Alecia told me how Ward became missing in action, about you driving him to that Bien Hoa air base and all, and about seeing that he got on that helicopter on time. Listen, son, you can't carry around all that guilt inside you for something you never could have done anything about anyway. Hell, Ward Crampton might have been court martialed or worse—if there could be anything worse—if you hadn't gotten him up that fateful morning and driven him to the air base like any good buddy would've. How could you have known that he'd get shot down by a VC rocket? Well, at least Ward is still officially MIA. Where there's no death certificate, there's still hope, son.

Remember how all those reporters flashed pictures and questions at you all because you didn't sign with the pros like poor, dead Turkey Locklear? Some say he didn't even get a chance to cash his bonus check. The way his mother tells it, only a few days passed after he signed before he died of lymph gland cancer. Nobody even knew before that! His mother also tells me that the day after Ward's mother shot herself with the twelve gauge Henderson had given to Ward for Christmas a few years back—you remember it don't you? The one with the persimmon inlaid stock . . . a beautiful shotgun.—Anyway, the day after she blew her face off in her front yard under that American flag they always had flying—then it was at half-mast for Ward—Henderson came home from a medical convention in New York with this story that a young man who could be Ward's twin was working as a waiter part time in some restaurant near Columbia University. Well, after Ida's funeral, Henderson flew straight back to New York to find out for himself. Naomi Locklear says he found that restaurant, but when he asked the owner about Ward and showed him a picture, the radical-looking bastard with a Garfinkle African hairdo said, "No, man. He's never been in here, man. Never worked here, man." How did he know? Henderson had asked. "I memorize every face that comes through my doors, man. Even yours, man. How else would I know, man?" Henderson told Naomi that the boy was downright rude. Those Yankees got no raising. Everybody knows that.

I wanted to surprise you with that news. You'll be real interested in who Henderson got the story from. And probably very surprised! Just come home for a short visit, son, and I'll tell you where the restaurant is and who told Henderson about it.

It's been months since Alecia told me how you were "just passing through" while on leave from Vietnam before going back to Fort Holabird. She says you only stayed long enough to go to Oakwood and put petunias on your Mother's grave. It's not your fault that your Mother died when you were born, either, even though you seem to think it somehow is. You weren't any more responsible for your Mother's death than you were for Ward's.

Alecia told me that you're finally going to be a teacher, an intelligence instructor at the Army Intelligence School. But Alecia told me also that there was not a word for me. Matthew, don't shut your father out, son. After all, we're the same flesh and blood. All that's left of it is in your veins. I'll put some flowers on Estelle's grave for you and me. Next time you're home, maybe we can visit her together like we used to back in the old days. Okay?

Oh well. Did I say I'm as proud of you as I was when you hit that grand slam against the Raleigh Caps in '63? Well, son, I am! Guarding the Pentagon. Damn!

May God bless you and keep you safe from the commie radical hippie queers.

Sincerely,

Jason Parkrow
Mayor

Matthew refolded the letter along already-tearing creases and stuck the six pages of stationery into his starched jungle fatigue blouse pocket. Poor man. Jason had been measuring him against that three-hundred-and-thirty-foot home run ever since he hit it. He had tried to tell his father, even then, that it was a foul ball, that the umps didn't see it or didn't call it for some reason. But Jason had given him the same song and dance that Ward had. If it had really been a foul ball, then why didn't one of the three best high school umps in the entire state of North Carolina call it?

Matthew had no answer for that question then. He didn't have an answer to that question now. But, he knew what he knew. After all, the ball was off his bat. No one else's. It was a foul ball. Not that he complained all that much about it at the time. After all, that grand slam had made him the big hero of the year. It had helped land him a grant-in-aid to State. More importantly, though, it had been an invaluable lesson in life. An *entelechy* kōan regarding actuality as opposed to reality. The grand slam had actually been a foul ball. But, as the result of a missed call, it became, in reality, the game winning home run for the state baseball championship.

He glanced at the date on his Seiko watch: OCT 21. "How the hell did Jason know four days ago who the security personnel for the Washington anti-war march would be?" he muttered. That had been "Eyes Only" Top Secret shit! He remembered what his roommate Kip Klopps had said earlier when he'd asked him the same question. "It's a club thing, man. You know, all those hot shot elected officials are in it. The Tri-Lateral Commission or some such shit. They tell each other everything, you know?"

In his periphery, Matthew spotted Colonel Otis Flanger striding past the row of jeeps, troop transport trucks (not so affectionately known as cattle cars to GI's), and operations vans along the ridge. His crisp cadence carried him toward their special MI mobile van with a sense of purpose reserved only for those men who, like Jason, approached everything in a self-righteous vacuum. Matthew, Specialist Five Donaldson, and Buck Sergeant Kip Klopps manned Colonel Flanger's intelligence van and comprised his primary instructor cadre. The van was Flanger's pride and passion, the training innovation he'd been working for. On the scene practice. An on the scene model for students.

Flanger had been touring troops through since six hundred hours yesterday morning. They were from the school at Fort Holabird where Matthew and the other van personnel were instructors, so he knew most of them. At least, he knew their faces. He even taught some of them in his present "Order of Battle" and "Surreptitious Entry and Surveillance" courses. Eddie Donaldson instructed classes in materials classification and handling of classified materials, and Kip taught imagery interpretation.

Each was a citizen soldier filling in the last days on his "Short Timer's Calendar" in magic marker and grease pencil colors. Matthew colored in days sixty-four and sixty-five with a blue grease pencil on his photocopy of the calendar which he had duct-taped to the inside front cover of his olive drab notebook. There he stored his lesson plans, lecture notes, and his personal diary entries and comments.

Damn! He couldn't believe that he might actually have a lead on Ward after all this time. But, it was through Jason. Did he really want to go back to Jason's house only to find out about what was probably just another wild goose chase? Could he abide his father's rattle, prattle, and chattel?

With the same grease pencil, he entered the Julian date 67294 into the Daily Log and marked a big blue X at the Washington Monument where—according to the latest aerial reconnaissance photos and intelligence summaries—the tribe had gathered for today's march on the Pentagon.

The last time they had gathered like this was in sixty-five for the "I have a dream" march. He'd been a senior at State University then. An ex All-American second baseman after he quit the team to become one of the tribe. Not one of the pigs like now. He'd given up his grant-in-aid in protest of a war he later fought. He still did not have an answer to that contradiction or the feeling that a part of him was still out there with them, even now. And, he also knew that he was already so short that he needed a hand up to get over the threshold of their Quonset hut door each morning. He only had thirty-five days left. Short!

"Great infra-reds!" Klopps chuckled as he attempted to hand some photos directly to Matthew and by-pass Donaldson's tight-assed classification syndrome.

Donaldson snatched the blurred shots of heat mass before Matthew could reach them. He slapped them onto his desk, protecting them from Klopps and Parkrow with hunched shoulders turned away from their only potential avenue of attack—from behind his desk and to his left. Like a dog sniffing out a place to piss, Donaldson perused the infrared photographs, first under various magnifying glasses, then under a stereoscope. "These are, most definitely, shots of the gathering storm. These must be classified SECRET!"

"Christ, Donaldson!" Klopps stomped back toward his desk and developing lab in the dark rear corner of the van, shaking his skinned blond head and muttering loud enough for anyone to hear. "On what fucking basis, Donaldson? On what fucking basis, man?"

"Kiiip! Come on, now. These photos deal with enemy troop movements. Regulations require that they be classified accordingly."

"They're pictures of fucking heat masses rising from the fucking pavement, for Christ sake!" Klopps howled from his dark corner. "If that's the 'gathering storm', Donaldson, I'll kiss your fucking ass. And, believe me, man, I don't want to kiss your fat ass."

Colonel Flanger's spit shined boots hit the first metal step at the van door. "Ten hut!" Matthew bellowed out the command like his Drill Sergeant in basic training used to do it and probably still did. Flanger was pretty gung-ho about that kind of shit. He liked loud commands, snappy salutes, and starched, pressed fatigues. So give them to him for the next thirty-five days and counting. Why not? Short!

"Good morning, gentlemen." He popped a limp-wrist salute toward Matthew, his senior NCO, as he crossed the threshold. He was right proud of Staff Sergeant Parkrow. Almost like the son he'd lost in Nam.

Matthew's salute was crisp and not the least bit limp-wrist. He noted with some humor that the Colonel didn't seem to need any help getting over the threshold. He sure as hell wasn't short. He was in for life. Matthew fought back a chuckle. "Good morning, Colonel Flanger, sir!" Must maintain decorum, act out the scene according to the rules and regulations, even classifying Donaldson's photos of heat waves if that was what it took. Play the role scripted for him even if it didn't suit him. Only thirty-five days left. Short!

"Good morning, sir," Donaldson muttered.

In the shadows of his corner, Klopps nodded, then turned back to his developing pans to process the last of the early morning shots just delivered by special courier only minutes before from their photo recon unit.

"Continue to march, men." Flanger fumbled in his fatigue pockets for a match to light the cheroot he perpetually chewed from the right side of his mouth. As he found matches and lit the cigar, he continued. "Don't let me get in the way of operations here, Staff Sergeant. I'm just checking things out before bringing through the next batch of students for a tour." He swaggered around the fifteen-by-twenty-five-foot confines of the van, peeking at photographs hanging from clothes pins on a piece of line strung across the lighter corner near the door. He poked through messages and intelligence reports, shuffled papers on Donaldson's desk. Klopps followed him at a safe three pace distance, whispering something to the Colonel which actually made him cackle. Flanger turned back toward the front of the van where Matthew stood at ease. "Staff Sergeant Parkrow. I want to compliment you and your men for the way you've handled these tours." He paused, and the silence could have been spelled "b u t."

"Thank you, sir."

He motioned to Matthew. "Can you come back here for a moment?"

"Yes, sir." Matthew skirted Donaldson's inquiry-twisted face and his swivel chair—the only one in the van. He clomped over the metal floor to the dark room corner where Klopps and Flanger stood hunched over Kip's desk. They whispered and chuckled like a couple of school kids while they waited for something to finish in the final wash pan. It was time's like these when Matthew wished that he'd extended in Vietnam—bad as it was at times—forever, if necessary. He just couldn't get into the stateside Army life, the spit-and-polish bullshit, gawks from his civilian peers on the streets when he walked by in his uniform and his Flanger-required sidewall haircut. He was their enemy, now, just because he wore the Army green and short hair. Soon, he hoped, they would learn how many brothers were in the military just like himself.

"Sir?" Matthew leaned down, glancing over their shoulders at the clarifying photograph in the tray. A copy of one of the infra-reds that Donaldson wanted to classify SECRET. Flanger pointed to the slick paper with its heat zones becoming more visible as the seconds plodded. "This is what Donaldson wants to classify SECRET?" As he whispered his question, smoke from his cheroot puffed from the corners of his mouth like steam from under a locomotive in an Arthur Penn western.

Matthew attempted to hold back the mounting laughter, but he couldn't hide the giggles in his eyes as they both glanced around at Donaldson. "Yes, sir. I'm afraid so, sir. Night infra-red heat mass shots of traffic passing the Washington Monument, sir."

"Is that how you read them, Sergeant Klopps?"

"Obviously so, sir. I've got kids in my class who wouldn't fuck that up, sir."

"Are you sure, Staff Sergeant Parkrow, that this character's actually experienced?" Flanger's mouth continued to bellow smoke as he talked.

"Well, sir. His Military 201 File says that he trained at Holabird in sixty-six. That's the same year that Sergeant Klopps and myself trained there. He spent a tour in the Nam, Colonel, as an imagery interpreter for some MI unit out of Nha Trang."

"Did either of you . . . ." Flanger's beady black eyes darted back and forth, conspiratorially, from Matthew to Kip. "Did either of you know this character, Donaldson, before? At Holabird? In Nam?"

They both shook their heads.

"So it seems he just appeared out of nowhere." Flanger's eyes rolled in their oversized sockets as his thin blue lips chewed the cheroot that had gone out as usual after a few puffs. "Then, for all we know, my information that he's CID or something like that, could very well prove correct? His 201 file might well be a complete and clever fiction."

Klopps eyed his NCO-in-charge and his closest friend in the Army world. "I don't know, sir. What do you think, Matthew, ah, Staff Sergeant Parkrow?"

Matthew shrugged. "Beats me, sir." He wasn't going to get involved unnecessarily in Flanger's military-bound paranoia about being spied upon from within constantly. He knew that MI planted spies in the local bars on Holabird Avenue and Dundalk Avenue as well as on "The Block" to keep eyes and ears out for young recruits suffering from diarrhea of the mouth. So, it wouldn't be any surprise at all if everyone in the fucking van except for him was CID or CIA or GKW (God-Knows-What). Probably, even Kip. But. If you can't take a joke, fuck it! Thirty-five days until it all ends.

"I wonder." Flanger draped his starched jungle fatigue bloused arms over their shoulders. "I wonder if there is some way to, ah, shall we say get him to transfer out of Fort Holabird?" He coughed around his cheroot stub. "Just as a precautionary measure, of course."

"All I know, sir, is that if he is undercover like your sources say, then he isn't going anywhere very easily."

"Well, I must tell you, gentlemen, that he has been the only black mark on our van tours. The students don't seem to like him for some reason. They think he's dinky dao." Otis Flanger thumped the residue of cigar ashes into the classified burn can under the plywood counter which held Kip's developing trays as if for emphasis. "Maybe he is crazy, and that alone makes him a big threat to me and to my plans. Not even counting if he really is CID or whatever."

"Maybe he'll defect to the hippies, sir."

"Christ, Kip!" Matthew could no longer resist. "Don't hold your fucking breath! Donaldson's the most reactionary fucker I ever knew. He'd never do anything like that, especially if he really is an agent sent to spy on the Colonel."

Flanger smirked. "That's not a bad idea, though, Sergeant Klopps." He glanced over his left shoulder at Donaldson huddled over his desk rearranging the piles of reports, messages, photographs, maps, hand scribbled notes from Parkrow, Klopps, and officials inside the Pentagon down and off to their left. "Not bad at all."

The sun was just seeping through the door. Another brittle October morning snapped to life, languid as the Colonel's strides out of the dark corner of the van toward the light, his arms still wrapped around Klopps and Parkrow pulling them along with him. Matthew's eyes followed the Colonel, finally resting on Donaldson's red flat-top glazed with pomade he'd obviously hoarded from the fifties. It sparkled in a shaft of the sunlight now streaming through the door while he continued to shuffle through documents on his desk as though he were really busy instead of classifying nothing as he strained to hear their whispered conversation.

"If we could pull this off, gentlemen, well . . . ." He stifled what appeared to have almost been a shriek of glee. He turned toward Klopps, grinning, and released them both from the grip of his arms. Then, he motioned for Matthew to follow him outside.

Poor Donaldson, poor stupid bastard. Matthew shook his head as he followed Flanger to the van door and the sunrise, remembering the day that Brian Epstein died and their own private wake in Baltimore.

"I read the news today, oh boy . . ." wafted through the smoke and odors of beer and odors of beer and Philly

steak sandwiches smothered in grilled onions toward laminated plastic tables in the dim back room off of the main bar at the Holabird Inn. It was the only part of the traditional hang-out across from the main gate of Fort Holabird where battleship gray and OD green buildings could not stare at them as they sucked up their suds and slugged down their shots.

"Jesus, Donaldson!" Kip Klopps wagged his toe-head, then tossed off the dregs of his shot of vodka. He smacked his lips and sipped now tepid water as a chaser. It had been sitting there since breakfast. They had broken their fast with Bloody Mary's and screwdrivers over easy. "You mean to tell me that you still think we're all being spied on by the communists?" he smirked.

Matthew slumped on his elbows over his shot of Jack Daniels green label and the remaining half of an Iron City beer. He glared at the dancing red-white-and-blue spots in the Budweiser sign hanging from the pine paneled wall behind Donaldson who slugged down the last of his Schmidts beer like it was the very last of the Schmidts in all of Baltimore and perhaps all of the east coast which would probably make it all of the Schmidts anywhere. Matthew felt outside of himself like he was on acid, as if he were perched on the glittering sign watching them around the table. He felt like he had when he first came back from the Nam, like they all had, he guessed. He had felt a lot of distance . . . a lot of detachment.

Matthew sloshed down the shot of sour mash. His body shuddered. He didn't bother with the beer chaser. He had given up on that shortly after lunch—A Mai Tai and all the pretzels he could wolf down. Besides, he liked the after burn in his throat and stomach, especially on a night like this one when the rain drenching the Dundalk area stung like sleet. Best anti-freeze known to man. "Shit," he heard his numbing lips spit at Donaldson. "You still think Dana is one of those spying on us, don't you?"

Kip snatched Matthew's beer and gulped it. His face contorted. "Ugh!" He gyrated his head, rolling his slate eyes, and shoved the glass back at Matthew. "You can bet your ass, my good man, that your fucking beer, here, is about as palatable as Donaldson's fucking paranoia."

"Okay. Okay!" Donaldson's meaty fingers tore at the smoke above their heads. "You don't believe me? Watch this!" He glared at

Matthew and Kip. "Nurse! Help, nurse!" His hazel eyes dulled by beer and fumes that, at times, seem to be absorbing them instead of the other way around. "Soooo, you don' believe me, huh? Don' believe old Eagle-ears Donaldson, huh? Nurse!"

"Woke up; fell out of bed; dragged a comb across my head."

The blond toothpick, Dana, finally shuffled across the scuffed linoleum floor toward their table. It was her fate not only to look like Twiggy but to also have their table for the evening, for most evenings. "Watch this, goddamn it," Donaldson spluttered again. Dana bent beside him, touching his shoulders and pocked neck with her handfuls of heaven held in place loosely by a scant blue halter. "'Nother round here, Dana, if you please."

"Sure, Eddie, honey." She winked a blue eye at Kip and Matthew as she purred in Donaldson's pixie ear. They were her regulars. Eddie was an occasional tag-along. "Anything else you want, Eddie, honey?" She allowed her breasts to move just slightly along his shoulder.

Doanaldson's face flushed lavender in the iridescent lights filtering through the smoke. "W . . . what would you take for a Dana sandwich on clean sheets?" The baby fat that still clung to his jowls seemed to vibrate as he continued to redden and giggle.

Dana jerked up. "Why, I'm just plain insulted, Eddie Donaldson." Her scarecrow arms askew, her gaunt, child face portrayed shock. She adjusted her halter to show him more breast tops and hooked her thumbs in the belt loops of her bellbottom jeans.

"Mitch Ryder and the Detroit Wheels said it best," Kip gurgled. He ruffled Donaldson's flat top. "Oh, fuck," he muttered, wiping the pomade on Donaldson's own charcoal wool slacks.

"Yeah!" Matthew seemed to be returning to his body after that last shot had settled his stomach and his head. As he leaned toward Donaldson, both he and Kip bellowed in ragged harmony: "Devil with the blue dress on. Ah, devil with the . . . ah . . . blue . . . ah . .. *jeans* on."

"Well," Dana sighed against Donaldson's flabby cheek, affecting a Russian accent. "If you inzist on paying'k me, darling'k, maybe you can let'z me read one of your lit-tle training'k books or zomezhing'k. I'm juzt fazinated widz military men and zhings." She touched his chest hair curling up under his neck between the open collar of his powder blue Gant shirt left over from Jasper State College fraternity days. "But, really, I juzt vant to know more about you, honey." She grinned, winked again at the other two. "And your vork." Turning on the heels of her boots that were made for walking, she stomped back across the floor to the doorway, glancing over her shoulder once quickly as she disappeared through the opening into the main bar room.

"See!" Donaldson's red hair glistened. It seemed to collect smoke making it look almost silver. "What'd I tell you?"

"I read the news today, oh boy . . . ."

"No more!" Kip raised his hands in front of his face, then covered his ears. "Please, now Dana's a spy? Please, no more of this communist spy shit at the wake," he mumbled.

"Wake? What wake?"

"Jesus H., Donaldson. Where've you been all day?"

"In the midst of paranoia," Kip choked out between convulsions. He took another short hit of Matthew's stale beer. "Phew!"

"But, paranoia's okay, Eddie. It's a Nam disease. We all suffer from it, poor devils that we are. Some just seem to suffer from it more severely than others." Matthew also tasted the beer, with caution, rolled the swallow around in his mouth, smiling. "Warm is how the Aussies drink it, too. No wonder they call it piss."

"But?" Donaldson bleared through the smoky haze at, first, Matthew and, then, Kip, his face truly blank. "What wake?"

"We'll fill you in on everything. Again." Kip did not know or understand why Donaldson seemed to have them both trapped the way he did. But, he did know it, somehow, had something to do with that night a few months ago when they were stumbling from the trusty Inn. A yellow and tan lop-eared tom cat came up to Eddie and began rubbing against his leg and all and purring like the cat was in heat or something. Of course, they knew tom cats couldn't be in heat. They were only capable, like he and Matthew and, perhaps even Eddie, of being perpetually horny. As they stumbled into the treacherous boundaries of Holabird Avenue, the cat tried to follow. Eddie kept shooing him back to the curbing. Once they were safely on the fort side of the Avenue, they reeled off toward the front gate. The tom cat meowed and lurched into the street after them.

"Go back, Tom Cat!" Eddie had gurgled. "Go back!" He flailed his baby-fat arms at the cat in the road. The cat eluded a Ford pick-up, then a Honda 175 motorbike. "Go back, goddamn it, Tom Cat!"

Brakes squealed. A fifty-nine Buick with save the animals stickers all over it burned rubber for fifty feet or more to no avail. Thunk. Tom Cat's skull cracked like a coconut on the bumper of the Buick.

"Why didn't you go back?" Eddie wailed, his alcohol-dulled eyes transfixed on the spot where the cat jerked like a marionette controlled by a spasming hand. "Go back, please." He slumped to his knees on the concrete sidewalk, bawling. "Please."

"Nurse!" Matthew slumped back in his chair almost knocking it over as he moaned. "Nurse. Help! I'm returning to my body, and I'm soooo thirsty. Perched on that Bud sign over there, I didn't know what it was to be truly thirsty. But, I sure as hell know now that I'm back sitting in this fucking chair where thirst is a veritable way of life much like the Tao."

When Dana brought more drinks, she made change for Donaldson's ten in saran wrap silence until Matthew shoved four quarters across the table at her. "Play more songs for Brian Epstein, okay, Dana?"

"Sure, Matthew." She half-smiled.

"Whostein?"

"Epstein. Donaldson. Brian Epstein."

"We're having a wake for a Jew?"

"Yeah." Matthew tossed off half of his double Jack Daniels, blew through pursed lips which he smacked as he poured his new frosted glass full of chilled Iron City. "It's called a jakewee by us Micks."

Kip was nearly in tears he was laughing so hard.

"Next round's on the house, Matthew. Want me to go on and bring them now?"

"Sure, Dana. I, for one, am going to need it simply to get by." Matthew stumbled to his feet, pushed his plaid shirt tail back into his jeans, whistling along with the juke box: *Without a little help from my friends.*" As he reeled around Donaldson, he clawed at his beefy shoulder for support. Unwillingly, Matthew sunk his fingers into the thick folds of fat surrounding Eddie's shoulder blade. "It's a wake ritual. Drink. Piss. Drink. Piss. Drink, piss, drink." He lunged toward the back corner of the room, beyond the Budweiser sign still blinking red, blue, and white on the shellacked wall. "Brian Epstein's car hadn't moved all weekend. That was how suspicions were first aroused that he might be dead," Matthew hurled back at Donaldson over his shoulder.

This door handle doesn't pull. "Remember. Drink. Piss. Drink." He hurled the words over his shoulder at Donaldson like grenades. "This is the piss part." This door knob must not've moved all day long either. Poor, neglected bathroom door. It cannot be what it is unless we use it. "And, Donaldson. And, occasionally, drink, piss, sing!" Come on, Matthew. You're not cracking a safe in front of twenty students now. You're just opening the fucking latrine door. He grasped the brass knob with both hands. Ah ha! He turned it counterclockwise. "If you'll just open up this once, I promise to make more use of you later on." The knob turns!

The door rattled as he continued to push and pull. "I will no longer ignore you. I swear it!" He accidentally turned the knob the other way. The door flung open, bumping him against the wall. "Thank you, god of latrine doors. Thank you," he muttered as he stumbled to the urinal beside the single stall, unzipped his fly, pulled out his aching penis, and flung his hands above his head against the scrubbed black wall tiles. His head dangled between his shoulders above the porcelain urinal.

He shuddered with relief as he flooded the clear water with dark yellow urine. "Ah, first piss of the day!" Still had breakfast's Bloody Mary's stacked up for their exits like airplanes for landing at la Guardia, O'Hare, or Friendship. If I don't get completely fucked up sick this day, then I guess I never will. God, I pissed all the way through the never ending chord . . . . Matthew shoved himself away from the black wall, watching his reflection totter on its tennis shoes for a moment. Whew! Maybe they would have to carry him across the street tonight and sneak him past the gate guard by holding him by the back of his jeans for a change. He probably could give a shit less, but it was one way to pass the time.

Kip slugged down half of Donaldson's Schmidts while Donaldson passed out as he sucked in a deep gulp of smoky air as if he were about to say something. Matthew stumbled back to the table, downed the rest of his double and swizzled a mouthful of beer through his teeth before he swallowed it and flopped back into his chair. "Nurse! Help! One DOA. Two barely snorting!"

"Donaldson defecting to the hippies rings ironic enough to me, Staff Sergeant."

Flanger grinned around his still unlit cheroot into the sun rising out of the Potomac like a huge florescent tomato beyond the hundreds of acres of lawns and terraces that stretched about the world's largest office building—a moat of vegetation separating the Department of Defense from the web of super highways weaving from Virginia into the capital.

"It wasn't an idea, sir. It was a sarcasm."

"No matter, Staff Sergeant. No matter."

The sun beat through white clouds, showering golden light on the manicured oak and cherry trees which clustered on the hills behind the lines of OD green vans, jeeps, and quarter-ton and duce-and-a-half trucks with olive drab people scuffling in and out of them. Some of the olive shades carried M16's slung across their backs. Others, forty-fives strapped on their hips like Matthew and Colonel Flanger as they leaned their shoulders against the MI-Mobile van and whispered above the steady drone of diesel generators.

"The real concern, Staff Sergeant, is not with how to classify Klopps's comment but rather with how we set up this 'sarcasm'—if you wish—as if it *had* been meant as an actual idea."

Matthew fidgeted with the bill of his OD green baseball cap even though it already sat as squarely on his knotty head as the creases from the forceps would allow. He was scaring himself by realizing that he actually understood the gibberish Flanger had just flung at him. "Well, Colonel, if you're really serious about this, ah, there are strategies that could be employed."

"Well, then, Staff Sergeant." He nearly swallowed the stump of his cigar as he attempted to chew and yell at the same time. "Out with it! What's the big secret?"

"No big secret, sir. Just something I learned early in 'spook' work."

"And, that is?"

"Okay. Even if he's an agent sent here to spy on you for some reason, you're still his CO. He has to obey your orders. So. Maybe. Let's see. Maybe, you could have him defect to the demonstrators under the pretext of infiltrating the enemy for you and providing you with inside intelligence. You know, sort of an undercover type assignment. Once he deserts, you disavow him and bust him for desertion."

"And you got paid to think up shit like that?" Flanger guffawed. "And, Donaldson would buy into this, you think?"

"I think." Matthew removed his baseball cap with the camouflage Staff Sergeant stripes tacked on its front and wiped his damp forehead with his starched fatigue sleeve. "For sure, sir. For sure. He'll go for it, sir."

"It all sounds so easy."

"It is, sir."

"Maybe too easy?"

"Someday, sir, we'll find out that memory is probably more about what we're told than about what we actually experienced."

"What the hell does that mean, Staff Sergeant?"

"Well, sir, it goes directly to your point of this maybe being too easy."

"Parkrow! Sergeant Parkrow! Come here, quick! Things are starting to pop!" blasted from the confines of the van in Eddie Donaldson's pinched voice.

Matthew looked at Flanger and shrugged toward the whining voice.

Flanger wagged his head, chuckling to himself. "Tell Donaldson," he mumbled around chuckles, "that this mission is a small but significant part of Operation CHAOS. He'll be 'under cover' and *in communicado*. Understood, Staff Sergeant Parkrow? 'Under cover' and *in communicado*."

Matthew replaced his cap and snapped off a quick salute as he turned to mount the steel steps back into the van. "Understood, sir. Nice touch, sir. He'll really get off on that scenario, for sure, sir."

"See that he does, Staff Sergeant!" Flanger guffawed again, turned on his heel in a perfectly executed 'about face' and stomped off toward the, now, nearly luminous horizon mumbling to himself as he walked. "See that he does. General Latch will be very pleased. That character's becoming a real danger to our operations with his wild notions. My God, he even reported spies in the EM Club and said that some waitress at the Holabird Inn made advances toward him to elicit classified information. He's a fucking lunatic!"

Matthew watched the Colonel's back jerk from side to side as he marched exaggeratedly toward the CP van. The MI-Mobile van door's own luminescence nearly blinded him as he stumbled on the top step, wedging his right boot between the step and the stoop. "Goddamn it!"

"What's wrong, Sergeant Parkrow?" Donaldson clucked at Matthew as he fell through the doorway after jerking his boot free.

"I've got incredible falling sickness, for Christ sake, Eddie!" Matthew leered at Donaldson as his hands hit the metal floor, absorbing the shock of the fall and keeping his uniform off the floor. "Like paranoia, it is also a Nam disease." He'd had the uniform washed and starched and pressed at the civilian laundry on Dundalk Avenue, just so he'd look STRAK, as an airborne trooper should. Heavily starched, all the creases were sharp and straight, not bent or off-angle the way they often returned from the post laundry, and he had to spread the legs of his trousers and the sleeves of his blouse with his fingers. He was, however, often puzzled over the oxymoronic implications of starched jungle fatigues.

As he shoved himself up on momentarily gimpy legs, he glanced at his name patch over his left pocket. Just above it, cloth replicas of his Airborne Ranger Wings and Combat Infantry Badge. Below, the weight of other cloth decoration replicas puckered the pocket. From bottom left to top right—the military convention of least to most importance—Good Conduct Medal, Vietnam Service Medal, Vietnamese Commendation Medal, Purple Heart, Air Medal with two oak leaf clusters, Vietnamese Cross of Gallantry, Army Commendation Medal with V device, Bronze Star with V device and two oak leaf clusters, and Silver Star. Matthew brushed off invisible dust. "A veritable Audie fucking Murphy," he smirked to himself. "I just can't walk. That's all. You know, like you get after two Schmidts." He tip-toed to Donaldson's desk and peered over his shoulder. "Okay, Eddie. What you got?"

"The insurgents are on Independence Avenue Bridge."

"Insurgents?"

"Yes. Insurgents!" Donaldson beat his fists on the metal desk. "Someone's been sleeeeping!"

"No sweat, Donaldson." Matthew perused the message in Eddie's scrawl, searching for the name of the source. "We'll just have this, ah . . . ." He finally found the name scrawled at the bottom of the Intelligence Summary. "We'll have this Spec Four Jeffers court martialed. That's all there is to it!"

"Yeah, that'll teach him to report faulty intelligence."

"Hell, yes. That'll teach the fuck!"

"Cool it, Kip. Leave old Eagle-Eyes alone, now. It's not his fault, after all, that Jeffers is so slow." Matthew clapped Eddie Donaldson on the back much too hard. "But, old Eddie's going to show us how it's done. He's going to be our man in the demonstration, aren't you, Eddie?"

"Mmmeee. Wwwhat dddooo yyyou mmmean?"

"You've never heard of the stammerer as hero?"

"Nnnooo."

"We'll fill you in later."

"Meanwhile," Klopps chirped, picking up on Matthew's game. "You're it!"

"Wwwhat?"

"The hero as stammerer." Kip quickly folded a photograph into an airplane. "You know, like LLLindbbberg cccrossing ttthe AAAtlllantic." He sailed the craft at Donaldson's head.

"Like AAAmelia EEEaarhart PPPutnam."

"And MMMax CCConrad."

"Huh . . . ah . . . ."

"And, don't forget JJJohn GGGlen."

"CCChuck GGGrissom and EEEd WWWhite."

"BOOM!"

The photograph airplane struck startled Eddie in the forehead.

"Wwwhat?"

Matthew wrapped his arm around Donaldson's twitching beef shoulders. "See, Eddie," he whispered in his ear. The Colonel's just been notified that the, ah, insurgents are going to try and get our troops to quit their posts, to defect, to join the demonstration."

"Yeah? So?" His dirty hazel eyes bulged from tiny sockets.

"Well, you're going to do just that."

"Wwwhat?"

"Pretend to join the demonstration. Your assignment will be to infiltrate the insurgents as part of Operation CHAOS. See?"

"N . . . n . . . no."

"Look, man. This is your big chance. The Colonel asked specifically for you to handle this job." Matthew hugged Donaldson's shoulders even tighter. "You'll be able to feed us inside information on what's going down out there among the tribe. Right?" He shook Donaldson's body as he talked. "Instead of analyzing pictures, like this . . . ." Matthew scooped up the fallen airplane folded from a photograph. "You'll become a part of them."

"Ohhh?" His baby fat jowls seemed to tighten with purpose as he pushed Matthew's arm from his squaring shoulders. He straightened in his swivel chair and cleared his throat. "Imagine? Me . . . ?" He rattled the floor beneath his chair with his boot heels as he jumped up and down, squealing in harmony with the echoing metal. "Imagine. Me. James Bond!"

"Hell no, we won't go! Hell no, we won't go! Hell no, we won't go!" rumbled across the

horizon long before the first marchers actually crested the northern terraces. The early sun dripped over them like liquid fire.

Begana. Kelud. Awu. Bulusan. Redoubt. The swelling mass of people was like a lava flow from volcanoes with names like those, scorching the corduroy lawns with sandals, boots, bare feet. Chants and songs were their eruptions.

"All we are saying is give peace a chance . . . ."

Cordons of troops stretched like firebreaks between the dull stone of the Pentagon and the flowing thunder of megaphone-amplified chants and songs. Mount Baker still steaming in Washington, while DC was becoming another Izalco. "The mountain comes to Pompeii," Matthew sniggered as he leaned against the van, smoking. Would it take another two thousand years to excavate them? Who would dust away *their* sleep like tons of ashes?

"The insurgents should be coming over the hill pretty soon now!" Donaldson's words were garbled by the metal walls of the van.

"Huh?" Matthew cocked his ear more toward the van walls. "Say again, Donaldson."

"I said, 'the insurgents should be coming over the hill soon.'"

"Christ, Eddie! They're already over the hill. Tell Kip."

"Oh, yeah?"

Klopps clattered across the van, piled through the doorway into the copper morning. He swung over the iron railing on the left side of the steps onto the grass. "Wow, look at all those people." His eyes were slits in the sunlight. He tried to shade them with cupped hands under the bill of his cap in order to gain a clearer view of the marchers. "We should be out there, man, you know. Not here."

"In sixty-five, it was 'We shall overcome,' and we didn't. Martin Luther King had a dream, but that dream was damned to nightmare in Memphis." Matthew pinched the fire off his cigarette and stomped it out in the damp grass with the heel of his jungle boot. He field stripped the butt from the filter and stuffed the stained tip into his right blouse pocket.

"I don't know about you, Kip, but I've been out there." He hocked and lofted an oyster through the crisp air like he and Ward

Crampton used to through the musty air in the baseball locker room to see who'd come closest to hitting a urinal. Now, Ward was only the best friend of his memories, probably lofting hockers at urinals in heaven or somewhere.

Or, was he? Jason's letter certainly opened up the possibility that Ward had somehow survived the fireball of that chopper crash. Maybe, he had amnesia or something. The sighting had been confirmed, anyway, by Ward's own father.

"People just get blown away out there, Kip. Shit! Look at what those Klansmen did to the freedom riders in Mississippi. Murdered three. Buried them, symbolically, near Philadelphia."

"But, they got theirs yesterday, didn't they?" Kip grabbed Matthew's left sleeve with agitated fingers, almost pulling him off balance. "Didn't you read the paper or see it on TV?"

"Yes, I saw it on last night's news at the motel." He toed the grass with his boot as if he were in the batter's box. "Seven out of twenty-one convicted. Not convicted of murder, mind you, but of violating the murder victims fucking civil rights, for Christ sake! Isn't that what the report said? Shit. Might as well call it the one-third's compromise of nineteen hundred and sixty-seven. Right?"

"Jesus, you're one cynical fucker. I never saw nobody so cynical, at least not since Sergeant Major O'Tool. Remember him? Ordinance at Long Binh?"

"Have I gotten that bad?"

"At least, Matthew. At least."

"Christ, he used to bet on how many mortar rounds Charlie would lay in on his own ammo dump." Matthew wiped his damp forehead with his sleeve. "And, he'd win, too."

"Not just once in a while but every fucking time."

"Hell, yes. He'd bet the Cherry Boys just off the planes over at 90th Replacement Company."

Matthew wagged his head. "I bet him once, you know?"

"You didn't?"

"I did." He glanced at the white gold Seiko on his left wrist: OCT 21 10:30. "Keep me informed, Kip, on anything new that comes in on the demonstration. Use Donaldson as a runner if necessary until it's time. I'm going to check out the cordon lines."

"Whatever you say, Sarge. But what about Donaldson's little mission? Doesn't he have to report to Flanger at the CP for his official marching orders?"

"No. He can't do that! No plausible deniability in that. Just tell him to be prepared to infiltrate at my signal. I'm his control for this mission, not Colonel Flanger. Okay?"

"Okay, Sarge. I understand."

"I don't know what my signal will be yet, but it will be unmistakable. I can promise our James Bond that much." With his right fist, Matthew playfully jabbed Kip on the shoulder in the center of his Big Red One combat patch. "We'll get him into the fray soon enough."

"Oh, hell! He's going to piss in his pants." Kip grinned at Donaldson's back slightly hunched, swaying off toward the CP van with messages. "Especially when he gets burned for desertion after thinking, all along, that he's been following Flanger's orders."

The terraces stepped down toward the Pentagon in wide graceful lines, geometric to a fault as the building they surrounded was. The grass was tight clumped and spongy carpet under his boots. Matthew slipped from the cover of the line of Army OD green support vehicles, down the turf steps. As the approaching flow of demonstrators blackened the whole of the top north terrace and rumbled toward the cordon lines of troops, Matthew ambled behind the firebreaks of OD green men, his hands jammed into his pockets, unconsciously humming the demonstrators' thunder.

"All we are saying is give peace a chance . . . ."

Cinders and ashes buried Pompeii, not lava flow. And they were here to make ash out of the tribe, right? Right. It was the order of the day: "If them peaceniks fuck up just once—just once, mind you— waste 'em!" After all, they ain't really Americans, anyway. Even their families won't miss the smell. What was his Daddy's last campaign promise? A hippie in every pot . . . boiling? And, he's just been overwhelmingly re-elected Mayor of Roanoke Park, North Carolina, a typical American town.

He had a dream, too. It turned into Tent City. It didn't much matter now that it had been Fort Jackson, South Carolina, not DC. He believed in God the Father Almighty, maker of heaven and earth, and in Jesus Christ, his only son, our Lord, who was conceived of the Holy Spook, born of the vagina, Mary, suffered under punctilious Pilot, was socialized, died, and was buried. On the third day, he was drafted.

"Bat . . . tal . . . i . . . on!" The command echoed down the ranks.

"Com . . . pan . . . y!"

"Pla . . . toon!"

"Squad!"

"Fix ba . . . yo . . . nets!" Shreesh. Long knives scraped against metal as a thousand hands unsheathed a thousand bayonets. Steel clattered as they snapped the bayonets onto noses of M14 and M16 rifles.

"All we are saying is . . . ."

"Bat . . . tal . . . i . . . on!"

"Com . . . pan . . . y!"

"Pla . . . toon!"

"Squad!"

'Pre . . . sent h'arms!"

Ballooning cumulus clouds rolled in from West Virginia. Rifles rattled in cloud-filtered sunlight. Unsteady hands slapped stocks. Metal barrels hitting palms boomed against the clouds.

" . . . . Give peace a chance . . . ."

Two poles. War and peace. Order and chaos. A swirling double helix of human beings. Like Crick and Watson, discover. Like Jefferson and Paine, create. Grow up, for real. March on Washington now that we're a nation of our own. So easy, too. But, the hippies want your soul just as much as A R M Y, I B M, G M C, A B C, C B S, N B C, C O R E, S N C C, N A A C P, K K K, Y A F, S D S, A D A, M I C - K E Y . . . M O U S E . . . .

Pain in Matthew's stomach knocked him to his knees on the spongy turf as if one of these national guardsmen had stuck him with his still-sheathed bayonet. He felt flu-like rushes from his toes, flushing his cheeks, his eyes, his brain. He had believed every fucking word of "Spin and Marty" and look where it got him. His stomach tied up in knots, on his knees in the grass surrounding the fucking Pentagon in the uniform of his enemy.

To salvage that much from their wreckage on that Scylla and Charybdis shoreline. Just that much only. To ascend from their parents' maelstrom of good intentions with only white hair and a startled look.

"All we are saying . . . ."

"Bat . . . tal . . . i . . . on!"
"Com . . . pan . . . y!"
"Pla . . . toon!"
"Squad!"
"Or . . .der h'arms!"
"Or . . .der h'arms!"
"Or . . .der h'arms!"
"Or . . .der h'arms!"

". . . . Is give peace a chance . . . ."

Again, rifles rattled. This time against their shoulders. Butt plates thudded to the turf. Palms slapped thighs.

We are the basic structural unit on which are founded powerful nations. Out of us came hamlets, mayors, sailors, soldiers, massacres, tribunals, witch trials, pesticides, genocides, the rockets that knocked down Ward's chopper like a hunter shoots down a quail with a twelve-gauge, always using the one thing we know is power to place our own hobby horses in history books.

Fear. A germ in the jungle after all. *For the summer's here, and it's time for fighting in the streets, boy.* The time is right for valid revolution, if you can find any. Upheavaloution. Sounds like something you would do in the privacy of your own bathroom. Thought actualized. Ideas. The ground of all determinations. We are what clusters around the cores of churches and PTA's, Marches of Dimes and prime-time TV, messiahs of all sizes. If we change, if each of us changes, then everything else necessarily changes. When we finally realize that the ground of being is simply the butcher's waste products, when we accept that the deliverer isn't coming, then it's ourselves we'll have to see slouching toward Manhattan to be born.

Tears began to burn Matthew's cheeks. "Oh, God help us!" He struggled to his knees, then to his feet, stretching his arms toward the marching mob. "It's up to us!"

The flow of demonstrators seemed to dam up a few thousand yards in front of the cordon lines. Matthew approached the troop lines from the rear. His baseball cap tilted low over his eyes creating an impenetrable mask. The Lone Ranger rides again. His eyes had dried. His stomach still hurt. His chest throbbed. "We have to help ourselves," he muttered. His ears rang a steady penetrating C sharp which he was sure would blow his ear drums out at any moment. "Each of us must change."

He seemed to regain control by the time the guard battalion commander became aware of the temporary stalemate and allowed his soldiers to break ranks. They milled around in clumps of three or four or five, smoking, playing some fast hands of five card stud or gin with soiled, cracked cards. Few traded the expected war stories, for very few, if any, of these guardsmen and reserves had ever seen war.

The demonstrators huddled across the battlefield. Nearly every one of them had been to war, at least on battlefields like Little Rock and Birmingham. The blue X on the Order of Battle map in the van now breathed, perspired, sang. No longer a grease pencil mark on acetate, the X pulled at him like the sun pulls meteorites into it. Thirty-five thousand and growing. He could not help himself any more than those meteorites could help themselves. The X impelled his body through jabbering troops heavy with the smell of fatigues becoming wilted and soggy in the unseasonably hot morning. He skirted bayoneted rifles stacked in teepees. This was insane. The next thing you know they would be issuing "unsheathe bayonets" orders. He had to do something now.

"When in the c . . . course . . . ." His voice cracked as he stepped past the cluster of troops. "When in the course of human events, it becomes necessary for one People to dissolve the Political Bonds which have connected them with another . . ." he shouted. "They should declare the causes which impel them in the Separation." His voice now seemed to echo off the terraces of demonstrators.

The sun seeped through the cloud cover as Matthew passed beyond the troop lines, unsnapping the metal catches which held his pistol. Behind him, the already jeering mob in OD green. He could hear JAG's charges now: Willful loss of Army property; desertion in the face of the enemy; incitement to mutiny. He turned back to face his comrades-in-arms, cautiously stepping backwards as he continued his recitation. "We hold these Truths to be self-evident, that all M . . . PEOPLE are created equal, that they are endowed by their Creator with certain unalienable Rights, that among these Rights are Life, Liberty, and the Pursuit of Happiness—That to secure these Rights, Governments are instituted among M . . . People, deriving their just Powers from the consent of the Governed, that whenever any Form of Government becomes destructive to these Ends . . . ."

The demonstrators on the terraces began to cheer as his words became understandable to them.

"It is the Right of the People to alter or abolish it!" With those words, Matthew fumbled at his left pocket, heavy with the weight of his decorations. He slipped his father's letter out and set it afire with his lighter, waving it above his head. Through the flame and smoke, Matthew could make out a figure in fatigues stumbling madly down the terraces from the line of military support vehicles which almost formed a horizon of their own.

Jesus. Donaldson had mistaken this action for his signal. Guess it was pretty unmistakable at that. At least it couldn't go unnoticed, even by Donaldson.

The great blue X embraced them both with song.

"All we are saying is give peace a chance . . . ."

The tribe had been singing ever since Matthew and a handful of demonstrators were arrested at the Pentagon steps. The muffled-by-distance chant was the heartbeat of the moment as Colonel Flanger approached Matthew and his guard. The Colonel saluted the MP. "Corporal. As you were."

"Good evening, sir!" He snapped a salute against his helmet that was as crisp as his triple-starched green fatigues without ever letting go of the cuffs behind Matthew's back.

Flanger stepped directly in front of Matthew. His eyes squinted in the half-light and chewed on an unlit cheroot. "Uncuff the prisoner, Corporal!"

"But, Colonel, sir?"

"Don't 'but' me, you . . . ah . . . Corporal." Flanger chomped right through his cheroot.

"But, sir? This is a political prisoner. I have to know your reasons, sir? I'm accountable, sir!"

"I'm a Full Bird Colonel in the United States Army Intelligence Corps. You don't have a clearance high enough, young man. Just obey my order. Now, Corporal!"

Matthew rubbed his wrists involuntarily after the Corporal removed the cuffs. He knew it wasn't smart to show any sign of fear or discomfort. Flanger edged closer to his top sergeant and instructor. He leaned near to his Staff Sergeant's left ear.

"Just tell 'em, Staff Sergeant, that you were following my orders. After all, you were going after that renegade Donaldson, weren't you?"

Colonel Flanger's jaw lines sagged in the shadows of the flashlight beam shooting from the young MP corporal's hand directly into Matthew's haggard, smiling face. He didn't even try to avoid the light. He knew it would be useless anyway. MP's like this corporal would follow his eyes in any direction with the beam. He thought it had something to do with control.

Flanger remembered. At thirteen-thirty hours, Klopps banged on the door of the CP. "Sergeant Parkrow's defected, Colonel, sir!" Of course, he didn't believe even Klopps. Not for a minute! Parkrow had been his most trusted NCO for months now. "You mean Donaldson, don't you, Sergeant Klopps?" That *was* the plan. But Klopps knew that. It had been his sarcasm that had started the whole damn ball rolling. "No, sir. I mean Matthew, ah, Staff Sergeant Parkrow, sir. But, Donaldson did follow him like a dog after its master, all the time figuring that Matthew's defection to the hippies wasn't really a defection at all. It was his 'unmistakable signal.'"

Flanger poured over Matthew's face in the light. Goddamn it! Of all his troops, why Parkrow? He'd been like a son.

"But, sir?" Matthew shaded his eyes from the blinding light for the first time. He couldn't see the MP behind the flashlight and didn't care. He could barely see an outline of Colonel Flanger's face hanging in the darkness above and beyond the light beam. He couldn't seem to stop his voice from saying what it was about to say. "The plan was for Donaldson to defect at my signal. Not for me to defect. Right?"

Flanger remembered. At seventeen-forty hours, Klopps called his van. "Damn, sir. Matthew's really done it now." Flanger had swallowed hard. "What?" Static in the patch between vans garbled Klopps' voice for a few seconds. "Repeat, Klopps." He heard Kip clearing his throat.

"They've just arrested over six hundred demonstrators who tried to storm the Pentagon." More static. "And, Matthew Parkrow, Staff Sergeant, U.S. Army Intelligence Command, led the charge!"

"Jesus Christ!"

The silver haired Colonel with a passion for unlit cheroots and brandy shook his head, now, unable to look Matthew in the eyes, even though he knew Matthew could not see him through the glare of the flashlight beam. "You can level with the Corporal, Staff Sergeant Parkrow. You won't be breaking security. I'm giving you permission to say something in your defense here." Flanger tried to catch Matthew's eye and wink at him, but Matthew was staring directly into the light again like a deer mesmerized in the headlights of roadside hunters.

"But, sir. I was already leveling with the Corporal. I led that charge, and I'm proud to admit it!"

"You deserter! Commie bastard!"

"Corporal, that'll be enough. I'll handle this matter with your commander, Major Foldy. Your security clearance isn't high enough for this. You're dismissed!"

"But, Colonel, sir. He's under arrest, sir."

"That's all, young man! Now di di fucking mau, Corporal, before you find yourself suddenly on security patrol along the fucking DMZ!"

In the shadows, the MP snapped his heels together, saluted sharply. "Yes, sir, Colonel, sir!" He flicked the flashlight beam away from Matthew's face and stomped by him. "You'll get yours, fucking commie traitor!" The line of white light bobbed and weaved in front of him as he marched off in the direction of the MP headquarters where fuzzy yellow lights illuminated van windows and seeped through the cracks around the van doors like some kind of smog. "You'll get yours!"

Flanger groped in the darkness left by the departure of the MP Corporal and his flashlight. He touched Matthew's shoulders with his rough but manicured hands. "Staff Sergeant. Ah, Matthew. Listen to me, son. You've only got a matter of days left in this man's Army. An excellent record. Many decorations. Hell, most career soldiers would be envious of all that lettuce you carry above your left pocket." Flanger paused, chewing on his cigar butt that was no longer there.

"Son, I can take care of this mess, if you'll just go along with our little story here. Hell, spying on dissidents ain't nothing new. That's why getting rid of Donaldson that way seemed like it would be so easy. Of course, I didn't expect my best NCO to . . . ."

"Oh, well. The Old Man would believe your story, anyway, even if it wasn't backed up by me, his most trusted commander. We infiltrate groups like that all the time. You knew that didn't you?"

"Yes." Matthew shrugged off the Colonel's shaky fingers. "But it's not my story, Colonel. It's yours, and it's a lie."

"You've lied before, Matthew. Everybody has. In fact, you lied to Eddie Donaldson just this morning. Didn't you?"

"Yes. But that was expediency, not a matter of conscience."

"Bull balls, son! Bull balls! This ain't no philosophy 101 class where you can split vagina hairs all day long and never cut your finger. This is real life where vagina hairs are more like piano wires. They just might cut you good, son. JAG'll damned sure cut you no slack at all in these times. They'll hang your young ass, son. Don't you realize that?"

"That's the . . . ." He shuffled his feet, looking at the ground he could only feel beneath his boots but not actually see. "Yes, I do know that, sir."

"Sure!" Flanger snapped his fingers. "Of course, that's it! You want JAG to hang you, don't you, son? That's it! Sure. You want to be drummed out of this man's Army like Chuck Connors in 'Branded.' Right?"

"Me, sir?"

"Yes, son. You!"

"Aw, come on, Otis! I'm not some martyr."

"Then, why?"

"Maybe because they're my people. Not you." He waved toward the yellow cubes of light on the hill that were the windows into the military support vans. "Or them."

"Oh, you poor young fool." Flanger reached through the night air and grabbed Matthew's right shirt sleeve. "Don't you understand yet that 'your people' have got to be the people in power, son?"

Gasoline generators hummed and rattled louder, now, filling the silence between them.

"Maybe because they're right."

"Hear that sound, son?"

"What, sir?"

"That rumbling noise?"

"You mean the generators, sir?"

"No, Matthew. Something different. The sound of a jeep. It's that MP Corporal's commanding officer's jeep. We've run out of time, you and I. You must decide."

"But, I have already decided, sir."

"Christ, son. If you persist in this, you'll end up spending the rest of your life looking over your shoulder at every turn. Do you realize that? Do you fully comprehend that, Matthew?"

Matthew could no longer look at Colonel Flanger's face. "I'm sorry, Colonel Flanger. I truly am, sir."

"So am I, Staff Sergeant Parkrow. So am I."

Part Three

ALL THINGS ARISE FROM THE WAY

Tao Te Ching

The day before Bobby was shot in the kitchen of the Hotel Ambassador the spring

semester at Columbia was closing in an uneasy truce that settled over the university like the haze of smog and sun that embraced The City for much of the summer. Matthew's court martial convictions for willful loss of government property, desertion in the face of the enemy, and incitement to mutiny, as well as his subsequent dishonorable discharge were six months in his past.

He had completed his first semester in the graduate school on a combination of scholarships and his blood money savings from Vietnam. The Court Martial Board couldn't take those things away from him like they had his rights and privileges and benefits. And, all his medals couldn't wipe away his desertion to the hippies.

"Guilty! Guilty! Guilty!"

"No school for you, deserter swine! Not at the expense of this man's Army!"

Matthew scuffed his sneakers past the granite sundial along College Walk toward the Amsterdam Avenue gate. Fortunately, Columbia graduate school had taken a different view of his acts of conscience. He muttered thanks to the graduate school admissions board for not only admitting him but for granting him some scholarship and fellowship money and to the invisible Students for a Democratic Society for arranging personal recognizance releases for himself and the more than three hundred brothers and sisters busted at FayerWeather Building when he decided to challenge them, even if it meant losing his university financial support.

Two PeterBuilts rumbled side-by-side, snaking through traffic Broadway bound, rattling like worn shock absorbers. Matthew leaned against the gate irons where something like a force field had separated the campus from the streets of Harlem until Martin Luther King was assassinated in Memphis on April fourth.

By the fifteenth, there had been riots in Washington, D.C. and over a hundred other cities. By the twenty-third, there was an intellectual riot in Hamilton between the whites and the blacks over who was leading the student uprising at Columbia. By the thirtieth, the force field was shattered by New York police charging the Sundial. "Let the niggers be; go after the freaks in FayerWeather," the police whispered among themselves as they marched toward the

Sundial. Those were the orders. Divide and conquer. Old as Alexander, but the Students African-American Society took the bait of power. It was too easy. It was a "Donaldson." That was how Matthew perceived it.

After five months in Harlem in a third floor walk-up studio, it still shocked Matthew when he left campus to see so many black faces scrambling along the 116th Street sidewalks as the red PeterBuilt cabs with golden streaks along their doors roared by when there were so few blacks inside those university walls.

The police were shocked as hell when they kept dragging them out one by one long after they thought that there shouldn't be any more freaks left. Fools, they thought that there was only about three or four hundred students in Hamilton, Low Library, Math, Avery, and FayerWeather combined. There were more than that in FayerWeather alone. And, all of them seemed to be in the same cell at the precinct station.

"Matthew?"

Honey among smog-constricted throats. "What?" Matthew rubbed the bristles of three days stubble with the back of his right hand as he stopped in the middle of his turn toward 116th Street. "Oh, hey. Is that really you, Emmy Lou?" The lines of her angular face were fuzzy like a photograph washed out by bright sunlight. Her lips and cheeks flushed in the afternoon heat. Her nostrils quivered.

"Yeah, it really *is* me."

Her jasmine perfume masked out the desperation behind the smells of gasoline and pizza that flooded the avenue and the street.

"I heard that you were in jail, Matthew."

Down the block someone whistled for a cab. Matthew watched a yellow-and-black taxi whip across three lanes of traffic on Amsterdam. Tires squalled as the taxi slid to a stop in front of Slick Santos, dressed for a circus in his pastel yellow velveteen suit and matching musketeer hat with an ostrich plum stuck in the band, wilting already from the humidity and heat.

"When I heard at the Wherein Doas Cafe that you'd been busted along with Sundial People . . . ." She crinkled her upturned nose and shaded her blue eyes from the hazy sun behind Matthew's head. "I thought . . . ." She shrugged. "I just got these vibes that I ought to come look for you here, for some reason."

"Yeah, I was. But somebody fixed PR's for us."

"Wow. Santos came through then?" She motioned at him entering the taxi. "That's far out."

"Yeah, that's far out, but, it was the SDS that got us out, not Santos. He reneged. When we called the bondsman Santos told us to call, the guy said he never heard of any Santos. And, on top of that, he never even showed up at the station. He denied us three times last night, Madame Bovary!"

"Sorry to hear that."

"Me too, but that's what happens when you count on money people to do the right thing."

"I imagine your father's going to be mad as hell about you doing the right thing, don't you know?" Emmy Lou tossed her taffy hair off of her shoulders which were damp with sweat down to the sun halter that covered her breasts in blue to match the jeans slung around her slender hips. "He hasn't forgiven you for getting drummed out of the Army yet."

"I know." Averting his eyes from her flat, palpitating stomach, bare and moist in the sun and thoughts of how her body trembled when he touched her navel with his tongue, Matthew fumbled with memories of guilty unless proven innocent, objections, motions for dismissal by his lawyers, rulings and over-rulings. Empty faces with marble eyes overwhelmed his thoughts. The judges sat at attention. Their gold leaves, silver birds, and golden stars flashed from their collars like sunbursts. Those were *his* peers? He threw his hands up toward the sun. His court martial had been a sunburst, too. Or was that a supernova? "From his perspective, I guess that's understandable. After all, his once vote-producing hero son has turned into a vote-losing radical, queer, commie who has been stripped of his rank and honors and marched out the gates of Fort Holabird to the incessant snare of drums like Chuck Connors in 'Branded.' Jason believes I'm a complete failure." He leaped into the air and landed in a sloppy pirouette on the sidewalk, shrieking. "And, look at me, Madame Bovary! I'm proving him to be exactly right, aren't I?"

He stumbled. Emmy Lou hugged him to her, her perspiration dampening the T-shirt she had tie-dyed purple for him as their stomachs pressed together. Matthew steadied himself against her, pulling her tight thighs against his. "Why don't we do it in the road?" he sang in his best quiet John Lennon voice.

"I think my place's better than the middle of Amsterdam Avenue, Matthew." Emmy Lou stuck the tip of her tongue between his lips. She loved to lure his tongue into her mouth with hers, then, nip it. "At least, it's air-conditioned."

> *Darkness at the break of noon*
> *Shadows even the silver spoon*
> *The handmade blade, the child's balloon*
> *Eclipses both the sun and moon*
> *To understand you know too soon*
> *There is no sense in trying.*

Dylan's nasal sounds bounced from the modular steel shelves she'd purchased at the Sears mail order outlet in downtown Manhattan. Imagine? She'd only had to look up the phone number in the Manhattan Yellow Pages Directory, dial it, and place her order. "You can pick it up here or send a check and we'll deliver via the mail," the Dietrich voice of the clerk had informed her. "Please, send the order by mail. I'll get the check out today." Funds were no problem. Jason was very generous to her. She wasn't at all sure why. After all, she was merely the maid's niece. And, he didn't help Matthew at all, and he was his blood son. Matthew, however, helped himself. Sandalwood incense smoldered in the hollow of a tiny bronze mushroom. Emmy Lou's hair fell like shredded shadows over Botticelli breasts as she adjusted the position of the mushroom—a little to the left of the Garrard changer. "There's no need for you to go to the Cafe if that's all you're going for, Matthew."

> *Pointed threats, they bluff with scorn*
> *Suicide remarks are torn*
> *From the fool's gold mouthpiece*
> *The hollow horn plays wasted words*
> *Proves to warn*
> *That he not busy being born*
> *Is busy dying.*

She'd lined her studio apartment's off-white walls with Beatles White Album photos, posters of Buddy Holly, Bob Dylan in black leather, Jimi Hendrix setting his guitar on fire at Monterey Pop, Janice Joplin, Che Guevera rattling a rifle in his left hand, Jerry Rubin smoking a joint in front of the gymnasium at his old Cincinnati high school, Eldridge Cleaver leaving jail or going to jail, and a hand-painted sign—SDS—in day-glo red on dull black cardboard which she'd added to her wall collection as soon as she'd heard about Matthew's bust.

Until then, she still hadn't been sure how far Matthew would go for politics, ideologies, truth, beauty, revolution. The fact was, there were a lot of people around who hadn't been sure either, even after what he'd done at the Pentagon rally. You could never be too careful when it came to who might be an undercover government agent rather than what they seemed to be, even when you've known them all of your life. Hell, especially if you've known them all your life. Before, she knew Matthew like you come to know a tree you climb every day or a prayer you say each night. You know the bark or the words but not the sap or the meaning. This year she had come to know something of Matthew's true sap, something of what his words really meant. Now, she was sure. She trusted him. She respected him.

I . . . love him.

"What do you mean, Emmy Lou?"

"About what?"

"About not needing to go to the Cafe ?" His fingers floated over Emmy Lou's thighs, her firm buttocks.

"Fiend." She grinned as she reached behind and slapped at Matthew's hand. "Stay on that mattress! Don't waste all that testosterone on a woman when she's walking away from you." She giggled as she skipped out of his reach, following wisps of incense smoke toward the kitchenette at the far end of the apartment where the refrigerator whirred and the air-conditioning wheezed in the ninety-four-degree heat. It was already proving to be a long, hot summer even with air-conditioners.

In the black light violet of the room, her muscles rolled like a Di Vinci drawing, creating velvet shadows on her golden skin. Her hair, now flung over her shoulders, splashed down her back to her hips like copper strands.

"Want a Bud?"

"Sure."

She opened the door. The white light glared like a sun a million light years away in nova or an MP's flashlight in the darkness. Her body seemed to melt for an instant. She fumbled for two cans of beer. Her sculptured lean curves disappeared as she slammed the door and snuffed out the light.

"So, what *do* you mean?" Waiting for her answer, he reached above him for the stone hash pipe on the night table behind the head end of the mattress lying on the floor. His fingers also located a small piece of tin foil containing the last of her Lebanese blonde.

One tab swishpopped on the kitchen counter, then the other. Emmy Lou tossed the aluminum tabs into a Dietsch grocery bag leaning against the wall next to her fridge. She turned with the beers in her hands and slinked back across the shag carpet toward the mattress, singing along with Dylan.

> *Temptation's page flies out the door*
> *You follow, find yourself at war*
> *Watch waterfalls of pity roar*
> *You feel to moan but unlike before*
> *You discover that you'd just be*
> *One more person crying.*

"Quick! Something's burning!" Matthew choked out the words as he held in smoke and offered Emmy Lou the warm stone pipe. It glowed amber in the muffled violet light.

> *So don't fear if you hear*
> *A foreign sound to your ear*
> *It's alright, Ma, I'm only sighing.*

She traded him one Bud for the pipe, took a long hit, and flopped beside him on the sheets. Matthew clamped the can of beer between his bare knees. He shivered momentarily from the coldness of the aluminum, then finished the pipe and tapped the bowl on a Holiday

Inn ash tray liberated from some motel or another. He refilled it with another pinch of hash. "Here, Madame Bovary. Have another hit." He pushed the cardboard drawer from its matching blue box cover, selected a safety match, shoved the Ohio Blue Tip cover back over the drawer containing the few remaining kitchen matches, replaced the box on the night table. Then, he snapped the pale blue tip on his left thumbnail. The match flared in the dim light.

"Where did you learn that one, boy?" She sucked on the cooling stone as he held the match over the top of the bowl. Hot sweet smoke tickled her lungs. She coughed as she tried to hold the smoke in and handed the still-smoking pipe back to Matthew. He finished it as she sucked on her beer, a luxurious sigh swelling in her chest.

"Not down home, honey, that's for sure. They only know how to strike matches on their tar heels."

"My, my." She smacked her lips and tickled his feet. He jumped. "Now, ya'll know that ain't so, boy."

Their lips touched, parted. Their tongues rolled around one another. A part of Matthew seemed to perch on the night table, leaning against the ash tray. Jesus, as much as he loved sex, all that slobbering and swallowing each other's spit. Uggh! Licking sweaty skin coated with The City's smog. A deadly affair, fucking. Shit, you never see Romeo and Juliet or Rogers and Astaire or Roy and Dale and Trigger or Tonto and Kemosabe fucking, bucking, sucking. Not only did they not go to the bedroom, but they also did not go the bathroom, unless they had to get their raincoats to face another night of frigid drizzle on the range. No, that would be the mud closet or the medicine cabinet, places where the raincoats of various kinds are stored.

Matthew shuddered. Emmy Lou trembled. Matthew convulsed. Emmy Lou convulsed. Clinging together, they rolled onto their sides, trembling, then quiet, then trembling again, somewhat less each time.

> *You lose yourself, you reappear.*
> *You suddenly find you got nothing to fear.*
> *Alone you stand with nobody near*
> *When a trembling distant voice, unclear*
> *Startles your sleeping ears to hear*

That somebody thinks they've really found you.

"Whew!" He reached for his Winstons on the parson's table. This time he used the striking surface on the side of the Ohio Blue Tip box. The match flared blueorange. He lit his cigarette, then smothered the flame with the smoke he spat out between his lips. He dropped the charred matchstick over his head into the ash tray. "So, is this why," he yawned, stretching from his toes, "I don't need to go out tonight?"

Emmy Lou returned his smile, then pinched his right inner thigh just below his groin.

"Ouch!"

"That's only one part of it, Mr. Parkrow!" She curled her buttocks against his stomach, her head in the crook of his right arm. Beyond her flowing hair, her jasmine scent, hanging on the wall was her latest art class project—a painting of sixteen virgins dressed in habits of seaweed. Their ghostly heads seemed more like skulls peering from beneath heavy hoods than real faces as they bowed in prayer around a table similar to the one the disciples gathered around in *The Last Supper*. Their shrouds were streaks of black and green overlapping, mixing. The table cloth gleamed as white as their skulls.

"The other part is that I have another lead on that guy you hope might be Ward."

A question in your eyes is lit
Yet you know there is no answer fit
To satisfy, insure you not to quit
to keep it in your mind and not forgit
That it is not her or she or them or it
That you belong to.

"What?"

"Yeah. Some guys down at Wherein Doas finally believed your story. I guess because you got busted yesterday. Until then, just about everybody at the Cafe was still suspicious that you might be undercover FBI, CIA, or some kind of special operations intelligence somebody trying to find this guy and bust him.

Although the masters make the rules
For the wise men and the fools
I got nothing, Ma, to live up to.

"Everyone there's been paranoid ever since old man Henderson Crampton came snooping around last year. I wish I'd never told him, you know, that I'd seen this guy who looked like Ward. But, I really felt so sorry for the old guy what with his wife dead and all. Weakness of mine, I must admit. He was up here for some doctors convention or something. Called me up. Took me to dinner. I just couldn't bear watching him break down in front of me, dribbling huge tears onto the dark bread in the Brocheteria at Eighty-sixth and Lex. Then all of a sudden you show up. It spooked them.

"Anyway, Marty, the owner, he said that this guy was real secretive about who he was and all, and he split as soon as Ward's father came nosing around."

"Shit, that's a really cold trail by now."

"Not as cold as you might think. Come to find out, the reason he was so spooked was because he's supposedly some big shit underground leader, and the heat's after him all the time. They're continually trying to set him up for some kind of bust or another. And, the reason the trail's not cold, honey, is that Marty's pretty sure that this guy will be at the demonstration in Chicago."

"That's coming up soon. Maybe I should . . . ."

"Do you have to go after him, Matthew? Why couldn't you just finally let this thing go and spend the rest of the summer between these thighs?" She rolled over to face him and pushed her mound against him. Her eyes were agates in the black-lighted room, a pouting smile nibbling at the edges of her lips. "We both know that Ward Crampton died in a helicopter crash in Vietnam."

"No *we* don't!" He fumbled behind for another Winston and lit it quickly. The smoke curled blue spirals and helixes toward the ceiling. "What *we* do know is fuck, argue; argue, fuck. Fuck; argue; fuck."

"Well, doesn't that beat the hell out of most things?"

"Like what?"

"Like playing doctor down in the hole at twilight when everything was lavender. The pines swished in the evening breezes."

"Is the hole covered over yet?"

"No, it's still there. In fact, when I was down to visit Aunt Alecia last month, I spent an entire afternoon sitting down near the sewer pipe we used to pretend was a cavern. Remember?"

"Yeah."

"I just sat there soaking up memories and the good old North Carolina spring sun. There isn't anything like that here."

"I know. Probably the closest is the Cloisters."

Emmy Lou wriggled on top of Matthew, basking in the warmth of his body like she had in the warmth of that sun and those memories of when they were children and their world was still full of rabbits and sparrows and black snakes and miles of pine forests they had roamed for what, then, seemed would be forever.

"Little by little he's killing it all, you know?"

"I know that, too."

"But no one can take away what we once had, Madame Bovary—you and me and Ward and old Turkey Locklear."

"I get this awful feeling sometimes, Matthew—you know, right here in the pit of my tummy like a kind of morning sickness only it strikes at any time of the day or night—that we're all that's left of the old Roanoke Park, the only organisms that haven't yet been gobbled up by civilization as we know it." Her words trailed into the whirring silence of the air-conditioned apartment three flights up at 201 East 83rd Street.

Matthew felt the wet warmth of her tears on his chest. He stroked taffy waves that fell down her back and leaned up to kiss her salty cheeks. "We may be, Madame Bovary. We, very well, may be." His eyes glazed over like a high jumper readying for his approach to the bar. The slightest touch and the bar might fall. He blanked his mind except for the quivering, intense creature now devouring his being. He'd known her, it seemed, forever. Ever since Alecia had brought her to live with them after a three-month vacation with her relatives down east near Williamston. He vaguely remembered the pink bunting she was wrapped in that day. In those times, he was only aware of a baby in the house. Alecia's niece.

"At least we've got each other, now. That mustn't ever change, Matthew."

"For sure, Emmy Lou. For sure." He snubbed out the half-smoked Winston and snuggled under her weight down into the bed.

> *Walk upside-down inside handcuffs*
> *Kick my legs to crash it off*
> *Say all right, I have had enough*
> *What else can you show me?*
>
> *And if my thought-dreams could be seen*
> *They'd probably put my head in a guillotine*
> *But it's alright, Ma, it's life, and life only.*

"Let's get a little shut-eye, what you say?"

"Okay. If you really think you can sleep with this hot body beside you." She slipped from the mattress to the hardwood floor, bounced to the record changer and flicked the switch to off. Then, she snapped off the black light and crawled back between the sheets, snuggling close to Matthew's back.

"The only name he ever used was Crayon."

"Who?"

"The dude that looks like Ward."

"Crayon? Must be a nickname." Matthew scratched his lightly bearded chin. "Guess I'll have to go to Chicago and find out what color Crayola this guy really is, huh?"

Emmy Lou sighed. She pulled him closer to her. "Not tonight, I hope." She kissed him and fell asleep almost immediately.

Three hours later he couldn't find any paper in the dark. He hadn't been able to sleep, thinking about Crayon in Chicago and him, maybe, being Ward. Could it be possible after all this time? He might not even know it, himself. Matthew knew that he had to find out. He prayed that she would understand. No, he knew that she would. Matthew tip-toed out of her apartment, having scribbled a hasty note on the back of the Dylan album jacket.

Dearest Madame Bovary,
Sorry to fuck and argue and run. Going after Crayon.
See you in a few weeks.
Matthew

"The whole world's watching! The whole world's watching!"

" . . . . But you will all know what I am full of, if you don't see me on other marches," The Reporter concluded. He was the last of the artists and writers to speak. All around Matthew people cheered his words that careened out of the microphone on the band shell stage. A young speaker in a fringed leather vest took the podium after The Reporter had finished his speech.

Matthew closed his pocket-sized spiral notebook and stuffed it into the right pocket of his jeans, patting it in place, then checking the left pocket for his wallet. At night, during his court martial proceedings, when everyone else slept, he would slip into the latrine where the lights were always burning and smoke a joint or two on the shitter while transferring every word from his military notebook into the new spiral one he had purchased at the Fort Holabird PX. He was afraid that the Army would try to confiscate his military notebook. They didn't disappoint him. By the time he had to give the notebook up, however, he had completed the transfer. His wallet was still in place. He thought he might've lost it in all the commotion.

"We ought to know already what you're full of, Mr. Reporter," he sneered as The Reporter, squeezing his way through the webs of hippies surrounded by Black Panthers, stumbled against Matthew's shoulder. "Fight's now, old man, not at the next march!" Matthew startled himself that he spoke directly at The Reporter. After all, here was a writer revered by himself and his fellow students over the years. "Just look at all their hardware, man! Just look around you, Mr. Reporter!" He leaped at The Reporter's white collar. "This is Armies of the Night, Part Two." His head reeled from morning hash as several panthers tore his fingers from The Reporter's shirt and throat, shoving him to the ground. "You know, man, like Toppsie!"

"Hey, man, be cool. Be cool," his black brothers urged as they held him down. "Make love, not war, brother," one of the Yippie guards soothed. The Reporter straightened his collar and brushed off his shirt, gazing distractedly through the crowd toward flashing neon lights of a bar beyond the barbed wire barricades across the street.

Matthew wanted to . . . . "My God, man! We are at war!" He wanted to smash that Yippie's cat-licked face in, to tear out the Panthers' fangs, to rip off the old Reporter's balls, that is if he could find them. He glared into the sweat-stained face of another Yippie guard holding his right arm down. "They've all got to go, stupid! Not just the politicians, but the tit-fingered writers too!"

Three hippie nymphs who looked like they'd been cloned from the Blind Faith album cover smothered him in the grass with choruses of strokes and kisses.

"Be mellow, man. Be mellow," they chorused.

"Make love, man, not war, man."

"Be mellow. Make love."

Matthew writhed against them as they replaced the force of his brothers with their own straight jacket of softness and flesh. His struggles against their restraint made them believe that he was getting worked up sexually. So, Nina, the youngest at seventeen, talked him into walking with her to the river, hoping to divert his attentions. Cool him out. Save him from himself.

The young speaker who replaced The Reporter at the podium had tears in his eyes. He pleaded for silence over the din of the masses. "Please, brothers and sisters, I have something important to say to you. Please."

Matthew hesitated, his eyes locked to the speaker's eyes as he struggled to sit up. He stood up by holding onto Nina's tanned shoulders.

"Our brothers and sisters in Czechoslovakia have been completely mauled by the Russians. In France, our brothers and sisters have been placated by shrewd old De Gaulle reforms. The Mexican government is planning to gun down our brothers and sisters in the streets of Mexico City if there's any trouble during the upcoming Olympics. The revolution is left on our shoulders now! We stand alone! It is up to each of us." He shoved his right fist above his head, his long black hair flowing down his neck past his shoulders like a shadow. "Power to the people!"

"Power to the people!" shouted the front rows of the just-hushed crowd.

"Power to the people!" The young speaker thrust his fist again into the demi-shadows of the band shell.

"Power to the people!" the masses echoed.

Matthew felt the power surge through his body like acid. "Power to the people," he yelled along with the hippie girl, Nina, whom he clung to and with all the other sweaty, sticky people surrounding him in the park.

"Power to your prick," Nina giggled softly into Matthew's ear. She squeezed his crotch. The throng erupted. Matthew allowed Nina to drag him from the park, through the streets choked with demonstrators and citizens of Chicago where the power of the Daley machine lined the curbs: troop trucks, Daley's Dozers, barbed wire barricades attached to jeeps to mow them down like trees on a construction site, knots of National Guardsmen surrounding the Hilton.

"What do you expect from him?" Nina's voice cooed like a turtledove amidst the revving of truck engines and the clamor of steel butts of rifles against the concrete streets and sidewalks.

"Expect out of whom?"

"The Reporter."

"Him?" Matthew spit at a truck tire jammed against the curbing. "Exactly what I got . . . . Nothing!" They walked faster to get past the clumps of soldiers.

"I used to be one of them," he muttered, nodding his head toward six soldiers bent over a poker game at the corner of the Hilton. "But, I quit."

"A National Guardsman?" She looped his arm in hers and squeezed it against the heat of her contained under a blue work shirt she wore loose, with the shirttail out flopping over her jean-covered hips.

"No." He forced a smile. She was, after all, trying to be very nice to him. And, she had saved him from probably getting his skull cracked or something equally undesirable. The Yippies and those two Panther dudes would've at least tried if he'd been able to get back up and tear at The Reporter's jugular vein with his teeth like he wanted so desperately to do. "I was the real thing as Henry James would say."

As her violet eyes that gleamed like polished stones clouded over, small wrinkles etched their sockets. Her rainbow lips drooped and quivered ever so slightly. "Vietnam and all that?" Her contralto voice broke.

"That's why I'm here. At least that's part of it."

"You've got more right than anybody. Ah, what is your name, anyway?"

"Matthew."

"A biblical name, huh?"

"Yeah, my father's a religious nut among other fanaticisms."

She laughed with him. "I'm Nina."

"Yeah, I know. I heard one of the other chicks call you that when you all had me pinned down in the park."

"Sorry about that, Matthew, but we were afraid you'd get hurt."

"It's okay, Nina. I probably would've." He paused and lit a Winston. "Or worse, I would've hurt somebody."

"You know, Matthew, if you'd rather, we can go to this pad down the block here. Some fiends . . . ." Her laughter interrupted herself. "I mean, some *friends* of mine have a place there, and I've got a key."

"Sure. Beats the hell out of this heat. Long as we're back at Grant park in time for the march."

"Sure, baby," Nina crooned against his shoulder as she nestled her shagged auburn hair against him.

They walked along the river bank toward her friends' apartment. Her hair smelled of Dr. Bronner's pure Castile peppermint soap and hashish.

"Sure. Just don't be so uptight, baby. We'll do some dope, take a hot bath, and maybe get it on a little."

He could feel her face smiling against his shoulder as they strolled along. "I'm hip to that, Nina. I'm sure as hell hip to that." He knew he'd have to struggle against the straps of Nina's sensuality, maybe even snap them, to get back to Grant Park on time. But, he had to be there. Some McCarthy people had told him earlier that they'd seen a guy setting up one of the aid stations—they couldn't remember exactly where—who looked just like the picture of Ward he had shown them. After all this time . . . and nothing. He wasn't about to miss out on a lead like that. He'd be at Grant Park tonight, for sure. Matthew clung to this thought like he, later, clung to Nina's herb scented thighs.

"The whole world's watching! The whole world's watching! The whole world's watching!" the mass chanted as it swirled and swelled against dams of troops surrounding Grant Park. Their candles flickered like a mammoth necklace of molten jewels clinging to a dark throat. Nina guided Matthew through the swaying, sweating throng which seemed almost as one organism. His notebook was safely snug in his jeans, and Nina's friend's Nikon hung around his neck and over his shoulder, swinging back and forth across his left hip. *So you think you want a revolution, we-ell . . . .*

"Just pretend you want an interview with him, Matthew. That way you'll get a chance to talk to him up close and personal." Nina's violet eyes sparkled like capsules suspended in her upside down pill bottle face. He'd made the analogy first when Nina turned that aspirin bottle containing two black beauties over, popping them into her hand that popped them into her mouth. That instant when the hits of speed began to drop from the bottom of the overturning bottle was when the powdery glass reminded him of the shape of her face and the pills, of her eyes.

Man, what luck. Damn. She was this Crayon dude's old lady, sort of. She thought the pictures he showed her were of Crayon. Didn't believe that he was Ward, though. She said he was from Billings, Montana. That he went to Berkeley. Got his start in underground politics in the Free Speech Movement. Never went to Vietnam as far as she knew. He was opposed to the war. But, what the fuck did Nina know? She'd only been with him for a few months. He knew that he must talk to this Crayon directly. "I'll make like an interviewer for the *Rolling Stone.*"

"Yeah. That's hip. But, Crayon really digs *The Voice.*"

"That's cool. A reporter from *The Voice.*"

"Hey, look who's coming, Matthew." Nina's slender fingers waved toward a large table on the grass at the edge of the park. The Reporter reeled forward and struggled with a bull horn. Nina suddenly wrapped her arms around Matthew, squeezing her body close, her lips brushing his right ear. "You're not still gonna tear out his jugular vein, are you?"

"No."

'That's good, baby, 'cause Crayon ought to be showing up here any minute now, and he just loves The Reporter."

"Crayon loves The Reporter?"

"Yeah, man. He really does. He's read everything that man's ever written."

"We all have, and we all used to love him, Nina."

Matthew and Nina pushed through the last three row-like clusters of people surrounding the table. The Reporter paused, glanced his way. Was there some recognition hidden behind those blood-shot, cataracting eyes? The Reporter was cleverly setting it up so that he wouldn't have to march with them tonight against Daley's thugs. If he could only get three hundred of the conventioneers in the Democratic Convention to march with him, he said. Then, he promised, he would march with them. Oh, yes, then he'd march through the Daley Dozers and the Daley thugs and the National Guard even through Dante's Inferno. Oh, yes!

Of course, that would be impossible. People were already scared shitless of repercussions from THEM and revolution from US. He'd never pull together three conventioneers much less three hundred, and he knew it! Poor convention fuckers, dilemma-riddled, waiting for Godot to tell them what to do. And, Godot didn't fucking know either.

Matthew stopped to watch The Reporter return the bull horn to the table and stumble off through the crowd. Matthew's head slumped for a moment. "Jesus, I really feel sorry for him."

"Who?"

He nodded toward the table and toward where walls of people had already closed around the path The Reporter had shoved through them like a fast-healing wound. "The Reporter."

"But, I thought you wanted to kill him?"

"Not any more. I just don't want to have to look at him."

Suddenly, Nina squealed. "Crayon!" She dodged a knot of hippies on the right side of the table and leaped into what seemed to be Ward Crampton's arms. "Crayon, baby! What's happening, man?" The tall, lanky man smothered her words with long kisses.

Ward or Crayon, he was obviously happy to see little Nina. Then, who wouldn't be? Hell, she gave everything, took only a little speed. Didn't even have to feed her.

Matthew pushed his way through the growing clump of hippies by the table as a dozen Panther security guards slipped closer to the platform. So far, so good, he thought. No replay of Columbia. Not yet, anyway. If we could only realize why *Peter Pan* hasn't played in fifteen years on TV or at the movie houses, then we'd understand why we can be strong, can survive, maybe even prevail as Faulkner said between benders.

The young man Nina called Crayon was rangy in his patched Wranglers and rainbow work shirt. His face was one of those square-jawed, blue-chinned types Matthew would have expected to see sauntering along Madison or Park Avenues or along Wall Street in subdued pinstripes. Except for his auburn hair being pulled behind his neck in a long ponytail, he looked exactly like Ward's photographs which Matthew always carried in his wallet. This was just plain eerie, he thought. He felt like he was about to interview the man he had driven to his death over six years before. As he emerged from the knot of people, Nina spotted him. She waved and began dragging the young man toward him.

Matthew's eyes focused on Nina and Crayon scuffling in his direction. The people seemed to congeal around the edges of the open space just past the Panthers and the hippies massed to the right of the improvised stage, ringing the three of them with the white iridescence of their candles. He sensed their closeness to each other in the way their hands clasped, fingers entwined, only loosening as they neared where he stood, transfixed in the white circle of light.

Instinctively, but without ever having had such instincts before, Matthew unsnapped the leatherette camera case dangling against his hip. The front fell open, exposing the camera's covered lens. He popped off the lens cover, adjusted focus, ASA, shutter speed. Then, he dropped to his right knee and began clicking shots of them until they stopped only a few steps away. He smiled at them through the single reflex lens. "What's happening?"

"Crayon, this is Matthew. He's a reporter for *The Voice*. He wants to do an interview with you or something." Nina began shoving him toward Matthew's outstretched hand.

Crayon balked. "Yeah? You for real, man?"

"Oh, come on, Crayon, baby. Come on now. Don't be like that. He's a nice enough guy with a job to do."

Crayon's perse eyes seemed like holes in his head in the circle of dull, creamy light. Matthew shivered in the muggy Chicago night although it was far from cool.

There's no way to know where it starts, a shiver. >Sensation >Reaction >Thought >Action >Results. You can pick it up anywhere, it seems. Just like an itch. You sense the itch; your hand scratches; you think: I've got an itch. You put calamine lotion on the irritated skin; the itching stops. Consequently, you feel no more itching; therefore you no longer scratch your skin. You think: I no longer have an itch. You begin pecking at the keys of your antique Underwood elite (all your mother left you); you describe the process you've just experienced.

"Come on, Crayon. Be cool, baby."

Nina reminded him of Emmy Lou's passion and softness. Awash in space. Sharp breath. Helpless, helpless, helpless. Sucked up between her briny lips. Life ring on this angered sea.

Crayon finally clasped the back of Matthew's hand. Their thumbs hooked. His wiry lips rippled in a hesitant smile. "Matthew?"

"Crayon."

"Yeah, man. Folks started calling me that after Nina tie-dyed this shirt for me."

Matthew fumbled with the camera in his left hand. "What's happening?"

"Not much, man. Just getting it on with this little revolution of ours, man, you know?" Crayon's slender, callused fingers searched his left shirt pocket for cigarettes. He extracted a Lucky Strike and lit it off of Nina's lighter which she had waiting for him. "Thanks, baby." He turned back to Matthew, still scrutinizing him. "You know, man, I don't much like that picture-taking shit. I mean, there're warrants out on me in twelve fucking states!" He paused, dragging deeply on his Lucky. "You dig?"

"Sure, man. I dig. I'm sorry, man. Just trying to get some candid shots, you know." He grasped the camera again which he had let drop back onto his hip. "Here, man, I can pull the film out right now," he continued. He popped the back of the Nikon open and reached for the film inside with his fingers.

"Hey, no, man. Like, that's cool. If it's really for *The Voice*, that's cool."

Matthew closed the camera, letting it drop again to his hip. The people surrounding them surged forward like a wave that has crested and rushes toward the shore. The ring of light shattered into a thousand small flickers.

"You'll have to interview him later, Matthew," Nina interrupted. "The march is starting." She winked at Matthew and clung to Crayon's left arm and Matthew's right.

"He's not the guy I'm looking for, Nina," Matthew whispered, "but thanks. I owe you both. I'll clear things up with Crayon after the march. Okay?"

"That's cool, Matthew. That's real cool."

The mass of demonstrators carried them toward the barricades around the park, manned by the National Guardsmen. Their terrified young faces glowed in the candle light like devil masks formed from fire and deep dark shadows. As the mass swayed and stumbled forward in the tide of the march beginning, they were surrounded by low hoarse voices:

"The whole world's watching."

Matthew wasn't sure if he'd made himself clear to Nina. The chanting had become instant thunder, erupting from Grant park. He took up the chant with the others.

"The whole world's watching. The whole world's watching! The whole world's watching!"

Invisible people shoved lighted candles into their hands. Matthew held his candle aloft with his left hand. His right hand clenched in a fist, he thrust above his head.

"The whole world's watching!"

The march on the Amphitheater was going down.

* * * * *

"So, Crayon. I'm really sorry about my little deception, man. But, I'm really desperate to find my friend, if he's still alive." Matthew grasped the cell bars in frustration. He had real problems with being confined, no matter how many times he found himself behind them.

"It was really all my fault, baby." Nina leaned against the carbondium-like bars which, at least temporarily, defined their universe. "I believed his story about this friend that was missing in action in Vietnam and all and that he really believed you might be that friend. Hell, Crayon, he showed me a picture that I would've sworn was you. And you've always been so secretive about your past. Anyway, I remembered him from the March on Washington and his court martial and all. So, man, I believed him. But I just knew that you would be too paranoid to believe such a story. So." She shrugged against the bars. "We came up with this idea of Matthew posing as a *Voice* reporter. It was harmless, man."

"Hey, it's okay, baby. Look around you. We're all in this place together. We know each other in the only way that counts."

"Right on, Crayon," Matthew muttered, extending his hand.

"Right fucking on, Matthew!" He grasped the offered hand, locking thumbs and wrapping their fingers around each other's hand in the handshake of the revolution. "You know, man, speaking of right on, what I want to know is who was the pig you laid that right hook on?" Crayon chuckled.

"Yeah, baby. You almost put his coccyx between his balls," Nina smirked, running her thumbs THUNK THUNK THUNK THUNK along the bars of their cell which smelled like it was normally used for a drunk tank.

"I'm really sorry about this, too." Matthew squatted on the concrete floor, propped his elbows on his knees, his bearded chin seated in his palms. He shrugged, stuffed his notebook into his back pocket. Pigs had confiscated the camera, but they didn't discover his notebook . . . . "Listen, Crayon. Nina. Everybody." He turned slowly on his heels until he'd locked eyes momentarily with each woman and man in the cell. "I truly apologize."

"For what, man?"

"For trashing a pig, man?"

"Bullshit!"

"No, listen to me. If I hadn't taken that cop out, then none of you would be in this cell right now. It's because of my lack of control that all of you got busted!"

"Fuck, Matthew, don't you think we can accomplish such feats as this without outside intervention?"

"Oh, I'm sure you can, Crayon. But, we're very likely stuck in this particular cell on this particular night because of one particular lie that this particular hippie told so very long ago." Matthew paused. "You see, man, what you do does come back to you, usually when you least expect it and in ways you never could've predicted."

Crayon leaned down to him, wrapping his arm around Matthew's sloped shoulders. "You really hit that pig like you knew him, man. I mean, you know, like it seemed like a real personal kind of hit?"

"It *was* personal," Matthew stood slowly, staring past milling students to the bone white back wall of the tank.

OFF THE PIGS!
BAIL FOR THE BALEFUL: 666-3333
OR
ESCAPE BY READING INSTRUCTIONS BELOW

Of course, the instructions below had been painted over with battleship gray paint leaving a glossy gray swath where escape once lay. The truth is chiseled on the drunk tank walls. The history of humans. No different from his own. Christ. Couldn't believe his eyes when that baby jowled face leered at him through the glare of the search lights. Covered in a riot helmet, his head looked like a bowling ball. His eyes and mouth were the finger holes. A bath of blinding white light emanated from spot lights behind their barricades and cordon lines. Just when you think you've got something buried, it appears to haunt you.

The bowling ball beast spotted Matthew when he popped up like a cork on a wave into the front line of demonstrators. The beast broke ranks, screams of rage tearing from his throat. His uniform seemed aflame in the lights as he tore through the barricade nearest Matthew, and, swinging his club above his helmeted head, he bore down on Matthew's startled face, also aglow in the blazing lights. Matthew instinctively side stepped the beast's charge. Donaldson? He brought his fists like a single club into his attacker's back knocking him to the pavement.

Suddenly, tear gas clouds floated toward them as the cordon lines swept past the barricades with the unblinking yellow lights. The faces of the police were covered with gas masks. Creatures from the Black Lagoon grabbed him by both arms from behind. They slapped cuffs on him, Crayon, Nina, and others who were marching close to them as they carried Donaldson to a medevac vehicle and led their prisoners off to one of the dozens of paddy wagons lining the curbs of the streets of Chicago.

"I thought I heard you yell his name. And I know he yelled yours?" Nina sucked on one of Matthew's last Winstons as she leaned forward from her perch behind Crayon on the only cot in the cell."

"Come on, Matthew, tell us."

Matthew's lips curled involuntarily. "Wish we had a few good joints to pass around while I tell you this one."

"Tell us the story, man."

"Come on, Matthew, baby, tell us the story about you and the Chicago pig." Nina chucked his bearded face. "Sounds like it should be playing on Broadway," she laughed.

Her smile reminded him of how much he had taken. Couldn't he give a little back, too? Even if it was nothing more than a story?

"Okay. Here goes." He lit a Winston which he periodically waved in the air like a conductor's baton as he recited his story.

> *Listen my children, and you shall know*
> *Of the trials and treasons of Matthew Parkrow.*

He paused to allow for the good-natured groans of the few in the cell who still remembered Longfellow.

> *It was twenty-one October of sixty-seven—*
> *Most of us still under heaven*
> *Remember that infamous day as the one*
> *When America charged the Pentagon.*
>
> *Matthew was confused, on the wrong*
> *   side of the field.*
> *As the battle raged, he knew he'd*
> *   soon yield*
> *To the incessant truth of Amerika's chant:*

"All we are saying is give peace a chance."

Matthew lit his final cigarette off of the one he was smoking, which he, then, snuffed on the heel of his sneaker.

"Right on, man!"

"All right, man. All right!"

"Get it on, baby! Get it on!"

"We can dig it!"

At least fifteen bodies huddled closer in the corner of the tank where Matthew paced as he continued his story.

> *Eddie Donaldson, marked for strife,*
> *Never important in anyone's life,*
> *Was picked to be the man*
> *To spy on the hippies first hand.*
>
> *Matthew had authored the plan,*
> *So only he could stop Donaldson.*
> *He felt alive again as he charged the line.*
> *He was real once more, getting busted at*
> *The Pentagon.*
>
> *Somewhere the sun is shining;*
> *Somewhere the game is a rout.*
> *But, there was no joy in Amerika*
> *That day,*
> *For Mighty Peace had struck out.*

"Cool it! Turnkey's comin'!"

> *All the doors were closed to him*
> *Except for those that closed around him.*

The guard's boots ceased their hollow thumping. Matthew heard a clanking of metal against metal as a key rattled in the lock to their cell door. "What's this jive-ass shit you're talking, honky freak?"

Matthew wheeled around. Opening the cell door was a slick faced man about twenty-one or two. His taffy face showed nothing of his feelings, if he felt anything. Dull brown eyes looked out at them from smoky whites.

Matthew swept his right hand under his chest as he bowed in the direction of the mulatto turnkey and continued his recitation.

So, he turned his mind to newer things
That could not, so soon, drown him.

"What is this shit, honky freak?" Turnkey shoved Matthew and others aside like tree branches blocking his path along a trail as he stepped inside the cell and peered around the tank, seemingly looking for someone.

"Your grace, sir." Matthew groveled on the concrete at Turnkey's feet where the guard's shove had landed him. "Have mercy. I'm just a poor troubadour, a bard of America the beautiful and the home of the grave." He pretended to shudder. Everyone in the tank was in hysterics. "Have mercy, please, massa!"

Turnkey's thread like lips sneered, showing parts of silver fillings in his teeth. "You didn't have none on me." He kicked Matthew's chest with the instep of his boot, pushing him onto his back on the concrete floor and leaning his weight on his foot, thus pinning Matthew helplessly to the floor. "When you was massa!"

The cement was cool through his T-shirt, but Turnkey's heel seemed to brand his chest with fire just over his heart. His heart thudded like kettle drums in the 1812 Overture. Matthew choked out words around short painful breaths from his crushing chest. "I don't . . . don't . . . even . . . know . . . you . . . ." Suddenly, he was seized with coughing and could hardly get his breath at all. He became so desperate for breath that he forced Turnkey's boot from his chest which caused Turnkey to stumble. He grabbed the bars next to the still-ajar cell door. Crayon and Nina immediately knelt over Matthew to protect him. They were joined by four others in the cell who were black.

"Hey, man. You okay?"

"Can you breath now, Matthew?"

Matthew nodded. "The VC couldn't kill me. For sure, this asshole can't," he spit toward Turnkey.

Crayon glared at Turnkey as he straightened himself against the bars and edged toward the door. The demonstrators began creeping toward Turnkey, too, a communal snarl welling in their collective black and white throats. Crayon flashed his hand in the air. "No. Let it be. He's the one who's got to live with what he is." He turned back toward Turnkey, whose face was flushed and sweaty as he slid toward the open cell door. "Better get out of here while you still can, Screw!"

Turnkey bolted through the open door of bars, slammed it shut behind him, and hurriedly locked it. "Christ, you people are crazy!"

Everyone in the tank whooped, yelped, crowed, squealed, and banged bars or thumped the graffiti muraled walls. Matthew struggled to his feet, clinging to Crayon's arm. His chest felt like it was concave over his heart, but Crayon said it was only a bad bruising.

"It'll hurt like hell for a few days, man, but no broken bones or anything."

Trance-like, Matthew began mumbling a new poem as it boiled in his oxygen-starved brain.

> *Turnkey, oh, Turnkey,*
> *Won't you let me go free?*
> *Turnkey, oh, Turnkey,*
> *Don't you know it's just me?*

In the back of the clump of prisoners, a guitar began picking a tune by single notes, then chords, and they all began to sing while they heard Turnkey's scuffling feet hurrying away from them to the cell block door.

> *Turnkey, oh, Turnkey,*
> *Won't you let me go free?*
> *Turnkey, oh, Turnkey,*
> *Don't you know it's just me?*

Whirrrrrr. The block door slammed open. Quick boot steps. Hushed words, echoing inaudibly in the hall. Whirrrrrr. The block door slammed shut.

They told stories and sang songs through the night just as they used to around campfires when they were kids growing up in places like Roanoke Park.

Matthew searched his father's eyes for a sign . . . some hint of something, anything.

"I'm so tired, Jason, so weary. I'm all beaten up, and I need some real R & R. I need . . . ."

These are the pearls that were his eyes.

"Hell, I only came here because you invited me, you know. Well, didn't you?"

"Christ, son. That was over a year ago. Long before all this." He flailed his arm like a bird in a cross wind. "All of this . . . ah . . . 'mess' you've gotten yourself into."

"Goddamn it, Jason! I've given you the best I've got to offer. We all have. We've given you our courage. We've given you our honor. We've given you our individualism. We've given you our hearts and minds. We've given you our lives, for Christ sake!

"So, we went to Vietnam, in spite of ourselves—out of honor and duty to god and country—just like the Boy fucking Scouts of Amerika. Now, parts of us are scattered over those rice paddies and jungles, because *you* said it was a righteous war.

"Yet, nothing seems to be enough for you. You treat our offerings as if they were gifts from Cain."

"Son. Son. Son. But, when it comes right down to, specifically and only, you—not some abstract 'they' or 'them' or 'your generation', but you—then what are you going to do now with this . . . ah . . . 'mess' hanging over you? And your record?"

"I'm going to teach English, Jason. I just have one semester left until I get my masters degree. That's what I'm going to do specifically now. Teach English."

"And, how long do you think that you'll last at that before you get a hold of some cause or another and get yourself booted out of the teaching profession altogether just like you did the Army?"

"Why would you say something like that, Jason?"

"'Cause. Just 'cause." He fidgeted on the end of the couch, as if anticipating what would be a most welcomed interruption by the telephone. "Well, look at your background, your past history, son. Look at your record." Jason leaned forward, counting on his fingers as he began to tick off his list.

"First, there was you not being satisfied with hitting the game-winning home run. No siree, bobwhite! Not my son! No! The

Mayor's son had to try and convince the whole world that his home run was really a foul ball.

"Second, you quit the State University baseball team in your junior year even though you were a scholarship All-American second baseman to protest a war you later fought in." Jason wagged his head. "That's one I'll never figure out." He twisted his laced gnarled fingers.

"Third, you deserted your military post under combat-like conditions during the Siege of the Pentagon. You, a much-decorated war hero. And you were teaching then!

"Fourth, you've led demonstrations against the very university which was open-minded enough—too damned open-minded if you ask me—to accept you into their graduate school despite your dishonorable discharge and general military disgrace.

"So," he shrugged and reclined into the corner folds of the couch, totally self-satisfied with his presentation of the facts. "Why should I expect anything but your eventual self-destruction as a college English teacher as well?"

A factual deboning, to be sure, Matthew thought. But, he was struck dumb more by how the facts were coming in conflict with reality more and more and more lately than by the factual force of Jason's argument.

The telephone rang. Jason snatched up the receiver. "You're too late, now, goddamn it!" Jason hocked into the receiver behind the barrier of his left hand. "What? Oh, Christ!" He slammed the receiver down. "I've got to run, son. We'll talk more, later. I'm sure we can work something out together."

"But, it's Christmas Eve, for Christ sake, Jason. Can't you get off the political treadmill for just one night?"

"Just a little flap with some environmental extremists. Shouldn't take very long. Have Alecia hold our Christmas Eve dinner until eight. Being from the big city and all, I guess you prefer eating late, anyway, don't you?"

"Yes, sir, I do. Maybe we can open presents afterwards by the tree in the living room just like we used to."

"We'll see, son. We'll see. Gotta run, now."

Although the meadowlark couldn't fly or stand, it beat tan blackspeckled wings, stirring up the snow-like flakes that coated the hole they'd lost so many baseballs in. Claws clutched invisible branches of the loblolly pines leaning over the deep gouge in the earth which Matthew and his friends used as a meeting place before most of the meadows that once surrounded Roanoke Park were seeded by city annexation and sprouted more homes for the home-coming GIs who beat the hell out of Hitler and Mussolini and devastated To Jo and Hirohito. The place where he and Ward and Emmy Lou had often pretended to be cave explorers or pretended they were part of the expedition in *Journey to the Center of the Earth*.

Matthew knelt by the rasping meadowlark flopped on its side, now, eyes glazed and crossed. He shook his fists and screeched at the four crop dusters buzzing Roanoke Park for the third time since he had come out at sunrise to take a long muffled walk in the early morning snow, the first snow he'd seen in a long time. "Goddamn it, what are you doing, you fools? It's Christmas morning, for Christ's sake!"

He scooped up a fist full of accumulating snow. It crumbled like powder in his fingers as he put it to his nose. No real smell, yet a vague almost-scent of some sort of chemical. Deadly perfume. He sniffed it in the gelid air, sensed it clinging to his scraggly beard and collar-length curls and permeating his black-and-yellow flannel CP jacket and his Levis. "You're seeding the fucking snow with poison, for Christ sake." Matthew touched the bird's yellow chest, searching for signs of life. It's wings, now rigid. It's labored breathing, arrested.

Although it was after sunrise, it was not yet light out due to the snow clouds packed in overhead. The crop dusters sputtered and buzzed in the distance. Their sounds seemed muffled in the snow stuffed air. The telephone jangled again past the loblollies. Tears erupted down his cheeks, harlequined by the seeded snow as the meadowlark's stiff cooling body was. Beyond the pine stand separating the hole from his father's gardener-manicured lawn, the jangling telephone continued. "What child is this?"

By the twenty-sixth or so time the telephone rang, Matthew's fingers had clawed an opening in the foot of the south wall of the hole where pine saplings bowed to the ground under the weight of the mysterious poison snow which still poured from the clouds. He gathered enough stones to cover the opening after he had nestled the meadowlark in its final resting place. Is that how Ward died in the chopper—arms flapping, mouth gaping, flames consuming his breath, then his body, as, in time, the earth would consume this bird felled by a white Christmas rather than by a VC rocket?

That must be the fortieth call, he guessed. Something was rotten in Roanoke Park and he was—oh shit!—no prince Hamlet nor was he meant to be. More likely the son of Willie and Loch Loman—the son of the fucking Mayor. Matthew jammed the final stone into the top of the mound of stones now marking the meadowlark's grave. His face screwed against the bitter breeze beginning to swirl the snow around him as he knelt on the floor of the hole. His field jacket and face were beginning to turn paste white as the snow clung more and more to him. He trembled with despair.

Dead like Ward. Matthew's jeans, too, were spattered white. Like dead Ward. He stumbled to his feet and scrambled hands-over-feet up the clay bank to the pine and honeysuckle thicket where Roanoke Creek now trickled only a hundred feet or so before being diverted by a reinforced concrete cul-de-sac into the sewer at the north end of the hole: a contracting oasis in a desert of VA and FHA housing.

Matthew was nine when his father gave him that Pee Wee Reese four-finger Rawlings PMM. The glove was so big for him that he scooped more sand than baseballs at second base for the Roanoke Park Nomads. Then, Roanoke Creek rushed over a bed of smooth white and gray pebbles and mossy rocks, through the pine woods dense with honeysuckle vines, under an oak bridge where the dirt road shoved a one-car-wide clay gash to the power relay station two miles further into the woods. Thick black cables danced, even then, above the forest canopy to the several isolated settlements just a few miles north of Raleigh. This was the direction things would grow, he'd heard his father say at their dinner table discussions. Jason had encouraged him to ask any questions or to discuss any subject at the dinner table, usually the only time they had together.

"That's why I'm busting my fanny to buy up all this land around us, son." Jason would pull at his stiff white shirt collar, loosen the string tie he wore to ingratiate himself with his rural customers, and puff his chest just a little before he continued in answer to Matthew's persistent dinner table question: What's going to happen to the woods when things grow this way?

"I sell more lightning rods than any salesman in the whole country so I can save this. All of this." He'd swoop his gangly arms in circles as he spoke. "Save it for you, son. Don't you worry none. Nothing's going to happen to your woods, Matthew." He would smile, reach across the blue-and-white checked oil cloth, over the worn Wedgwood platter still containing fried chicken wings and rumple Matthew's hair. "I'll buy it all. I promise, I'll buy it all for you, son."

The telephone was ringing again as he crossed the rolling yard which used to extend over a dirt path into a large meadow where the Nomads practiced for their games against the neighborhood teams from other communities at the ends of the other black cables that ran pole to pole from the relay station.

Now, Creek Drive replaced the dirt path. The crab grass meadow beyond had been obliterated by expansions of the original housing development as well as the recent construction of the world's largest ChamCorp distribution plant. When Turkey Locklear first organized the Nomads, there was no field they could call home. The meadow was fine for their practices but the wrong shape for a baseball field.

"We'll play anybody, no madda where or when, long as they got a field!" When Turkey shouted, his Adam's apple bobbed like a turkey when it gobbled, and his voice would break on the high syllables of his deep south accent touched by a year in the Bronx with his birth father when he was ten. "Abner Doubleday invented baseball in a fucking meadow just like ours." That was why Turkey Locklear was their leader. He knew all the impressive information and words you could ever want to know about baseball and owned more baseball cards than anyone else. At thirteen, he was the oldest boy who lived at their end of one black cable. The only one whose voice was changing. The only one who'd had an actual wet dream. And, most important, the only one who'd actually been to New York City, to Yankee Stadium where he had watched his daddy go two for three and a walk with three runs scored and two RBI's to lead the Bronx Bombers to victory over the Chicago White Sox. Turkey's horn rimmed glasses glinted in the sun as they did every time he twisted his head toward his right shoulder just before he threw a curve.

Matthew entered a side door on the northwest side of the house. The door opened directly into Jason's den. It doubled, for all these years, as his office.

"It's aldrin, madam. To destroy those blasted Japanese Beetles, madam. The very ones you've all been complaining about. They would've done to this town what their Zeros did to Pearl Harbor, madam!" Jason Parkrow's swarthy face dripped perspiration as he shouted into the telephone. "I know this is Christmas morning, madam. I have a son whom I still have to play Santa Claus for this morning, myself. That is, if I can ever get off of the telephone, madam!" He pulled at the open collar of his red flannel bathrobe. His matching slippers plopped along the pine-tar colored shag carpet while he paced the length of his new cowhide couch and back continuously as he talked, listened. Suddenly, he flopped his gangly frame onto the couch in mid-stride. He beckoned for Matthew to wait, then whispered into the receiver. "It was an invasion, madam. Our aircraft have been on alert for three days, but this morning was the first morning that it snowed, the first time we could seed the clouds safely. Yes, thank you, madam."

Jason abruptly dropped the copper-trimmed receiver back onto the copper-trimmed base as he leaped from the couch. He stumbled toward Matthew, grabbing his shoulders. "My God, son, you've gotta help get these damned radicals and environmentalist freaks off of my ass! Now that you've given up on all that teaching foolishness or whatever and you've come home, you'll be my number one staff assistant. Your first assignment: Get those fuckers outta my hair, at least what there is left of it."

"What the hell are you talking about, Jason?" Matthew pulled free of his father's grasp. "I never said that I was leaving Columbia or giving up the idea of teaching!" Matthew touched the sore spots left by his father's bruising fingers. "And, I certainly never said that I'd go to work for you. Christ! All those phone calls? Japanese Beetle invasions? Jesus, Jason. Look at my face, will you. My clothes." He sucked in a deep breath. "Look at your hands where you grabbed my shoulders."

Jason tripped back onto the couch as he, first, really noticed his son's End Man face. "What you up to, boy? Imitating Al Jolson?" He forced a quivering grin, ignored Matthew's denial, and lit another Camel, his tenth of the morning already. One still burned in the alabaster ash tray in the middle of the mahogany coffee table in front of the fat couch where he sat. His eyes sought the safety of the Remington hanging from the white oak paneled wall surrounding a shellacked limestone hearth.

The Remington wasn't an original, either. Only a print of *Calvary Charge on a Southern Plain.* Hell, Jason Parkrow, himself, was only a print. That, Matthew reasoned, made him the son of a print. Nothing very original there either. "What are you destroying, now, Jason?" He scowled as he stepped closer to his father's averted face. "I just buried a bird, a meadowlark, in the hole." As he continued, he felt his lips beginning to tremble. He clutched his CP jacket tighter around him as if he were chilled. "That poor bird was covered with the same stuff that I've got all over me. The same stuff that you've got on your hands. Will it drive me insane, then kill me like it did that meadowlark?"

The phone rang.

"Will it, Jason?"

"Mayor Parkrow, here." He lit another Camel from the butt of the one he, then, squashed in the ash tray as he fidgeted in his seat and his face clouded over again. "I have not poisoned Roanoke Park! Quite the contrary, I've saved it from pestilence!" This time he slammed the receiver onto its base. "Goddamned communist bastards!"

"Who, Jason?" Matthew smirked.

"The Audubon Society!" He lit another cigarette, forgetting that he had one burning in the ash tray. "Alecia! Where's my breakfast?"

"Almost ready, yoah honor."

From the other end of the ranch-style house, Matthew heard the maid's muffled voice. Maid? Hell. Alecia had been more than that. She'd been his mother, his nanny, his maid, and, quite often, his conscience all wrapped up into one. "The Audubon Society?"

"Yessss! The Audubon Society and the Veterinarian Association and the SPCA and Mrs. Pogowaller across the road. She's helping Naomi Locklear on this bird sanctuary business."

"Mrs. Pogowaller, Jason? That woman wraps flags around her fat ass quicker than mu'u-mu'u's, and she worked that same flag-covered ass off for Nixon just like somebody else in this room did."

Jason tried to smile as the telephone rang again. "You worked for Nixon, son?" he chortled, picking up the receiver. "Why, I'm right surprised at you, son. Hello, Mayor Parkrow, here."

Matthew rose quickly, hoping to escape to the relative safety of the kitchen during this phone call. Jason caught his eye and motioned for him to stay. He sat down again. After all, it was Jason's house. "Japanese Beetles, sir! Is this Adam Gaffendale?" Jason nodded to himself. "Oh, it is. Well, Adam, son of councilman elected on my coattails Gaffendale, your goddamned nursery would've looked like fucking Pearl Harbor if my aces hadn't done their jobs this morning!"

"You used Pearl Harbor before," Matthew muttered.

Jason waved him to be quiet. "Thank you. I'll be expecting that token of your support and appreciation in the mail real soon, now." Jason smirked as he spoke. He suddenly seemed to realize the expression on his face and altered it to a Christmas morning Santa Claus smile as he recradled the telephone for the umptieth time.

"Son, you heard me say to somebody earlier that I still had a little Santa Claus playing to do myself, didn't you?"

"Yes, Jason. I do believe that, somewhere in the blur of this jingle jangle morning, I heard something like that. I was puzzled then, I must admit. And I'm still puzzled now. I mean, you didn't even get home in time for Christmas Eve dinner after we waited and waited for you."

"Well, son, I am real sorry about Christmas Eve dinner and not opening presents and all that, but . . . ." He pulled an envelope from his robe pocket. "Ho! Ho! Ho!" He shoved the large red envelope at his son. "Merry Christmas, son. Mer-ry Christ-mas!" He waved the envelope in front of Matthew's startled eyes. "Here, son. Take it! This is the best Christmas present anyone could ever hope for."

Matthew did not reach out for the proffered envelop. Instead, he glared at it as if it were possibly booby-trapped. "What is it?"

"Now, that would spoil it. It's a Christmas present, just like I said, son, from ole Saint Nick Jason for you to open and see."

The flap was unsealed as Matthew very hesitantly accepted the envelope with the tips of his fingers, holding it at a distance as if it might be diseased. Opening the flap, Matthew spotted folded typed pages of what appeared to be some kind of legal document. "What the fuck is this, Jason?"

"It's a document setting up a trust of all I own in your name, son. It's all for you, son. It's always been all for you, son.

"The trust will continue to pay all household and estate expenses, and provide for Alecia and Emmy Lou. And, I'll live off of my Mayoral salary and retirement when that time regrettably comes."

"I can never accept this, Jason." Without even extracting the document from the red envelope, Matthew pushed it back at his father.

Jason put his hands up in protest. "No. Everyone's taken care of, son. But, it puts you in charge. Please, son. This is for you. For you like I always promised."

"You know that I could never . . . ." Matthew dropped the Trust, unopened, into Jason's lap. "That would be, somehow, like sanctioning what you've done all these years, and I just can't do that. Not now, not ever!" Matthew stomped from the den, through the narrow hallway to the living and dining rooms. There was no talking with Jason, so it seemed. He had his agenda, and there was no reasoning with it or with him. No answers. He took a left into the dining room where Alecia was setting the table for breakfast. Her head was almost cone shaped as if it had been bound by twine when she was a baby the way she'd told him, when he was a small child, that her tribe back in Africa did. Her hair curled close to her scalp like gray wool. Her black lips were like saucers. She'd raised him like her own from the time his mother died at his birth. Jason used to joke that his mother had died of fright after taking one look at him. Jason's jokes might win him votes, but . . . ."

"Lordy, Master Matthew. "Wha's dat all over yoah face and coat and look at yoah trousers." She shook her head as she turned from Matthew and the set table and shuffled across the emerald carpet, through the swinging doors into the kitchen.

"I'm playing a reverse Al Jolson in the school play."

"Oh, go on with you now, Master Matthew."

"How long before breakfast, Alecia?"

"Any time, now, Master Matthew. You go on in and wash up first, like a good boy."

"If this shit'll actually wash off. Who knows. I may be permanently stained." He scuffed the carpet until he'd separated the nape enough to see the porous material that the carpet threads were woven through. "Actually, Alecia, the Mayor tried to poison me this morning, I believe." Should serve him the roasted body of that poor dead bird for his breakfast. Bastard! He giggled, however, as he continued. "Tha's why Ah'm sooo white, Ms. Alecia, honey!" he teased.

"Now, Master Matthew, hush yoah mouth!" Alecia slumped back through the pastel green swinging doors, a platter of country ham and redeye gravy in one hand and a large bowl of lumpy grits in the other. Steam swirled from the platter and the bowl as she placed them in the exact center of the Carolina-blue lace table cloth. Folks is gonna think yoah crazy, Master Matthew."

"Folks already do." He hesitated. He had always really hated it when she called him that Master Matthew shit. He needed to stop that once and for all. And, maybe this would be the last time he'd even be in this house. So, it had to be now or never. "They already do call me crazy, Slave Alecia!"

Alecia's cloudy brown eyes welled up with tears. She turned away from the young man who had been like a son to her for all these years and started for the kitchen again. "Master Matthew," she sniveled, hesitating at the swinging doors. "Why you go and say such a thing to somebody's been like a momma to you all yoah life?" She continued to mumble under her breath as she exited into the kitchen.

Matthew bounced across the carpet, burst through the doors like a gunslinger into a saloon. Eggs were frying in ham grease in a cast iron skillet on the gas stove. The pungent odor of salty ham smothered his senses. It hurt him, too, to say these things to this woman he loved like a mother, but now was the time. "Why do you call me Master Matthew?"

"'Cause you is Master Matthew!" Flinging her head back, Alecia caught two pieces of toast, flung from the toaster, in midair and began to butter them on the Formica counter top across from the stove.

"No damn more than you're Slave Alecia. And I resent being called Master Matthew just as much as you do being called Slave Alecia. Okay?"

Alecia's tiny frame shivered in the kitchen despite the heat. She dropped the butter knife onto the counter top and turned on Matthew. The soft yellow light from the clear dome on the ceiling flattened the lines of her cheeks in shadows of her wide nose. Her eyes were bloodshot like the eggs in the crystal bowl beside the frying pan on the stove waiting for their turn to swim in hot ham grease.

"I just plain nevah thought about it like dat, Mas . . . ah . . . Matthew. Your daddy . . . ah . . . ." She stammered about for words to express her feelings.

"Goddamn it, Alecia! You have to hatch those eggs to make the hens to lay the eggs to make my breakfast or what?"

"No, yoah honor! Ready right now. Come and get it!" In her shouts, Matthew could not detect even a taint of her frustration. She turned to Matthew and whispered, "I'm sorry."

"Me, too, Alecia." He reached out and embraced the aging black mother, the only mother he'd ever known. "But, I don't like it any more than you do. Can you dig where I'm coming from?"

"Yes. Okay, crazy boy." Her lips popped open in a wide smile. "Now off to the bathroom with you a'fore you mess up my whole house and not just my smock."

Matthew glanced at her calico smock, now spotted with white, powdery patches where he had touched her. "Oh, God! You, too, Alecia. That stuff really is poison. I'm not kidding you about that. It killed a meadowlark out by the hole earlier this morning. I buried it in the hole. You'd better change, too."

"Yes, Mas . . . ah . . . Matthew. Soon as yoah daddy's eatin'."

She should shake that shit all over his eggs and grits like salt, Matthew thought. Let the Mayor of Roanoke Park eat aldrin.

"You go on, now. I'll save these eggs in the bowl for you."

The picture on the midget television compelled Matthew to switch the sound from FM radio back to the television: "Frank Bormann, James Lovell, and William Anders are into their ninetieth hour of Apollo Eight, man's first flight to the moon, climaxing, appropriately, on this Christmas day, 1968, with these shots of the lunar surface from the Apollo Eight command module."

The first lunar shots faded to a commercial about letting IBM do your thinking for you. Matthew's leathery skin tingled under a shower of steaming water. The four-inch black-and-white screen above the faucet handles was edged in the same stainless steel which the faucets, the shower nozzle, and the shower door casing were made of. Its screen was protected from moisture and heat by a sealed plexi-glass covering masoned into the walls of ceramic surrounding him except for the door to his left. Until Jason had the television installed last week as the house's Christmas present (he didn't want to miss any of the news just in case he was mentioned), the alternating red-and-white tiles covering the walls and floor had reminded him of a shower stall in the gym at Roanoke Park High School. Jason had it built that way for him when he and his new friend from Florida, Ward Crampton, were the only sophomores to make the high school baseball team in the ten years of the school's existence.

"The astronauts are on the dark side of the moon now. Another American first! So while we are in communications black out with them, we'll go to Jules Bergman at Houston Control for an update on this most recent turn of events right after the following commercial messages."

Marching mechanics filled the screen, singing "Atlantic keeps your car on the go, go, go."

Matthew lathered his scalp and winced when the hot water hit too directly on some of the numerous recurring bumps on his back and arms. Chloracne the doctors were calling it. Jungle rot was all he knew.

"A . . . T . . . L . . . A . . . N . . . T . . . I . . . C . . . . Atlantic is the very best." His lips curled back from his teeth, his face a hideous mask of white paint-like streams and suds spilling from his hair.

It was Ward who made him believe he was a Nellie Fox with power, that the two of them were Tinkers and Evers though their only Chance was a dufuss first baseman they called Stretch because he couldn't. Luckily, they both had strong and accurate arms. They could hit Stretch in the letters most every time so he didn't have to stretch. And, old Stretch did have pretty good hands.

Instead of Jules Bergman's smiling face, film footage of the Pueblo being seized in the Sea of Japan by the North Koreans flashed across the screen. "Eighty-two of the eighty-three-man crew of the U.S.S. Pueblo were released in time to be with their families for Christmas." The Johnny Appleseed like announcer took a deep breath on camera before his beak mouth continued. "Here is a look at some of the happy reunited families on this Christmas morning."

Matthew pushed in the on-off button to the left of the screen, turned off the shower, pulled open the door, and stepped onto the bathroom carpet. Steam hung in the air like the clouds over the earth that brought the poisoned snow. Jason laid the red-and-white indoor-outdoor carpet squares himself after that game-winning grand slam for the State Championship. That way the floor matched the walls, he had explained.

It had been their first game under the lights that year, and they all had trouble hitting until the late innings. They were having trouble picking up the white ball against the backdrop of the lights. Down three to nothing in the bottom of the ninth, Ward started things off with a blooper to right center which he turned into a double with his speed. The clean-up hitter walked. Next at bat was the center fielder, Eddie Mason, who could put one out of the park on his knees when he connected. More often than not, however, he would strike out. There was a hurried confab at the mound between the Capitol City General's coach and his battery. Matthew knew what had to be going on. Walk Mason. Load the bases. This guy, Parkrow stings the ball but has less power and he hits left handed against their lefty. Even a base hit with the bases full is better than a home run with two men on base when you're ahead three to zip. Play the ball home for the force out.

Matthew remembered how his stomach knotted up when that lefty pitcher walked Mason intentionally to load the bases. As he dug his left foot deep in the batter's box, Matthew heard his father's shrill voice above the noise of the home crowd. "Smack it, Matthew! Kill the ball, son!"

He concentrated on the pitcher's eyes just like Ward had told him to do. He had concentrated on lefty's eyes once before in the West Side Presbyterian Church parking lot before a dance being held after their football game with the General's last fall. Lefty had been the ring leader of the guys who tried to rape Emmy Lou that night. As lefty began his wind up, Matthew cranked his bat clockwise once, shifted his eyes toward where he knew the ball would be released. He felt sure that lefty also remembered the ass-kicking he had received from Matthew on that fall night. Lefty's blond head twitched toward his pitching shoulder just a little, like Turkey Locklear's used to—dead of lymph gland cancer at seventeen only weeks after he'd signed with the Cardinals. Lefty's hand flashed through the glare of lights on the ninety-eight percent humidity hovering in Devereaux Meadow like smog. Matthew cocked his bat at the very last moment. A blur of red stitches tumbled toward home plate. The ball was coming straight at his head. The bastard remembered all right. He was throwing at his head!

Bail out! That had been his instinct. No. Curve ball. It was a roundhouse curve. He was just trying to fake Matthew out, trying to get him to bail out of the batter's box, playing on their past history to make him think the pitch was aimed at his head. Fuck him! Matthew remembered thinking. Stand in tough. Dig back foot in. Begin stride with right foot forward. Commit hips and shoulders but not bat and wrists. It was breaking high. Pull it! Right foot a little more down the line. The blur of stitches was upon him. Commit bat and wrists.

This is for Emmy Lou, you bastard! He didn't feel the concussion of horsehide on thirty-four inches of well-lathed black Duke Snider ash in his clutching fingers, through his forearms, into his shoulders like he expected. As he leaped down the line toward first base, not yet looking at the high line drive sailing for the chain link fence in the right field corner, he wasn't even sure he'd hit the ball except that he'd heard the sound of ball against bat and the roar of the crowd. After he rounded first, he glanced toward the foul pole stretched like a piece of starched tape fifteen feet above the fence. The ball was far above the pole. It seemed to be drifting foul! Goddamn it! He pulled up. Roanoke Park fans in the stands seemed to be applauding, stomping the ivy-choked bleachers surrounding the field on three sides. He started to walk back to the batter's box and pick up his stick when he realized that the ump was waving the ball fair. Somehow, no one else seemed to have seen what he saw in the glaring lights of the ball field. A home run. A grand slam home run. Hot damn! He jogged around the remaining bases and stomped on home plate. Then, he turned and glared murderously at the lefty rapist pitcher as Ward and his team mates mobbed him. But the knots in his stomach wouldn't untie.

As Matthew toweled off, he mumbled to himself. "Even the home team crowd cheered. Ever since Castro had that picture taken on some pitcher's mound in Havana, then took over Cuba as a communist dictator, people in the States had had it in for pitchers. Bay of Pigs, the grand slam that went foul and was called by the umps." He sucked in a deep draught of steamy air. Like a Sai-Gon sauna, for sure.

"You gonna be in there all day, son?" Jason's voice faltered through the mist from beyond the locked bathroom door which had a large color photograph of his game-winning grand slam decoupaged on the upper panel. "We've gotta talk about my . . . ah . . . our . . . ah . . . about your future, son."

Who was he trying to kid? Any talk they would ever really have had already taken place. Anyway, Jason couldn't talk now, or, probably, ever again with his voice so hoarse from all those phone calls. He may even become known as Jason Parkrow, the Mute Mayor.

"Think I'd better just slip the hell out of this place called home," he muttered to himself, "and di di fucking mau back to Manhattan, back to Columbia, back to Emmy Lou's air-conditioned sanity."

"Please allow me to introduce myself, I'm a man of wealth & taste . . . ."

"Please . . . . Let me through, please . . . . I'm a medic." Matthew Australian crawled through the crowd. "I must get to the stage right away!" Fat chance that anyone would believe that he was a medic if they got a look at his pupils. But, he repeated the words again and again, anyway, as if he were chanting his mantra. He continued to slide and shove his way through the crowd of three hundred thousand. There wasn't time to explain that, well, he wasn't really a medic, just a Vietnam vet who had patched up enough buddies that he figured he might be of some use up there on the stage where all hell seemed to be breaking loose.

When he came home from the fighting, he had a key to the town awaiting him. "From Roanoke Park with love, pride, and devotion to our beloved Matthew in whom we are well pleased." A symbolic key had been wrapped in those words on official Jason Parkrow, Mayor stationery. His key. But, they never actually gave him the real thing.

Matthew worked rock festivals with the Red Cross and in OD tents when he was able. He felt that it was one way to give something back to his people at a time when they really needed it. And, his war experience made him much more calm under the fire of sprains, cuts, overdoses, and the occasional birthing than most "lay" help the volunteer doctors and nurses could get otherwise. Yet, in all those festivals, he'd never seen anything like Altamont. At least, not since Nam. The vibes were . . . . Christ, the vibes were very bad. Like steel bands tightening around his temples. Shit, since before the idea was conceived to have this free concert at the Altamont Raceway, the anthropomorphization of the idea was doomed.

"Medic! Let me through, please. Medic! Must get to the stage." He parted a couple wrapped in a Navajo blanket. They were simply in the way of his shortest distance between two points as the crow flies, straight ahead, point blank. He wedged between them.

"Hey, fuck off, man," the redheaded boy challenged.

"Yeah, fuck off, man!" his blond companion mimicked.

Matthew felt a warm damp breast and a hard nipple against his left arm as the blanketed couple parted unwillingly like the Red Sea. The dude's prick slapped against Matthew's right thigh like a Billy stick. Jesus! "Christ! I'm sorry," he shouted over his shoulder. "I didn't realize. Sorry!" He fell forward through the next wall of swaying, sweating people.

Inside the acid in his head, flecks of blood were imbedded underneath his fingernails, deep in the quick, as he inserted an oversized "Key to the city" into the lock on the door to Roanoke Park. The dream was always the same, whether in sleep or on acid. When he tried to turn the key, it wouldn't budge. Sirens fractured his stirrups and hammers and anvils like ear aches used to when he was a small child. His father . . . no, Alecia . . . of course, dark comforting Alecia came to him in the night. Her musky odor, sweet like the meadows deep in the pine forests when the meadows were ripe with hay. Alecia. She brought the warm liquid in the square blue bottle. The warm thick liquid which soothed his aching ears. How it quivered his inner bones at first. Then, the heat began to soothe. Within hours, he could hear again without pain. Sirens spit neon words into the sky around him. THIS LOCK HAS BEEN CHANGED TO PROTECT AGAINST TRAITORS! DO NOT ATTEMPT TO USE YOUR KEY TO THE CITY AGAIN! Matthew dropped the key. Is anyone inside? he asked. This is Matthew. Matthew Parkrow. Son of the fucking mayor. He groped for words, for thoughts. He groped for where the fuck was that voice coming from that spit neon words at him like rockets?

"Excuse me."

"My pleasure, I'm sure," the woman giggled. She winked a volatile violet eye beneath black flowing lashes. Her face was tanned like the rest of her. She stood naked in front of him. A veritable Venus. Her skin breathed. Her face seemed to spread as she pulled him against the hair of her vagina. "Please, baby. Don't run in and out of my sex life like this. Stay awhile with me." She tried to hold him, her vaginal lips pursed for his lips.

"Sorry." He stumbled from her grasp when he saw that head again bouncing around over top of the crowd like a Mitch Miller sing-along dot. That was the third time he'd seen that head. "Ward!" he hallucinated that he yelled as he tried to move toward the bouncing dot head. The Purple haze rushed through him like . . . . He wasn't . . . . Was he? Or . . . . The purples and violets in front of him were lines of infra-red photographs of people. Then fluoroscopes of lines of people in pulsing purples purples purples purples. Oh, soothe sooth sayer, seer, sayers, Gale . . . smooth delicious violet and the growing, uncontrollable smile. Where going? Somewhere going?

Near a stage. To the stage. "Medic!" Help has found its way. "Medic!"

Orange and yellow and red splashed the stage. Jungle drums. Bird calls shook the sound waves. Grunts. Driving piano. Then, Jagger, trying, again, to start *Sympathy for the Devil.*

> *Please allow me to*
> *introduce myself.*
> *I'm a man of*
> *wealth and taste.*

Lights flashed, flared, and zipped across the sky like tie-dyed lightning. A red-orange-and-black cape dervished about Jagger's lithe body. Matthew noticed separate movement off to the left side of the stage. Nothing more specific. The crowd closed in on Jagger and the stage. The Hell's Angels guards held off about two hundred more from getting onto the stage. The Angels had been beating up on hippies all day long like it was their concert, their stage, their rules. What the hell were they doing at the concert, anyway?

> *I've been around for*
> *a long, long time,*
> *helped many a man*
> *seal his fate . . . .*

Rhythm piano and congas counterpointed his words.

And, there was no one in the town. They had all vanished with the installation of the new lock on the town door. There was . . . only . . . the voice. And, the neon staggering stick men he saw in front of him now, the last line between him and the stage.

"OOOH . . . OOOH! OOOH . . . OOOH! OOOH . . . OOOH!" the crowd cried in rhythm to the music.

The left side of the stage heaved with more motion. Angel's clubs or something else flashed in the white spot lights now beaming down into the crowd. What was that?

"OOOH . . . OOOH! OOOH . . . OOOH! OOOH . . . OOOH!" the crowd moaned.

Matthew couldn't remember at this point how long it had been since the announcement came over the P.A. for doctors on stage.

Suddenly, Jagger interrupted his song. "Cool down!" Instead of singing to his audience, he was yelling at them. "Be cool! Be cool!"

Hell, the Angels weren't being very cool, were they? People in general weren't being very cool, were they? The acid wasn't being too cool either, was it? It was jumping him around inside his own head like a Mexican Jumping Bean in a yerba pod. Suddenly, he covered his eyes with his hands as stage left rippled again with new movement. "Oh, no! It's blades they're flashing." The blades shimmered in the orange light. Music stopped completely. Began again. Stuttered again. Then stopped.

Why had the music died? "Medic! Let me through, please. I'm needed on stage!"

It would be the next day before Matthew would read in the newspapers while on a train to El Paso that the scuffling he'd seen on-stage had been the beginnings of what came to be called the Meredith Hunter stabbing and stomping party held by the Hells Angels. Invitations only.

"This sure ain't no Woodstock," a chick to Matthew's left complained to everyone around her and to no one.

"If they'd only consulted an astrologer like they did for Woodstock, then they would have found out that today is absolutely the worst day for a concert like this, what with the moon in Scorpio and all. Like that's really heavy, man."

"Hey, that is heavy, man."

"Hell, it ain't been no Woodstock from Santana's set on, man."

Then it hadn't been a whole lot different from what Matthew had expected. Fracases. Minor incidents between the Angels and the hippies. Somebody said the Stones had requested the Hells Angels as security for their concert. No one planning Woodstock would've ever entertained such a thought . . . of giving Angels police-like authority over 300,000 hippies!

"Medic! Medic! Clear the way. Medic coming through!"

It was definitely going to get worse, not better, as the weekend wore on. As best he could, through the violet and purple acid haze he had become accustomed to looking at the world through after being up for about three hours on Purple Haze, Matthew focused his attention totally on the knife flashes and eruptions of blood on the left side of the stage.

"What's this shit?"

Matthew heard the scowl in the hoarse voice behind him as he felt a large hand vice-grip his left shoulder in its penetrating fingers.

"A reporter for *"The Voice"* in Chicago? A medic at Altamont?"

"Oh!" Linda shrieked as she fell over a large man holding Matthew from behind by his shoulders. "Please, don't hurt him. Please, don't." She cowered against his sandaled feet. "Don't hurt us . . . . I'll do anything . . . ."

Matthew felt the fingers digging into his shoulder, then, suddenly, relaxing.

"Oh, miss. I'm terribly sorry. I didn't mean to frighten you. I'm just fucking around with old Matthew, here. We know each other from Chicago, and we shared a cell together, didn't we Matthew?"

Matthew knew that voice all right. "Goddamn it, Crayon! You crazy fucker!" He turned and embraced the big dude. "What are you doing here at the end, man?"

"Same as you, I guess, man," Crayon responded as he returned Matthew's hug. "I had to come and see it for myself, you know what I mean, man?"

"Yeah, man. Empirical proof. I know . . . ."

Crayon nodded his head. "I'd hoped that . . . ." He swallowed hard at the words as the two friends pulled apart. "I'd hoped we'd have a little more class than this." He nodded toward the stage and the seeming pitch battle going on up there between Angels and the crowd trying to protect Meredith Hunter. "You know, Matthew?"

"I know, Crayon." Matthew fumbled for a cigarette. "I know, man!" He lit a Winston off of a lighter Crayon offered him. "I'm afraid that it's war on the home front for them that wants it. For the rest . . . . I don't know, man. For the rest of them . . . . Fuck me. I've done my share of the fucking fighting and shit."

"Me too, Matthew. I don't think I can fight still another war . . . . The underground's dying piece by piece . . . scattering out of fear of persecution, man . . . out of fear . . . ."

As they caught up on what had happened to each other since Chicago, they seemed to misplace the purpose for Matthew's desperate attempts at getting to the stage.

"And, what's that on your ass, Crayon?"

"It's a Nixon, man." Crayon spat into his palm and slapped it on the ass patch on his tattered Wranglers. The patch bore a caricature of Richard Milhous Nixon. "A good likeness, don't you think?"

"Think so, do you?

"Yeah. I do."

"Me too . . . ." Matthew seemed to be gazing off into the encroaching night. "What about Nina, man. What does she think of the patch, man?"

When Crayon grinned, his white teeth seemed to explode across his face. "She also agrees with me. She better, man. She's my old lady now."

"How is she doing?"

"Great. She's in school at Kent State. Wants to be a teacher of kids, you know. Like grade school kids and shit, man."

"Great, man! We need good teachers."

"Dig it! Teach your children well . . . ."

"Right on, man. Right fucking on!" Matthew was trying, with some difficulty, to focus on the conversation. "Ah . . . . When does she graduate?"

"Seventy-one . . . spring semester."

"Cool. You planning to do the marriage thing then?"

Crayon grinned that infectious grin of his. "Yeah, I guess we do."

"That's a long time to wait, man."

"Yeah. But, it'll be worth it." Crayon nodded at Linda. "Your old lady?"

Linda's ears perked up.

Matthew shook his acid head. "No. We just met at Atlanta jam last summer. Just happened to run into each other on the road to this cultural cul-de-sac."

He could at least have lied a little, she fumed to herself. To make her feel a little better . . . to not embarrass her.

"Still hung up on the girl from down home, huh?" Crayon whispered, turning them away from Linda's view.

"Yeah. Emmy Lou. After this cultural joke, I'm on my way to Alamogordo and then to meet her in Denver. I didn't want her here. I was afraid for her safety."

"Same here with Nina. Good thinking as it's turned out, yeah?"

"Yeah. Too damned bad though."

"You know, man, there's this dude in El Paso. He goes by the name of Don Amerika. Runs a gun shop . . . among other things. He can get anything you want or need for your trip into the desert, man, and he's very cool. Crazy but cool. Just tell him I sent you, man."

"Well, I will be going into the desert for a while, so I will be needing some supplies. Thanks, man.

"And, what does this Don Amerika dude say about your Nixon ass patch?"

"Definitely digs it! Says it's the spitting image of the fucker. Shit, then again, he better think that. He's the one who sold it to me," Crayon cackled. "And, he'll say just about anything to sell you something, man . . . . That's probably his biggest fault."

"Well, it sure goes along with the Nixon ethic, man. And, that's definitely what's 'in' these days."

"Well?"

"Well what?"

"Well, you can't camp out in the desert forever, man. The rangers won't let you. So, what are you going to do after that, man?"

"That's true, man," Matthew laughed. "We'll try Denver for a while or Boulder . . . or maybe Georgetown up in the mountains. There's lots of hippies around there and in the mountains nearby. We'll just hang out and keep our heads down and our names and pictures out of the papers and off TV for a while, I guess. I'm going to try to get a teaching job, too."

"Be careful, man. Lots of cowboys out there, too. Not just hippies. Lots of them! Watch out for the cowboys, Matthew!"

"Guess they're just a different version of the Angels." Matthew's eyes rolled for a moment in recollection. "Jesus. That's where I was headed!"

"Where, Matthew? Where?"

"The stage, man. The fucking stage." He tugged at Crayon's gangly frame, trying to somehow pull him along toward the stage with him. "I came here to work the OD tent and Jagger called for doctors or medics a few minutes or a few hours ago. I was on my way to try and help . . . . There's something bad going down on stage. I think the Angels are killing people up there."

"That means getting past those same Hells Angels, man!"

"Guess it does, at that."

"Well, man. I can get you to the stage pretty quick now, but even old Crayon ain't got no pull with them fucking Angels. They've always been out of control, and now that Jagger's given them official status by hiring them as body guards, they're impossible."

"Mick Jagger hired Hell's Angels?" Linda whimpered, still at Crayon's feet.

"Shit, yes!" Crayon looked at Matthew. "Where the hell's this chick been, anyway, man?"

"Obviously not with the Hell's Angels."

"I don't believe that about Mickey!" Her black eyes glazed over as she glared up at Crayon. "How would you know that, anyway, Mister Crayon?"

"Just Crayon . . . ."

"Crayon knows lots of people, Linda. Inside people, if you know what I mean . . . ."

Crayon skinned her alive with his eyes. "Don't believe me! Ask Mick your own fucking self the next time you bump into him over cocktails or something, honey. The revolution's been bumfucked, honey . . . by you, by me, by Matthew, and by everyone here at this race track including, and most especially, Mick fucking Jagger!"

Linda felt her bottom jaw drop, and she couldn't seem to take up the slack. What an asshole . . . . Matthew, too . . . . Matthew, too, hell. Matthew most of fucking all.

"Come on, Matthew. This way to the stage, man."

Crayon hugged Matthew's slender shoulders with his huge left arm, pulling him through the crowds like a rag doll, away from Linda and toward the Hells Angels. As people in the crowd noticed Crayon, they automatically moved aside for one of their most recognized leaders.

Linda did not try to follow Matthew. She wasn't going to do that any longer. Serape or no serape, you could bet your ass on that! She turned in the swarm of humanity choking the Race Track infield and stalked away from the Meredith Hunter knifing that was still taking place on the stage.

> *Why ask who killed*
> *the Kennedys,*
> *when, after all, it*
> *was you and me . . . .*

Knives again flashed in the flood lights. "We'd better hurry, Crayon!"

So, it must have been Crayon's head he saw bouncing around on the shoulders of the audience earlier. Not Ward's. No Ward in New York. No Ward in Chicago. And, now, No Ward at the end of the fucking world being staged at the Altamont Race Track. There must be no more Ward Crampton anywhere. Blown to bits in a helicopter in Vietnam. R I P . . . .

"OOOH . . . OOOH! OOOH . . . OOOH! OOOH . . . OOOH!"

"WOOH WOOH! WOOH WOOH! WOOH WOOH!"

A train whistled in

the distance. It sounded like a city version of a coyote's howl. Matthew thought that it could easily be the same train he had arrived on only an hour before he faced racks of rifles jamming the pine paneled walls of Don Amerika's Gunshop.

The glass storefront bore the shop's name in day-glo red, white, and blue matching the American flag carpet. Every seven feet in each direction a stars-and-stripes stood out against the basic uranium gray of the carpet. Standing behind each flag was a life-size fiberglass figure—Jesse James, Wild Bill Hickock, Buffalo Bill Cody, Pat Garret, Davy Crockett, Daniel Boone, William Travis, Sam Houston, Steven Austin, James Bowie, J. Frank Dobie, Frank Robinson, Dwight David Eisenhower, Chester Nimitz. Each figure displayed a glass-and-aluminum case in its belly, locked with a polished Yale lock and containing certain specialties of the shop such as Seiko watches with compasses, hollow point shells, and western style pistols. Beyond these figures, a triumvirate displayed shelves of various caliber cartridges in their bellies. Lyndon Baines Johnson, Katharine Ann Porter on each end and Richard Milhouse Nixon in the center, his hands reaching out to bless the adjacent NCR register. A fourth figure lurking just behind the register was arrayed in a Captain America costume. But, the Captain America figure had no display case in its belly. And, its arms, legs, and head began to move, turning toward Matthew. It spoke.

"Hey, man."

Matthew stared hard at the statue that moved and talked as it sauntered from behind the cash register between Crocket, Boone, Travis, and Austin toward the statue closest to the entrance near Matthew, Chester Nimitz. His name, as all the others, was engraved in bronze on a slave necklace locked around his neck: Don Amerika. He offered his wrinkled hand. "Don Amerika. This is my shop. Need something to shoot?" he giggled. "And these . . . ." He waved his arms about, seeming to indicate the figures. "And, these are my creations."

"Hey, man, that's cool!" Matthew grasped the wrinkled hand in his, expecting it to be weak and fragile but finding instead a sturdy grip. "I'm Matthew. Crayon from Berkeley recommended your shop, man."

"Hey, that's cool, man. Crayon is a righteous dude, man, a real righteous dude! So, welcome, then, Matthew, friend of Crayon's. My place is yours, man."

"Are you for real, man, with this get-up and," Matthew swept his arms indicating the entire store, "And this place?"

"Hey, Matthew, man." He shrugged and leaned against Nimitz. "You gotta survive, man. Like everything's gonna start coming down real heavy, you know, man . . . like real soon, man . . . . For freaks, you know, like you and me, man, it's gonna be a real 'freak out,' man!"

"You're probably right, Don. But, right now, I'm heading out into the desert. I need a few things, Don . . . like a rifle . . . rounds . . . ." He chuckled. "A horse . . . ."

"The horse you'll have to get from Hickock's livery across the street. I don't deal in horses. But, I can help you with the rest, man. Come on back, man. Let me show you what I've got, man."

As he followed Don Amerika toward the back of the shop, Don disappeared behind Katharine Ann Porter. A metal door screeched on its hinges and scraped the concrete floor behind the counter as it opened. The door slammed shut. Don's boots clomped across the cement floor. Then, silence.

"For the rattlesnakes of all kinds out there, man." Don winked his glaucous eyes like pieces of atomic glass in the sand as he emerged from behind Katharine Ann Porter. His arms spilled over with a Winchester, six boxes of thirty-thirty shells, and a matchbox he said contained one hit of organic mescaline and about fifteen grams of golden smoking powder as well as a few rolling papers.

"Wow, man. This is perfect!"

"We aim to please, man." Don's eyes, rather than penetrating, seemed to surround Matthew, sucking him up.

"How much?"

"For a friend of Crayon's, man? Let's say seventy-five even for the rifle." Captain Amerika hesitated, cracked his knuckles. "The rifle's hot . . . from Morocco. So . . . ." Don Amerika shrugged his shoulders again. "You pays your money, and you takes your chances, man . . . . Say . . . one fifty for the whole stash . . . ."

"Okay, man. Sounds good to me." Matthew paid him from the clip in his left front pocket.

"If you like the merchandise, man, let me know. I've got a very cool connection there."

"Where?"

"Morocco, man. Morocco. I can get you guns, dope . . . the best black hash . . . Lebanese blonde the color of a monk's robe."

"Cool, man."

"So . . . you really are going into the desert, man?"

Matthew nodded.

"What the fuck for, man. Ain't nothing in the desert but sand and sidewinders . . . and ghosts, all kinds of fucking ghosts, man."

"What else does a guy do with an MA in literature?"

"MA in lit, huh?"

"Yeah. Just finished my thesis defense a few weeks ago . . . or was it a few years ago? Can't keep time straight anymore."

"I know what you mean, man. Too much acid, man."

"Too much of everything, man."

They both chuckled.

"Lots of pilgrims used to pass through here, man, on their way over the Franklin Mountains to Alamogordo." When he finally asked Matthew if he was looking for the cradle endlessly rocking, too, like those other pilgrims, Matthew snatched up his packages and the rifle and flung himself past Bowie, Crocket, Houston, Nimitz, out through the remote-controlled doors without even saying good-bye or thanks.

Don's square soft face hollered after him as he fled to his rented jeep. "Happiness is black hash, man. Happiness is a Lebanese Blonde, man. Happiness is a warm gun from Morocco, man!"

Matthew couldn't be sure what roused him from his trance, that jet crashing the sound barrier or the noiseless steps he sensed shuffling through the red dust near his campfire. Now, it was only glowing coals. The cinders were cities crumbling and new ones rising from their ashes. Maybe, it was the mescaline finally kicking in. He'd been sitting for hours or seconds just staring at fiery masks. They glared at him from the fire. Next to them in the night, the silhouette of a hunched figure, slumped cross-legged in the mesa dust with hands outstretched over the dying embers. A faint stench permeated the otherwise clear desert air. It was a smell Matthew knew but couldn't recall what it was.

Jason? Sorry, I left without us having that talk you wanted or even saying good-bye. No. How can I be sorry for the inevitable. You even said that much yourself.

The stench grew stronger as Matthew continued to feign sleep, trying to place that smell. His right hand crept from under the blanket wrapped around him. Fingers groped until they touched the linseed-oiled stock of his Winchester. He had had a vision of Ward somewhere in a desert like himself. His hand eased the rifle from the case and lifted it onto his blanket.

Remember. Flip the fucking safety off before going for the lever. These people are capable of anything. Fathers. Not the least of which is that they produce sons like me: personifications of the Cartesian dichotomy. Wellstones and the water they enclose. I am a wellstone. My spirit is the tanictinctured water oozing through my panicpunctured walls like White Water Bay in the Everglades spills through cypress into the Gulf of Mexico. Careful! Fathers are the well-ripping roots.

"Won't be a'needin' that, sonny." The shade's words crackled like dry lightning. Crouched by the fire, it turned from its waist, peering past what was left of the flames through the night. Out of the fireflush, eyebrows leaped like whiskbrooms from the figure's brow. Its disheveled beard cascaded down its chest like clumps of sheared wool. The stench was becoming overwhelming. The shade's clothing seemed to smoke as if about to catch fire.

"Don't mean you no harm, sonny." The words still crackled. He backed away from the heat patting himself all over to quell the almost fires in his clothing. "A little too close to the fire. You do that sometimes if you can't see, you know, sonny."

How did any man hear him going after his rifle? He made no sound? "Who the hell are you?" he heard his voice say with a strong tinge of protecting his territory as he stared at where the figure's eyes should've been gleaming in firelight. The old man's eyes were flatblack holes. There was no gleaming in the firelight. The stench gradually dissipated into the snappy desert air.

Beyond the old man, a puma hissed. Snap. Matthew flipped off the Winchester's safety. Clickclack filled the rifle chamber with a round. When he bolted up, the army blanket fell from his shoulders. All he needed was a dead fucking horse. He aimed from the shoulder toward the increasing hisses.

"No!"

Matthew gaped as the old man struggled to his feet, blotting out the golden crescent moon that still floated through clouds over project Manhattan behind him. It had only been days since Buzz Aldrin walked on that surface. Occasional slivers of moonlight flashed off the chain link fence in the distance and danced along the old man's shoulders like St. Elmo's Fire through a schooner's rigging. "That's my puma. She ain't gonna hurt you either, sonny."

Matthew dropped his aim momentarily, but he did not relax. "Who are you?"

"I'm the one what knows the truth. I'm the only one what saw it!" He grinned and shook his head. "Poor old Estevan."

"Hell, we've all thought that before."

The old man did not speak.

"Okay, old man, what truth?"

"*The* truth!" Estevan stabbed at the blackness above his head with withered hands. The puma's fangs suddenly gleamed in the firelight from the shadows behind his knee. She hissed. "Quiet, No-cat. Quiet!"

Although Matthew could see only shadows of the cat's front haunches, he could tell from the level of its chartreuse eye slits that it was still sitting like a dog behind its master's left heel. The rifle slid from Matthew's loosening fingers onto the army blanket bedroll bunched up around his hips. "The truth? The truth? What the hell is the truth, old man?"

"I'm the only one what knows it. Poor old Estevan. The only one what saw it! Poor, blind Estevan." He stomped up dust with rag wrapped boots. "The truth blinded me." His dried fig fingers clawed at empty sockets. He slumped again to the ground, red dust splashing over him and faced the fire. No-cat slouched into the darkness beyond the firelight's reach.

Matthew's horse snorted and pawed at the stone ledge where he stood, hobbled. A night hawk bolted for the moon. Its wings thrashed ancient desert air. Old as Daedelus . . . Icarus. Old as the envy swelling in Matthew while he followed the black dot as it streaked past the yellow crescent into the darkness yawing out of his reality. DiVinci knew their quest. He drew fliers patterned after what he observed in birds. If we peel the secret like rings from a tree, we'll be able to fly, the right brothers had, finally, to think before they could command a concrete pylon erection on Kill Devil Hill because they had flown the first time with power of their own driving those wooden wings into the outer banks wind. Wright on!

Blasts of thunder echoed over the mesa from somewhere near White Sands. "Damn, that jet sounds like the Saturn rocket taking off," he muttered. Buzz Aldrin flies through space in Apollo and aldrin snow flakes permanently ground a meadowlark in Roanoke Park.

Estevan, startled from his stupor-like infatuation with the heat of the flames from new wood Matthew had placed on the fire as he sat beside him, grunted in response, then retreated further into his meditation. Jests and jets were nothing new to the uranium prospector. Jests were his nightmares where he could still see with his own eyes, not just through the eyes of No-cat and Jackass. Jets, they were the condors of his visions, forever tearing at his eyes. Already a memory fading, the afterburner roar of the jet seemed to hover over the desert for minutes, rippling toward all horizons like water in a pool after a dragonfly touches down.

Even the sounds of the jet had vanished when Matthew pulled a large flaming splinter from the fire and lit a joint of Don Amerika's finest, tossing the splinter back into the flames when he was finished. It flared like the trail of a shooting star. "Tell me, Estevan. Tell me how the truth blinded you."

Estevan turned toward the sound of Matthew's voice. His withering body rustled inside his baggy plaid shirt and sunbleached overalls. "Okay, sonny. Just remember, you asked old Estevan. He didn't *offer* to tell you nothin' . . . ."

"Yeah, sure, sure . . . ." Matthew smiled in the firelight at how Estevan's empty eye sockets wrinkled up with mystery as he spoke. "Anyway, I like stories, Estevan." The way Estevan leered at him through the light, he'd swear there were eyes that could actually see sunk very deep inside those wrinkled sockets. A sudden breeze from the north chilled the air. Matthew laid on another piece of wood and wrapped Linda's serape tighter around his shoulders. Across the mesa, his gelding whinnied at the puma hissing at sounds in the night and the burro braying at the puma.

"Poor, blind Estevan . . ." the old prospector grunted again, wagging his shaggy white head.

"Somewhere around 1539," he began, "a Franciscan, Marcos de Niza, explored this territory in search of gold. With him he brought his trusted slave, Estevan. De Niza only desired more of what he already had more than enough of . . . gold . . . silver . . . precious stones. Living in the de Niza household, Estevan had not only taken the name of his master, but he also had learned what it was like to have wealth, to want for nothing. He, too, wanted wealth and all it could purchase. Estevan had become as greedy and impatient as his master.

"These treasure-mad pilgrims wandered across the bottom of what, now, is known as New Mexico, moving eastward toward what we call Texas. They had been out of food for a full day and had only one goatskin of water left dangling from the left side of the lead burro when they spotted the Black Mountains to the north of their trail. De Niza had heard stories of mountain dwellers whose cave floors were tiled with gold and silver.

After a full day of travel in the direction of the Black Mountains, they came upon a clear water pool at the base of the cliffs called El Morro. A group of Indians from the Big Sky pueblo, located near where the city of Acoma is today, were watering there. A desperate de Niza lied that they were peace ambassadors from a great king in a land across the great waters to the east who had come to the Indians' country to meet them in friendship. He offered the Big Sky pueblo three of their four remaining burros as tokens of peace.

"Now, the chief had often heard the drum messages in the night telling of hoards of olive and white people ravaging the lands far to the south for gold and silver and turquoise. They murdered like Apaches. They wore crosses of gold like the one de Niza wore on a matching gold chain around his neck. But, the chief was a fair-minded man. He refused to be swayed by the drums alone. Afterall, these men had not even violated the nearby sacred place—Keva. And, with only one burro remaining, they were truly at his mercy. So, the chief welcomed them and accepted their burros. De Niza and Estevan were accorded places of honor in his household once they had returned to the pueblo and passed around the locoweed-filled peace pipe carved from the thigh bone of an antelope."

"Would you like some?" Matthew interrupted.

"Some what?" Estevan's voice sounded shrill. "What?" His withered sockets seemed to twitch at the interruption.

As he turned more directly toward Matthew, Estevan seemed to actually glare at him. "Some locoweed? Top grade shit from one of the best underground connections in the country. Here, smell it burning?" Matthew shoved the joint under Estevan's drooping Romanesque nose. Coarse, white hairs bristled as the old man's nostrils flared.

"No. I can't smoke that stuff and tell my story straight." Estevan turned back to the fire. His nostrils curled back from their dusty bristles.

Matthew shrugged and sucked on the joint "Do your own thing, old dude. Do your own thing . . . ."

Estevan picked up his story, his voice a resonant monotone as if he had memorized the words of his tale without any inflections. "Now, the chief had a beautiful daughter. She was fifteen with a figure like twenty-one. Her hair was raven in color, and her eyes glistened more beautiful than gold in the morning sun when she would stroll to the washing well.

"The young princess was the only thing which drove the obsession for riches from Estevan's mind. Each morning he stalked her at a safe distance, dodging in and out of pueblo doorways, until she reached the well and began cleaning. First, the family's laundry. Then, herself. When she washed her body, she opened her hide dress by unstrapping the leather string which tied it down the front and dropped hand scoops of water from the stone bucket down her chalice-like breasts.

"One morning, during their second week in the pueblo, the princess was slinking down the dirt path when she suddenly turned around and began retracing her steps. Uncharacteristically, she wasn't carrying any laundry in her arms. Her move took Estevan by surprise. He was caught in the middle of the path. He dove for the nearest doorway. His heart pounded. He thought it would tear open his chest as he huddled in the doorway of the Medicine Man's pueblo.

"She must have seen him, he thought. She looked straight at him. As he peeked around the stone jamb, he saw her again walking down the path, dust puffing from behind her heels as she wiggled toward the washing well. It seemed to him that she was exaggerating her walk purposely, so he decided to follow and see what happened."

Estevan paused. He coughed and spit in the fire.

Matthew reached for the last log beside him and cradled it on the firecircle of rocks so that it straddled the flames. "You mean to tell me that old Estevan would not have followed the girl that morning if he hadn't thought she was walking in an exaggerated fashion? Come on, old dude. You can't be serious?"

Estevan's words continued to drone on through the fire and smoke as if Matthew had not spoken. But, Matthew was sure that he knew what would happen next. It, too, was as old as dreams of flight, like Estevan and "divide and conquer." As Estevan's monologue continued, Matthew's mind swirled through its own vortex.

There is a certain predictability in the human process. Estevan talks. He is talking as each moment of the continuing present is future, present, then past. The words, the results of his process, the sensation of mine. Are we no more than products of each others' minds? Matter shaped from the patterns of our thoughts? He wished Estevan would skip the rest of the obvious stuff and move on to 'the truth', as he called it, whatever that was.

'The truth', indeed, Estevan! It can only be that there is no truth, and that can only be said with qualification, because we can't know anything truly enough to say we can or cannot know anything truly. The search for truth which the philosophers always lament is dying with them is just that, a search . . . as much for Eisenberg or Einstein as for Santayana or Sartre . . . the human process as closely as we can describe human process . . . life impetus.

What allows this process to exist as we understand it? Time. Time yields the results of process . . . . A knot on the new log popped, spraying red and blue sparks into the darkness above the fire. What was the old man saying, now?

"Poor Estevan tried to tell the chief that his daughter had tantalized him beyond belief. She had stripped herself at the well, pouring a full bucket of water over her shoulders and stroking her breasts, satin like the desert hills under the breaking dawn. She had opened her thighs in his direction and touched herself. She had known that he was watching. She invited him to enter her. He had been unable to control himself. It had been as if he had become someone else . . . someone completely obsessed with having her.

"Estevan pleaded with the chief. The chief pretended that Estevan was a liar. Estevan pleaded with de Niza. De Niza pretended that Estevan was a stranger.

"With spike-like stones—maybe even some of the stones here in this fire circle—the medicine man gouged out his eyes as he lay spread-eagled on the sand, tied by wet leather tongs which would shrink as they dried in the sun and tear his arms and legs from their sockets. Through his pain, Estevan could hear them dancing around him and chanting for the sun to rise bright and hot. Suddenly, they were gone. He felt the sure death of the sun's heat caking the blood on his cheeks like a mask. Yet, he held one hope . . . that he would be born again from the princess's womb.

"According to the way the story has been passed down from father to son over the centuries, the way it was told to my father by his father and to me by my father, the first Estevan's bones are buried somewhere beneath these very rocks." He pointed a trembling hand toward the heat of the fire. "In fact, all of the Estevan's are buried here."

"Jesus!" Matthew gawked at the blackened stones which formed the firecircle, the altar, the grave marker. "Really?" He had recognized the formation as a fireplace, entertained the simile of an altar of smutted rocks reminding him of the old man's empty sockets. An altar built of holes. Matthew shivered. "I'm really sorry, Señor

Estevan. I honestly didn't realize. I just didn't know . . . ." He tried to pull the serape which Linda had given him tighter around his shoulders, but it was as tight as he could make it already. "Jesus . . . ." He whistled softly, almost to himself. "Buried right here, huh?"

Estevan nodded at the fire.

"Well, at least you know where the bones are. They are right here on this mesa. My search has been for a friend. A friend whose death I fear that I may have been responsible for. Yet, I continually hear rumors about someone who looks just like him . . . who might be that friend. That he may, somehow, still be alive. So, I have not been able to stop looking. I have no mesa to go to where I know the bones of my friend are buried."

Estevan nodded. His head reminded Matthew of a lion's in the firelight and shadows.

"For four hundred and thirty years the first Estevan's dying hope has been a curse to my line," the old man continued. They were all born blind and doomed to be outcasts from their societies because of a common lust for gold which also seemed to be born in them. I was the first," he laughed bitterly, "to be born with eyes that could see. Ever since I can remember, my father told me that the curse of Estevan had finally lost its power . . . even though my mother did die at birth like all the others before me . . . ."

"Mine, too, Estevan. Mine, too . . . ." Matthew nodded his head. "Did you feel kind of responsible, somehow, once you knew about it?"

Estevan's creviced face turned toward Matthew again, his gnarled fingers clasping Matthew's knees. "Sometimes, I still do."

"Yeah, I know what you mean, old dude. I know what you mean. It's a hard thing to get mellow about."

Estevan, turning back to the fire once more, fumbled in the air near the flames until he touched a stick of wood. Grasping it between his fingers, he poked at the fire, sending sparks into the night like meteors and comets shooting through galaxies he could not see.

"My father taught me what he called a new way. Gold was no longer the thing of value, he told me. Something was beginning to take its place. He lectured me about a fellow named Klaproth discovering it way back in seventeen eighty-nine, and how a whole bunch of fellows—physicses or something like that . . . ."

"Physicists," Matthew interjected.

"Physicists, then," Estevan spat at the fire. "They discovered this theory about it the same year as the four hundredth birthday of the Estevan curse. This was a sign, he said. But, he never said a sign of what . . . .

"So, he taught me how to use this new-fangled contraption that buzzes like a rattler when it spots this new gold . . . this uranium stuff. I can even do it without no eyes, you see." He gurgled in his throat like a warbler at his own little play on words.

"A Geiger counter! You have a Geiger counter?"

"Yeah." His voice was strained, accusing. "That's what it's called." His shoulders bunched under the blue-black plaid of his frayed flannel shirt. "How'd you know what I was talking about, sonny? Huh? You some kinda prospector coming in here to jump my claims?"

"No. Nothing like that, Estevan. Geiger counters are just something I learned about in college or in the Army or somewhere along the way, you know?" He scuffed his boots in the red dust. "Do you think I could, maybe borrow it later on, just for an hour or so? I want to make a few readings over at the bomb test site. Ground Zero. You know where I'm talking about?"

The moon was fading over project Manhattan. "Yes, I know." Estevan's voice seemed to gargle a sardonic laugh as he waved the flaming stick he held in his left hand in the direction of the Southwest as if he could see it. "Ground Zero." He flung the stick into the fire and dropped his head into his hands. A snarl of pain tore from his craggy lips. "That's where my story ends . . . ."

"Odd," Matthew muttered, more to himself than to Estevan. "That's where my story begins . . . ."

The old prospector, then, continued with his story, again, almost as if the interlude of their dialogue had never taken place. "Every year my father brought me to this place overlooking that desert out there to commemorate the end of the curse with a sacrifice. We always came here the day before the ancient Estevan supposedly died. We would make camp. The following morning we would burn a blood offering on this very fireplace . . . always the eyes . . . of a prairie dog . . . of a lizard . . . of an owl or a hawk . . . . My father used to say that it reminded him of the story of Abraham and Isaac in the Bible. I would always answer that I hoped that God would never ask him to sacrifice me. He would laugh from real deep in his flabby belly. 'No, son," he'd say. 'You don't have to worry none about that. You're blessed by God, son, not cursed like the rest of us.'

"Of course, I believed him. After all, he was my father. I was his son. Why would he lie to me?" Estevan sighed as if he were about to cry. The puma's pads thumped in the dust in the darkness as she glided to his side, it seemed, to comfort him.

"All of a sudden, I was twenty-one and left alone to hoist my father's corpse over his burro, strap it down with hemp rope, and make the three-day trek from our base camp to this place. Rattlesnake bit him. Damn slithering creature bit him right in the jugular vein."

Morning was beginning to edge into the sky in streaks of gray and amber on the eastern horizon. The sun would be coming up soon. Matthew coughed. He poked at the edges of the fire with his boot toe to try and hide his impatience. "So, Estevan, what is this 'the truth' you've been going on about? What is 'the truth', really?"

Estevan sucked in a deep breath to damn the sobs flowing through his words. "A few weeks later, I led an expedition of white men into an old burial grounds less than a day's ride from here. They was looking for uranium, and I knew where there was a bonanza! I was cocky at twenty-one, blessed by God, you see. And, I never thought that burial grounds would still be considered sacred around here . . . in the United States of America . . . not anymore. Not even my own family's burial grounds . . . ." His lips curled into something between a sneer and a grin.

Matthew sat forward and started to respond, to say, again, how sorry he was, but Estevan held his hands up palms away from his body and toward Matthew. "No need, sonny. No need."

Matthew sat back, and Estevan continued.

"But, the old Sky tribe did. They captured me after the white men made camp and bedded down for the night. They brought me here almost a full day's ride. They knew that this was my tribe's burial ground. They tied me down with wet leather tongs, just like their ancestors had tied down my ancestor more than four hundred years before. According to our family legends, at this very spot.

"I knew I was as good as dead, but I was real puzzled when the Medicine Man didn't poke out my eyes with stone needles or something. I had expected that. They just vanished with the first morning breezes across the desert. I was left alone on this mesa with the rising sun already getting hotter by the minute. When I turned my head I could see a small herd of antelope grazing on the other mesa which was covered with scrub brush and prairie grass rather than dust like this one. Wings of vultures beat overhead.

"It seemed like hours later when I heard the explosion ripping through the morning light. The concussions shook the mesa under me. I jerked my head southwest for a look at what was causing the loudest explosion I'd ever heard in all my life.

"A glowing jade cloud mushroomed into the rose sky. The antelope herd stampeded. Existence smeared like paint on glass. My eyes dribbled from their sockets. In a matter of seconds, the antelope vanished and I was blind."

Matthew placed his arm around Estevan's slumped shoulders. The old prospector's chest heaved. "It's okay, old dude. It's okay . . . ." For an instant, in the fire light and shadows, Estevan's face seemed to reshape itself . . . . Was it Jason he saw lurking somewhere in the depths of the old prospector's face?

"Blind. Blind. Poor, blind Estevan!" He twined vine-like fingers around the boy's arms that embraced him, holding him fast. "I'm the only one what knows. The only one what saw!" He released Matthew with his left hand and stroked the puma's head as she sprawled in the shadows by his left leg. "No-cat, here, saved my life, though. She discovered me about noon. I was better than half dead. My lips were cracking open, sort of raw like. My eyes had dried on my cheeks. The drying tongs had stretched my arms and legs to near their limits but hadn't, yet, ripped them from their sockets. No-cat, the evil fiend, thought she'd found herself some easy eatin', didn't ya girl?"

Estevan scruffed the dome of the puma's head with his gnarly fingers. "But she felt sorry for me, I guess. She must've been able, somehow, to sense my helplessness like she might one of her own cubs, because after she scared the shit out of me growling and purring and hissing and sniffing around my body, she began chewing through the tongs one by one rather than chewing on me.

"And, she's watched out for me ever since. She's been my eyes, my protector. Haven't you, girl?" He again ruffled the scaly fur on No-cat's head. "Helps me hunt out my uranium. I swear she can smell the stuff. Uranium, that is." She purred. "She's about half dead now, herself, poor old No-cat."

Matthew wagged his head, poked at smutted stones with his boot toe. "I've got news for you, Señor Estevan. It's no longer uranium that matters. It's information. Information is the new gold, old dude. The new uranium . . . . Let No-cat sniff around in the desert for that . . . ."

"No!" Estevan's bowed psaltery lips sneered, eyeless gouges above them blooming like abysses in the growing morning roseness. "I'm the only one what knows the truth!" He leaped to his feet, fumbling for Matthew's arms again. "I'm the only one what saw it!"

GODZO.

Matthew instinctively reflexed backwards, yanked his left arm free of the closing vice of Estevan's groping fingers, combat crawled from the fading glow of the fire toward his bedroll near the east ledge. His combat instincts told him he was suddenly in trouble. He could see the Winchester's silver barrel beginning to take on a luster in the dawn light.

GODZO.

A low, slow wind drifted from the southwest over dryrotting outhouses, disintegrating concrete bunkers, crystalized sand, and rattling chain link fences carrying the memory northeastward like the fragrance of enchiladas.

GODZO.

Estevan stalked the sound of the boy . . . the scent of the boy. He could smell him like the puma could smell uranium. "I'm the only one what knows it. Poor, blind Estevan." He howled like a pack leader getting wind of prey.

GODZO.

"Your eyes, sonny! They've got to go on the fire!" The prospector's gravel voice became Yosemite Falls crashing onto the mesa. "You don't need them to find your friend. He's dead just like you are, boy. Just like all of you are!" Maniacal laughter shredded his lips. He raised his hands like a falcon's talons above his mangy head. "Now, that's 'the truth!'"

Matthew's hair bristled on his neck.

Estevan's hulk blotted out the glowing coals of the fire as he lunged after the sound of the boy's reacting body. He could hear him scrambling on his stomach back to where he had been before. The old man stumbled in the direction of Matthew's bedroll.

GODZO.

Finally, Matthew felt the cool metal of the Winchester between his clawing fingers. Forgetting that the rifle was loaded, he levered a round into the chamber, expending an unused round into the red dust, now chocolate in the violet dawn . . . and letting Estevan know exactly where he was located.

GODZO.

Estevan leaped for the sound of the lever, landing on his belly atop Matthew's blanket. "Your eyes, boy! I need your eyes!"

Matthew rolled to his left, again into the browning dust, chalk in his mouth, like a barium milkshake.

GODZO.

"Got to have your eyes!" Estevan flailed stick arms and legs tangled in the army blanket like that dying meadowlark had flailed its wings under the weight of Jason's aldrin snow. Each had been crazed by a different poison.

GODZO.

Matthew set himself in a prone position. He pressed the linseed-oiled stock against his cheek and shoulder, took a deep breath, released his breath evenly. He did not hold his breath at all. He simply ceased breathing. He squeezed the trigger.

GODZO.

The sound of the rifle shot seemed to echo off every mesa. Blood spurted from a volcano in Estevan's chest. Rocinante whistled, reared his hobbled hooves.

GODZO.

Jackass squalled. Rocinante whinned.

GODZO.

No-cat never moved or made a sound. She just peered through the morning air in the direction of Estevan sprawled spread eagle in the chocolate dust near the eastern edge of the mesa.

GODZO.

Matthew crawled toward the old prospector, his rifle dragging behind through the luminescent rust of years that covered the mesa.

The earth had been warm when Matthew began. Now, in his hands, shards of Estevan family grave markers still gouged at cooling mesa dirt as he carved out a hole in the charred, fire-softened soil underneath the dead campfire. While he dug with sharp stones that could be the very ones that gouged out the eyes of the first Estevan, he could not avoid thoughts of another more hastily dug grave in The Hole near his father's house. The hole where he had buried the meadowlark his father had murdered with his poison snow last Christmas. Now, he was burying the old prospector he, himself, had killed. Both father and son claimed self-defense.

Was this, then, a beginning or an ending? he wondered as he rolled Estevan's corpse into the hole. While he shoveled dirt with his hands to cover the body, he realized that he was burying much more than Estevan in this shallow grave.

Matthew broke camp in the funereal silence of the desert dawn. He unhobbled and saddled Rocinante. Before mounting, he stood beside the grave, staring at the charred stones, now, marking a new burial in the Estevan family burial grounds. The final Estevan.

He suddenly was struck by the fact that he had not spoken any words over the old man. He had left no written epitaph. He reached for his saddlebags. Rocinante whinnied. His left flank twitched as Matthew opened the leather bag. He pulled out his pen and the Rolling Stone. Its pages constituted the only available paper other than his diary. And, he was already writing on the backs of those pages. He thumbed through the tabloid rock 'n roll paper until he spotted a Sam Goody's ad with lots of available white space. He began to scribble in the white spaces. When he finished writing, he tore the ad from the paper and replaced the Rolling Stone in his saddlebags.

He had written the words. Now, how did he preserve them against the slow onslaught of the desert? Searching his saddlebags again, he located the plastic bag which had previously held his birthday eggs. The plastic was clean and dry. He folded the page from the Rolling Stone with his words scribbled on it to fit the baggie, pushed as much air out as he could, then sucked out the rest. He sealed the words safely inside. That would protect the words from the sun and the winds. Safer than it had been for the meadowlark or for Estevan . . . or for Ward . . . . Safer than it would ever be for him or for those whom he called "brother" and "sister."

Here lie the ashes of Estevan
Blinded by the bomb,
Crazed by the sun.
Murdered by my gun,
Rest with your uranium,
Blind, mad, dead, last Estevan.

Matthew slipped the words-in-a-plastic-bag underneath the stones he had used to dig the new grave. Here, old Estevan. The stones will protect these words against predators . . . .

"It's no Beowulf, old dude. No *Nibelungenlied*. But it relates the essence of our encounter here on the mesa in the desert. 'The truth', if you will, of our night and morning together.

"How did we put it, old prospector? This was where your story ended and my story began? That was what we agreed, wasn't it?" Matthew mounted the bay. "Adios, Señor Estevan. Adios! I'm really sorry that it had to end this way. I really, really am . . . . Adios . . . . Adios . . . . Adios . . . ."

He cantered the gelding into the purples and pinks showering the desert from the morning sky as the sun began to rise above the still-gray eastern edge of the earth. He turned back in his saddle just once. The monument of charred stones appeared as a lumpy black hole in the mesa.

After Matthew's horse had negotiated the descent from the mesa table to the desert floor, he reined the quarter horse in. Up to that point, Rocinante had known the best way. Now, he had to take the reins. Hell, the livery place had a deposit for the value of the horse anyway. He'd call them from Denver and let them know that he had absconded with their prize bay gelding. What were they going to do? Hang him in the square for horse stealing?

Matthew clicked his tongue and pulled lightly on the left rein. The horse turned one hundred and eighty degrees. He touched his heels to the mount's haunches. Rocinante galloped northwest. Matthew did not look behind him this time, so he did not notice the silhouettes of two riders on the eastern horizon. They were riding hard toward the twin mesas as Rocinante galloped toward Denver. Toward Emmy Lou and far beyond the letters on the sign the desert wind had finally uncovered:

GROUND ZERO.

Book II

The Second Coming

Turning and turning in the widening gyre
The falcon cannot hear the falconer;
Things fall apart; the centre cannot hold;
Mere anarchy is loosed upon the world,
The blood-dimmed tide is loosed, and everywhere
The ceremony of innocence is drowned;
The best lack all conviction, while the worst
Are full of passionate intensity.

Surely some revelation is at hand;
Surely the Second Coming is at hand.
The Second Coming! Hardly are those words out
When a vast image out of Spiritus Mundi
Troubles my sight: somewhere in sands of the desert
A shape with lion body and the head of a man,
A gaze blank and pitiless as the sun,
Is moving its slow thighs, while all about it
Reel shadows of the indignant desert birds.
The darkness drops again; but now I know
That twenty centuries of stony sleep
Were vexed to nightmare by a rocking cradle,
And what rough beast, its hour come round at last,
Slouches toward Bethlehem to be born?

"The Second Coming," William Butler Yeats

Part One

THE EASY WAY SEEMS HARD;
THE HIGHEST VIRTUE SEEMS EMPTY.

Tao Te Ching

Spiderman leaned on his burl handled walking stick. After three years in this desert he was finally beginning to feel at home. As he hobbled up the stone steps that spiraled into the sand hills toward his sandstone fortress south of The Plain of Souss, he knew that, at least if nothing else, he was safe here. As much as two days from Agadir and more than three from Marrakech, depending upon your mode of transportation and the desert storms, it was safer here than most places. After all, he lived surrounded. Dunes rippled to the north and east like foothills to the Anti Atlas Mountains. South and west of him, the Sahara where Berbers still wove rugs and molded pottery in the old ways. They also made killer hashish which they would obligingly conceal in those same rugs and pottery, as well as in handcrafted Thuya wood pieces and other Berber jewelry as well as camel leather goods.

Until he came to live in this desert, Spiderman had not realized that Berber was used as a generic name for a lot of nomads who crossed the desert on camel caravans laden with spices and riches. Spiderman brokered between these new Berbers and his contacts in the two major cities just as the old Berber traders had done. His service provided authentic Berber handicrafts, pots, and rugs to merchants. He provided hash-filled items for smugglers, particularly rich American smugglers, who were normally importers and exporters, art dealers, doctors, lawyers, librarians, and even cab drivers. He occasionally brokered weapons shipments as well for individuals and even for small revolutionary groups.

Spiderman often thought of himself as being a lot like his great grandfather, Zebediah. He had been a mountain man with Jim Bridger. He also had helped smuggle whiskey and guns with shipments of seed or dried beef bound for their Indian brothers. Of course no one in Morocco knew who his great grandfather was or what he had done. Spiderman liked it that way, too. He let no one close enough to find out. His life had become a trail of breadcrumbs since he escaped from the war and went underground. He had learned to trust only his own instincts when it came to dealing with people and, then, only when people could not be avoided. The rest of the time? Avoid people at all costs? That was what he paid Ranier the big bucks for. To help him avoid people.

I Ching had told him only this morning to be careful of a feminine stranger ("one bearing shade on her back") who would prove to be sly and strong-willed in her purpose. *I Ching's* hexagrams had drawn it plainly enough on the rug covered floor. And, he knew he was closing a deal in Marrakech in a matter of days for twenty Berber rugs and ten pounds of black hash with some jet set nymphet who had contacted Ranier. Not that he really believed any of that *I Ching* stuff anyway. He didn't. For him, casting his hexagrams each day was like people reading their horoscopes in the daily newspaper. He didn't see a current news paper very often. On the other hand, *I Ching* was as current as his last toss.

He was, however, always cautious. As a matter of course, he wove a web of information around prospective customers before ever committing himself to a deal and another web of disinformation around himself and along the customer's path to him. When he was ready to do business, then, and only then, would he allow that web to unravel in the least. Even at that point, he only allowed it to unravel just enough to consummate the deal. From the information his partner, Ranier, had compiled, this jet set chick seemed credible enough, a used-car chain heiress from Memphis, seemingly indulging some cheap thrills because she had the whim and the money to satisfy it.

The wind began to blow up from the south, spreading a rippling carpet of fine sand just inches above the desert floor. Spiderman fingered the dog whistle dangling from a camel hide necklace. He paused, again leaning on his walking stick. Finally, he put the whistle to his dried lips and blew. You never knew, he thought, if the damn thing worked until you saw Lazlo.

A dark shadow shot from the horizon toward where Spiderman still leaned on his stick, waiting. Lazlo was a blur. The black-and-tan Doberman bounded over velvet dunes burnished under the setting sun as if they were cast in bronze. He studied the pincher as he ran, admiring his length of stride, the incredible quickness of his turns. "A man ought to be able to live his whole life the way that fucker runs," Spiderman mumbled to himself as he wagged his head beneath the hood of his dark Berber cloak. As he began to limp along, his left leg stiffened forever by a VC rocket, he continued to mutter into the wind. "That's the only way to get what you want and live to enjoy it."

The dog bounded at full speed down the last dune between them until he was only a few strides from his master. Then, he leaped straight into the air. His momentum carried him the last few lengths in the air. He nipped playfully at Spiderman's jugular before dropping onto all fours back in the sand, standing with his head pointed up toward his master's face, his tongue lollying out of the left side of his half opened mouth.

More like a cat than a dog, the way he always seemed to land on his feet no matter how high he jumped. "Heel, Lazlo. Heel." The pincher scurried to Spiderman's side. His ears laid back on his sleek black head as far as the requisite ear operation would allow. He had actually left the labyrinth and gone to Marrakech to a veterinarian Ranier had recommended for the surgery. He laughed as he stroked the dog's tan chest, then his black muzzle and head where only the eyes were marked tan just over the brows. Lazlo's tongue dripped with saliva. His razor white teeth glistened around it. "Good, fella. There's a storm coming. Don't want to get separated in the flying sand." With surprising tenderness, he ruffled Lazlo's head again. "Good boy, Lazlo! Good boy!"

Spiderman, with Lazlo at heel, continued along the stone steps, deeper into the labyrinth of dunes known among the desert tribes as the spider's web. Because it was constantly shifting and changing shape, many had been trapped or lost in the web before the stone house and its permanent stairway were built by the ruling Spanish in the eighteen-seventies. It was now, however, until just prior to the outbreak of World War II that the solid stone markers rising three feet out of the sand were sunk into place so that the steps could always be found, even in the drifting sand. The Berbers avoided the web still. For them, the pillars represented a time of constant war, a time of little freedom.

Lazlo followed just off Spiderman's right heel. His head constantly shifted left to right to left as he trotted. His ears stood straight up except when he growled at the silky squeaks of a burrowing sandfish lizard's body before it swam away through the sand like a tadpole through water. Then, his ears lay back as flat as they could. When allowed, Lazlo loved to chase the sandfishes down. He would capture them and then release them again and again, also much like a cat.

The wind was rising when they reached the marker where the stairs split in two directions: right to his house; left to the *souk* oasis, one kilometer to the north. A sand storm seemed to be brewing. Too bad that he and Lazlo didn't have stilts, like old T.E. recommended for walking above such a storm. He chuckled at the picture of him and Lazlo on stilts, fumbling along the granite stairway above the swirling carpet of sand beginning to take shape around them. They needed to get inside before the wind got much worse.

"I guess we'll have to put off going to the oasis until the morning, Lazlo. Buy some figs for the trip to Marrakech with Ranier to close our deal with Ms. Linda Tallefero." Yes. Ranier liked figs fresh from the desert, grown the old way, not irrigated. Of course, his poor westerner's palate couldn't tell the difference, but Ranier's could.

Won't he be happy when he drives up in that rebuilt monster Nazi half-track of his to see him standing on the bottom step at the entrance to the web with a sack of fresh, non-irrigated figs as well as their merchandise. "Have to keep old Ranier happy, Lazlo. After all, he's the only person who could possibly . . . ." The pincher glanced up when his master's voice trailed off like his black robe billowed in the increasing wind as he hobbled along the right path in the direction of the center of the spider's web.

But, Ranier hadn't betrayed him yet, not in all this time. When did he begin to really trust the old Berber turned Arab? Christ, Ranier turned him on to the best hashish and arms connections in Morocco. The guns and ammunition were always predictably impeccable. And, the damned hash was downright hallucinatory after just a hit or two. Ranier labeled it "AP" for Astral Projection. Spiderman could attest to the appropriateness of the name for he had, himself, experienced such hashish propelled flights through space while sitting on piles of rugs in his Kasbah. "Fucked up" or "ripped" is what he, himself, called it. "Hell," he muttered to the building wind, the swirling sand, and the hassling Lazlo. "For over three years now he's been trustworthy. Isn't it time to begin trusting him just a little?"

Linda Tallefero sashayed into the Kasbah Marrakech full well knowing that

every eye in that second floor slice of Moroccan café nightlife was ogling her, and, why not? She was model beautiful after her failed suicide—"her fall," she called it—and her rebuilding and rehabilitation thanks to Mr. Bow-Tie. He kept telling her that she only felt more beautiful because the beauty now came from within. The outer beauty, he reiterated, had always been there. The inner beauty had not. But she knew full well that she was now a stunner. Before, she had been merely "not bad." She also knew that "inner beauty" had very little to do with her halter top and mini skirt, and how she filled them, although she was beginning to realize they might be just a little overstated for Marrakech, even if they were Moroccan originals, even if one was on the prowl as she always was even while working. Hell, being on the prowl *was* her work.

She spotted Ranier reclining on a pile of rugs and a divan of cushions at a low table in the rear, beyond the kitchen. Scents of cumin, cinnamon and ginger bubbled in a stew of smoke thick air. His private Kasbah was secluded by rows of dangling glass beads that shimmered ruby and azure in the radiance of the oil lamps that filled the half-moon shaped café. The Kasbah occupied a wide balcony looking down upon the labyrinth of streets known as the Medina. Evening braziers were beginning to sparkle in the twilight like new stars. The Atlas Mountains were fading to dark purple peaks in the sunset. A perfect romantic Moroccan night was embracing Marrakech more perfectly than the travel brochures could ever portray. And she was going to have to spend it with this overstuffed Moroccan drooler. Oh, well. She didn't know what Arab tastes were, but she was sure that, whatever he wanted her to do, she'd figure out a way to enjoy it. Maybe even more because he was repulsive. Sometimes that got her off more than the hot muscled beauties who always thought they were God's gift and in complete control. At least the Raniers of the world knew better.

Linda had not yet met him face-to-face. She had only talked with him over the telephone. But, she knew from CIA and Interpol photos that the man grinning and drooling all over himself as he stared at her from behind the sparkling wall of ruby and azure beads was, unfortunately for her, *Ranier ibn Al-shaikh*. Ranier of the "I've got the dribbling hots for white western women" variety of semi-grounder. He wasn't above ground. He wasn't underground. He was somewhere in between, this swarthy man wrapped in robes of the desert tribes. He was semi-ground. An easy mark.

Ranier grunted loudly as he rose and parted the glittering beaded wall. Linda entered. A few of the strands of ruby and azure beads slipped through Ranier's pudgy fingers, snagging for a moment on Linda's left breast. He inhaled her musky scent and bowed his head slightly from the top of his neck, never once losing sight of those beads glistening in the lamp light like jewels slipping over the fullness of her breast and her erect nipple. He felt as if he could almost see them beneath her lemon spandex halter that left her midriff completely exposed. A golden dollar sign dangled from her exposed pierced navel on a seven link golden chain.

"Mademoiselle Tallefero, yes?" He grinned. Drool crusted the corners of his mouth.

"Mademoiselle Tallefero. Yes."

"Please be coming inside my little Kasbah, as it were, and be making yourself comfortable." His head turned toward the bar. Again, the man seemed to isolate all his directional movement to the top of the neck. Nothing else of his body moved in coordination with his head movements. "More wine. And, a glass for the lady. She is being hot and she is being thirsty. Do not be dallying!"

Despite his slovenly piggishness, Ranier's baleful brown pools that were his eyes would have engulfed her if they had contained any flicker of life. However, the pools did seem to somehow snap to life momentarily while he was giving orders. He obviously liked controlling business and social situations. On the other hand, he seemed to be completely controlled by this mysterious Spiderman character. A man of contrasts in a land of contrasts.

"Please, be reclining on my ottoman, Mademoiselle. Be relaxing. Be listening to the music and be watching the dancers while we be talking. They are magnificent."

Linda slithered onto the ottoman that curved around two sides of the private area enclosed by the strands of beads. "What are those divine aromas coming from the kitchen, Mr. Al-shaikh?"

His eyes popped wide and his lips smacked with simulated pleasure. "Ah, it is being the tagine."

"Tagine?"

"It is being like your stew, I am thinking. Tonight we are celebrating your arrival with seafood tagine. It is being the specialty of this café."

"Sounds delicious?"

"We will be having some very soon, my sweetness."

She crossed her legs. Her white hose hissed. Her white bikini panties flashed before the drooling Ranier's baleful eyes as she reached across her body and extracted a cigarette and lighter from her purse. "Why, Mr. Al-shaikh, I just get all hot and bothered anticipating that stew of yours." She held the cigarette to her lips.

"Allow me, my sweetness." Ranier gently extracted the lighter from her fingers and lit her cigarette.

"It smells so very spicy!" she exhaled bluish smoke.

"That it is being, my sweetness. That it is being!" he chortled. "And, you may be calling me Ranier."

"Okay, Ranier." She laughed softly from the bottom of her throat. The fingers of her hands glided down to the hem of her matching lemon yellow mini skirt and lightly tugged it back to just below where her legs came together. "My Daddy's a big shot used car dealer back in Memphis, you know. That's in the state of Tennessee, you know, in the United States? Well, really, I guess he's sort of the president of this huge corporation there."

"MemCar Corp?"

"MemCar Corp. Yes. But how?"

"I be knowing, my sweetness. I be checking. It is being my job."

"So, Ranier, my teddy bear Moroccan sleuth. You've obviously checked me out thoroughly. Very smart of you." She slid her right hand along the folds of his robes slowly toward his vulnerable crotch. "And, I do check out, don't I?" Everything she'd learned about this man indicated that he would be a pushover for a sexy, hot, American woman. She grinned as he squirmed under her touch. "Don't I, teddy bear?"

"Well, ah . . . ."

She bent toward him.

"I, ah . . . ."

Her breasts nearly pushed their way out of her Moroccan original top that she bought especially for this occasion.

He wiped sweat from his dark brow. "Well, yes. You do be checking out."

"So?" The nipple of her left breast slipped partially past the edge of the lemon spandex.

"So?" Ranier's tongue flicked across his sausage-like lips time and again as if he were tasting that hard dark brown nipple.

"Your wine, sir." The swarthy squat waiter seemed to appear out of the lamplight and smoke. The glass bead strands that enclosed the small private Kasbah did not move. He placed a bottle and two glasses on the table. "May I pour for you?"

"Thank you." Ranier exhaled his gratitude in a sigh of relief.

The waiter filled both glasses and set the bottle back on the table. "Your tagine will be coming soon, sir."

"Thanking you." His head turned back toward Linda. "Morocco, my sweetness, in many ways is being a country apart much like tagine is being, in its own way, spicy. It is nestling on this northwestern tip of Africa here, and it is being separated from the rest of Africa by the huge Atlas Mountains and by the Sahara itself.

"In the north, we are having fine beaches, lush highland valleys, and romantic old cities. In the south and east it is being the beautiful ranges of the Atlases and the Sahara stretching out to the horizon."

Linda licked her glossy pink lips in return as she almost shyly pulled her halter back over her breast. "That's all just wonderful, teddy bear, but I want to meet your partner. I want to meet this mysterious Spiderman."

"I am being sorry, my sweetness. I would be denying you nothing, Ms. Tallefero. I am being sure you know that, after our time together this evening. But, I cannot be doing this thing, Ms. Tallefero. Mr. Spiderman would be impaling me on a stone directional marker in the labyrinth surrounding his house."

"A labyrinth you say?"

"Ah. No. I am not saying. No, I am not saying."

"But, you did, teddy. You did."

"But, it is being here in the Medina. That," he spewed, waving his arms toward the balcony and the encroaching night, 'is being the labyrinth."

He remained paralyzed by her touch and now speechless as well.

"Is it that this Spiderman person won't meet with just me? Or, is it that he won't meet with anybody?"

"Oh, no, Ms. Tallefero. Mr. Spiderman is not meaning to offend you alone. He is meaning to offend everyone equally in these matters. He is meeting none of our clients under any circumstances."

"But," she murmured. "I thought you told me that if I checked out, then you'd try to arrange a meeting?"

"And, honestly, my sweetness, I did be trying. I am thinking that he might make an exception this once, since you knew of him directly from Captain Amerika. But . . . ." He shrugged.

"But what?"

"But, I am being very sorry to inform you that Mr. Spiderman will be making, as he said: 'No exceptions.' Not even for you." He bowed his huge head briefly as if he were praying. "I am being truly sorry."

"Me, too, Ranier. Me too."

"But, my sweetness, be taking in a deep breath now. Here is coming the tagine. I am smelling it."

As the waiter approached and set a rust color glazed earthenware platter with a tall conical lid onto the low Thuya wood table, the scents of cinnamon and cumin wrapped around the aromas of fish and shrimp overwhelmed her, even relaxed her a little. She would relish this spicy stew and then she would ravish her Moroccan teddy bear. She would see just how resolute he could be at resisting her own version of tagine.

As Lazlo crested the final dune, moisture dribbled from his Canines. He bolted ahead.

Below, Spiderman could see the granite block house sprawling close to the sandy valley floor, forming a one-story wedge with a tree-level tower at its apex. The center of the web. Legend had it that the house was used as a temple of some sort until Morocco gained its freedom, finally, in fifty-six.

Somebody was in his house. That wasn't possible. Not in all this time had his security of isolation been breached. But Lazlo was not snarling at some lizard boring into the sand. The pincher's snarls increased as they descended the dune to the sand floor some fifty feet below. He sensed something, smelled something. Lazlo leaped toward the tower door, growling deeper in his throat as he ran. Spiderman followed slowly. Lazlo reached the door and began clawing at the varnished wood. Finally, Spiderman snatched open the bronze inlaid oak door.

"Control, Lazlo! Control!" The pincher sprang through the doorway opening, howling and snarling as he tore across the polished stones of the entrance hall. "Control!"

Spiderman stumbled into the tower behind his dog, peering through twilight into the hallway where Lazlo disappeared. He could hear the dog's paws raking across polished stone along the hallway that led from the tower into the two wings of the house. Spiderman could also hear him still growling deep in his throat as he ran. He pulled the door shut behind him. Brass hinges squalled like a vault closing. Thunk.

"The Kasbah." That's where Lazlo was headed. Seemed to have stopped running now, just snarling. He's got something or someone cornered there. Spiderman bolted for the long shallow cupboard on the north tower wall. Fumbling with a large ring of keys in his left robe pocket, he located the cabinet key, snapped open the cinnamon-scrolled door of the converted cupboard, and glanced quickly down the arms rack. In a matter of seconds, he scanned the gun rack. One of the twelve gauges? Too messy. Could ruin his rugs. Twenty-two? Not much stopping power except at short range. Not always lethal. A Winchester. In his mind, he slid an oil-darkened thirty-thirty from the group of twelve rifles and balanced it in his hand, his index finger in the trigger housing, his other three fingers resting just inside the lever. He smiled as his mind's fingers caressed the barrel, as blue as the Mediterranean, and the stock, as smooth as his hand-rubbed stone floors. Fine piece, but lever action's too slow. Aim at close range can be erratic. A couple of twenty-two target pistols. A three-fifty-seven magnum. Two forty-fives—inaccurate even at hand-to-hand range. A stack of metal clips beside his treasured M16 he'd carried with him all the way from Vietnam. Cartridge boxes stacked edge to edge across the bottom of the cupboard.

He pulled the sixteen from the rack, locked in a nineteen-round clip, shiny from recent oiling like stagnant puddles among the cobblestones of Marrakech after one of its occasional rains, snapped the bolt back and released it twice, ramming a round into place. As he clicked off the safety and set his selector on autoget'em, he carefully stalked Lazlo's diminishing snarls.

When he approached where the hall forked, sleeping quarters to the left and living quarters to the right, he heard Lazlo's snarls turning to whimpers. Then silence. His eyes narrowed. Muscles twitched in his cheeks, pulling his lips back from his teeth as he turned to the right and slouched on his legs and left arm into the Kasbah. He sensed whispers in the dimness. "If whoever it is has hurt my fucking dog, I'll fucking waste them for sure," he mumbled without realizing that he was talking aloud.

A faint odor of musk clung to the evening shadows, cloaking the Kasbah in strangeness. He had not smelled that scent in his house before. It was quite different from the lavender toilet water worn by nearly all of the occasional nomad women he would invite in for an evening or the ginger and cumin and cinnamon that often filled the breezes from the *souk*s at the oasis or his own kitchen. An easy task for him—acquiring women when he wanted them. Nearly every Berber chieftain and their respective tribes within a radius of five hundred miles owed him for the business he provided.

Spiderman inched his way along a marble ledge that surrounded the sunken room, keeping in the shadows so his black robe made him nearly invisible. Musk flushed his nostrils. In the far corner of the Kasbah, he saw a lump of shadows that, somehow, evoked images of a past he would rather not be reminded of, acts he wanted to pretend he had not committed but could not.

"But, Colonel Ting, I can't fight Lieutenant Jesse. He was my bunk mate at the hospital." Spiderman could still smell the burning kerosene in the torches just as surely as if they were now lighting his way through the labyrinth, just as surely as he could smell the musk now in his Kasbah. "He's . . . he's an American, Colonel Ting. He . . . he's my friend."

"You will fight. Both of you will fight. And, one of you will kill the other, or I will have you both shot!" Ting flipped his hands skyward as if tossing something into the winds blowing off the mountains. "Then," he howled in a kind of cracked laughter, "I will just order two more of your swine to fight. And, they will do so willingly." The camp commandant leered up at him as if he were looking down on him. "One way or another, whether you are alive or dead, we will have our little fights here in the evening for our entertainment."

He still remembered the look in Jesse's jaundiced brown eyes. The only life left in them seemed to be the flames of the torches reflecting from his terror-widened pupils. His body still quaked with malaria without warning. He could tell by the poor man's eyes that he knew he was going to die. And, finally, he did.

They fought, if you could call it that—a gimp and a malaria-ridden skeleton—while the VC cadre made their bets and cheered their favorites. After a couple of minutes of this combat, he began to understand something of how to use his bad leg to his advantage. He began to pivot on the leg, away from the charging, palsied Lieutenant Jesse. On one charge, as Jesse missed him, he was able to club Jesse on the back of the neck, knocking him to the ground. The cadre cheered in the darkness beyond the torches. He landed on his knees in the small of Jesse's back. He straddled the already semi-conscious Jesse and grabbed his head between his hands, ready to snap his neck. He remembered looking across the dirt circle at Colonel Ting. Ting had stared back through the dull orange light of the torches. "Kill him!"

"Kill him!" the cadre chorused. "Kill him! Kill him!" echoed in the jungle darkness.

He hesitated.

"Kill him or die yourself!" Ting screamed. He drew his pistol and aimed it at his head. "Do it now!"

He heard the hammer click back. The kerosene smoke burned his eyes. He huffed in agony and complete frustration. He sucked in a deep breath, and, with one swift twist of his wrists still strong from a lifetime of baseball, snapped Lieutenant Jesse's neck. The last tears he ever shed flooded down his burning cheeks.

He soon became a living legend in the POW camp in the jungles along the Ho Chi Minh Trail near the Cambodian border long before he had been able to engineer his escape. He parlayed his stiffened leg into a lethal instrument in his bouts with destruction of another fellow prisoner or an occasional traitorous NVA guard. After that first fight with Jesse, the killing came to him almost too easily. It was as if accepting the inevitability of his situation somehow allowed him to enter a kind of amorality zone similar to that of a soldier in combat. In the end, it was always him left holding his vanquished and dying opponent in his arms. He became an expert at holding men he had killed in his arms.

"Mr. Spiderman?"

A husky voice matching the musky smell lilted toward him as he continued to crawl along the ledge. It was the voice of no Berber girl, that was for sure.

"Mr. Spiderman. I'm . . . ."

His sigh cut her off. "Ms. Linda, I presume?"

"Yes."

He stopped, turned his body in a line facing the lump of shadows near the only windows in the room. A wall of plexi-glass picture windows had replaced the entire front wall facing the sand dunes he and Lazlo had just crossed during their evening walk. The original stone wall had been destroyed by nomads over fifty years before in some fight or another. An oil millionaire from Oklahoma had purchased the fortress and repaired the damage by having the wall of windows built simply because he was infatuated with the sight of the desert. Ranier heard through his grapevine that the oil magnate, who had planned to live in the house, soon discovered that he couldn't handle the isolation and living without indoor plumbing and electricity even for short periods of time. Spiderman had been able to make a very good deal on the place. Another one he owed Ranier.

He aimed his sixteen in the direction of that shadowy corner from where the voice emanated. "You got a light on you, Ms. Linda?"

"Why, yes, Mr. Spiderman. I surely do."

"Okay." He sucked in a deep breath. "There's an oil lamp on a low table just to your left. It's covered by a small rug." He could hear her fumbling in her purse for a light, then stumbling a few steps across the floor until she located the lamp. "Find it okay?"

"Uh huh."

"Good. Now light it and freeze. And, I do mean hands-behind-your-head kind of freeze, Ms. Linda. I've got a fully loaded M16 trained on you right now!" He could hear the glass dome being removed from its brass stand. A lighter clicked. A flame flare blue, then red orange in the semi-darkness. Tracers of light trailed through the air as a partly visible arm touched the flame to the lamp wick. It spit, then glowed into yellow light. Now he could see her outline and Lazlo's. After she replaced the dome, the diffused light focused and he could see them both more clearly.

Lazlo sat near Linda's feet like a porcelain statue, his tongue dangling out of the left side of his mouth. Linda stood straight. Her hands clasped behind her head caused her naked breasts to point toward the stucco ceiling. She seemed to have been painted on the wall by Talal or Yacoubi.

Christ! He hadn't expected. He hadn't anticipated a naked angel in the lamplight. His face flushed. His loins tingled. Loins. Lions. Just reverse the vowels. His index finger relaxed on the trigger.

"I'm truly sorry, Mr. Spiderman, for this unannounced intrusion, but your door *was* unlocked."

"What the hell would you expect out here in the middle of the fucking desert? Bolted doors and burglar alarms?"

Undaunted by his interruption, Linda continued, arching her body in a way that the lamplight seemed to caress her. "And, I'm here to get right down to business, as you can plainly see."

"Yes." He cleared his constricting throat. "Well, I can plainly see you, that's for sure. Naked as a jay bird as my great grandfather used to say."

"May I ple-ase put my poor little arms down now, Mr. Spiderman? They're starting to hurt, and, surely, it is obvious,even to one as suspicious as you, that I am hiding nothing."

He could hear the pouting in her voice even though he could not really see her pouting clearly from this distance. Yet, he was sure he also heard a smile play across her pouting lips. As his eyes adjusted to the light, her lips were rubies in the lamplight. His eyes locked on her round breasts, slim waist, slightly heavy hips. Curly black hair covered her mound beneath her sloping stomach. "Ah, okay, sure." He cleared his throat again. "You can put your hands down by your sides, slowly, and keep them there. I am walking over."

"Oh, goodie!"

He approached her from behind the lamplight so that he was still invisible to her. Close up she seemed less like a Talal or Yacoubi shrouded in the mists of myopia and more clear like the curves of the moon's surface so familiar to us all now that astronauts have walked on it, their cameras stripping it of its mystery. Her olive skin, tanned even around her crotch and nipples, glowed in the light. Black hair streamed in thick curls down her back and over her shoulders, highlighting her breasts like shading in a painting.

Without a sound he passed out of the shadows of invisibility into the lamplight of sight and stopped directly in front of her, poking the cold barrel of his sixteen into her slight bulge of a navel where Linda's trademark gold dollar sign dangled. That and a brown birth mark that looked like smeared shit on the inside softness of her left buttocks that shivered when the barrel touched her skin—not out of coldness or fear, but more like an orgasmic shiver—were the only blemishes on this creature.

A veritable Diana.

As he stepped closer, the goddess lifted her right hand from her side very slowly so that her hand and arm seemed to float gradually upward. He could feel the heat of her naked body nearly overwhelming him. "Linda Tallefero, Mr. Spiderman. I'm so very pleased to finally make your acquaintance."

His lips stuck together as he mumbled. "Me too, I guess."

"Now what's that you all say in the Army, Spiderman, honey?" Her voice trembled still. "This is my rifle." She caressed the barrel still aiming at her navel. "Ah, this is my gun." She touched the darkness between her soft thighs. "This one's for killing and this one's for fun." As her voice mellowed into throaty tones and trailed off into the closing-in twilight, she again caressed the barrel of his M16, then his black-robe-covered crotch.

"I wouldn't know, Ms. Linda. I was never in the Army." Spiderman jerked out of her reach, then lowered his rifle. "What the hell do you think this is, anyway? A fucking game!"

"Hell, honey. I sure hope so." She giggled as she glided closer to him, pushing the rifle aside as she smothered him with her bubbling warm, musky flesh. "What say we get down on this pile of Berber rugs here and negotiate?"

As she stepped toward him, Spiderman instinctively drew down on her. "I'm sorry." He dropped his sixteen to the floor. It clattered against the side of the marble ledge. "I think you'd better put some clothes on Ms. Linda Tallefero. You've got a lot of explaining to do."

"There's a *souk* at the oasis near here tomorrow."

Spiderman sprawled beside Linda on a divan of red pillows. It covered nearly half of his Kasbah. First, several layers of Berber rugs covered the polished stone floor. Pillows piled on top of the rugs and against the marble ledge facing the windows. The windows overlooked a desert of burnished bronze dunes gradually disappearing into a sunset curtain of swirling rose sand.

"A *souk*?" She pulled a cigarette and lighter from her purse. "What's a *souk*?"

As Spiderman took the lighter, snapped it open, ignited the wick, and held the flame out toward her, he recalled the first *souk* Ranier had taken him to in a remote region of the Atlas Mountains. The village of Imilchil where his favorite cousin was getting married. In fact, the people of Imilchil were celebrating a festival of marriages. Ranier had explained it to him as he drove the half-track across the desert in the direction of the snow-capped mountains he could barely see in the distance. "It's sort of a get-together or gathering of desert people. Sometimes it's family. Sometimes it's trade. This time it's marriages. So be careful," he chuckled.

Spiderman remembered Ranier's story verbatim. "Every year, by tradition, the Ait Hdiddou tribe are gathering in Imilchil to trade, socialize, and marry. In many ways, not being too different from *souk*s in the desert here. Traditionally, this was being the time after harvest and before winter, when the nomadic Berbers would be leaving their farms and flocks. People of marriageable age, accompanied by chaperones of course, would be coming to Imilchil to be having the chance to meet just like here at home. Nowadays, most meeting and courting are occurring throughout the year, but the marriage ceremonies still be taking place during the festival, as with my cousin.

"You will be seeing performances of Berber music and dance as lines of dancers like you have never been seeing are standing shoulder to shoulder, chanting in honor of the gathering and in praise of Allah. They are raising their shoulders up and down in time with the music, lifting their knees while dancing in line, weaving from side to side. The singing can be going on for hours at a time."

The tip of Linda's cigarette glowed as she pulled back from the lighter's flame and inhaled deeply. "So, I sort of conned your partner, Ranier, into bringing me on out here instead of waiting back in Marrakech for another couple of days. I was just getting more and more bored by the second. You know?"

"Bored, in Marrakech? I can't imagine ever being bored there. Freaked out by the press of too many people maybe. Sensory overloaded, sure. But bored? Never."

Ranier's monologue from that day continued in his mind. He seemed unable to stop it. "My people are having a lot of history in North Africa. Our ancient ones were settling in the area just inland of the Mediterranean Sea to the east of Egypt. Many early colonial accounts are mentioning a group of people collectively known as Berbers living in northern Africa. My people.

"Our Berber society is being divided between those who tend the land and those who do not. At one time, tilling the land was being considered the work of the lower classes, while the upper classes were being merchants. Usually, groups of sedentary Berbers were paying allegiance to a locally appointed headman. He, in turn, was reporting to the noble who considered the village his domain. As time is being passed, however, these farmers are being able to accumulate wealth even when the Saharan trade routes be diminishing in importance. They were also being given political status by colonial and postcolonial administrations."

"Well," Linda pouted. "I just wanted to see how a real live and dangerous 'romantic hero' like yourself actually lives from day to day." She fluttered her eyelids in an exaggerated but awkward manner simultaneously mimicking and mocking what she had seen silent screen actresses do when they flattered and flirted. She exhaled a silver stream of smoke that curled its way toward the ceiling like a helix. "Ranier told me that he wanted to visit some of his family that lived near here. So, he just came a little early, you know."

Spiderman sucked in the last hit. The glow in the hookah bowl flickered for the last time like the twilight outside the windows. Nothing was left in the large bronze bowl but ashes. "Yes, well, Ranier thinks of himself as Arab, but his racial roots are aboriginal, you know? Berber. Either way, he knows better god damnit!"

"But, just think. Now, you don't have to travel for three days up to Marrakech if you don't want to." She grinned and flipped ashes into a bronze ashtray Spiderman had found somewhere among the pillows and carpets. He had explained that he normally put ashes from the hookah into it. "See how much easier I've made things for you already?"

"Yeah, right." He slammed a karate jab into the pillows beside him, tearing the cover of one. "Nobody's ever supposed to come out here." The pillow's shredded wool stuffing puffed into the still air of the room. "Most of my customers never even have the opportunity of meeting me, even talking to me directly, much less intruding into my sanctuary." Lazlo jumped to his feet, whimpering. Spiderman reached out in the growing darkness and stroked his flanks. "I mean, nobody, Ms. Linda! You're just damned lucky that I didn't simply kill you before you were even able to identify yourself."

Linda coughed another silver smoke strand into the last of the rose twilight. "Damned Kyriazi Frères. Thought I should try Egyptian cigarettes since I'm part Egyptian myself."

"The Cleopatra of used cars?" Spiderman avoided her face, continuing to stroke Lazlo. The pincher twitched his paws as he slumbered, running again in another sand dune dogmare. "Is that right, princess?"

Linda ignored his sarcasm. "Why are you so protective? So secretive? Why have you isolated yourself like this, Spiderman, honey, out here in the middle of the desert hills of Morocco for Christ's sake?"

"This is exactly why." As his voice trailed off, he waved his free arm in her general direction.

"What's why?"

"Too many questions from people just like yourself." He refilled the hookah bowl from a cream-colored pouch that lay on the table beside the water pipe. "That's why!"

Linda's fingers touched him beneath his robe as he packed fine golden powder into the bowl with his fingers. Over the marijuana, he crumpled a thumb-and-forefinger-size pinch of black hash. Her face was a sadness mask, one she hoped asked for forgiveness for her intrusion. "But, Spiderman, honey, like I said, I was bored and now I get a chance to go to an authentic Berber tribal market and . . . and I met you which," she grinned, "seems to be no mean feat."

"I'll twist that frog's legs off when I see him tomorrow." He struck a stick match and lit the mixture in the bronze hookah bowl.

"Frog? What frog?"

He passed the hose to Linda as he held sweet smoke in his lungs as long as he could. "Frog Ranier!" he spit out with bursts of smoke. Just when I was thinking I could finally trust him. Damn! Isn't that about par for the fucking course? "Ranier! That's what frog! I do have the correct amphibian, don't I? The one that can be changed utterly by the kiss of a princess?"

Linda snubbed out her cigarette in the bronze ash tray. "Aw, come on big, bad Spiderman, honey." She tiptoed her fingers down his chest, bare where his robe was not closed. "Don't be so hard on poor little Ranier. I mean, you aren't doing such a hot job of resisting little Linda's Egyptian magic yourself, now are you?" Her bow-string lips pulled back from teeth very slightly stained by nicotine into a smirk that, at the same time, seemed to drip Sourwood honey.

She used her lighter to keep the bowl burning and sucked on the hookah hose like it was Spiderman's penis. She, too, held the smoke in her lungs though not as long as Spiderman. Little did he know, if he could drop the right names in the right places he could also get Ranier—or anybody else for that matter—to do, well, whatever he might want them to do. She'd known the right names. The right places took nearly two years to discover. God, it seemed longer, much longer, than two years.

"This is my lighter that I give to you," Matthew had said. "Whenever you light up, remember me." She remembered. Yes, she remembered how Matthew Parkrow's laughter had throbbed in her brain while she hid in her bedroom in her parents' home in Memphis—a solid brick colonial with four white plantation columns across the front entrance on a hill overlooking the river and the psychedelic bridges spanning it to Arkansas. Used cars were her Daddy's business. That was the one thing Memphis had in addition to Gracie Mansion. Used car lots. Why, Memphis seemed to have more used car lots than churches, and her Daddy owned all or a piece of most of them. She remembered Matthew laughing. No, shrieking was more like it. Something about returning to the cradle endlessly rocking and rolling like Sha Na Na. That had been the last time she had heard from him.

Spiderman felt as if he had no choice, no will of his own left. "You really want me to shove my sixteen up you and empty the fucking clip, don't you?" He sank his teeth into her shoulder just short of drawing blood as he crumpled into the pile of rugs and shadows from which he had come, lying on the rugs with Linda Tallefero who tore at his robe and mumbled something about filling her vagina full with his M16. Flinging his robe into the darkness of the ledge that trailed out behind them, she straddled him, her arms and legs akimbo like a crab. Queen of Pentacles. Beware of a dark woman *I Ching* had said.

And, only last week, a desert gypsy reeking of lavender had told him the same thing. She swore that she was the daughter of Madame Thriceblessed in the direct line of Cassandra. Hell, of course, he didn't believe her any more than he believed this morning's hexagrams, but it didn't hurt to have insurance from whatever source might be available. Like most followers of Islam in northern Africa, Ranier and many of his Berber relations believed in the continuous presence of various spirits, *djinns* as they called them. The *Quran* was their means of Divination, not horoscopes or the *I Ching*, and most men, like Ranier, wore protective amulets that contained verses from the *Quran*.

Linda's nipples seemed to cut into his palms as he touched her hanging breasts. Bit by bit she seemed to squat onto his penis as she began to lubricate. He could feel the sticky soft wet hot of her slowly gobbling him up. He writhed under her sucking throbbing presence allowing it to take him over completely. He clutched at her, nipping her with his teeth. He had forgotten how it could be . . . .

She bit his neck, his shoulders. Her nails raked his chest like Lazlo's paws had earlier raked across the hallway floor. She urged his thighs off the rugs as she finally dropped onto him completely. He felt the end of her around him. He swelled with her vaginal contractions. His hips arched. She lifted her haunches and dropped them again and again. Shrieks tore out of her mouth from between clenched teeth each time she shuddered with round after round he shot into her like spurts from his sixteen.

The musky odor of her flesh suffocated him. Her hands now urged him up like a potter's fingers molding clay on the wheel. What we used to do in Nam. Yeah. The girlsans always got off on it, even the most seasoned and hardened harlot. Why not? He sneaked his right hand behind him, groping for his rifle.

He crawled on top of her body, drying salty in the darkness just out of reach of the oil lamp's glow. He forced her thighs open with his knees and plunged. She oozed warm fluid inside. He struck deep and swift like a guerilla attack. She whimpered beneath him like Lazlo who slouched on all fours only a few feet away.

Spiderman clutched the M16 over his head. His index finger curled around the trigger. He reared on Linda like riding a spirited mare, rammed the bolt forward.

"Oh, God! No!"

He lunged his hips down against hers and emptied the clip, not into her vagina as she had asked, but into the thick ceiling, showering the room in plaster snow.

She felt the twisting convulsions in her spine of relief and pleasure of an unknown species, something like she had never experienced. "Oh Christ! Fuck me more, Spiderman, honey! More!" Seeming to fragment, she shrieked and tremored among the red pillows, spasming in a lump. Her eyes rolled back into her head as he slammed spermcanos against the rippling walls of her womb. Darkness, sweet darkness, like the darkness of that night after Matthew left her at the race track with all those fucking Hell's Angels.

They collapsed, limp among the rugs and twilight shadows in the Kasbah of Spiderman's fortress at the center of the web among the bronze sparkling dunes of the desert at 321 00 N, 51 00 W in the land of lions, *Al Mamlakah al Maghribiyah*, Kingdom of Morocco.

Linda's first night back in Memphis after Altamont, she was in the midst of a four-way hit of Window Pane when she became obsessed with being joined into the same force that had, somehow, torn her Matthew away from her. So, she decided to jump off one of those flashbulb bridges to Arkansas, hopefully, to be swept up into the Mother river's current like Matthew must have been. He'd mumbled something about not wanting to be a witness to the end but having little choice. Then, he just walked away from her as if she wasn't even there, as if she had never even been there.

Instead of falling into the river, her plunge dropped her smack dab in the middle of a cruise party up from Natchez. Several of the party suffered broken bones—a collar bone, a couple of ankles, one arm, a leg, and even a coccyx as a result of her falling on top of them as they sipped mint juleps on the afterdeck of the authentically restored paddle-wheel river boat, The Natchez Queen.

The debutante with the cracked coccyx was the real ass of the bunch anyway, with her snot-assed airs she put on while Linda chewed her tongue and frothed at the mouth like a mad dog. God damn. Like debutantes didn't ever try to commit suicide. Linda remembered slobbering something at the time. Yes. About. Yes. It was. Yes. "Don't fuck with me. I was a Debbie darling, myself, Ms. Coccyx."

When she realized she had come out of the whole fiasco with no worse than some repairable cuts on her face and neck, a badly chewed tongue, a headache, a good hit of abuse from the debutante, the possibility that her chromosomes would be fucked up in any baby she might conceive, several personal injury lawsuits before they became fashionable, plus a few rather shrill snatches about the trip that continued to, unpredictably, short-circuit her synapses, she just knew that Providence had intervened.

After all, she was alive. She was, more or less, in one piece. She was destined ever since she had passed out after her fall in the arms of a man in a dark blue three-piece suit with an American flag pin in his lapel. A Madras Bow-Tie bobbed around his thick neck. Yes. She had been destined all right. But, destined for what she did not truly know.

Christ. Is she dead? Spiderman jerked out of her limp body. Necrophelia was not his thing. She moaned from the depths of her crotch. She still breathed. Her hips moved, reaching up for him. His sperm showering over her in the darkness seemed like a flow of pearls splashing against her olive thighs.

"Oh, Spiderman, honey. Yummy." She shook between sighs. "I really never got off like that before in my whole fucking life. Wow!"

It had been the guy in the red-white-and-blue Madras Bow-Tie that came by to visit with her while she was recovering at Saint Jude's—a private Memphis hospital she had never heard of—from plastic surgery. She was housed and treated, however, in the Alcohol and Drug Abuse facility which was more like a five star hotel than a hospital. He had promised her that he could assist her in finding her destiny in life, her purpose, so that she would never again feel the need to throw herself off of a bridge. He brought her reading materials from his church. Baptist, he said. But, it all read like government propaganda.

Later, this man, into whose arms she'd fallen into from that Mississippi River bridge, approached her about working for the government under cover. She could help Uncle Sam destroy the arms and drugs dealers, and, thereby, crush the revolution that threatened the very fabric of America. As it turned out, the Bow-Tied gentleman from The Natchez Queen cruise party was a CIA station chief working on a very special project code named CHAOS.

Linda was overwhelmed. She jumped at the chance, although she wasn't exactly sure why. Even now. She agreed to help in any way she could. For months, she spent hours nearly every day with a tape recorder and with the Bow-Tie station chief who, by then, had a name: Bow-Tie. She recorded everything in chronological order just as he had suggested. In that way, she was able to recall details about almost every person she could think of whom she had met while still a wild hippie girl before her "fall."

Finally, after more than a year of work and rehabilitation at the facility, a tape she made concerning the boy friend she met at Atlanta Jam interested Bow-Tie. She remembered him grinning for, perhaps, the first time. She certainly couldn't remember seeing him grin before. Smile a little, maybe. But never overtly grin.

"Good girl," he had whispered through his grin. Then he shouted, "Good girl, Linda!" She remembered being, somehow, happy, too, because Bow-Tie seemed happy, but about what she wasn't all that sure of in the here and now of her memory.

Spiderman studied her carefully. Her mouth sloped down at the edges of her lips like the edges of red paper. Her flared nostrils still quivered. The gap between her top front teeth would put the Wife of Bath's to shame. The only somewhat flaw to her otherwise spectacular sensual beauty. Her tongue vacuumed his mouth as he leaned over her, sprawled among the red pillows and Berber carpets nearly unconscious like a tapestry or one of the mosaics covering the walls of the spare bedroom at the end of the other angle in the stone wedge house. He called it the Kama Sutra bedroom realizing that it was probably an inappropriate name for it considering the country he was in.

After mating is when the female is most dangerous. Stay clear of her fangs, that's all. "Yeah, it's a real trip, ain't it? Even better when you're ripped. Right? The fear rushes and the sex rushes just collide and collide and collide." His head tilted back as though he were nodding out. "Wow. It's been a long . . . ." Shut up, fool! Keep a closed and free mouth. No running off at it like you were Lazlo with rabies.

"Where did you learn that trick anyway?"

"Not down home on the farm, that's for sure," he chuckled.

"Where, then, silly?"

"Nam." He stopped laughing as he spoke the monosyllable mistake.

"Vietnam?"

"Vietnam?" He mimicked her surprise. "Listen, GIs brought back a lot of things besides PTSD and the clap, you know?"

"Really?" Her nose twitched. Her dense bluish gray eyes glowed like old stars. "I thought you said you'd never been in the Army, Spiderman, honey?"

"I. Ah . . . ." He mentally sat on his real thoughts, not allowing them to transport to his tongue. "Lied."

"When were you there?"

"Oh, sixty . . . ." He stopped himself. "See, you're back to questions again?" He drew in a deep breath and drew back from her star pools. "Let's talk about something else. Okay?"

"Sure." She shrugged. "Okay." The hair, which piled above her shoulders on the pillows under her head, spilled down her teak breasts almost to her navel. Her eyes sparkled. "Let's talk about the *souk* at the oasis tomorrow," she squealed. In her mind, Linda focused on the scene of her first remembered Christmas so that she would squeal convincingly. He had to believe that she would chance smuggling—insane as it might seem—simply because she was a naïve used car heiress from Memphis out to cop some hash on a lark and, consequently, to get a first-hand look at the real native culture along the way. So far, it was working.

"Sure." He winked. "You'll really get off on it, I believe."

"Great! Then, you're not mad?"

"Hell, yes, I'm mad. But not much I can do about it now. I will just have to talk to Ranier about this serious lapse of judgment on his part." He began to chuckle again. "The little froggie."

"Oh," she pouted. "A lapse of judgment. That's what I am?"

Spiderman continued to chuckle.

Linda turned on a radiant smile. "Oh, I almost forgot. I have a couple of messages for you from the froggie. He tied them up in a string. I presume to keep my curious and possibly untrustworthy eyes out. They're in my purse." She vaulted to her feet. "I'll get them for you, Spiderman, honey." She fumbled around among the carpets for her leather purse, snatched off of a Katherine Ann Porter wax figure in Don Amerika's Gun Shop.

"Yes, ma'am. Now that we've fucked a bit, I do remember a dude like what you described."

"And what," she hissed in his ear, "do you remember about him, Don honey?" She rubbed his red-white-and-blue clad crotch as hard as she dared without risking pain to his testicles.

"Well, he bought a rifle and shit. Said he was going into the desert up near Alamogordo for a few days. Hell, Ms. Linda, that was about all there was to it."

"Are they important?"

"What, Spiderman, honey?"

"Ranier's messages."

Don Amerika had told her she'd have to "get in real tight with this dude in Marrakech named Ranier" if she wanted to get to Spiderman. "Ranier'll lead you, sexy mama, to Spiderman or anyone else for that matter just for a little promise or two along the way. He's very freaked out that way on foreign women. Especially sensual, sexy American foreign women like yourself."

"Oh, Spiderman, honey. How would I know that unless I untied the froggie's little ole string and read them?"

He spread his arms toward her under the yellow glow as she fumbled through her purse. Her moon-curved body shimmered in what seemed to be gaslight on a stage. She'd sucked his brain into his balls. That was what she'd done. No doubt about that. If she could do it to him, then she certainly could do it to Ranier, even better, perhaps. After all, he did freak out over white American pussy. He became completely unglued. As Linda turned back into the shadows, she became a shade flowing in the direction of his arms. She grasped the two messages and pulled the string loose. Her hands, outstretched, spilled the notes onto his thighs like blades reflecting the yellow light behind her of the lamps and the moon light beginning to settle on the tops of the dunes.

"Cleaver, my dear. Quite cleaver!"

"I thought so, myself."

She plopped beside him looking over his shoulder as he tried to catch enough of the dim light to read Ranier's fastidious printing. She waved her arms toward the bank of windows in front of them. They shimmered as the moon oozed from behind the fat dunes, gradually spraying the desert hills and the blowing sand a hazy silver with golden yellow highlights. "Moonlight so you won't strain your eyes, Spiderman, honey."

"Do you command the moon, as well, you little vamp from Memphis, you?" He turned the first message toward the moonlit windows. Sand pelted the plexi-glass giving the impression that the moonlight was pelting the window. He had not really noticed that sound before.

MEET ME AT OASIS. NOON. BRING MS. LINDA TO *SOUK.*

She shook her head. "No, I don't command the moon, Spiderman, honey. I just use what's there."

"Me too."

The second message was in Ranier's same neat block letters.

BEWARE, TARANTULA!

"I don't need your money, Spiderman, honey," Linda softly whispered into his ear. Her voice vibrated as they jostled about in the rear seat of Ranier's modified Nazi half-track as it weaved two dark parallel swaths across the moon glow sand, north in the direction of the Vers Laayoune road that would take them to Tiznit and ultimately to Agadir. The Berber *souk* had been everything that she imagined and hoped, even more. Nomads and those who lived in permanent villages throughout the upper Sahara and Lower Atlas regions came there to barter and sell their wares, livestock, and contraband as well as to socialize with old friends and family seen only a few times a year at other *souk*s. And, at dusk, the carts of oranges, figs, and roasted grains were replaced with hot food stalls. One after another, acetylene flames glared out into the dimness just like in Jemaa el Fna Square in Marrakech.

Linda touched Spiderman's arm, nodding at the pile of packages and bundles on the floorboard. "We made some good buys, huh? Saved a lot of Dirham." Her nails gripped firmly, but did not penetrate, his skin.

Spiderman shook his head mentally. She had just about bought the fucking *souk* out all by herself. Well, the Thuya wood pieces anyway. She had fallen absolutely in love with the rich mountain cypress textures and shades she saw in the chess and domino sets, ash trays, note, card, and pen/pencil holders, decorative and tissue boxes, book ends, and picture frames. She had bargained for and purchased a chess set for her Father, four ashtrays, and a dozen each note, card, and pen/pencil holders. "They would make good Christmas gifts," she explained.

In the driver's seat, Ranier sat like a Muslim robot, but one with a brain that thought in Berber, even when he spoke English or one of the other languages common to his country: Spanish, French, and Arabic. From his studies, Ranier knew that Berber languages formed a branch of the Afro-Asiatic linguistic family. Differences between the three hundred or so local dialects could be considerable, due to geographical distances. In Morocco there were three main dialects. Riffan, spoken in the Rifs and down along the Algerian border in eastern Morocco all the way to Figuig. The dialect of the High Atlas and Middle Atlas, had many names, like Berber, Amazigh, Zaian or Tamazight. The dialect used in the Anti-Atlas and southwestern oases was called Chelha or Tashelhait, Soussi or Chleuh. Out in the Sahara the Berber language was called Zénète, his native dialect.

Berber identity, he knew from a life of experience, was strongly linked to the language. That was why in so many areas where being a Berber was considered a bad thing—principally because many Berber societies were less developed than the cities where almost all inhabitants saw themselves as Arabs—many North Africans, like himself, called themselves Arabs even though they were truly of Berber origin.

Visiting with his Berber family and friends was usually so refreshing that he was stimulated for days, sometimes weeks, afterward. But, that damned vamp from Memphis, U.S.A. forced him to cut a very short visit with his family, many of whom he had not seen in months or years, even shorter.

In the shotgun seat beside him, Lazlo sat on his haunches like a Lladro figurine. In fact, he'd moved very little since he'd first encountered Linda in Spiderman's Kasbah, and, then, only when that damned woman told him to. She'd ruined a good dog, and, like Lazlo, the dog's master had also been taken under that damned woman's spell. Her Spiderman potion seemed to be a brew of moonlight and sexual fantasies. Ranier did not know what Lazlo's spell was cast from, but he figured it was probably quite similar. That was certainly something like the spell she cast on him that seemed to force him into actions that he knew he should not take like bringing her to the center of Spiderman's web.

Ranier drove with no lights under the soft lemon flow of the desert moon. The only smell on the desert was the half-track's burning gasoline. The stench trailed behind them like Gretel's crumbs.

"As I'm sure you know, Spiderman, honey, I have all the money I could possibly ever squander. A filthy rich CEO Daddy, don't you know?

"I don't want anything from you, honey, except . . . ."

The half-track engine shut out all but Linda's giggles echoing through Spiderman's nerve endings as she slipped her cool fingers under his robe, unsnapping, unzipping the jeans he always wore underneath his robe when he ventured out in public. "Except your body!"

Behind his bulging brown robot eyes that stared at the sand stretched out ahead in the moonlight, Ranier fantasized her naked on the beach south of Agadir. Her olive skin dripped lemon sea water as if she were under a moon shower. She ran toward him, her arms flung wide to him, her cat-like eyes leaping from her head to enter his, to steal his very soul with a stare. Spiderman was gone somewhere. Forever! And, he, Ranier ibn Al-shaikh, was alone on the beach with his Egyptian princess from Memphis.

Ranier was aware of the cool fiberglass of the new steering wheel he had installed just last week after their first legitimate rug and crockery deal in years. Spiderman was trying to go clean, now. He'd made enough. Ranier had made enough. This Tallefero thing was supposed to be their last smuggling transaction.

Suddenly, her image was upon him, again, like a sandstorm, sucking his breath from his body, his thoughts from his mind, his prayers from his lips as he basked in her flesh of warm, sweet pain.

Linda urged Spiderman up. "Christ, Linda! Ranier's right up there, driving."

"No matter." She pulled her hand away, untied the sash around her matching turquoise toga and shrugged it from her shoulders. In the moonlight, she knew her skin glistened like fool's gold. She began to sing in whispers to one of the songs from *Tommy*. "He can't hear us. He can't see us. Anyway, he couldn't bring himself to come between us."

Hot flashes wracked Ranier's body as he recalled how she had played him in Marrakech. Fulfill your every wish, your wildest fantasies, she had promised. And, she did sit on his face and allow him to enter her every orifice with dildos.

The half-track swerved. Ranier jerked the steering wheel back, held firm, and the vehicle skidded back onto a straight course for Vers Laayoune. He thought he had heard a scream, more like a shriek. Linda? No, she waited for him on the beach near Agadir. Hearing nothing else, Ranier settled back into the pleated leather bucket seat. His inner vision transported him, once more, to that beach just outside of Agadir. Her body waited for his there, a quivering mass approaching a quivering mass. She had promised.

Spiderman and Linda fell into the heap of packages, no longer able to control the behavior of their outer extremities, which seemed to have individual minds of their own. Howls that emitted from deep in their groins stumbled almost silently from their laughter-constricted throats.

"What was that?" Ranier's head darted from side to side. "Did I hit something, Lazlo?" As he looked back, he observed that both Linda and Spiderman were missing. He muttered an unintelligible invective in the Zénète dialect of his ancestors and slowed the half-track. He whipped the wheel, skidding in a semi-circle back in the direction of the oasis.

After half a mile or so, he stopped the half-track and pulled up the emergency brake. It was somewhere around here that the truck had swerved. That must have been when they were thrown out. The engine, rebuilt by Ranier and his mechanic cousin, idled like a continuous cough. He jumped to the ground with a flashlight in his left hand. His right hand slipped a magnum from inside his robe as he stumbled off in the direction where Linda and Spiderman must have been thrown clear.

Shrill laughter shattered the desert night from behind him. "Goose it, Spiderman, honey! Make tracks! Haul ass!"

Ranier whirled toward the sound of her voice barely audible above the distant engine cough. Lights blazed orange through fog lamp glass. The engine revved. The half-track skidded around in the sand and sped off toward the Vers Laayoune. Two naked people were stealing his half-track. He fired twice into the air before he tumbled face down into the desert sand. The magnum flew in one direction, the flashlight in another, both lost, he was sure, forever in the sand and the darkness. Even with the lemon moonlight he was convinced he would never find them.

"Make half-tracks, you mean, don't you, Linda?"

"Guess you're right, Spiderman, honey." Linda grinned. "Lazlo! Back!" The pincher leaped into the back as his mistress sprawled back in her bucket seat beside Spiderman. "We can drive this baby right smack through Agadir. Naked as jay birds as your great granddaddy used to say. Right?"

"But, won't Ranier be in trouble?" Spiderman tossed his head toward the part of the desert behind them now that was already out of their moonlight. "Out here?"

"Hell, Spiderman, honey." Linda ruffled her black hair with her fingers, arranging it in thick strands down her naked breasts. "He's a Berber, isn't he?"

"Yeah. So?"

"So. He'll be all right out there . . . out here. This desert is his home. It's in his blood. And, we can be a l o n e."

"Yeah." Spiderman's face, touched by the dry wind, smiled, a ship at sea on a calm lemon moonlit night. "You got the money, honey, and I got the con-nec-tions!"

"A real matched pair, aren't we?"

"Dig it!"

Linda fumbled for her lighter. She'd spotted it on the floor under the packages where they had fallen earlier. Her buttocks reached skyward like Siamese moons. When Spiderman tickled the hair protruding from her panties, she almost toppled into the rear seat with Lazlo. Not necessarily a totally unpleasant unintended consequence of her actions. She caressed Lazlo's snout as he fawned on his back, transfixed by his penis erect and unsheathed. "Christ, Spiderman!" She struggled back into the bucket seat on the "shotgun" side of Ranier's Nazi half-track. She snapped open the Zippo, flicked the flint wheel igniting the wick. The flame glowed orange with blue tips in the wind as Spiderman turned the half-track right onto the Vers Laayoune road to Agadir. Her lips twitched a joint between them as she tried to hit one of the blue tips of fire. She sucked deep into her lungs as the end of the spliff finally sparked, snapping the lighter shut as she sucked another hit off the joint and gazed at the script initials engraved on her lighter. L.T. on one side and M.P. on the other. She passed the joint to Spiderman and began to cough uncontrollably.

"Aaaggghhh!" Smoke spewed from Spiderman's mouth and nostrils as he tried to spit out the bitter taste. The truck swerved off the road and back on again until he finally caught his breath and regained control of the steering wheel.

"What's wrong, Spiderman, honey?" Linda's fingers touched his heaving shoulders as her own coughing subsided.

"Jesus Christ, Linda. For a girl so rich, you can sure be one stupid bitch, you know that?" He flung the joint straight above his head. They both watched it flicker and flare, seeming to fly off behind them into the darkness like a space shot or a meteorite.

She slumped back into her seat, her lips spread fiddle strings. "What the fuck are you talking about, man? You're the one who just threw the fucking joint away!"

"Aw, shit! Ouch!" He jerked his knee as she kicked him in the shin. The half-track groaned, slowing to a camel's walk. "That wasn't good kef, baby. In fact, that was hardly kef at all. Mostly black tobacco."

"How was I to know that?" she pouted. "Ranier's the one who sold it to me." She huddled tighter in the seat, her arms crossed over her breasts, her feet under her almost like she was squatting. "I thought that I could, at least, trust *him*!"

"So did I, Linda." He shrugged, settling his right foot back on the accelerator. "So did I."

"Protect, Lazlo! Protect!"

Pink flamingos hardly fluttered their wings in the nearly flat green sea at the sound of Spiderman's command. And, Lazlo did not respond as Ranier approached them on the ruby beach. Whimpering, he buried his tail stub between his rear legs and covered his snout with his forepaws.

"I guess that be leaving just you and me. Am I being correct, Spiderman?" Ranier brandished a machete he had retrieved from the half-track before confronting Spiderman here on the beach between Inezgane and Agadir where Linda had promised him she would be only for him. Yet, she was here, on *their* beach, with Spiderman instead. He would make her pay, too, somehow.

"May Allah be damning you, Spiderman! Allah be damning you and the whore, Ms. Linda Tallefero!"

"Hey, Ranier. Come on, man. It was just a joke, man. You know, like the black tobacco laced shit you sold to Linda as top grade kef."

Ranier flung the machete at the sand. The point stabbed into the beach near where Linda huddled in low dune shadows as if it had found a human target. Spiderman had shoved her into the safety of the dunes uncharacteristic of the normally flat and wide beaches when Ranier first came charging down the beach waggling that machete of flame in the sun setting into the sea. His wild Berber yodels had made her spinal fluid curdle. She scrambled across the still warm sand, further into the violet shadows of the dunes as the last sunlight skipped across the low waves and the agitated flamingos.

"I am walking miles and miles and miles to the Vers Laayoune road, Spiderman. I am walking all night and part of the day.

"Finally, some drunken tourists—a French couple also speaking Spanish and living on a yacht of Dutch registry—are picking me up. It was being easier than trying not to be running over me, the way they were driving. And, it was they that was driving as one. It was taking both of them just to be keeping the gas on their jeep accelerator and be steering a somewhat straight line at the same time."

"So, we didn't have a god damned thing to smoke until I copped in Agadir before coming back down here to this beach I knew would probably be deserted this time of year. I actually had to go out of our way all the way into Agadir and back here because of you and your own little joke. So, Allah damnit, yourself, Ranier!"

"I am being all alone in that desert night. No flashlight. No gun. Nothing."

"You had your magnum. I heard you fire it as we drove off."

"I am losing it in the sand when I am running after you and falling."

"And I saw a light?"

"The fall. I am breaking the flashlight when I am falling. I am being left naked in the desert of my ancestors."

"We didn't take your clothes, man."

"No. I am being just a—how are you saying it?—a figure of speech."

"Well, then, as long as we're talking about being humiliated. That is it? Right? Humiliation? Then imagine me, Spiderman, *the* Spiderman, reduced to haggling with a mere street dealer at sunrise. Now that's fucking humiliating! That's what *that* was. Downright fucking humiliating!"

"I am seeing my half-track back there along the beach road by the hotel." Ranier jerked his thumb over his shoulder indicating the path along the lumpy dunes that ran south to another oasis where the old Spanish Sahara began. "Back there." He never took his pudding brown eyes off of Spiderman. "There could not be existing another one like it. And, *her* things were being in the back." His voice began to splinter like the last sun rays on the ruby waves and pink flamingos before they, too, would gradually be engulfed by the onslaught of the evening. It betrayed tears that he was too proud to shed. "I am knowing it was you!" he wailed. "Would you be thinking you could be hiding from a Berber in his own land?"

"It was all just a fucking joke, Ranier. Like I said before, just a crazy fucking joke, man." He took a step in Ranier's direction. "Look, man. I'm sorry. Really sorry. Okay, man?" He put out his right hand, all the time keeping one eye on Ranier's eyes and the other on the machete sticking handle up in the rosy sand. "Okay?" Ranier wasn't Lieutenant Jesse but this was just as important to his continuation of life.

Ranier pivoted on his right heel in the direction of the path along the dunes. "I am getting you for this, Spiderman!" He stalked away, toward the rose and shade black dunes. The heels of his sandals sprayed sand behind him like sparks. "I am getting you both," echoed up and down the otherwise deserted beach as Ranier mounted the dunes a few hundred yards down the coast. He disappeared on the other side where the path would lead him to his half-track.

He had to laugh the last laugh here. He had his half-track. He had their packages. He had her rugs and vases stuffed with top grade hash and kef. That was the best way he could think of to begin his revenge. Money was so important to Americans. Often, it was more important to them than their own immortal souls. He had witnessed this with his own eyes more than once. Otherwise, he would not have believed it himself.

"Is he gone?"

Linda's question barrel-rolled out of the dune shadows. Spiderman shuffled his bare feet toward her words, still hyperventilating as he shoved one foot in front of the other through the sand. "Yes." Jesus. Ranier could've probably killed him. Them. Right here. Why didn't he do them here and now if that was what he wanted? Certainly, it wasn't due to Lazlo's intimidating presence. "Christ, woman! What have you done to my fucking dog?"

"Nothing, Spiderman, honey." She was crooning and crying in the cool darkness behind the first dune. He knelt beside her. His robe opened at the top. The collar flapped in the sea breeze of the rapidly encroaching evening. She felt his body heat as he touched her. "Does he mean it? Will he try to get you, to get us?"

"Sure, he means it. Wouldn't you? I just don't understand why he didn't go for it now? He had the edge, no pun intended," he chuckled in spite of himself and involuntarily glanced over his shoulder at the fading rose reflection of the dying sun off Ranier's machete blade. "Then, again. He knows me better than he should, and he's got all your stuff in the half-track. That's worth a small fortune to him."

"Oh, so it's all my fault, now?"

"What? No." Spiderman stroked her dark musky curls even as she tried to pull away. His fingers followed them past her shoulder to her breast mostly exposed under her rumpled toga. "Now, don't go blaming yourself, babe," he muttered, seemingly oblivious to the real intent of her words. "It wasn't anybody's fault." He kissed her eyelids and the infant crow's feet at the edges of her eyes. Briny. Damp. The sea. "It was just the *I Ching* of it all or . . . ." He chuckled once more and tickled her extremely sensitive underarms.

"Oh, stop it now. This is a serious situation here!" She jerked away from his touch, not yet ready to give up the fear for the fuck.

"Or the phase of the moon." Suddenly he reached for her chin and turned her face toward the desert. "See. It's rising early tonight. A good omen wouldn't you say?"

"I don't know what's a good omen from a bad one," she spat at him. "Do you?"

"Okay. Okay. No, but, it'll all work out. We've had our little differences before, Ranier and me."

"But?" She could no longer see the beach. She could only feel it as she kicked at the sand with the heel of her foot. "But, the other times weren't exactly like this one, now were they?"

"Well. Not exactly." He guided her hands to his genitals. "Guess it's sort of my fault, really."

"How so?" She tried to pull her hands back, frowning as hard as she could, but the increasing darkness now seemed to hide all subtleties of facial expression. "Damnit! This is important, Spiderman, honey. Really important!"

"Well, I guess the big difference is that this time it's over a woman, ah, you, that is."

"Oh?"

"Yeah." As if you didn't know what you were doing all along. "I've made a fool of him in front of you." Spiderman shook his head in disgust with himself and his foolish but inevitable behavior and released her hands. "That's sure as hell how he has scoped out the situation, anyway."

"Is this going to end up like some kind of duel or something?"

"Or something, maybe. Likely."

"Poor Spiderman, honey. I'm so sorry."

Her musk odor overcame him there on the invisible sand as the sun sizzled finally into the sea. She buried her face in his shoulder, tears soaking his robe. "It's all right, babe. Like I said. It wasn't anybody's fault unless it was mine. It was just fate."

"Fate," she shuddered. "Or whatever it is makes me really scared, Spiderman, honey."

"No need to worry or be afraid, babe. Just hurry!" He grabbed at her breasts crusted with oil and salt and sand. Leaping to his feet, he pointed in the direction of a stack of lights several thousand feet down the beach past where Ranier had disappeared into the dunes. "I've weathered worse, believe me."

Linda grinned back at him through the intensifying darkness illuminated by yet another lemon moon. She dodged his still groping hands, then followed him to her feet. "Okay, my Moroccan love machine. Let's get thee and me to yon hotel by the sea and be what we can be."

"The clitoris is the most erogenous human body part. Did you know that, Spiderman, honey?" Linda sipped fresh squeezed orange juice from oranges they had purchased at the *souk* and brought to their room along with their clothing when they checked in. She licked the specks of pulp from her lips with a tongue tip as pink as her clitoris in the sun beginning to rise over the desert while the moon was still setting in the ocean. Its soft light poured a tangerine aura through the glass doors leading onto the balcony of their hotel suite with a view of both the desert and the sea. The scent of olives ripening stroked the morning breeze with a lover's touch.

"How so?" he half-mumbled, his nose buried behind the pages of the latest edition of the English language newspaper from Tangiers.

"Well, you see. The penis cums and pisses. The vagina cums and pisses. But, the clitoris just cums and cums. It doesn't piss anything away," she laughed. "I guess the only other guy I ever discussed my clitoris with was this hippie I met at one of those happenings. You know? Like they used to put on in the sixties—Monterey Pop, Woodstock, Altamont?"

He nodded, never looking up from the paper except to grasp his coffee cup and take a leisurely sip. "Wasn't around for any of that . . . ."

She sighed. "Where I met him was . . . ." Her eyes rolled toward her brain for a moment. It had taken an entire night's worth of fucking for her to get basically no further than she had gotten at his web fortress. The best she'd been able to do so far was to maneuver Spiderman into letting her ramble on about guys she'd known. He almost seemed to enjoy the stories. At least he didn't try to stop her once she started. And, she needed an opening desperately. It was time.

Spiderman gulped some Kenyan coffee made two spoons of grounds to one cup of water as he continued to peruse the Tangiers paper's headlines, avoiding as best he could Linda's near nakedness across the tangerine infused glass table top from him. He had heard her sneak out before dawn. He'd heard the door latch click when she left. When he arose, freshly ground Kenyan brewed on the hot plate. The weekly paper and a huge joint awaited him by his place at the table. The news would be two, three, even four days old sometimes. But, it was not much different as history; and the date on the paper itself, at least, was current. The glass top wicker breakfast table between them reflected light from the rising sun under their plates crusted with scraps of eggs benedict and pastries like a bed of coals.

"I think it was Atlanta Jam. Yes. The festival in sixty-nine." Sixty-nine. An appropriate number. With it, the birth rate began to drop. "We were both working with OD's in the medical tent. Man, did he ever have vibes shooting out from him. He sent goose bumps to my brain when I brushed up against him while helping him to force a thorazine down a freakout's spasming throat."

Spiderman rattled open the pages of the newspaper. August 6, 1974. He flipped the front page over to continue the headline story on page two. His eyes found the column where the story picked up. "Cool," he muttered without actually having heard what she was saying. The paper was only three days old. Cool.

Nixon Tapes (cont'd from p. 1)
Butterfield alleged that the President had taped all of the conversations in his offices since 1971. Butterfield testified that, to the best of his knowledge, the tapings commenced in March.

Linda continued to sip at her orange juice, rolling the small glass between her palms as she spoke. "He's the one who gave me my Zippo, you know?" She clasped the juice glass in one hand and lifted the lighter off of her package of Egyptian cigarettes with the other.

When Spiderman heard the metallic click of the lighter opening, he leaned around the newspaper and over the table to light the joint. Linda lit the Zippo, and Spiderman fired up the joint, inhaling deeply. "Want some?"

She shook her head as she closed the lighter top extinguishing the flame. "The Zippo has both our initials on it. See?" No oxygen. No light. "See?" Linda offered the lighter across the table for him to look at.

"Yeah," Spiderman choked out in an automatic kind of response having already retreated with his joint behind the newspaper. "The one with the initials on it." She smiled, almost indulgently it seemed to him, as he allowed his eyes to stray from the article on the Nixon tapes over the top edge of page two.

"Yes. These initials. L.T. for Linda Tallefero and . . . ." She gulped the dregs of her now tepid juice almost swallowing a seed.

She spit the seed into her glass. The glass clattered as she set it on the table. "M.P. for . . . ." *En gard!* Her fingers trembled as she held a cigarette to her twitching lips. Too late to get spooked now. Everything was in motion already. She had to keep control of the situation on all fronts. She lit the Zippo again and touched the flame to her cigarette. That was what she had to do now. She released the inhaled smoke as she spoke. "M.P. for Matthew Parkrow."

God damn he's good. He must have a tough hide. He didn't even flinch. He just sits there behind his rattling news pages, smoking his joint, as he scours those pages for more news. Got to get this done, get him in my clutches and into the street by eleven. "He gave it to me when we split up at Altamont." As she continued, smoke curled from her nostrils and mouth. Her fingers steadied.

Now for the peri! "Actually, I believe he said he'd bought this lighter at a place in El Paso. You may have heard of it? Don Amerika's Gun Shop?" Jesus! This guy had nerves of steel or no nerves at all like in his bad leg. Not even a twitch around his lips or eyes which, according to Bow-Tie, was usually a dead giveaway when all other observations failed to show any reaction. Nothing. "This Matthew Parkrow was some serious dude, you know? He was carrying around some kind of real heavy burden. All I could think of was a line from that Beatles song: *'You got to carry that weight, you got to carry that weight for a long time.'* Remember that? From *Abbey Road*, if I remember correctly. Anyway, doesn't matter. It seems that this Matthew believed he was responsible for his best friend's death in Vietnam. That was the weight he carried."

"Lots of people walking around with something like that on their heads. Walking guilt, I think you call it." He made a production out of shoving the paper onto the table. As he continued thumbing the pages, he sighed.

Very cool, indeed. Like ice. "Once I asked him what he was really looking for. He replied immediately: 'Forgiveness.' It was so sad, the way he said it."

"Aren't we all looking for that, Linda?"

"I hope so." Thrust. "Ward."

Pages of newspaper swooped like gliders from the table onto the sunrise-polished tile floor. The joint fell from his fingers. His usually squared jaws sagged momentarily but long enough for her to notice.

"Whwhat didid you call me?" His lips twitched around the stuttered broken words.

Finally Linda reached across the table pressing his icy fingers between her toasty hands. She smiled soft, warm in the sunlight that dissolved around her from orange to coral pink shafts as it passed through the glass doors, the glass table top, onto the marble tile floor. She had him now.

His slate eyes reached out for her. "How did you ever?"

She averted her face. Off to her right was the drawing room where they had drawn each other to the squirming edge of one orgasm after another on the teak card table, behind the bar she couldn't now see, and wrapped together in the silver silk hammock hanging directly in her line of vision in the center of the room where Lazlo still jealously sniffed their lingering scents.

Ward Crampton leaped to his feet overturning Spiderman's wicker chair. It clacked on the marble surface several times and then was silent. "You!" He wagged his finger at her, still slumped in her chair, still staring off toward the silk hammock where Lazlo still sniffed around where they had been fucking. "You conned Ranier. We know that. Probably fucked him too just like I'll bet you fucked poor Lazlo so that, now, he's good for nothing but whining and whimpering after you. You seduced me, even against my own will. You've turned Ranier and Lazlo against me." Ward coughed into his right hand, clearing his throat. "And now you tell me this bullshit!" He threw what was left of the opened paper over the table at her. Pages sailed across the now coral pink glass top, fluttering into her lap. How can she know this? Nobody knows about Ward Crampton and Spiderman. Nobody!

Except himself. He knew. He remembered all too well. You damned right he did. How could he *ever* fucking forget that rocket from a portable fucking launcher hitting his fucking chopper that fucking morning. He'd been flung through the low morning fucking mists rising out of the fucking jungles like a human fucking cannon ball. He cleared the fucking wreckage by more than a hundred fucking meters before a huge fucking mushroom of gas tanks and ammo exploding nearly fucking simultaneously consumed the rest of the fucking crew and blew the fucking inferno hull into kingdom fucking come, or Vin fucking Long.

The only obvious problem with his being thrown clear and being the only one still alive after the second explosion was that a significant portion of his left knee cap had been left behind, consumed by the blazing skeleton of a helicopter. For a soldier flung into the midst of his enemies that was something other than simply crippling. He couldn't even think about running or hobbling or even crawling as the VC point man approached his smoldering body, his bayonet readied. The hot pain twisted like a serpent through his leg into his groin. The stench from his own burning flesh fouled his nostrils. For a ballplayer, this had become something more than simply a "ticket home" should he survive this shit. It was about to become his death certificate. And, even if he somehow survived, it was a ticket to the bleachers rather than to professional tryouts.

"Oh, Christ!" He slapped his stiff knee with his palm. Ranier. Of course, Ranier knows enough to piece it all together.

Linda shifted in her skin. She faced him. Though tears matted her hair to her cheeks, she smiled and shrugged.

Ward snatched Spiderman's chair from the floor and slumped into it, his elbows resting on the glass table in front of him, his head in his hands. Or were these Spiderman's hands? Was this Spiderman's head? "Damn!"

Yes. He sure as hell remembered. How could he do anything but remember? Sure. Maybe if he'd been MEDEVAC'd out by U.S. chopper and shipped straight to their Japan medical facilities, then he might've even been able to pick up on his Cubs contract. But, there was no MEDEVAC. The way their chopper blew when that VC rocket hit, it must've looked, for sure, like everyone on board was dead. And, in a sense, they were. The VC came around looking for salvage and survivors. They took him prisoner without a struggle. He had no struggle left in him. So, he ended up in a subterranean VC Field Hospital instead. There the medical care was suspect even for their own much less for an enemy *My* soldier.

Then, on top of that, there was no rehab. Just straight from the hospital to a POW camp deep in the central highlands canopied forests near the Cambodian border. All he could think about every single minute of every single day—both waking and sleeping, it seemed—was what it would feel like to be on the other side of those mist shrouded hills in the distance. Cambodia was on the other side. Freedom was on the other side.

He became aware, gradually, that he was not just thinking the words. He could hear his voice speaking to her, but it was as if someone else were saying the words. He spoke of himself in the third person as though he were telling someone else's story. In a sense he was.

"He only endured because of his obsession with escape. For nearly two years he was harnessed to the Wheel of Power like an ox along with nineteen other men or partial men for five hours a day, seven days a week. As they turned the wheel, it generated power for the camp. For nearly two years he was subject to fights to the death with fellow U.S. and ARVN POW's in order to stay alive. If he wouldn't fight, then both him and his opponent would be shot. If he didn't win, he would be killed by his opponent. So, determined that he had to fight and he had to win, no matter what, yes, he had killed. How many was it? He thought that he would never forget that number. Yes. A baker's dozen before he escaped. ARVN's mostly, but some of his own. The very first fight was with one of his own. A friend, if one could say that about anybody in a prisoner of war camp. Lieutenant Jesse.

"But, God damnit! He had survived! He made it through the Wheel of Power and the fights for long enough to observe how things worked in the camp. And, finally, he formulated and began to execute a subtle but daring plan of escape. First, over the next several months, he leaked disinformation about escape plans and POW plots to sabotage the camp's generator and storage facility next to the Wheel. He knew that whoever was in bed with their captors would pass on the information. The others would not. He didn't care who was who. He just wanted the information passed on to the camp Commandant. After several situations arose where the informants provided bad information, the informants' reputations became tarnished. Soon, they were no longer credible to the VC camp Commandant.

"Then, and only then, he leaked the information that he would attempt to escape that next morning on the daily supply truck when it left the camp. He knew he was taking a calculated risk. He realized that timing was everything. He understood that he had assumed a great deal. But, he knew that even if he miscalculated and was captured while attempting to escape at least he would have made the attempt.

"The next morning, just before zero six hundred he sneaked into the back of the supply truck after it had been unloaded. He remembered the guards spoke rapidly when the truck approached the gate, but he could understand enough Vietnamese to get the sense of what they were saying. 'Let the truck go!' one guard shouted at the other. 'It's orders from the Commandant!' Just as he'd predicted in his plan, the supply truck with him stowed away inside slipped out of the gate without inspection. The Commandant, not wanting to lose face again by giving any credence whatsoever to the latest rumors passed on to him by informants who had already caused him to lose face several times over the past few months, had ordered the guards specifically not to search the truck.

"Once the supply truck entered the cover of the forests, Ward jumped, a shelter half, a ruck sack full of supplies, and an AK-47 and a captured M-16 strapped onto his back as well as a canteen of water, K-bar knife, five full ammo pouches and a forty-five dangling from his pistol belt. It had taken him months of scavenging and trading to accumulate all the supplies he needed. After one look back to make sure he had not been detected, he limped off toward the misty hills of Cambodia and beyond.

"He crossed Cambodia and Laos into the Burmese jungles. He thought he'd be safe from pursuit there. But, he was soon found out and reported to some local communist leaders who were in with the NVA and the VC. So, it was on to Decca. No peace there either. That was, after all, Bangladesh, where the only peace seemed to come in what was often agonizing and humiliating death. His path led him next to Katmandu where he was able to rest and heal and stay stoned for a few months. From the highs of Katmandu he descended into the lows of India, Pakistan, and Afghanistan as well as the mania-driven Teheran and Baghdad. Of course, all he had previously known about Baghdad was *Aladdin*, Ali Babba, and *The Thief of Baghdad*—shit like that. But he was truly disappointed with the lack of any authentic magic carpets in those cities. Next was Jordan.

"He looked over Jordan and what did he see, coming for to carry him home? It was Jerusalem and, finally, Tel Aviv, coming for to carry him home. In Tel Aviv he had planned to stow away on a boat to Barcelona. Once in Barcelona, his plan was to turn himself in at the local consulate or embassy or whatever the Americans had in Barcelona as an escaped prisoner of war trying to return to the States.

"After only a few days in Tel Aviv, having no luck on locating a boat, he remembered Tanya, the prostitute he had hung out with in Kuala Lumpur when he was on R & R. She'd given him her brother's name and address. He remembered the brother's name: Ranier ibn Al-shaikh. And, he lived in Marrakech."

He paused. His brow furrowed. Damn! Why, Ranier? Why? After all this time together, why betray me now just for some woman?

"Ward?"

"Yes. I remember him like I would a dead brother. He didn't realize how much it was going to cost him to cross those thousands of miles from Vietnam to Marrakech."

"And, if he had understood the costs?"

"He might never have attempted it."

Linda shook him by his slumped shoulders. "Ward!"

"Yes. I remember my dead brother. He saw babies in Biafra, the skin around their swollen bellies so thin he could've torn it off with his hands. He'd seen the soldiers peeling the babies just to hear them shriek and their mothers wail. Disgust settled in his brain like oxygen as he sneaked his way to Nepal."

Ward seemed to stop breathing. "Ward!" Linda shook his shoulders again. "Ward! Stop this!" Again. "Do you hear me?" His eyelids twitched somewhere inside the privacy fence of his hands.

Like a recording, he continued from inside the safety of his hands. "Without delay, he was off to North Africa toward Morocco and Marrakech where, somehow, he would find Ranier ibn Al-shaikh, son of the elder, a man whom he hoped could help him to become a new person. A changeling wiggling into the desert sand like a manta ray into the ocean floor.

"I see my brother stoned immaculate and still reeling from the unexpected Arab hospitality extended to a mysterious American stranger on the run. From your Egypt to Algeria and even Libya in between, he was treated with kindness and respect even though also with a healthy bit of suspicion. Because he was escaping the American war in Vietnam, they all saw him as some kind of hero in an anti-hero sort of way. He represented, to the Arabs who fed and clothed and protected him on the final leg of his journey to Morocco, the abject failure of Americanism. Their own young men were running away from their criminal war.

"He stood gazing at the Straights of Gibralter thinking of Molly and Leopold "the lion" Bloom dashing about in the curves of Joyce's brain like the streets terracing the rock island itself." Ward shivered as if suddenly wracked by dysentery. A light breeze filtered through a crack between the glass doors leading onto the balcony. "As my brother sucked in deep breaths of ocean air, he believed that he could see the Spanish beaches across the water purple in the afterglow right after sunset. He wondered what there was left to live up to now that his leg was stiff so he couldn't bend over to field a ground ball or drive his hips forward into a swing at a fast ball. Can you imagine a Chester at shortstop? Should he reconsider the Barcelona option? He knew his politics would be suspect. He'd been in an NVA prison hospital and an enemy POW camp for close to three years. In that amount of time, certainly he would've been brainwashed. Plus, no one would believe his wild tale of a journey from Vietnam to the northern Morocco coast where ships passed him as if he were seeing them through an infra-red scope.

"Who in their right mind would ever believe that he went that distance just to get back into the race with a bum leg? But, Ward was scared, man. Real scared as he leered across the water still hoping to see the shore of Spain before darkness closed down his vision. He liked the notion of being somebody new since he couldn't remain who he had been. You see?"

Linda nodded, lighting another cigarette. She knew. "So. He became Spiderman?" She held the cigarette between her lips as she placed the Tangiers paper back on the table beside her lighter and cigarette pack.

"Yes. Spiderman." He trembled as his voice did while he opened and closed his fists over the pinkish glass. "So. Ward Crampton is dead. After seven years, even the Army pays off on his insurance. And, it was seven years last May!"

Linda grinned, her lips like ruby wires. "It was only six years last May, Mr. Ward turned Spiderman. Check your calendars, man!"

"Let's see. Two years eight months as a POW. Ten months to get to Marrakech after the escape. Three years and four months in this desert. That's, ah, oh shit! Six years and ten months." He allowed an unintentional whistle to escape between his teeth. "Hell, six years, seven years. What's the difference? Spiderman emerged from the skin of Ward Crampton. And, Ward Crampton died while staring across the Straights of Gibralter thinking he could see Spain in the infra-red darkness. He was already a husk drying in a tattered web."

"But spiders don't change when they shed their skins like a caterpillar becoming a butterfly. Spiders just outgrow their skins, don't they?"

"This spider defied natural laws then. Okay?"

"And man-made ones too, I guess?" Linda's fist pounded the glass top after each word. "You're not dead, Ward Crampton. That's the significance of the six years instead of seven! Legally, you're still alive as Ward Crampton, whether you like it or not." She fumbled in her purse on the chair between them, extracting a photograph. She shoved it in front of his eyes. "See. And, like the spider, you even look the same. Take a close look at Ward Crampton, All American. Just another skin, Mr. Spiderman. Just another skin!"

"No!" Ward averted his eyes.

"That's the only way you won't see yourself in this photo!"

It was like looking into a mirror when his averted eyes finally returned to the photo—allowing, of course, for eight or nine years of hard living. The photograph was a chest up shot of him in his State University baseball uniform, grinning around a wad of Bazooka bubble gum. The Roanoke Times used that shot in their coverage of his signing with the Cubs. Lines drew tight around his mouth and eyes. His jaw muscles rippled. Teeth ground against teeth. "It was a bizarre metamorphosis, Linda. Only the insides were changed utterly."

"Oh, you mean like a conversion or something?"

"Yes. And no. Conversion in the more tangible sense. Like Ranier's half-track, for instance. It looks like a Nazi half-track on the outside. But, take a look at its insides, under its hood. It is completely different from a Nazi half-track and more like a NASCAR racer.

"Can that really happen? To a person, I mean?" 'Well, Linda, honey,' she had to ask herself: 'How did you go from jumping off a Memphis bridge into a CIA station chief's arms to where you are now?' She had to admit that her photographs of that time would look pretty much like she looks now—taking into account the plastic surgery after her fall. "You're right, of course. It could happen." She was, herself, after all, living proof of it, wasn't she?

"Of course it can," he snorted.

In spite of his forced levity, Linda sensed his tension as she watched him fidget with a cigarette he had unconsciously taken from her pack. Finally, he lit it with her lighter. The lighter with his past's initials engraved on it.

When Ward glanced down and saw the initials, he flung the Zippo across the table as if the metal had burned or shocked him. It skidded across the rosy pink glass into the folds of Linda's open lap, coming to rest near her rose petal clitoris. He barely avoided her eyes by looking out over the azure waves, white foam running along their low crests. The flamingos again frolicked in the rolling sea almost as if they were extensions of the pink tints of sunrise flashing in the surf.

Each time he looked back she was there, grinning, her pulsing clitoris once again between her fingers. In spite of the fact that he was right and she knew he was right, she summoned Ward Crampton out of the grave Ranier and Spiderman had dug and filled years before in a Marrakech restaurant. "Damnit! How'd you find out about Ranier? About me? I mean, you had to find out about him from somewhere or you would never have known to pump him for information about me." Information. Cursed blight. It builds and destroys worse than gold or uranium ever did.

Linda stood, began pacing behind her chair. Three paces toward the bedroom. Then, three paces back to the chair and three beyond almost to the slightly ajar sliding doors that led to the balcony. "When the CHAOS agent who saved my life urged me to try locating Matthew Parkrow, I ran across an interesting character in El

Paso, in the very store where Matthew stopped on his way into the desert near Alamogordo after he had left me cold at Altamont."

"Who?" Damn, Don Amerika.

"None other than the same Don Amerika whose decal is on several of your rifles in your rifle rack." She pointed toward where the tower area would be if they had been at his desert fortress.

"But, he didn't know anything about Spiderman really being Ward Crampton. All he knew was that I was the connection through Ranier. We'd met a couple of times early on."

"You're right. He didn't know about who you really were. But, I knew something about Ward Crampton being missing in action, remember, and Matthew being obsessed with finding him alive." She shrugged. "When I met him that was nearly all he could talk about. I just added up a couple of things here and a couple of things there. My hunches began to pay off big time when I finally made contact with Ranier by using Don Amerika as my reference." She stepped toward him. "After all, finding you, in this case, is like finding the buried treasure."

"Christ, and I thought my tracks were damned well covered."

"And they were. But, even trails of breadcrumbs don't always get completely eaten by the birds. If you know what I mean?"

"Apparently not."

"Anyway, believe me, Ward, honey. I'm on your side. I'm your friend." She touched his clammy hands with warm fingertips, walking them up both his arms until he shivered. "I dig you, honey." She tousled his hair, kissed him. "Lean on me."

The lobby clock read two minutes after eleven as Ward and Linda sauntered from the Hotel of the Lemon Moon, arm in arm, into the late morning heat, down the nine stone stairs, then along the side of the cobbled road of the small nameless settlement that had grown up around the hotel over the past hundred and seventy-five years and five renovations. They had left Lazlo snoozing in the sun that still beat down through the balcony doors.

"Look, Ward." Linda covered her mouth momentarily as if acknowledging her mistake. "I'm sorry. I guess you'll have to remain Spiderman for now. But, look, Spiderman! There on the horizon!" She pointed in the direction of a camel caravan far inland swaying its way across the dunes. The camels were ambling spots on the inland horizon. "Isn't that a truly amazing sight?"

Spiderman shaded his eyes with both hands to get a clearer view. "A caravan right out of the *Arabian Nights* or some other such tale." He attempted to count the camels, but they began to run together after the first two or three into an impressionist blur. "Yes, Linda. As long as I've lived here, I'm still amazed by it all just like a little kid reading books about mysterious caravans and cloaked desert horsemen."

Ranier had told him the story of the camel becoming important here as a beast of burden, particularly for trade. It began when the caravan trade picked up around and across the Sahara long before the so-called Christian Era. Three main trade routes had developed between the southern and northern borders of the desert. One of those routes brought the caravans directly through Morocco. This road he stood on now, Oasis Road, connected with the Agadir Highway which was a spur off that original caravan trail from Morocco through Adar to the middle Senegal and Upper Niger. It didn't take many trips across the Sahara for the traders to realize that camels, not horses, were well adapted to their long, waterless desert treks, and a camel could carry a considerably larger pack load than a horse.

Spiderman hoped he and Ranier could be reconciled. He had always liked Ranier's stories. But, Ranier had his Berber pride. He understood that by now. But, for Spiderman, understanding this Berber and Arab pride thing was like understanding the saving face thing. Understanding them didn't make them any less inscrutable.

Spiderman studied the inland horizon. Linda glanced back toward the hotel. In the shadows of the alley between the hotel and a bazaar, a figure covered in a dark cloak muffled a cough with trembling hands. Spiderman wiped his forehead with his robe sleeve. Those traders handled loomed cotton, lost-wax casting in bronze and brass (now, they used the art to craft pipe bowls), delicate ornamental work in silver and gold. They traded for manufactured Mediterranean silks, beads, mirrors, paper, swords that they bartered for dates and salt from the Sahara. With the Sahara products, they bought West African gold, grain, gum hides and skins, kola nuts, ivory, ostrich feathers, and slaves. Much of the same traffic Linda had seen at the *souk* except for the slaves. What remained of that trade was accomplished in secret. He glanced at her.

Linda surreptitiously glanced over her shoulder again, trying to pierce the shadows of the old hotel walls, then hooked her arm in Spiderman's, hugging him close to her, and kissing him on the cheek.

Recognizing the pre-arranged signal, the dark figure leaped from the hotel alley, a dagger raised high above his head in his right hand, running at them from their rear.

"Ward . . . . Spiderman, honey! Watch out!" She waved toward the charging cloaked figure. "He's got a knife!"

The darkly cloaked man shoved Linda to the ground, then lashed out with the dagger handed down to him from his father. Despite his game knee, the old fighting skills Spiderman had relied upon in the POW camp flooded through him. He dodged the attack and stumbled backward as the dagger swiped near his neck. The cloaked figure tripped awkwardly and fell forward onto the cobblestone road. His legs jerked several times. Then, the figure lay still beneath the dark Berber weave cloak.

Linda crawled to the figure and pulled back the dark cloak. "My God, it's Ranier!" Blood oozed through Ranier's gray robe. "He fell on his dagger." Quickly she checked the body for life signs. "Jesus. He's dead." Linda leaped to her feet as a crowd began gathering around them. "We'd better get out of here." She pulled Spiderman back from the corpse. "Now!" She clasped his left wrist in both her hands. "The natives are getting restless." She jerked her head back toward where a crowd was already gathering around the dead man. "Quick! This way!"

The half-track was nearby. She'd spotted it a few hundred yards down the road when they first left the hotel. She bolted for the other side of the road, Spiderman in tow. He hobbled behind her as fast as he could so he wouldn't fall on his face.

"Jump in! Slide over! You have keys?" Linda barked as she settled into the driver's seat. "I'll drive."

Spiderman fumbled in his robe pocket for the keys and flipped them to her. She inserted and turned the key. The engine coughed, fired. Slamming the transmission into first, she popped the clutch. They bounced beside the road as the tracks grabbed at the sandy shoulder. "Stay down!"

The tracks spewed a dense screen of sand and rock back toward the crowd now clustered around the fallen and bloody Ranier. As the crowd closed around him, Linda hit second and skidded onto the sand and cobblestone road heading for Agadir. Spiderman slumped in the passenger seat, his head, again, in his hands.

Once they were out of sight of the hotel crowd, Linda slowed the half-track, allowing it to cruise along in high gear at about forty kilometers per hour. Mumbling to himself, Spiderman slouched still further into the seat.

Linda lit a cigarette, inhaling deeply. "The Moroccan police will be after you. You know that, don't you?"

"But, I didn't do anything, Linda. He fell on his own dagger, and he fell on it while *he* was attempting to kill *me*, for Christ's sake."

"And," Linda smirked, "do you think that the crowd back there or the Moroccan police are going to believe you? An infidel? Or give a damn?"

He struggled between nodding and shaking his head. "No, I guess not."

"Then, I think we should find you a good place to hide until we can get you out of this damned country. Don't you?"

He nodded.

"So," she began, hoping to divert Spiderman/Ward Crampton into an area of discussion that would be beneficial to her plan. "So, tell me about you and Matthew Parkrow. You really grew up together?"

He nodded again, still not looking up.

"You were good buddies, right?"

He nodded.

"And you are the friend he thought he'd somehow killed in Vietnam?"

Yes. He nodded once again.

"Boy, have we got some real down to earth talking to do."

"About what?"

"Oh. He speaks. Well, you'll see soon enough."

"See what?"

"Never you mind that now. You'll understand when we get to Agadir." She smiled when she saw his eyes peeking from under the hood of his robe that he had pulled around his head. "Crawl on out of that old Spiderman skin, Ward Crampton. Nobody's within sight. You can tell me all about you and Matthew." Again, she grinned as she watched his head burrow back, further into his robe. "Why you two must've been a regular pair of Hardy Boys."

The plains undulated under the half-track like a mistress under her lover's touch. The Haut Atlas range loomed to the east. "What did you two neo Hardy Boys do when you were children?"

He relaxed as much as he could which wasn't very much in the bouncing half-track seat. With all the blood on his hands from past deeds, he would've thought that one more death wouldn't matter much. But, this one did. This one was different from the others. This had been an accident. The victim had been a partner and friend. He had not meant for Ranier to die. Or anyone. But, no matter. He seemed to be totally in Linda's hands now. Somehow, somewhere along the way, that had happened. She seemed to know what to do, and he seemed unexplainably paralyzed.

"We met when we were nine. My family had moved from Florida. Father was going to be the community doctor. We both liked books and baseball. We liked to hike through the forests and build tree houses that we kept stocked with rusty nails, twine, pork'n beans, tuna fish, Vienna sausages, and as many candles and matches as we could "borrow" from our homes. Our favorite tree house was the one on this slight ridge just beyond the power station. It was up in the topmost branches of a mammoth oak. Must've been a hundred years old. Usually we could build a tree house in a couple of weeks, but we worked on that tree house for over two months."

The plains were quiet except for the half-track and his voice. The Plain of Souss seemed to roll in waves under the late-morning sunlight. "I remember Matthew saying that we ought to know what the Egyptians who built the pyramids felt like. They had to transport huge stones over long distances. We had to raise building materials and supplies thirty feet in the air into the lightning split near the top of the tree. It made for a perfect almost level foundation for the tree house. There we stored our Captain Midnight decoder rings, our pact signed in our blood ala *Tom Sawyer*, as well as rabbit and squirrel skins we salvaged from animals we trapped and cooked when we camped out. We used all the animal if possible just like we learned in *Jim Bridger: Mountain Man, Kit Carson: Indian Scout*, and *Buffalo Bill: Plainsman*. There was a whole series of those books bound in brown leather-like covers. We read and lived them all.

"We also kept Matthew's telescope at the special tree house. His dad had given it to him that first Christmas we spent together in the tree house after all the Christmas morning rituals were over. We would take turns looking at the stars and fancying ourselves transported to the red planet or the blue star or the north star or the moon. The telescope germinated our watching Flash Gordon Saturday matinees at the one town theater. We usually took Emmy Lou along to the movies even though she was a girl and good for little else than bossing around and playing with in one of the lesser tree houses. At the movies, she would always get us free popcorn and candy from Mr. Sasser who took tickets, sold the goodies, and ran the film all by himself—a grand old one man show. He just wanted to stare at Emmy Lou and have her talk to him a little like he was really human or something. No one else thought of him that way. But, Emmy Lou was like that. She saw the human being in everyone."

The plains rolled by. Each mile seemed like ten to Linda. She knew that she had to get him underground before he discovered . . . . If that happened, if he uncovered her plan . . . . She shoved the accelerator to the floor.

"After our voices changed, we became more interested in girls in other ways, so Emmy Lou was sort of left to her own devices. Flash

Gordon matinees and our tree house camps were, more or less, abandoned. Once we hit high school, we were pretty distant from her. You know. Different schools, different friends, and all that kind of stuff.

"However, when she entered Roanoke High in our senior year, we took her to ball games when we weren't playing or made sure she had a box seat behind our bench. And we always met her at after-game dances. You know, stuff like that. She couldn't get dates because of being Alecia's niece. None of the guys would be seen dating what was known in those days as a colored or high yellow girl. If Jason hadn't been Mayor, she would've never even been allowed to go to our schools at all." He shrugged somewhere inside his robe. "But, come to think of it, you know, those people who didn't know that she was Alecia's niece took her for Jason's daughter every time!"

"There must've been a strong resemblance."

"Well, maybe so. But, anyway, we were sort of all-everything in high school. All-American baseball players. But we played football and basketball too. And, ran track, sort of, to keep in shape. Our influence and popularity usually protected Emmy Lou from those who would try to hurt her because of her background. But, I remember once when we played Capital City in football, some Capital City players tried to rape her in the church parking lot where the after game dance was being held as it was after all home games no matter what town you played in. One of the assailants was their star quarterback and pitcher. We were just getting out of my white over Carolina blue '57 Chevy convertible after we'd showered and changed in the locker room. I remember, we won 42 to 3. Matthew had the game of his life at quarterback, subbing for the starting quarterback who had his leg fractured in the game the week before. He ran for two touchdowns of 67 and 83 yards and passed for four touchdowns. When Matthew saw what was happening, he went into such a rage that he beat up the six guys all by himself. And, he wasn't a big guy, either. I was going to help, but he just simply didn't need my help."

"Was this senior year the same year that Matthew hit that game-winning grand slam against Capital City?"

"Yes. That came later. The following spring in Devereaux Meadow, a crumbling Class B ballpark that served as the Capital City High home field. College scouts filled the rotting, sagging wooden stands that were slowly being swallowed up by kudzu and time. They came to see this state championship match-up between the two best baseball teams ever in the state. At least that was what all the media hype was calling it. And, all those scouts had their collective eyes on me and Matthew and the left-handed Capital City pitcher who'd tried to rape Emmy Lou. After hitting the grand slam and assuring himself and me of our college scholarships by delivering Roanoke Park the state championship and relegating the Capital City lefty to an ignominious college career at a lesser school, Matthew told me that he was sure the ball had gone foul. He said that he couldn't understand why the umps didn't call it.

"'Naw,' I said. 'If it had gone foul, then the umps would've called it. Right?' You were just seeing things, Matthew.'

"In college, I continued at shortstop and Matthew at second base. We both started as freshmen. Matthew played well, but I was selected ACC Rookie of the Year after hitting .333 with ten home runs, thirty-nine RBI's, and seventeen steals while making only three errors all season. For my final three seasons, I was first team All-Conference as well and also an All-American. I was named to the first team my junior and senior years. I signed a professional contract with the Cubs the day I received my draft notice. Talk about highs and lows in the same day. I just couldn't fucking believe that! I was being billed as the Cubs' new Ernie Banks. Instead, I was headed for the major leagues of Vietnam.

"Matthew, on the other hand, forfeited his scholarship only hours before the first game of our junior year. We had been the best keystone combination in the ACC since our freshman year, and he was scheduled to lead off the batting order because of his ability to get on base, no matter what. But he had suddenly become 'socially aware' or whatever, so he traded in his uniform for anti-war placards.

"His father, Jason, claimed that what happened had happened exactly because Matthew had fallen in with the wrong kinds of people—leftover beatnicks, peacenicks, artsy-craftsy types. You know? And, it was about this same time that Jason caught him cropping marijuana in the meadows surrounding the power station near the location of our most secret tree house when we were kids.

"According to Jason, Matthew would shut himself in his room and listen to that god awful nasal voice of Bob Dylan's and read and get stoned. And, he did march on Washington with the blacks—something I never understood 'cause they didn't give a pig's ass about him—even when Jason pleaded with him not to because he was afraid it would ruin his chances for re-election as Mayor of Roanoke Park.

"I don't know what I've done so wrong, my son. But, why couldn't you be more like Henderson Crampton's boy?' Jason would whine."

"Did you see each other much after Matthew quit the baseball team?"

"Oh, sure. Often. We both still majored in literature as we had planned since we had first started book-reading contests soon after I moved in down the road from him. Most of our professors characterized us as their top students—eager to learn, yet skeptical of what we were taught. We were creative in our criticism, and we participated intelligently in class discussions. Matthew was somewhat more withdrawn than I. Aloof may even be a better description. He seemed burdened with a more brooding view of life than myself—a more existential view, perhaps. I was, on the other hand, totally gregarious. Odd, when you look at me now and how reclusive I have become. When I offered a comment in class, it flowed. When Matthew could no longer refrain from commenting, he had to tear the words out."

"Were the two of you ever in real competition?"

"I guess. Yes. We were. Even though we both accepted that I was the jock who liked books and he was the bookworm who liked being a jock, there was always a kind of competitive edge between us."

"But you joined the Army together, didn't you? On the buddy plan?"

"That's true. But, even in the Army, we competed to see who got the most rank the fastest and the most decorations."

"Was it difficult for you to talk Matthew into joining with you?"

"Are you kidding? Matthew was an awakened pacifist. He was dead set on Canada. He was at the Union Bus Terminal, ticket in hand to Montreal, when I collared him and dragged him into the Men's room to start persuading."

"What kinds of arguments did you use?"

"God, country, Mother, apple pie. Matthew sneered and clenched his fists as if he were ready to bust his best friend in the mouth. 'I don't believe in god. My country is wrong. My Mother is dead, and I hate apple pie,' he retorted.

"Then I asked him: 'Ain't it undeniable fate, us getting our draft notices on the same goddamned day?'

"Matthew had to answer: 'Yes. It is fate—undeniable or not.'

"'Three years in the Army together is better than three-to-five in Leavenworth or forever in Canada.'

"Matthew smiled patiently, finally relaxing his fists. The restroom door opened. Voices bombarded our ears from the terminal waiting area. The compressed-air door closer whooshed as a wino stumbled past the urinals and sinks on opposite walls, sandwiching us in. His hands, jutting from under shiny sleeves of a tattered gray tweed jacket, fumbled with the latch on the stall furthermost from us. He fell into the stall, slamming the door closed behind him with a crack that sounded like a shot off the ceramic tile walls. The bolt snapped into place, locking the stall door from the inside. We could hear him heaving over the toilet.

"'Isn't that what you feel like, Matthew, every time you think about never being able to come back to your country again? Never being able to come home again? Think, man, how active you've always been. Could you still change things here if you are a draft dodger? Could you? From Canada?'

"While trying to shut out the wino's wretching from his own ears, Matthew was forced to answer: 'No, I couldn't.'

"'Could you write the great American novel about the supreme idiocy of Vietnam if you've never been there?' I had to smile to myself on that one.

"Matthew again was forced to answer that he couldn't."

"So you two did finally join together on the buddy plan?"

"Yes. I led Matthew to the recruiter's office that very day, and we joined before he had time to change his mind. We wanted, at least, to stay together while we were in the Army, and we did until my helicopter was shot down over the Iron Triangle. That was the first time one of us had gone out on an assignment without the other.

"And you say Matthew felt responsible for that?"

"Completely, I'm sure."

Linda lit a cigarette. "How do you think he could take on that burden?"

"My best guess?"

"Sure. Why not? At one time you knew him better than just about anyone."

"He probably reasoned that I was only on that particular helicopter rather than any other helicopter because he, Matthew, had awakened me that morning himself. If only he, Matthew, had gotten me up later so that I missed my scheduled helicopter flight, and then, had taken a later one, then I would not have been shot down and still be missing in action, presumed dead. Therefore, he, Matthew, was to blame for me, Ward, being shot down over it, the Iron Triangle."

"He could live with that?" She stifled a laugh.

"He would see no alternative in the void of existential solipsism. Only the guilt of Orestes. Only . . . ."

"Only?" Linda stared at Ward. He had gone silent for several minutes.

His head now peered out from under the hood of his robe for the first time since they had escaped. His nose sniffed the wind like Lazlo would have. Had he been talking in his sleep again? Had he been dreaming again? No. This was no dream, though it might be classified as a waking nightmare. "Only?"

"Only," Linda coached again but received no response. "Only your Mother committed suicide when you were reported lost in action and presumed dead. Your Father tried desperately to find you after this Emmy Lou character, who is now living in sin with your boyhood buddy, Matthew, told him that she thought she'd seen you in New York City, working at a coffee house. Helluva clever way to snare a man, I guess. I'll give that bitch an 'A' for originality, anyway."

"But," he nodded, chanting the rest of the story just like she had related it to him earlier. "This guy turned out to be one of the underground leaders in Chicago. A guy called Crayon. Matthew told you all this when you two did some sunshine together after that Atlanta Jam thing. Right?"

"You chant beautifully. Just like a native. And, you're right."

"But you've told me this already."

"Yes, but *I* actually *met* this Crayon guy at Altamont." She shook her head. "He looks more like Ward Crampton than you do. I can see how even that Emmy Lou bitch might have really been fooled by him, especially if she figured he had amnesia or some kind of traumatic brain injury or something."

"You said something about Matthew saying he was looking for his birth place?"

"Yes. He said that he was sure if he could find his birth place, then, there, he would also find you. He told Crayon that he was going into the desert to find that birth place." Linda chuckled as she guided the half-track with both small hands clutched near the top of the steering wheel. "I thought he was a little whacko, to tell you the truth, but in a nice sort of way, you know?"

"He always was. Still is, I guess."

"Oh, no, Ward!" Linda's eyes suddenly glared past her right shoulder at his face. "No, he's not!"

"What do you mean? He's not?"

"What I mean is this. Matthew Parkrow is a threat to the security of the United States of America. The FBI and CIA both have thick files on him and his subversive activities since 1963."

Ward was incredulous. Sure, Matthew had always been a man of conscience, but a threat to national security? He didn't think so.

"He's a known drug and arms dealer—not unlike yourself, I might add—and a much wanted revolutionary." She sucked in a tortured breath as if she were readying to throw herself into a possible line of fire or off a Memphis bridge. "And, he's also a deserter and a murderer."

Ward's head popped around. "No. Now, that's not possible. Not Matthew. A killer, yes. We all were. But a murderer? Never!" His eyes leered at this woman driving him toward god-knows-where or god-knows-what in a half-track stolen from his partner, the man he had just murdered, but in self-defense. It was an accident. He attacked and fell on his own knife. Yes. They'll believe you, son of a European, after the sins of France and Spain heaped upon these

Moroccans. If the Matthew he had grown up with had killed, then it had to have been under some kind of similar circumstances. There had to have been some justification.

"He shot a helpless old blind uranium prospector named Estevan out there in that desert where he said he was going to find you. Shot the old man in cold blood. He even left a confession note written in his own handwriting." She grimaced. "I can show it to you, if you don't believe me."

Ward shook his head. "I want to know how you know all this stuff about me and Ranier and Don Amerika and Matthew. And how do you know that Matthew is what you say he is? A terrorist? A revolutionary? A murderer? And what does it matter, anyway?" He shook his finger, then his fist, at her. "Who the fuck are you, Ms. Linda Tallefero? Who the fuck are you really?"

"Look!" Linda pointed across the plains toward what looked like a Berber fortress shimmering mostly white in the afternoon heat. "Agadir!" As the half-track closed on the city rebuilt upon its ruins from the 1960 earthquake, the plains burgeoned with lush orchards of figs, dates, and other fruits. "Oh, look at how the orange trees have both fruit and blossoms on them at the same time. How strange."

"Who. Are. You?"

The road sliced through the irrigated gardens to the city gate. "I'm a government agent working for CHAOS—an agency dedicated to the destruction of all known subversive elements in America." She watched his jaw slacken, his mouth dropping open with a dull pop like a dead man's. "We operate under a direct Presidential mandate. And, Ward, we need you!"

Ward threw his head from side to side as they entered the gate. "No. No. No!" gagged in his throat from his own anger and fear.

Just inside the gate Linda braked the half-track, pulling it to a stone curbing on their right. "We'll have to leave the truck here."

Two policemen appeared as if from nowhere in front of a carpet stall across the narrow street. She shoved Ward out of the vehicle. "Hurry! Into this alley before they spot us!" Falling out of the half-track after him, she nearly knocked him to the stone walk leading to the alley in front of them. She grabbed his hand. "Come on! It's just down this alley here!"

"What is?" Ward stumbled over his slightly stiff leg every time he took a step as Linda dragged him, too fast, across the walkway into an alley covered by overlapping roofs all the way into the maze between buildings as far as he could see. It was the shock of the sudden darkness that seemed to unsnap his lock-jawed brain. This was all getting too out of hand. Where the hell was she taking him? What the hell was this CHAOS shit? And them needing his help? He jammed his stiff leg against the jutting cornerstone of a hooka shop, jerking Linda back into his arms. He held her fast against his waist. "Linda!" The pipes in the window glowed like closing owls eyes. Their beaten copper fittings smoldered into red, blue, green, and yellow cords woven around the smoking tubes. "What the fuck's going on here, goddamn it?" Where the hell are you taking me?"

Linda pushed her fists against his chest. "Just a little further." A policeman peered into the alley. "You don't really have a lot of choice, now do you?" His arms relaxed. She wrenched free. "They'll want you for Ranier's murder, remember? And the only thing that's going to matter to them is that you're not a Moroccan and you're white. They won't care if it was an accident or not, and you know it."

Ward's hands dangled at the ends of his arms like the Ape Man of Morocco. Homos erectus moreorlessus, he mentally sneered as he limp stepped behind Linda in the direction of the end of the alley where four plain brown blankets hung stitched together over a wall. Each blanket had one emblem painted on it. A yellow grain of sand for earth. An aqua drop for water. A red spark for fire. And, on the last blanket, those three emblems swept up in blue wavy lines representing the wind. Earth. Water. Fire. Air.

"In here." Linda lifted the last blanket. She shoved Ward through the huge black hole in the masonry wall and followed, dropping the blanket back into place.

They were in a dirt floor room. Ward could smell the earth. Walls of sandstone and masonry patched in places like the one where the entrance had been busted through under the fourth blanket. Slate roof. His eyes were pulled through the dampness toward the only light in the room. A candle on the floor in the far corner smoldered red, then green, blue, and yellow as an invisible hand from an invisible body sprinkled incense into the flame. Sandalwood?

Linda placed a finger over Ward's opening lips. "Wait here." Stepping as softly as she whispered, Linda glided away from him into the darkness in the direction of the sputtering candle. "Bow-Tie?"

"Only with a cigar and brandy." The words emanated from somewhere in the blackness behind the candle.

"I have a lighter and a snifter."

"Vamp. My predatory protégé. And, who is that with you, skulking over there in the shadows?"

"That's Lazarus, Bow-Tie."

Lazlo with rabies. Ward fidgeted with the sash of black silk tied around his robe. Poor Lazlo trapped in that hotel room like he was trapped here. The two policemen ran by in the alley. "I'm sure it was him that I saw in here."

"That murderer! We'll get him!"

"Ah, yes, Vamp. Very good."

Lazlorabies. Lazlo.

"Are we to embark on the raising of the dead?"

"Yes, sir, we are ready to begin Operation Zombie." She shifted her weight to the left a little, trying to look around the light from the flame as she pushed Ward's photograph through the glowing air into the darkness. "Passport. CHAOS ID. The works. For the man in that picture—Ward Crampton."

A hand snatched the photo from her fingers, but she could not see it. She couldn't see anything in the blackness behind the flame. She couldn't feel the pressure of any touch at all when the picture left her fingers. All touches had some weight, didn't they? Yet, Bow-Tie's touch seemed weightless.

"What do you mean? Lazarus?" Ward shuffled forward a few steps. "What the fuck's Operation Zombie?"

"Shut up, Ward!"

"Yes, do shut up, Mr. Crampton."

"Shut up? Shut up?" Ward lunged past Linda's shadow in the candle light. "This is my life, you fucker!" Through the orange glow, his fingers clawed for Bow-Tie's already-vanished throat. The boots of the policemen, again, cracked along the alley way. "You're sure that was his half-track that you saw?"

"Yes, by Allah, praise be unto him! I am sure."

Linda motioned in the direction of the policemen's voices. "Not any more, it's not!" She snarled under her breath, enunciating each word as he grabbed her shoulders from behind and shook her until her voice vibrated like a bad soprano. She knew why they were there, of course. But, Ward did not.

"By morning, when Bow-Tie returns, you've got to decide. Either you go back to the States with me and help us set up this subversive murderer, and we'll all live happily ever after. Or you can remain here, and Bow-Tie will feed you to the Moroccan authorities piece by piece."

She shrugged from his still-grasping fingers. "It's simple, Ward. We need your cooperation, but we can't afford to have you running around loose if you refuse to help us." She shrugged again as if she couldn't help herself. "We do have to keep things tidy, you understand. So . . . ." She dragged out the word into a hiss. "You choose, Ward. Spiderman. Whatever or whoever you think you are. All I can tell you is this. You can rise from the dead as Ward Crampton and live. Or, you can keep Ward buried and rot until you die in a Moroccan prison for Ranier's murder.

"Either way, Spiderman, honey. By tomorrow morning, you will be Lazarus or you *will* be dead."

PART TWO

THE LEARNED DO NOT KNOW.

Tao Te Ching

Matthew First heard about synthesizers back in sixty-two when a music student at

Woman's College in Greensboro turned him on to electronic music. But, it wasn't until seventy—after Woodstock and Altamont had instilled the concept of self-parody into an entire generation—that he finally saw the music sizzle the collective consciousness of American pop culture the way that old uranium prospector Estevan's specter, time and time again, sizzled his. The musical Barbecue had begun with a rendition of an old standard, Schiller's "Hymn to Joy," upbeated for the speedier generation of the emerging seventies. All voices and instruments were created by the moog. Thus, Les Paul beget Peter Townsend who spat out Walter [AKA Wendy] Carlos who opened the door for Richard . . . Nixon or anyone else . . . to use the burgeoning new technologies as instruments just like you would use a guitar or a recorder.

During this dawning of electronic music, Matthew Parkrow and Emmy Lou Black moved into the Air-Conditioned Gypsy, a fifty-two-foot silver trailer located down a dirt-and-gravel path not on any map off Ebenezer Church Road south of Roanoke Park, a small town just west of Capital City, North Carolina. The Chicago Seven had been mostly exonerated, so they wrote. There was going to be a rock festival in Love Valley that summer to rival Woodstock, so they said. John, George, Paul, and Ringo were getting together in Toronto for a huge peace concert, so they rumored. Just let it be and everything was gonna work out fine, so they sang. Even the vestal beast, the invisible ghoul with Estevan's eyes glittering like coals of that desert campfire from so long ago, seemed to be at rest, so he and Emmy Lou hoped.

While they had unpacked that day five years ago, he had seen Emmy Lou's painting of sixteen vestal virgins which she had named "A Whiter Shade of Pale" after the Procul Harum song. It was the first time since they left Denver that he had seen the only painting he ever asked to tamper with. He remembered seeing a seventeenth figure as if it were already in the painting. That was May, sixty-eight, after he got busted at Columbia, before he ventured into the desert, before he actually saw Estevan face to face. Sometimes he felt sure he had never done any of those things as if the acts had been committed by someone else. Such things all seemed so far removed from his now tidy life. Oh, there were still loose ends like finally getting Emmy Lou to marry him and completing the last two chapters of his dissertation. But, damn it, he was finally getting respectability in the only ways this poor slob of a society could think of: position, prestige, and security. Even after four years at the University, his integrity remained in tact. He taught his way, learned his way, wrote his way, lived his way. What did it hurt to give way on some of the lesser important issues? Your life cannot, after all, be a second-by-second battleground, can it? There must be some respite. There must some respite be. His camp was his against all, even now, when all was empirically well.

The memory of seeing the painting that day triggered other memories of Emmy Lou's bone white apartment, chilled against the heat of coming summer. In the afternoons, especially, you needed the air most days. He could almost feel the air-conditioned whiteness of Emmy Lou's place on 89th and First. The bone white walls glared from around posters of Hendrix burning his guitar at Monterey Pop and Jerry Rubin, his fist thrust toward the sun, like the dazzling sands of the Sahara. The painting hung on the wall above her bed.

Emmy Lou pointed to the newly completed canvas. "No, Matthew, there are only sixteen faces . . . ."

He touched his finger to the oils, still tacky in places where the paint was thick, where he saw the hooded faceless specter with the flaming coal eyes.

"No, baby," she repeated. "There is no face there."

After he came out of the desert months later and met her in Yellowstone, he pleaded with her to let him paint in that face because he had finally seen it up close and as real as death itself. But it was only later, while they were living in Denver, that he finally persuaded her. He sketched the face as best he could. She helped him transfer the sketch to the appropriate area in her painting, peering over the shoulders of two vestal virgins at the back corner of a long table very much like the one in *The Last Supper*. As he described and re-described the face, she refined and re-refined until, at last, Estevan's face stared out at them from under the darkness of his blistered robes. His vacant eyes flared like volcanoes from inside the shadows of his hood.

Now the painting was stored in Jason's house. The only painting he and Emmy Lou had ever done together. But there just wasn't room here in the Air-Conditioned Gypsy for everything. Emmy

Lou's other completed canvases were also stored at his father's house along with letters he had written to Jason, Emmy Lou, and others and their replies while he was in the Army. Letters to Ward's father after Ward's chopper had gone down in flames. Jason hoarded too much of him in his damnable house. So much for all going empirically well. So, for the time being at least his camp would be safe from the onslaught of his extended normalcy slash and burn campaign.

Matthew felt as though he had lived in the Gypsy always. He felt that way the first time they pulled up beside the chain link fence in their canary-yellow International Travel-All that was about on its last leg or tire rim after the trip from Denver to Capital City. Once he had received his acceptance from the University and had been offered an assistantship, it had been easy to decide to move back. Together, they had crossed the country twice. Alone, Matthew had lost count of the times, the states, the cities, the cul-de-sacs, the jails. Jason knew Roanoke Park like the back of his hand. Matthew knew the country like the back of his.

By then, they were simply tired of wandering, of the feeling that they were somehow hiding out more than they were dropping out. They would have his assistantship money plus the possibility of teaching one or more summer classes. And the GI Bill money would be a half-assed supplement. It certainly wouldn't help any other way, though he had to really chew and swallow a lot of pride to finally convince the Army to change his bad paper to a General Discharge so he could receive benefits like other Vietnam Veteran heroes. They sure preached the hell out of those bennies when you were in. But, as his ACLU lawyer in Denver had told him in such apt terms, "You gotta crawl before you can walk, partner." So he determined he would combat crawl his butt until he reached the Ph.D candidate level where he would be paid more. Then Emmy Lou planned to go back to school. She felt a need for more formalized art training. It was time to try what Wolfe (Thomas, not Tom) had said you couldn't do. Go home.

Matthew had pulled back the flex-handle on the metal gate with his free hand while clutching his Fisher twenty-five-watt-per-channel tuner to his right side with the other. He pushed his boot against the gate, shoved it open into the yard shaded by a half-dozen oak trees and several lean pines that grew just outside the four-foot chain link fence. Alamogordo. Yet they barely canopied the trailer side of the yard by the driveway where Emmy Lou followed him, struggling under an armful of garment bags half-blocking her view. Matthew snatched up the suitcase full of books he had dropped to the ground while opening the gate. He shifted the weight of the tuner further up under his armpit while sidestepping through the gate to avoid their black-and-white springer spaniel, Molly Bloom, who was leaping into the air every few steps as she barreled through the gate ahead of Emmy Lou. He had named her that because Joyce had mentioned a springer in Ulysses which he was re-reading when he bought Molly for Emmy Lou's birthday last February . . . . "Woah . . . down, Molly!" Molly was fine. She drove the male dogs wild. "Down, girl!" Pine needles ruptured into odors under his boots. The breeze seemed to sizzle through the needles and leaves taking the smells to nostrils in another yard. Interesting stories surrounded Molly. Moly, drug of dreams. Nightmare Alley, now there was a place for having fun. Or under the cool shade of Myrtle's red rock. T.S. Just outside of Denver. Horseman, pass by. If only he could write lines like that. Walpurgisnacht. Goddamn it, Allegeri! Homer was blind, too. He stopped on the cement porch which ran the full length of the trailer balancing the weight of his suitcase full of books and his tuner. He closed his eyes. Is this what I have to do to see?

"I'm still here. Molly's still here. Air-Conditioned Gypsy is still here. You are still standing on a cement porch attached to the same trailer." Emmy Lou brushed by giggling and stuffed herself and the garment bags she carried through the narrow front door. The only door as it turned out. Luckily they had left it open after their first load of books and kitchen utensils and paraphernalia. Junk. God knows they had more of that than they needed, then or now. Some might say they had more books than they needed too. Fifteen boxes worth. Emmy Lou dropped the garment bags onto the beige tapestry couch in the narrow living room and slumped down beside them. Matthew wandered in, his eyes opened again. Molly lagged at his heels. "Jesus. Do you think we'll ever get all this stuff unloaded and moved in by the time classes begin?"

Matthew spied a sturdy case by the opposite wall from the door. Good place for the Fisher. Records underneath. Looks like it was built just for that. "Hell, Madame Bovary. We've got three whole months!"

She smiled. "Well, then, why don't you roll us a joint or three then, since we've obviously got forever and lots of time to waste . . . or get wasted in."

Matthew shuffled across the off-color carpet. "In which to get wasted . . . ." Used to be royal blue. Now it was somewhere between a dull Carolina blue and gray. Halfway across the twelve feet, he realized he was still carrying the suitcase of books. He plopped it down in mid stride, continuing to what had already become the record cabinet. It was built into the wall . . . more correctly, onto the wall. Stained dark . . . like cherry wood or something. The shellac on it was so thick you could peel it off in places with your fingernails. But it was sturdy. Hardwood of some kind. Could be beautiful wood underneath all that crappy veneer. "You are so clever, Madame Bovary, how you come in from left field with what you want." He placed the tuner on the top shelf of the case.

"Wasn't that what you guys always made me play? Left field?"

"No, no, no. Right field. Right field!"

"At any rate or from any position, I am willing to trade." She grinned. "I'll get Molly's food and water if you'll roll the joints. How's that?"

Her grin had always been too much for him. Ever since they used to make her play right field. She knew it too. "Fair enough. Her food's in the back seat, under the tent. Know where I'm talking about?"

Emmy Lou had vaulted from the couch and slipped toward the trailer door. "Every time, honey. Every time!"

Emmy Lou's jeans and flannel shirt still smelled of last night's campfire. His too. The last memory of their last night on the last road, living under the last stars. He quickly rolled two of his famous blimp-shaped joints. While Emmy Lou fed and watered Molly, he made two more jogging trips to the Travel-All for his speakers. Marantz. He wired them to the amp, snapped on the tuner switch and swirled the needle across the illuminated FM spectrum until he hit Eric Clapton's mellow acoustic guitar lead-in to a Blind Faith classic. The needle was around 180, WDBS out of Durham . . . Duke

University station. Matthew knew where he was going on that dial. He'd been born and raised in these parts.

> Come down off your throne
> and leave your body alone;
> somebody must change.
> You are the reason
> I've been waiting so long;
> somebody holds the key.
> But I'm weary and
> I just ain't got the time
> and I'm wasted and
> I gotta find my way home . . . .

He sang the words along with Clapton. "Somebody holds the key . . . and I'm wasted and I gotta find my way home . . . ." *April is the cruelest month, breeding lilacs out of the dead land.* Emmy Lou says that we're home now.

Home out of the dead land. Haven't been there—at least inside Jason's house—since I buried that meadow lark in the snow on my first white Christmas ever in all my travels. Even in Denver there wasn't snow on Christmas day. I've already seen more than I should've, been more than I could've. A dull head among windy spaces at merely twenty-eight. That I still live at all is no small miracle.

> Come down on your own
> and leave your body alone;
> somebody must change.
> You are the reason
> I've been waiting all these years;
> somebody holds the key.
> But I'm weary and
> I just ain't got the time
> and I'm wasted and
> I gotta find my way home

"A real fine song." Emmy Lou sucked on the joint then passed it to Matthew. He squatted "Vietnamese style," as he described it, beside her, his tail dangling near the ground between his legs bent at the knees. She sat on the floor leaning against the beige couch. "Makes me think of Woodstock. Running across the meadow to old Jasgar's woods where the lake was always shimmering in the sun. Then it rained. Remember?"

"Yeah. The lake got muddy as all hell."

"But it still shimmered in the sun, like milk chocolate."

Matthew closed his eyes and smiled as he let the smoke tickle his cilia. *I can see for miles and miles and miles and miles and miles . . . . breeding lilacs out of the dead land, mixing . . . .* "It still does." *And then went down to the ship, set keel to breakers, forth on the godly sea.*

"Don't mind if I do." She snatched the joint, again, from a dazed Matthew.

> And, I ain't done nothing wrong,
> but I can't find my way home.

"Take your hit from between my fingers, Matthew." Emmy Lou leaned forward. "It's getting too short to pass."

Matthew puckered his lips as best he could so as not to singe his beard or mustache. There was an art to it when the joint was too short to pass. The fire on the Blanco Negro rice paper almost burned his upper lip anyway. While he held in his hit, Emmy Lou reached behind her and snuffed the roach in the alabaster ash tray they'd bought when they had rendezvoused in Yellowstone. For months in Denver, it had been their single piece of furniture aside from a second-hand mattress, a yard sale special. Denver was a real yard sale paradise. Reasonable minds could differ, for sure, on whether a mattress without more would meet the test of furniture. For that matter, the ash tray could also be considered as something other than furniture. Maybe they didn't have even one stick of furniture back then. He exhaled. "How about a survey of our new domain, Madame Bovary?" And not much more now.

Emmy Lou nodded.

214

There was another gate at the back of the yard away from the driveway. It opened into the woods where they walked that day with Molly. Her black-and-white coat flashed in the streams of sunlight flowing between the mixed stands of loblolly pines, white oaks and hickory which seemed to stretch into forever around them. He was surprised to see so many hardwoods in what usually was heavy duty pine country. As they finished their second joint while walking through the forest, Molly discovered a small pond about half a mile due west of the Gypsy. Leave it to a Springer to find water. The north end was cupped by a steep red clay bank. Wide swirls of slate-colored clay accented the slick reddish bank choked with lichens. The south end was marshy. Cattails grew near the edge of the pond under the spread of a giant red oak. Its branches spewed like paint from a spray gun out over the edge of the pond. Matthew raked off the algae scum in one spot near the marsh end of the pond. Under the film, the water seemed clear, fed by an underground stream. He shook his head and laughed. Standing up, scummy water dripping through his fingers, he chanted, "April is the cruelest month, breeding lilacs out of the dead land, mixing memory and desire, stirring dull roots with spring rain . . . ." He flapped his hands in the air. "Circe's this craft, the trim-coifed goddess." Drops of green water flew into the air like rain. He wheeled around, bending over the marshy water and dipping his hands in again. "There is shadow under this red oak. Come in under the shadow of this red oak, Emmy Lou, and I will show you redemption in a handful of algae water."

She shuffled forward as if in some church ceremony, her lips twitching between serious and a series of belly laughs that she couldn't prevent from building up inside her. She knelt beside him and he blessed her with green water. She dipped her hands into the cool water, touching his head with her wet fingers. They had embraced, giggling as they knelt on the muddy bank of the pond. Molly yipped and pranced a semi-circle around them as she shook free the water that had soaked into her coat from her swim at the far end of the pond when she discovered it.

Following Molly back through the woods, they heard the bass from the tuner growing louder. When they entered the back gate, the announcer's voice cut off the crescendo of *Careful with that Axe, Eugene*.

"Dateline: May 4, 1970. Kent, Ohio. Today National Guardsmen opened fire on student demonstrators at Kent State University, injuring many students and killing at least four. The students were protesting the bombing of Cambodia by the U.S. At this time there are no further details. But we will keep you informed, Brothers and Sisters. I repeat . . . ."

Matthew remembered their shock that day as they stepped out of the woods into the yard of their new mobile home. A hundred and fifty a month for a lot of privacy. He remembered, too, thinking of Nina first thing. Had she been in that protest? And Crayon? Strange how events of the present so easily conspired to evoke deep and disturbing snatches from the past.

Emmy Lou had trouble sleeping that first night in the Gypsy reliving the announcement of the Kent State shootings, being over exhausted from a long day of unpacking and settling in, exploring for the right curves and angles on a strange mattress, and hearing tree toads and cicadas instead of the rhythm of the Santa Fe freight rumbling along the Platt River flats out of Denver and the blast of horns and clacking of snow chains and studs on the streets freezing in the darkness. Matthew had sworn more than once that Neal Cassady's ghost spent nights in that railroad yard under the Colfax Avenue viaduct. All she knew for sure was that the ghastly specter Matthew had added to her "Sixteen Vestal Virgins" spent its days and nights under Matthew's bridge. For some reason, they felt themselves to be "too far west." At least that was about the best she could get out of him even when drowned in one of his alcohol stupors or acid trips. It was going to be good, this move. He would come back out of himself again when he got to teaching. Those kids were gonna love him. He was such a natural. Right out of Malamud.

Now, in the eternal present, Matthew set the volume of his Fisher amp on two, flipping the selector knob with his other hand. As he fine-tuned the radio signal, a different announcer's fuzzy voice became clear.

"Alexander's Saloon brings you 'Sad Truth of the Day' for August 28, 1975 right after this message . . . ."

Five years. He snapped his fingers. Just like that. Standing on our heads, so to speak. God, it just doesn't seem possible that it could've been that long.

Blue grass fiddle and banjo filled the airwaves. "We bake our goods, serve vegetarian foods."

Christ. It's been five years now since they broke out the heavy arms against their own children. Doomstruck. Struckwood on Max Jasgar's farm where we denied their basic values but thrived on the artifacts their values produced. "Largest choice of suds, like Pearl, Schlitz, Bud." *I had a dream last night. What a lovely dream it was. I dreamed we all were all right, happy in a land of Oz.* Now Sebastian writes, "Welcome Back Cotter" for TV. The same man? Who knows, man. Are you? *Why did everybody laugh when I told them my dream?* Arlo, Woodies' boy, said, "New York State Thruway's closed, man." And Arlo laughs a little too to cover up the tears, like me, like you, like Sebastian.

"Alexander's Saloon." The fiddle skipped up the scale and skidded down.

None of us really knew why we let our freak flags fly. But we had a baby at Woodstock anyway as did every self-respecting rock festival ever after ala Clark, Graham, and Kirshner. In fact if you were nine months pregnant, you could usually hustle your way in for free—your old man, too. Nowadays you would be lucky if you could afford a ticket for yourself and half-price for the baby, *especially* if it was born during the concert. Proof of a nation, after all, is its progeny and, its wealth and not necessarily in that order. But none of that mattered now. The guns had come out in Oakland, Mississippi, Ohio as sure as the helicopters had that Saturday at Woodstock dropping food in parachutes on a hungry nation blockaded by its own cars. For all the world he thought he was back in Nam.

"Alexander's Saloon. What the others ain't got, we does!" The bluegrass banjo tinkled into the oblivion behind the announcer's carefully enunciated words.

"Radio news exclusive! Radio news exclusive! Remember last November when U.S. District Court Judge Frank J. Fattisti acquitted eight former Ohio National Guardsmen of all charges resulting from the 1970 massacre of four Kent State University students? Well, Judge Facist—excuse me, Fattisti—ruled that the prosecution had failed to prove 'beyond a reasonable doubt' that the guardsmen had willfully deprived the students of their civil rights."

Matthew nodded vigorously. Obviously, they only willfully deprived them, for sure, of their civil lives. He poured his first cup of coffee, muttering half-aloud. He had grown accustomed to having early mornings all to himself. He did not seem to require much sleep, so he looked forward to watching the sun come up after he slopped their red jersey porker with a mush of silage and garbage he or Emmy Lou carried home in the van in barrels twice a week from Mac's Diner. They'd been really great about keeping their food scraps separated from trash. He and Emmy Lou didn't buy into the don't eat pork fad of the day. They knew first hand that much of the pig was very lean meat, and the rest was, well, just yummy anyway. By then he would have already fed their layers with coarse corn meal while he gathered the chickens' fresh brown eggs. A dozen this morning. Emmy Lou didn't start classes till tomorrow. Thursday. She seemed to need the recommended eight. More sometimes. So, let her sleep. He sipped his coffee. "Phewww." Matthew quickly measured out two teaspoons of milk from the Melmac pitcher and one of sugar from the matching bowl. Some of the few things they owned that matched. He sipped again. "Much better." He shuffled to the door opening onto the cement porch which ran the length of the Air-Conditioned Gypsy. Hell, total self-sufficiency was a myth, anyway. Right? It went out with the fucking pilgrims or the pioneers or somebody. But we bust ass trying, and that's the thing that counts, goddamn it! The trying.

"Well," the disc jockey continued in School of Broadcasting tones. "If you remember, I guess you won't be real surprised at our sad truth for August 28, 1975. Late yesterday, an Ohio Federal Court jury acquitted Ohio Governor James A. Rhodes, former Kent State University President Robert I. White, and twenty-seven National Guardsmen of all responsibility in the shootings. That's right, Brothers and Sisters! That's *all* responsibility. Joseph Kelner, chief counsel for the former students and parents of the dead students, assessed it as [and I quote] 'a sad day in American justice.'

"Guess it's a real Dylan morning."

Oh, where have you been, my blue-eyed son?
Oh, where have you been, my darling young one?

"Morning, Matthew." Emmy Lou yawned behind him. Her chilled hands flopped over his shoulders as he stood in the aluminum-encased doorway staring at gray and rose swaths of horizon between trunks of pines. Dylan's words attacked their ears from the Marantz speakers.

> I saw a newborn baby
> with wild wolves all around it.

Sparrows and blue birds warbled old-fashioned songs among beetle-ravaged yellow pines. Beyond the parliament of fowls, the road ran.

> I saw a highway of diamonds with nobody on it.
> I saw a black branch with blood that kept
> drippin',
> I saw a room full of men with their hammers a
> bleedin',
> I saw a white ladder all covered with
> water,
> I saw ten thousand talkers whose tongues were
> all broken,
> I saw guns and sharp swords in the hands of
> young children.

"Morning, honey." He touched her hands. Clammy like the morning dew on their Better Boy tomato plants. He wiped down all of the tomato plants for the fifth consecutive morning. Otherwise, mildew could set in, and mildew was deadly. Stretching his arms above his head, he grabbed the aluminum doorjamb and yawned. Inferno . . . .

> And it's a hard, and it's a hard, it's a hard,
> it's a hard,
> And it's a hard rain's a-gonna fall.

"I'd hoped you'd be able to sleep this morning. It's your last chance to sleep in for awhile."

"Couldn't help hearing the news." She nodded toward the tuner. Her tousled taffy hair fell over her face in shifting wisps.

And what did you hear, my blue-eyed son?
And what did you hear my, darling young one?

"What does it all mean, for God's sake? Are the courts trying to say that Kent State never happened?"

"Well they *are* planning to build a gymnasium over the site, you know?" Matthew turned and kissed her.

"Five years ago. Remember, Matthew?"

"Remember. Jesus! Of course, I remember!" He turned back toward the dawn, her arms still cinching his waist. Memories like volts from an electric prod of those he'd laid down his life with on both sides of the uniform. "How could I ever forget?"

I heard the sound of a thunder, it roared out a
warnin',
Heard the roar of a wave that could drown the
whole world,
Heard one hundred drummers whose hands were
blazin',
Heard ten thousand whisperin' and nobody
listenin',
Heard one person starve, I heard many people
laughin',
Heard the song of a poet who died in the
gutter,
I heard the sound of a clown who cried in the
alley.

"There," he pointed toward the sounds of Dylan's lyrics, "is your answer." He pulled free of her arms. "They could be nineteen-eighty-fouring us, you know. Could be at that. Rewriting history. Maybe that's what the courts are doing. I mean look around us. Look! Revisionism is rampant. Is there any real concrete evidence that the sixties ever really happened at all? Except in our individual and collective memories?"

"Jimi. Bopper. Janice. Morrison." Her full ruddy lips frowned. "Just chanting the names of the dead. Isn't that proof enough?"

"It hasn't been enough for the vets, has it?" Matthew jostled down the five cinderblock steps to the ground without waiting for an answer and shuffled toward the fence. The front gate opened directly onto the gravel path that wound its way through the woods that hid them almost completely from Ebenezer Church Road. He always walked through the woods rather than following the driveway in the mornings after he'd slopped the hog and fed the hens and gathered the eggs and watched the sunrise. "Going for the paper. Maybe there'll be an article about a situation when chanting the names of the dead did some good." When he opened the gate, the hinges squealed in the still morning. Starlings, perched on the giant oak that stood alone in the center of a stand of pines, screeched. The pink sky blackened with their beating wings as they fled the oak for the morning breezes. Jason had not killed everything yet. He could hear Molly's four paws spinning their claws on the linoleum floor of the hallway, then the kitchen. She tore across the living room carpet and shot past Emmy Lou who was still standing sleep-dazed in the doorway wrapped in aluminum. Molly lofted off the porch, landing on all fours and at a full run on the pine-needle-cushioned ground. She bolted ahead of Matthew, out the gate, leaping like a gazelle between the trees. Springer. He still felt Emmy Lou's clammy hands on his shoulders. As long as he could feel her touch, he would be okay.

Oh, who did you meet, my blue-eyed son?
Who did you meet, my darling young one?

Matthew snatched a stick from the pine straw. "Molly!" She whirled in mid-air about twenty feet closer to the dirt-and-gravel path which connected them with an asphalt artery of civilization. Molly yipped and lunged toward his outstretched arm. "Go get it, girl!" She pointed. Waiting for him to throw, she swished her docked tail so rapidly from side to side that her entire rear end waggled. When he flung the stick through the air into leaves toward the road,

Molly hopped toward where she heard it whizzing into the air, her eyes wide, her floppy ears perked. With her last leap, she landed near the spot where the stick had landed. She snorted through the pine needles and oak leaves near the giant oak, making small overlapping circles as she searched for the stick . . . like a search and destroy mission. Finding it lodged between a twisted, torn root of the oak and the ground, she jerked it loose. Rolling it around between her "soft" mouth teeth with her tongue and holding her head high, she pranced back toward Matthew. She circled him twice, then deposited the stick near, but not at, his feet. Immediately she sat behind it, her tongue hanging out one side of her mouth. Her teeth looked like pearls in the sunrise, and in a sense they were. For Molly cost them fifty dollars only because she was the runt of the litter. But her lineage was excellent and her health incredible. She was worth thousands as a breeding bitch. One of these days. Maybe next heat. Most of all, she was smarter than most people.

"Aarrauf . . . aarrauf . . . aarrauf!"

"Okay, girl. One more." He threw the stick again, this time back toward the fence. Keep her away from that asphalt road or the cars'll kill her for sure. Molly gave chase as Matthew continued through the woods to where their drive met the dirt rut road. Beyond it, the asphalt highway. Spaniels hunt mainly with their noses. Encyclopedia Britannica, he thought, said that. But Molly seemed to spot things when she sprang through the air.

Where the roads crossed, two boxes were nailed to rough sapling stakes driven into the hard red clay. A plastic green cylinder was for the newspaper. Matthew referred to it as the Huge Disturbance. He ignored the galvanized box, the larger one with a red flag on the left side as you face it. Mail delivery wasn't until one or two in the afternoon. About the time of his second class. Finally, they were giving him a real literature class . . . after four full years of teaching freshman composition. All he'd done since his transformation into an ex-gunslinger, since Kent State, was teach freshman comp. Emmy Lou. It was her strength and love that helped him make that decision. He could still remember when he first heard that radio announcer telling about the massacre. He'd had to turn his face away from her as they approached the Gypsy from the woods that day because the mask they had been so carefully building for him was dripping from his face like molten wax. Under the mask was the hideous self, the killer. He pulled the newspaper from its cylindrical womb and popped the rubber band with his index finger. Unrolling the paper, Matthew could not avoid the headline on the front page

KENT STATE DEFENDANTS ACQUITTED

Can't let these things get to you now, my boy. Too much at stake here. Just one more year and two more chapters and you'll have it all! Assistant professorship. Ph.D. There will be time enough then to do something. Shoving his hands into his pockets, he walked barefooted along the crabgrass which struggled up through the gravel edges of the driveway. The grass was cool, damp with an unseasonable dew. It was like people, the way it struggled. Too cool for his feet. Clammy like her hands in the morning.

Molly was waiting for him inside the front gate, the same stick he had thrown held tight between her grinning teeth. As he approached, she began prancing like a prize colt. He entered the gate and ruffled her black-and-white hackles. He snatched the stick from her mouth and tossed it the length of the yard. Molly retrieved it from against the fence while Matthew walked along the porch past the converted Pine State ice cream freezer they used for storage of their garden vegetables, their chickens and their pork. Beef they still had to buy at the market. No pasture. Self-sufficiency, fini?

"What about that kid at Brown who created his own atomic bomb from materials he bought and information he conned, Madame Bovary? Now that's some kinda self-sufficiency, ain't it?"

As Emmy Lou's touch became distant, Matthew looked out over the florescent-lit faces of twenty-one young men and women seated at desks in the basement corner room in English. It pretty much had been his classroom for four, now going into five, years. He rocked onto the back legs of his chair, knees balancing him as they pressed against the blond table in front of him. Blond? Blonde? His hands clasped behind his head, hidden in his shaggy hair.

> *Ba . . . boo . . . boom . . . . Don't let me down, don't let me down.*

The new cotton work shirt scratched under his arms and around his neck. He'd forgotten to wash the shirt before wearing it as he usually did before he wore new clothing to soften them up and cleanse them of chemicals. God only knew what kinds of irritants were fiddling around inside the cotton at this very minute. The new Wranglers fit tight around the waist. Not stretched yet. Could hardly walk in them this morning after breaking down to Emmy Lou's pleas to wear something decent for a change. So stiff. Like a rusting tin man. We're all tin men to the OPEC nations. For most of these students, this was their first university class ever. In the overall scheme of things, this class was pretty important.

Behind him, his name was printed in block chalk letters on the green board that ran the length of the whitewashed brick wall. He'd gotten to class ten minutes early as he usually did the first day, telling Emmy Lou that he was just anxious, so he could print his name legibly on the board. His handwriting was something of a joke to past classes and to himself. In fact, it had become somewhat of a campus legend. But the students all seemed to adjust to reading his scribble. If they couldn't read some marginal notation or words on the board, they'd ask him. In a way, it became a part of his teaching process. Make them have to ask questions to survive. Create a friendly environment. Be human where possible. Make mistakes and admit them even if you're so goddamned perfect that you have to create mistakes. Get their interest and guard it jealously like a lover. Learning is creative and natural so make it seem so. Let them in on what it's like to make things with words . . . to be a wordsmith. Most of them have never known, never will if you don't show them. They'll dig it for sure.

They seemed to be even younger this year . . . . No. That wasn't right. Each year they seemed younger, but the freshmen and freshwomen remained the same age. Wasn't it, rather, his getting older? He flung his right arm behind him toward his name and the other information he had so painstakingly printed earlier. They have to be constantly reinforced on these things. "My name is Matthew Parkrow, Mr. Parkrow—if you insist—or just about anything short of SOB." He glanced around the room. Looked like it was shaping up to be a male semester. Only four women in the class. Then, there's the afternoon literature class yet to come. "Check your computer card printout before it self-destructs and make sure you're in the right section of Freshman Composition, better known to us computer robots as English one-eleven." He made robot-like movements as he again pointed to the board. "This is section zero-zero-nine of English one-eleven." He glanced over the class. "Anyone in the wrong section, the wrong course, the wrong university? The wrong universe?" The students giggled. Maybe a little self-conscious. Usual. Not used to this kind of a come-on from a college professor. Not used to much of any kind of come on from a college professor since this is probably most of the students' first class in a university. "Fantastic! Not one misplaced student and not a single alien . . . ." They laughed. "And everybody's all hung up on Johnny not being able to read!" They were belly-laughing now.

He paused, lit a Winston. "My office is on the third floor of this very building. It is known to all who inhabit this building by day as room three-ten. Those flawed few of us who often haunt the building by night and scare the night watchman call it the Instructor's Maze." He crouched over the front row of desks now, perched on his table soliloquizing. "Walk in and ask anybody where the resident freak's office is. They'll gladly point out my cubicle." He slouched back into his chair and propped his feet up on the table. "Office hours. Yes, that's something the administrators require of us. So mine are ten to twelve on Monday, Wednesday, and Friday. Any other time just make sure you check with me first to assure we'll be at the same place at the same time. You know how absent-minded professors can be." Cackles. Scattered smiles. They were actually still listening. "If, for some unknown reason, I'm not in my office when I'm supposed to be, I'll most likely be at Mac's—a diner two blocks up from here on the opposite side of Hillsboro which, if you don't already know about, then you soon will—or on the fifth floor of the library tower. I have an office there this year for the first time. It is office number 555. Perks of Ph.D. candidacy . . . finally!" He eyed them again, these new shiney-faced students. More smiles. A few whispers toward the back of the room. Word was filtering around already from the ones in the know. What can you do? "I can tell by a few knowing smiles that some of you are already aware that you have somehow struck the English Comp gold mine here. The great Computer God has seen fit to place you in Matthew Parkrow's class. And everybody knows he gives the best grades in English Comp. And I need straight A's for pre-med or pre-vet." Matthew leaped to his feet, flourishing his arms like swords. "But I don't give my students their grades! They earn them!

"What the heck, anyway. Grades are too relative to be of any real importance. What's an A for one student might be a B or even a C for another. However, I do understand how competitive it is out there where you guys are sitting. Grades are important in the real world. Grades are important in the structure we've built for ourselves, whether they are logically of importance or not. In this class, though, your grades are going to be based upon how you measure up against yourself—not how you measure up to some arbitrary and impersonal scale set up by some hung-over administrator and by business men and women and grad school deans who want your grades to serve their petty and discriminatory screening purposes." He put his hands up before they could react. "No applause, please. But thank you for thinking of me . . . ."

Matthew returned to his chair, leaned back again with his knees against the table, rocking back on the chair legs. "What we'll be doing in here is learning to write and to read literature at a hopefully better level than you have before which will prepare you for your continuing career as a student at this university. I know a little about these things, so the university gives me the opportunity to teach in these areas. We'll do some things a little differently. For example, we will listen to and analyze songs by Bob Dylan and John Lennon and Paul McCartney as our introduction to poetry. We'll have group study and group projects throughout the semester. I hope you'll enjoy this class in spite of yourself and your probable and understandable dislike for English. Any questions?"

Matthew searched the room for the one brave hand that inevitably wagged in the air about this time of the first class of the first day of classes. A few times he'd actually been blessed with entire classes of the maniacs. He drew on his cigarette, glanced from face to shining face. They stared up at him, shining-faced America, like he knew what he was up to or something. For some strange reason he affected his students that way. They were easily familiar with him. Friends in a way instantly. Yet, simultaneously, they were agog at his presence. Emmy Lou had said it was that he did have a certain presence about him. "That's what all those idiots in three-ten and people like old Beauregard Scythe fear, Matthew." She had said it so many times it seemed sometimes like a prayer. Such statements seemed to be coming closer together, like labor pains.

"Okay. Just a couple of things left. I believe learning is a rush . . . a trip. And we're going to try really hard to make English one-eleven a trip for you, too. I know it's going to be hard," he shrugged. "But let's try. That's all I ask.

"You're all here to learn. So it has to be something you can get off on or you ought to do something that doesn't require any learning . . . though I can't, for the life of me, think of anything that humans do that doesn't require learning of one sort or another." He paused. Sucked in another pregnant drag. "Can you?"

One of the young women waved timidly from behind the black guy who must be on a basketball scholarship with his vertical size. "Yes . . . . Please stand up and give us your name."

"Kathleen Jurgenson."

"Okay, Kathleen. Let's have it!"

She fidgeted. "Well. What you want us to say . . . . Well . . . ." She flushed a little, shuffled her feet. Her auburn hair pulled behind her in a ponytail. Gray eyes fluttered toward the tile floor permanently dirtied by the years of feet and desk abuse.

"Yes. Go ahead, Kathleen, please." She was onto it.

"Well, you want us to say, like, farmer or, like, mechanic or, like, something else."

Matthew beamed, sat upright in his chair. He was paying attention to Kathleen Jurgenson. She was the first student ever to unmask his gambit so quickly. "Yes, Kathleen. Do go on."

"Then you'd list a bunch of things that each of them has to learn, you know, in order to do what they do." Her pug nose crinkled over a set of grinning red lips.

"Take a bow, Ms. Jurgenson."

She curtsied.

The class laughed and clapped.

Matthew clapped and laughed. "What do you think, class? Is she right? Has she skewered the instructor to the proverbial wall?"

"Yes!"

"Okay, you got me, Kathleen." He raised his hands over his head, turned and spread-eagled his hands on the chalk board like he was being busted.

"Who's gonna frisk ya, Mister Parkrow? After all, you're the teacher."

Matthew turned back toward the class, dusting his hands on his new stiff jeans. He pointed at the young man who had spoken. "And, do I teach or what?" He laughed.

The class laughed.

"Seriously, haven't you learned something?"

The young man nodded, seemingly a little surprised that Matthew had been able to pick him out with his back turned and equally surprised at his own answer. He chuckled too.

Another young man who'd been staring out of the window until now was, however, the one who actually responded. "Yes. We learned that everything takes learning about . . . ." He grinned. The freckles on his nose almost glowed red in the florescent light of the basement room. "Even English, I guess." He sniggered.

The class chorused.

Yes. Okay. A quick group of kids. "Yes. That's the idea . . . ." They should be a lot of fun. *Na nana nananana nananana, hey Jude . . . . You're only looking for someone to perform with . . . .* "So, if everything takes learning about, then knowing how to learn is where it's at. Right?"

"Right," the class seemed to chant in unison.

"And, two of the most important tools we use in learning are reading and writing because through them we can order our own thoughts as well as come to understand the ordered thoughts of others. What's in this book . . . ." He scooped his copy of "Readings for Writers" off the table and shook it above his head. "What's here and what's in your own head are equally important." He dropped the book onto the bouncing blond/blonde table. Thudduddud . . . the cloth-and-cardboard cover. He clucked his tongue, pulled at the dark curls of his beard. "In English one-eleven, I'm afraid that all of this rhetoric still boils down to writing assignments, no matter how I try to package it."

The class groaned like green barns in a high wind, even Ms. Jurgenson.

"Okay." He stood, stretched his arms over his head. "What don't you like about themes?" He beckoned to them. "Come on." He pictured Mick Jagger prancing in red-and-blue spotlights across the sagging stage in Denver. "Give!" Jagger beat that stage to death with his scarlet scarf. *Please allow me to introduce myself, I'm a man of wealth and taste . . . .* Matthew pivoted toward the class ala Mick Jagger. "How can we have themes you want to write if you don't tell me what you dislike about them?" He shrugged and started toward the table again. As he turned the straight-backed chair behind the table to straddle it, he sensed a hand was up behind him waving in the air. Eyes in the back of his head just like their parents back home. When he turned back to the class, no hand was waving but a mousy brunette in the far corner, who'd been giving out her phone number or something to the guys as they came into the room before the bell, was whispering. "Please, Ms. . . . ah . . . ?"

"Cindy . . . ."

"Please, Ms. Cindy." The class giggled in a chorus. "Could you speak a little louder so we can all hear you?"

"Sure." She smiled. Her apple-like cheeks ripened. "I was just saying that we never get to write about things we like to write about . . . ."

Poor girl's crimson. He turned, walked to the board, snatched up a piece of chalk and scribbled 'Bad Topics' on the board. "Bad topics?"

"Yes." She giggled and sat down.

"So, that's what that says." Ron Dawson, All-American high school tail back and top recruit of the football Mafia on campus, guffawed as he pointed at the scribbled words on the board. The class chorus pointed and guffawed with him.

Matthew hung his head, feigning embarrassment. "Aw, shucks! I never did learn to write too good. But," he continued, raising his head, "this ain't no penmanship class neither." He grinned.

Another. "We don't ever get told what we did wrong. Not really."

"Yeah. We just get a bunch of comments and negative stuff."

"Or have things explained when we don't understand."

"Even if we write a good theme, they always grade us down on spelling or fail us for commas or something."

"It's like the teachers enjoy putting us down!"

"Okay!" Matthew threw up his hands in front of his face. He'd long since given up writing their suggestions down on the board. "Okay. Okay. You're going too fast for me to get it all down."

"It don't matter . . . Mr. Parkrow. We can't read it noway."

"It doesn't matter. Not 'don't'. And anyway, not 'noway'." Matthew shot an index finger at the fat boy on the front row. "Regardless would be even better."

The class chorus laughed and shot finger pistols at the fat boy who burned red in his jowls but laughed along with his classmates at his own stupidity. Of all places to talk wrong, English class was sure as hell not one of them.

"And if you'll work on that language problem, I'll work on my scribbling problem."

"Yes, sir," the fat boy chuckled. "That's a deal."

"Okay. Look, ladies and gentlemen. I'm going to try very hard and work with you on these complaints. I know that many of them are justifiable and reasonable. How about . . . ." He pulled at his beard. "How about a double-decker grading system to start off with? One grade for content and one grade for grammar/spelling . . . etcetera . . . etcetera . . . etcetera!"

A few of the chorus nodded.

"And we'll work out our grading in levels. The first few weeks will be looser. The next few weeks will be a little harder. The final weeks will be the hardest in terms of grading. That gives everyone a chance to become acclimated."

More and more nods.

They like that. "Well, let's give it a try. The main thing to remember about this class is that we'll work together. You'll learn as much from each other as you ever will from me. And I will learn something from each one of you because each of you is unique.

"Always be willing to be that unique person that you are. If, for example, there's something individual or unique bothering you— about this class or about something else—then please tell me about it. We'll talk it out. If at all possible, we'll try out your idea or suggestion if it's about the class, or we'll try to deal with your problem." Matthew wagged his head. "I'm late. I'm late." He picked up the watch. "I'm late for a very important date." He scanned the room, the question in his eyes.

"Alice in Wonderland . . . ."

"The white rabbit . . . ."

"What else?"

"A song . . . ?"

A couple of girls in the back row began to sing: "Just ask Alice. I think she'll know . . . ."

"Jefferson Starship . . . ."

Matthew smiled indulgently. "Airplane. Jefferson Airplane. That was before they got an overhaul for interstellar travel." He looked around as if startled. "Where is all this going?"

"Remember what the Door Mouse said."

Matthew grinned. Well, well. Ron Dawson, football player par excellence. Surprise, surprise.

"Feed your head."

Matthew lit another Winston and dragged deeply on it. These kids were beautiful. Ready. Far fucking out. "And that's what you can do in here, ladies and gentlemen. You can bounce off these brick walls as good as any white rabbit. You just gotta get loose. Now ya'll knows about getting loose, don't cha?"

Nods. Grins. Snickers. They knew all right. "SURE you do!

"In here, I figure we're going to be spending lots of time together, so we might as well start out by getting to know each other a little. Start getting loose with each other without extraneous stimulants. You know? What do you think?"

Blank. Tableau rasa. Skeptical. Cautious. Hope they approach learning in the same manner. "Well, let's give it a try. Okay?" Lost in the light of twenty-one smiling faces of America, he waved his arms in circles. "Let's form groups. Let's see. Twenty-one. Make five groups. Four of four and one of five. Okay?"

They stared at each other and at him as if they were unaware of what to do, or maybe they'd become glued to their seats. "It's alright. You're not glued to your seats, and the chairs and desks are not screwed to the floor . . . at least not this year." Kathleen Jurgenson giggled and began to shove her desk toward a growing knot of students. "The only requirement is that you get into a group where you don't know anyone."

Desks began to scrape one at a time across the tile, building to a din of squeaks and scrapes as they scrambled around to find a group. Matthew pulled at a few renegade strands of beard. The students began to settle like dust after a whirlwind. "Alright. What you're going to do now is get to know the people in your group, and they will get to know you. You might start off with your name and where you're from. That's usually a good basic beginning. Maybe what high school you went to. Anything unique about yourself . . . hobbies . . . whether you eat rutabagas or not." Matthew paused for the laughter. "It'll start picking up by itself as you get loose."

One group was stacked with Kathleen, Cindy, and Ron Dawson, All-American. They started immediately. The other groups he stopped at one by one and each began with a little coaxing. It wasn't a problem for these kids. It was just something very different. When Matthew left the room for a drink of water which he didn't really need, the groups were humming.

"Mistah Pahkrow?"

Oh shit! Matthew smirked his tolerant smirk as the dumpy supervisor of graduate assistants approached him from where he had been lurking in the shadows of the stairwell under the concrete-and-steel steps up to the first floor. Easily, he had been within hearing distance of his classroom. Was he at that snooping shit again? From the first fucking day of the new semester? No let up from this creep. Like Jason, another facet of the flawed diamond. And Estevan. Scythe had spied on him since he was voted Teaching Assistant of the Year his first two years at the University. He was like a . . . no, he *was* a parasite, desperately feeding off of the mistakes of his graduate assistant charges. He not-so-patiently waited for Matthew to commit his first damnable sin. Must be three years ago now. He came to observe Matthew's class one morning, and he found the room empty. Well, you can imagine. When was that? After the night of the Watergate hearings, Cambodian bombings. The Arab-Israeli soap opera war: A new installment? Must've been. Yes. The fall of seventy-three. A few of the graduate students—the new ones who still spoke to him at all—told him that Scythe nearly suffered a coronary when he stormed into three-ten looking for Matthew, and he wasn't there either. Poper Dryden, his office mate who doubled as the verbal newspaper among graduate assistants, swore over several large drafts at The Saloon across from Mac's that Beaureguard Scythe was frothing at the mouth like a mad squirrel. "If he'd only looked under the spreading chestnut tree in the quad behind English, he'd have found you and your class. Right?"

Poper never could hold his beer and seldom drank at faculty functions because his tolerances for whiskey or wine were even lower. He feared the demon would unleash the latent man behind the veil in public and ruin his career as a scholar. Poper's veil paralleled his own mask, so it seemed. The primary difference was that he knew about his mask, but he seriously doubted that Poper knew about his veil. Matthew remembered having smiled quietly, gently. The same smile he used to give Donaldson before Eddie had helped court-martial him. Couldn't much blame him though.

Matthew felt that he owed the University something for looking the other way on that one just like Columbia did. Nobody else had, even after he'd been cleared by the VA. But it seemed that his and Emmy Lou's luck was always to be tarnished with a little irony. Thus, Beau Scythe. A living embodiment of that tarnish. Four years in a row was just too much of a Teacher of the Year for the poor old bastard to take from a commie, hippie, freak like Matthew, given his mania for classrooms with walls and ceilings and desks and blackboards that are green and rules, rules, rules.

"Mr. Scythe." Matthew's eyes tore through the old man's facade as they faced each other in the shit-green hallway. Sunlight flooded through the open door leading to the stairwell outside. Scythe's washed-out eyes were like parched leather. The whites, bloodshot.

Darkening bags under them. Sagged like his jowls which were webbed with bursting vessels from too many whiskey sours at too many cocktail parties and too many in the secrecy of his bachelor apartment to stop his hands from shaking so he could drive to work or sneaked shots when alone in his office. In his mental ramblings, Matthew had once struck upon the idea that Beau Scythe was exactly what Jason might have been if he'd come from an aristocratic southern background and had been educated at Sawanee . . . down to the ripples in his peppering hair.

"Mistah Pahkrow, I was undah the impression that you had ah class at this houah?"

"For a change, Mr. Scythe, your impression is correct."

"Then, might ah ask," he sneered, "what you ahe doin' roamin' these halls?" Scythe paused long enough to light his Kent and puff at it to keep it lit. "Looking foh anothah tree to teach undah? Ha . . .haha . . .ha . . . haha . . . ." He tried to elbow Matthew in the ribs.

Matthew dodged. "Missed again, Mr. Scythe." He stepped out of further reach. "Class is going on without me, you see."

"Without the teachah? Impossible!"

For a moment, Matthew could have sworn that he saw steam rising from Scythe's ears as he bellowed again and again: "Without a teachah? Impossible!"

Instructors glared out of their classroom doors. When they saw that it was just Beauregard Scythe and his favorite target Matthew Parkrow at it again, they closed their doors and continued lessons on the dangling participle, the paragraph and how to use and abuse it, *The Wasteland*, or *Portrait of the Artist as a Young Man*.

"Yes . . . . I guess, Mr. Scythe, you might call me the Toscanini of Freshperson Composition."

"Huh?"

Matthew turned toward his classroom, muttering over his shoulder to the stammering Scythe. "I knew it. I just knew that, of all people, you'd understand!" Get back. What assignment for the kids? Some topics for an outline. Work on the outlines in groups on Friday. Rough drafts in class on Monday. Wednesday, first full in-class writing using the outlines. Okay. Sounds good. He stumbled into a left turn at the end of the hall ignoring Beau Scythe's voice squeaking behind him like the fan in the heating blower system just outside of his classroom.

Matthew figured that Scythe's muttering was really no more than his standard whimpering attempts at explaining why he was spying outside of his room. That was the only possible explanation for Scythe's behavior when put together with their history of conflict. This was the beginning of the fifth year of that feud. He completed his pentangle June 2, 1976. Then his shield would be complete. He would be able to walk through so-called real life protected by his armor of education and position.

The glare of the white doorway. Voices. Oh, yes. Class. Something interesting for their topics. Topic: Academic Spying or Politics. He laughed to himself as he stepped through the doorway.They wouldn't even understand that topic, hopefully, much less be able to write a paragraph or so on it.

Hell. He snapped his fingers as his right boot touched the floor inside the room . . . slick gray tiles shining today like they only did after holidays and breaks between semesters. The topic is on the front page of the newspaper today, for Christ's sake! Kent State!

His students hardly looked up as he bounced across the shining gray tile to his table. The groups were really animated. Cross-group discussions were going on too. Pretty loose now, aren't they? Only a few University Dailys were visible. Always would be a few. There's the other topic . . . on the front page of the University rag.

STATE UNIVERSITY SETS NEW ENROLLMENT RECORD

"May I?" He snatched an open paper from one boy caught unawares by his re-entry into the class room. "Thank you." Must give them a choice but not too much of a choice. Give them options, but I've got to have some stability for comparisons so I can see where everyone is regarding their writing abilities. He cleared his throat as dramatically as he could. "May I have your attention, please?" He leaned on his left elbow. "I really hate to break this up . . . but . . . if you want to get out of here a little EARLY today . . . ." He dragged out the "EARLY", letting it do its own work. "Okay. You'll get a chance to work these groups on Friday and again on

Monday. Makes things a lot looser, huh?" He paused. "You learn from each other as you go. Being in a room three times a week with a bunch of dull strangers isn't my idea of having fun. Is it yours?"

The class chorus shook their collective heads, some muttering "No." The one young man with daydreaming problems was again looking out the window at the legs of the passersby on the sidewalk above. "For next time, I want you to work up a rough outline for a one-page paper. In class on Friday we'll work on the outlines together in your groups. So have something here to work on. Monday we'll do rough drafts. Then on Wednesday we'll write in-class for the first time." Matthew shuffled the two steps to the greenboard. "Let's see. Texts . . . ." He wrote the names on the board. *Harbrace College Handbook*, twelfth edition; *Readings for Writers.*

"These are your required texts for this class. *Harbrace*, sometimes referred to by TA's as the Bible." He pointed to the second title. "*Readings for Writers*—basically supplemental materials. You may purchase both of them at the local school bookstore. *Harbrace* has a section on outlining. Check it out for the right form and so forth."

Matthew pulled at his beard, caught a tangle with a finger and worked it loose. "Oh yeah. What are you going to write about? Topics? That's where I was going."

He scribbled the topics on the board below the texts. "Topic number one: How it feels to be a new student in a large university. The second topic: Is anyone responsible for Kent State?" He underlined each topic as he read it. Hell, he had to read them. They were otherwise illegible. Good thing no one tests teachers for adequate handwriting. "There'll be more choices as we go along. But, in the beginning, I need to limit topics so we can see how each of you writes about the same topics. That way I can see how each of your skills matches up with the others in the class. Then I'll know how slow or fast to go, who may need special attention, and so forth. These are current issues, in today's headlines. You'll find all you need to know about Kent State and the shootings there in 1970 in this morning's local newspaper. There's a front-pager on the conglomerate university in the daily university rag." Matthew glanced around and then at his watch: 8:45.

"Okay. Do your best on this outline. See you on Friday!"

Soon after,
Matthew
splattered
the yolks
of two over
easy eggs
with the four
tines of a

stainless steel fork just recently washed for the first of several times today. He spotted two blood specks in each yolk as he spread the viscous liquid in rich cadmium swirls over the whites. Almost made it, didn't you? But I'd've gotten you one way or the other, you know. All grown up and Bar-b-qued. Old and stewed. Stuffed. Chick filleted. Kentucky Fried. Baked . . . trussed and dried. Campbell's chicken soup. Or grandma's for that matter. Prevent chickenplosion! Eat an egg today! Slicing off pieces of the hardened albumin, he dipped crisp hot toast into the liquid. A slurpy yellowish mouthful of crunch between his teeth. A bite or two of the white. Ad lib the bacon since he couldn't afford it anyway. The hash browns served nicely as a substitute . . . . Matthew slurped coffee, washing down the mixture of textures and tastes, both real and conjured. Wiping his beard and mustache, he nodded and muttered to no one in particular because there was no one in particular to mutter to. "From before birth to after death . . . . Chicken. The only way to fly . . . low to the floor of the coop, coupe: four-door or with guns?

"Gosh, damn. It's getting rather cold out for August."

Enter Poper Dryden's wimpy voice.

Matthew glanced up from his coffee. Politeness was his only reasonable response. "Yeah. Cold for August, for sure, man." He tried to avoid his office mate's jaundiced eyes. They were always asking for pity. They seldom got any . . . especially not from him . . . the ancient pitiless destroyer.

Twenty-five going on nineteen, looking fifty-nine and frightened. The first thing you had to notice about Poper wasn't his nose or his mouth or his sick eyes or sinking cheeks, protruding kneecaps, clavicle maximus. They were minimus. His crowning achievement and first noteworthy characteristic was his carrot hair which he kept close cropped just above the ears and collar line but allowed to curl naturally all over his head. The color was so livid that you'd swear he dyed it, except that you couldn't imagine anyone consciously choosing to dye their hair such a shade of carrot-yellow red. From the first second you saw Poper Dryden, you saw carrot-top. "How you been Carrot?" Poper's perpetually flushed face flushed even more as he pulled off his green ski jacket, wiped perspiration from his thin brow, and slumped into the chair opposite Matthew. As far as Matthew knew, he was the only person in the world who called Poper Dryden "Carrot" except for his dear Mother, Laura Lee Dryden.

"The first class of the semester is barely over, Matthew, and I feel rushed already . . . ." He dabbed his beet cheeks with a freshly laundered handkerchief imbued with a hint of lilac. He always kept one in his left trouser pocket. "I just sometimes wonder if I'm really cut out to be a teacher . . . . I'm literally exhausted, Matthew. Lit-er-al-ly exhausted . . . ."

Truth at least at last. Great God Almighty, grimy truth at last. Be kind. Why should I? Because there's nothing else to do. You can only wound him. But, he's wounding students every day. Maybe even killing them! I . . . I don't know about that . . . . "Well, when you get your doctorate, you'll soon be teaching less students for more money, so you'll have less of the teaching load pressures . . . more research."

"Yes, my God, there are the scholarly pressures, too." He sighed. "Publish or . . . ." He sighed again, from his toes this time. "Perish."

His voice trailed off into the haze of smoked sausage, bacon and brewing coffee as the urn continued to bubble, across the room and through the door into the counter room. Just off to the left, past the hallway to the bathrooms.

"Wonder where Ms. Mac is . . . ?" Poper's golf ball eyes darted from side to side, seeming about ready to pop out of their sockets. He turned in his chair, glancing behind. "Ah, here she comes from the pick-up counter."

Ms. Mac smiled at Matthew while she watched Poper settle back into his chair, his hands clasped together as he circled his forefingers around each other meticulously, occasionally changing direction.

"Until teachers are encouraged to be teachers instead of pedants and scholars out of touch with the vibrations of eighteen-year-old energy, there will be those pressures, Carrot. You know what I mean?"

Poper threw up his hands in the sign of a cross, fending off Matthew's words like the bite of a vampire. "Wait a minute," he whined. "I didn't mean to stir up a Matthew Parkrow verbal essay on the role of the teacher as catalyst . . . ." He shook his head. "Or anything like that."

Matthew smirked around the chipped edge of his coffee cup. The amber liquid was so hot, still, that he could only sip at it. "I just don't understand it." He wagged his head, almost spilling coffee before he realized that he should set the cup on the table, which he did immediately. "Nobody wants to discuss things with me any more." His eyes gleamed. "What you got to say about that, old Carrot?"

Poper shrugged, glanced around the room. "Nobody likes to be wrong all the time, Matthew." He shrugged again as if it were the only body action he could perform to express what was between— and in—the words. "And you're so damned right so damned often. It gets downright depressing."

Matthew shrugged. Must be catching. In a hurry, Ms. Mac refilled Matthew's cup without a word, only a hanging head and a baleful look in her hazel eyes. At sixty or whatever, her eyes had more zest in them than poor Poper's. Matthew was sure of that. What about the zest in your own eyes? He forced a grin. "What can I say?" It's been a hard life . . . . He chuckled.

Poper tried really hard not to shrug, but it seemed to be a part of the molecular structure of the moment. He could not help shrugging. Hardly had he shrugged, he uncontrollably began to giggle. And only coffee to drink, too . . . .

All this shrugging shit. You'd think they were a pair of . . . yes. There are thoughts that you have and don't realize you have them. There are thoughts that you have which you realize you have, but you refuse to recognize that they are your thoughts. There are thoughts that you have which you realize you have and which you embrace as your own thoughts. And there are thoughts that you simply don't have? Or do all people have the same thoughts? Each person embraces all thought. The native wisdom of the masses? But that's before we replace their native wisdom of the masses with what we laughingly call education. He glared at Poper from behind the wall of fingers he had erected by clasping them together over his nose. Like Poper, they all think that learning can be measured by computers and tests so dull you can't even stay awake long enough to do them properly. Hell, I fell asleep during the Army Intelligence testing at Fort Jackson but still did well enough. At least, I qualified for Nam. This idea that individuals have to adapt to a certain frame of reference to learn is absolutely Caligulean. Yet, I'm the one who's considered mad? Who says? Jason says. Scythe says. Alecia says. Emmy Lou, though she loves me, says. Poper says. Of course, he is discountable. Isn't he? Two-thirds of the English faculty say. Can I discount them too? If I'm not careful, I'll soon be fractioned out of existence. Poper's lips moved. There were words . . . .

"He said that he'd stop by your . . . our . . . office just before nine."

"Who?"

"The guy that stopped by earlier. Aren't you listening?"

"Sorry, I guess not."

"This guy stopped by. Didn't say who he was. Just said that he was looking for Matthew Parkrow."

Matthew smiled, wagged his shaggy curls. "Can't imagine who it could be."

"Well, he's a new teaching assistant . . . but only at the M.A. level. Didn't Scythe tell you? Hell, he was there!"

"No. No he didn't." Maybe that was what he was mumbling about behind my back earlier.

"And, his wife is really sexy!"

"Oh, really?"

"You know. No offense. But I think your Emmy Lou is the hottest. But, God, you could almost carve this woman's vibes with a knife."

A slice of breast? Oh, you prefer the darker meat inside of the thigh. Some thigh, so Poper claims. "Really, now?" Matthew finished his coffee with the last bites of egg and toast. "Ms. Mac?" Ruddy-cheeked, she turned from the silverware tray by the wall where she had been wrapping knives and forks in white paper napkins, attempting to ignore Poper's repeated attempts to get her attention. Her hair braided and wound in a bun on the back of her head looked like silver rope. "Refills for Mr. Dryden, poet-laureate of eighteenth century Capital City and for myself."

Ms. Mac beamed as she waddled toward their table. "Ah just love the way you talk, Matthew. Ah could listen all day."

"A woman of taste, obviously."

She giggled as she took their cups and waddled off toward the coffee urns in the small front room of the restaurant where the counter service was. She and Poper were a lot alike, though she obviously did not like Poper. And he wasn't too sure about Poper liking her all that much either. Both were from Capital City, yet neither of them realized that there was essentially no such thing as eighteenth century Capital City. It wasn't even created as a capitol until seventeen-ninety-two. Eight years hardly a century makes. Both liked him, in their own ways, though each felt they shouldn't but didn't know why. After all, he was mad, wasn't he?

"Anyway, how have you been, Matthew?" Poper fidgeted with his carrot curls, flashing a clean smile, one right off of a 4H poster. "Haven't seen you all summer in the stacks or the office."

Smile's fit for a toothpaste commercial complete with Bucky or Leave-It-To Beaver brushing them. After those hundreds his Mother had doled out for caps, they ought to be. Another day-to-day twist of the iron mistress, mixing between the flower and the bud. Or is that flour? How do you answer such questions when you know they're only being read off of cue cards. "Okay, I guess . . . . And you?"

"Your coffee, boys. Talk later. Gotta run."

"Got you hoping . . . hopping I should say."

"I should say!" she cackled at poor Poper over her shoulder. She was taking another order two tables away by the time she finished chuckling at poor Mister Dryden's bad joke. And if she thought it was bad, then it must be pretty bad . . . .

Poper sipped his coffee, his line-drawing lips just off the edge of the chinked white cup. He couldn't bear to actually touch it to his lips. All that old grease and dirt—not to mention human saliva—packed down between those dark cracks. God, he wouldn't serve his maid in this . . . . Well, he wouldn't serve his maid in anything, but . . . . He sort of dropped the cup into its saucer and quickly dabbed his lips with the white paper napkin which had covered his lap. God, it was likely as germ-ridden as the cup. Sometimes he wondered why he ever left his apartment at all. It had to be the only truly clean place in Capital City. Maybe in the whole country . . . except, possibly, for Laura Lee's. Nobody could've had a better Mother for a teacher when it came to being impeccable in one's housekeeping. "Emmy Lou tells me that you came down with a case of woods fever this summer. Is that right?"

Matthew covered his face with his hands, his elbows slouched over the table. The boy'd learned well from his Mama. His line of reasoning departed from fastidiousness and led to order. But at what cost? There's a kid right now living inside a bubble because he has no resistance, no immunities, no anti-bodies. That's the logical absurdity. All of us humans bouncing around in our very own hermetically sealed little self-contained bubbles. And us humans are sure as chitterlings bound to take anything to its logical absurdity . . . at least once. He hoped that Poper had not seen the disgust pulling at his lips like a snarl. It wasn't meant for him . . . at least not specifically for him alone. Inside his hands his words sounded like echoes rather than the source. Rudy Valle . . . . My time is your time . . . . Winchester Cathedral or 73. "Yes. Wood fever. That's as good a name for it as any." He cocked his head, controlled his lips. Could he let his hands down now? "I'm pretending to be a cro-magna."

"For God's sake, why?"

Safe now. Snarl's gone. Dropping his hands, he revealed a full-lipped grin. "I want to be able to understand your world . . . ." He waved his arms about to indicate the world all around them. Wish Emmy Lou wouldn't talk to him so damned much. But who else is there for her to talk to? Really. Alecia? Jason? No help. Me? Just ironic that he's also the gossip of the university's English department.

Oh, God! Here it goes again. Another Matthew Parkrow sermon on something or another. What this time, I wonder?

Every fall it's the same. 'Emmy Lou says you came down with something-or-other. She said you couldn't get anything done. A shame . . . .' That should be coming next. For four fucking years now, Christ. A change in this script is in order.

"She said you couldn't get any work done." Poper wobbled his tiny head. "A real shame, I'd say. I was so looking forward to reading it . . . ."

Whatever it might prove to be, right? Matthew nodded. Patience. He nodded again for emphasis. Sipped his coffee. "I have to learn to think like you before I can write anything for you to read. Thus, my cro-magna act." He watched Poper light a Vantage. It was inserted into a Water-Pik filtered mouthpiece: An opaque plastic cigarette holder. Once the sign of sophistication or snobbery depending on which end of the holder you were on, the cigarette holder had become relegated to symbolizing addiction and the nasty task of filtering out nicotine and tars so people like Poper could pretend to quit smoking. Poor Poper was on his fourth fourth filter. He'd made it through the first filter easy enough, and the second. It was by the third filter that he began to become grouchy, fidgety. Matthew couldn't even get papers graded in peace. That fourth filter, though, was the killer. Practically no tar and nicotine at all in the smoke. He was working on his fourth one of those filters now. This was supposed to be the level at which he would be able to quit.

Poper wanted desperately to stop, but he just couldn't. It was such a nasty habit. The only one he had. But people like Matthew and his own Mother made it practically impossible to stop. He needed something to chew, to gum, to knaw, something to do, to drum, to draw, something to do with his hands, some kind of shield. They both agitated him so . . . Laura Lee Dryden and Matthew Parkrow. Come, Matthew, what park do you row? What social rash do you itch now?

"I just can't—for the life of me—understand a society that can let those people go free."

"Huh?"

Matthew felt his body tremble. He sucked in a deep breath, held it, let it out slowly. Only a little more and he'd begin to shake outwardly. He breathed deeply again and exhaled slowly. If it were only socially acceptable behavior for him to reach across the lunch table and strangle poor Poper Dryden rather than have to tolerate his existence any longer.

"What people?"

Blank face, blank eyes. Like a ghoul. The seventeenth figure. Dry-rot robes falling like Spanish moss from his limbs. "Those people . . . ." He bit the tip of his tongue. Don't say 'Stupid!', stupid. Leave him alone. He can't help it. Matthew pointed toward the headline on the Durham Sun front page which was being held up in front of Stanley Slater's face by his nicotine stained fingers. You could recognize the chairman of the Philosophy Department anywhere even with his face hidden by KENT STATE DEFENDANTS ABSOLVED. He always wore his university red-and-white Adiddas just in case he could scare up a quick set or three of tennis.

Poper slumped further into his chair. Oh, God . . . . "God, Matthew. That's five years old, for Christ's sake!"

"That's today's paper . . . ." He bit his tongue again. No. This time say it. He banged his fist on the formica top attached to a steel stand. It rattled the cups in their saucers. Everyone for six tables around turned to see what had caused the noise. All but Stanley Slater, that is. He only turned the page of his Durham Sun and contemplated being and somethingness. "Today's paper! Today's headlines! Today's news!" Say it! "Stupid!"

No, don't do this to me, Poper shuddered. Why me? Why me, Lord? Please. No. "Now, Matthew. Calm down, Matthew. Please. Let's be rational . . . ah . . . let's reason together . . . . Okay?"

"Reason!" He stopped yelling and began whispering almost in the same breath, suddenly aware that he had disrupted everyone's breakfast. "Rational . . . reason . . . shit. That's based upon the assumption of two rational people. Right?"

Poper nodded, almost as if hypnotized.

"So, how in the hellll . . . . ." He threw up his hands, completely exasperated.

"We've just got to go on, Matthew," Poper responded, seeming to snap out of his trance-like state. "Forget such things as Kent State . . . ." He shrugged toward Slater's paper. "All that's in the past now. Let's forgive and forget. Let it rest." He smiled, an indulgent smile. "Like your revered Beatles said: 'Let it be' . . . ." The only times he could ever feel superior to Matthew Parkrow were the times when he was like this, struggling to remain in control. He was almost contrite, now. Enjoy it . . . .

"That's not what they were talking about, you fool." Matthew seemed to almost whimper. Poper's answer for everything: forgive and forget. What would happen, then, to history? Where would the tension needed to charge life come from? 'If you'll just forgive Jason, just blank out his sins from your memory, then you'll be free of all guilt.' How? Forget that he sold the forests he'd promised to save for me and my children in order to build himself a goddamned chemical plant, a housing development, and an industrial park? Forget the chemicals that fell from crop dusters in the Christmas sky? That was what dear Poper had told him more than once. He had read it right out of a book on abnormal psychology or abominable philosophy, so he said. What was the title? Guilt is Better? Something like that. Matthew would snarl in his mind when he said it. That wasn't going to stop these breakdowns or outbursts or whatever they were from happening. Nothing would. And the spells were coming more often and more unawares these days. Sneaky bastards would outburst without warning. Like here. He had been in the midst of this one before he realized what was happening. Usually, he had some warning. "Sorry for being so loud. But, damn it, that's why I can't do anything . . . write . . . anything . . . ."

"Why?"

Zombied eyes washed out gray as the sea before a hurricane. "I don't understand the language and logic of your planet." I don't understand your dead eyes, your programmed speech, your tailored clothing, your capped teeth . . . . Matthew pulled at his beard as if the strands were worry beads. "I don't understand . . . ." *Those are the pearls that were his eyes . . . .*

Yes. While you still can, before Matthew fully recovers, do something drastic! "Ms. Mac!" Order more coffee. Say it quick. The moment won't last much longer. She's standing right there, just two tables away. She must hear me. "Ms. Mac!" He waved. "Refills please." She hears me, damn it. I know she does. "Ms. Mac?" Why is she always ignoring me?

"Two refills please, Ms. Mac, when you get a chance?" Matthew's voice was not much above a whisper yet Ms. Mac's head snapped around.

"Sure, Matthew. Just a couple of minutes."

"Thanks . . . ."

"I'll take a fresh cup myself, Ms. Mac."

Ms. Mac beamed over her shoulder as Emmy Lou walked by her and patted her flabby shoulder bunched under her white daycron and nylon waitress dress. That Emmy Lou was pure sunshine, she was.

Matthew heard her breathless voice drifting through smells of ham and eggs, sausage, bacon, hash browns, grits dribbling with margarine and the sputter and roll of coffee in the urns. The rattle of other morning voices packed the dining room again. Her arms bulged with school supply store bags. "Jesus, never knew I'd need so many books," she muttered toward Ms. Mac as she glided across the room, tossing her taffy hair off her face which was flushed from the nippy breeze just blowing up. It was unseasonably cold for August.

"Hi, baby," she whispered in his ear before she pecked his lips. "Ummm . . . egg yellow . . . ." She plopped packages into the empty chair next to Poper. His eyes saw hers. "Poper." She hardly looked at him as she crossed behind Matthew and settled into the chair between them. It wasn't that she disliked Poper or anything. In fact, like Matthew, she felt more pity for him than anything else. And he was a good listener when she needed one. Everyone had their good points. But damn it, the first day of classes and they can't even leave him alone long enough for them to have breakfast together . . . alone. Soon enough Matthew's new students would become regulars at Mac's. They would swarm his table in the mornings. Soon enough he'd become public property again. Spring vacations, the summers, Christmas . . . sometimes. That was about it. Eight months of the year he belonged to his students and, when he could muster up the courage, to his writing. Four months a year was all she was able to grab any real part of for herself. But she knew this was the order of his passions. And nothing held her other than herself. She could walk out the door of the Gypsy whenever she wanted to. But she had accepted that order of things because she loved him and because she, too, understood the lure, the needs . . . . She sensed his genius but also that he seemed to need . . . . What? A steadying hand? Some kind of true focus. She turned to Matthew. His face was pale, tensed around the jaw muscles. His breath was shallow. He had a spell. Ignore it. If you say anything, then it'll just embarrass him. "Guess who I saw this morning?"

"Who?"

"Alecia. I had coffee and sweet rolls with her after I dropped you off at English this morning."

"Hell. I thought you were going to say you had snorted cocaine with Mick Jagger . . . or something."

"Ppppppp!" She stuck her tongue out at him. She had done that when he teased her ever since she could remember.

"So?"

Poper stiffled a belly laugh as best one can stiffle a belly laugh.

"So . . . . Jason was there, too."

Matthew averted his eyes. For a moment, her face seemed to have no eyes, only sunken sockets with blue and purple veins palpitating where the eyeballs should have been. He pretended to read the autographs on the photograph hanging on Mac's wall. State University's first National Championship basketball team. What a year . . . seventy-four. We won the NCAA and Nixon got the sack. "God, Matthew! He looks like a skeleton with waxpaper skin wrapped around its bones. He's just wasting . . . ." She struggled with a quiver in her voice. "Wasting away . . . ."

He could see the moisture in her crystal eyes. He had always felt that he could see right into her brain through her eyes. However the one thing for sure he couldn't read through those eyes was why she had such an emotional committment to reconciling him and Jason.

"What's wrong with Mayor Parkrow, Emmy Lou?"

"Ma-yor Park-row, shit," Matthew mumbled underneath his coffee-stale breath.

"Matthew," she chastised. Her face flushed. Turning to Poper, she fought for control of her skin color. "The doctors, Poper, are saying he's developed all the symptoms of cancer . . . but they can't find any cancerous cells anywhere in his body." Her head suddenly heavy, dropped into her hands.

Poper shook his head, clucking his tongue like the hen he sometimes was. "That's really unusual, huh?"

"Unusual. Indeed," Matthew snarled, no longer mumbling. "You are the master of understatement, Poet Laureate Dryden. I was under the distinct impression, myself, that cancer was a disease of the living."

"Matthew!"

That snapped her head up out of her hands. "Matthew . . . Matthew . . . Matthew . . ." he crowed in a falsetta which cracked with every th syllable. His hands flapped wildly.

Emmy Lou grasped at his flailing hands, caught them in hers, and stared at his eyes until they seemed to be pulled into hers. She felt him beginning to breath deeply, holding each breath and letting it out slowly. "Baby, he says he's gonna die soon, and he wants to see you just once before he dies, you know, to talk about some things . . . to make his peace with you . . . Matthew . . . his only son . . . his only child. If it was any one of your precious students, you'd be there in a flash."

"My precious students take me for what I am. Jason—my precious father—couldn't accept me for what I was when I was only a radical, commie, pinko queer, now could he? He couldn't accept my not wanting to sully myself with the filth of his house . . . oh, the murders . . . the murders he's committed in the name of the people . . . ." He trembled, clenched icy fingers around Emmy Lou's vice-like hands. "Not real murders, mind you. Oh, no! He doesn't go out and assassinate opposing candidates or little old lady's who disagree with his point of view . . . oh, no!

"He's too fucking smart for that! He kills birds and fish and cats and dogs . . . things that can't fight back. He kills them with chemicals. He kills them with ordinances and statutes. He kills wilderness with power stations and subdivisions. He kills communities like our Roanoke Park with the absurdity of power." Matthew gasped a breath almost like an asthmatic and enunciated the words he spoke as he exhaled very deliberately. "Jason *is* the cancer!" The words hissed from his larynx.

"But, baby . . . ."

"Think of Jason as a cell, and you'll see the cancer which the earthling doctors cannot perceive!"

"But, Matthew, he's a fellow human being . . . your father!"

"Yes, Matthew. Your father . . . ."

"I'm an anti-body. Jason's the infection I'm programmed to fight."

"Baby, he's desperate for your understanding . . . ."

"That is my understanding . . . ."

"And . . . your forgiveness . . . ." Her head drooped. Taffy curls spilled over her shoulders, hiding her eyes, her cheeks. He couldn't take the tears. That wouldn't be fair, especially with him in this state . . . . She rubbed her hands over her face as if she were tired. "Can't you give a little for your own father?"

Matthew shook his head.

"Maybe that's what makes him a disease, Matthew. Did you ever think of that? That his disease is your lack of forgiveness?"

"That's all very Greek, Madame Bovary, but . . . ."

"Of his failure in his own mind with his only son . . . ."

"But also . . . a genuine crock!" Matthew smirked and shoved his chair back from the formica top table. As he stood, he snatched his legal pad and stack of note cards and stuffed them, along with his Flair black ink pen, into his plaid cloth back pack. "I've got to go to the tower." He touched Emmy Lou's hands with his fingers as he moved off behind her. "I'll see you after my one o'clock class for lunch." He kissed her neck. "Okay?"

Her heavy lips pouted. "Okay . . . I guess . . . ."

"Okay."

"I presume then that I must tell Alecia that you decline her invitation to dinner this evening?"

"If she ever thought otherwise, she was fooling herself and you and Jason . . . and she damn well knows it!" She knows better. She remembers the forests Jason promised to save for me . . . for us! And the meadowlark I had to bury in the hole . . . the Christmas of sixty-eight. Aldrin walked on the moon and killed that meadowlark.

"I'll keep a close eye on Emmy Lou for you, Matthew."

"I'm sure you will, Carrot. Just don't keep the kind of eye on her that you said you were keeping on that new TA's wife," Matthew smirked as he ambled toward the open doorway which connected the dining room with the counter service area.

"No. Never. Of course not, Matthew."

Snapping his fingers, he turned eyeing the packages in the chair between Poper and the chair where he had just been sitting . . . empty now. "You have any money left, Madame Bovary?"

"Yes." She still would not look up at him.

"Will you take care of the check, then?"

"Don't I always . . . ?"

He turned into the steamy front room, seeming to dissolve in the vapors.

"He sure wiggled out of that one, Emmy Lou?"

"He always does . . . ." She wagged her head, her eyes straining to follow Matthew's form in the steam as he groped his way to the front door leading out of Mac's onto Hillsborough Street. Across the street, the tower, awaiting him. "He always does."

Poper slumped over his stained coffee cup, the steam rising around his face. "I just don't understand him Emmy Lou. I only wish I had a father . . . ." His gray eyes moistened as he ran his hands through red curls. "Mine ran out on us when I was just two. Can you believe that? Left me and my mother because he wanted one mint julip . . . and another . . . and another . . . ."

"I'm really sorry, Poper . . . ."

"Yes. I was, too . . . ."

"I had no idea . . . ."

"It's okay, Emmy Lou. Practically nobody knows, so how could you?"

"Well . . . ." She pressed her fingers against Poper's arm, softly. She almost flinched against the pain she felt coming from inside him.

"I guess I still am sorry, you know, because, when I heard the hatred in Matthew's voice directed at his father, it made my insides knot up and go all numb. You know what I mean?"

"I know what you mean, all right." She scratched the back of her neck under her taffy hair. "I never knew my father at all . . . or my mother, either, for that matter. Jason and Alecia have been my family . . . my mother and father, so to speak." She smiled reluctantly. "And, of course, Matthew . . . ."

"Of course . . . ."

"Refill anyone?" Ms. Mac waddled by their table with a Silex pot in her hand full of fresh steaming coffee.

"Thanks, Ms. Mac." Emmy Lou looked up from where her eyes had been riveted to the tabletop. "You, Poper?"

"Yes, please. I think one more'll do it." That Ms. Mac. The old bag won't come near me usually, but as soon as Matthew leaves she starts hanging around with the coffee pot to keep an eye on Emmy Lou for her precious Matthew. My, my, my. I made a rhyme.

Ms. Mac eyed Matthew's half-empty cup. The milk seemd to gather at the top of the coffee as it had cooled. "Will Matthew be wanting a refill too?"

Emmy Lou swirled a spoonful of sugar into the amber liquid in her thick cup. "No. He's gone over to the tower to do some more research on his dissertation, Ms. Mac."

"Oh?" Ms. Mac's pastry jowls flopped. The smile which burst onto her face was parental. "He finishes this year, doesn't he, Emmy Lou?" He'd become like her own substitute son, the one she and her husband never were able to have. No children at all, in fact. And they never knew why. Was he sterile? Was she? A quick trip to the doctor would have given them their answer. And, they'd made appointments with their doctor on five different occasions when they were still young, still eager, still feeling the primal urge to procreate.

And, five times Mac had cancelled out at the very last minute . . . too much work at the restaurant . . . or something . . . .

"We hope so, Ms. Mac. We surely do hope so. Right now everything depends on him getting that dissertation completed and approved . . . ."

Ms. Mac understood why Mac was always too busy or something. What if it was him? He never would've been able to live with that. Maybe it was better that they never knew. So, she smiled, thinking of the times past when Matthew would come in and write for hours at one of the tables off in the corner away from the crowds. That was before he'd become sort of a living legend (her lips twitched into a grin). "Then he can get back to writing again like John-Boy on 'The Waltons.'"

"Yes. I hope so, yes."

"I know. I remember when y'all first come in here. What's it been now? Going on five years, ain't it? He used to sit here for hours every afternoon scribbling page after page and drinking cup after cup of my coffee . . . . And smoking those cigarettes . . . ."

"Ms. Mac!" A bass voice rumbled from across the room next to the fogged picture windows by the sidewalk bordering Hillsboro Street. She waved. "See y'all later." She stared hard at Poper, then waddled toward the fogged plate glass windows.

Poper, stirring his coffee rather than drinking it to avoid further contact with the cruddy cup, stared after Ms. Mac, not really seeing her or the windows or Hillsboro Street or the brick walkways and buildings of the State University across the street. "When did he quit writing, Emmy Lou? Was it connected to when those spells of his started?"

Emmy Lou turned toward his words. They sounded hollow, recorded. "Hell, Poper, he's been like this ever since we've been here just about . . . at least as long as Ms. Mac remembers, right? Any mention of his father sends him into these fits. But, God, how he is with those kids is just magical . . . ."

"I know." Poper stopped stirring, placed the dripping stainless spoon on the saucer. "I've watched him in action a few times when he had classes out under the trees while the rest of us sweltered in our class rooms. It was almost scary, like watching Socrates with his following, though Matthew'd probably prefer the analogy to Lao Tze."

Emmy Lou nodded, sipped her coffee. A chill shattered her spine, filling every pore of her flesh with ice. What a strange day for August. Windy, damp, cold. Not cool, but cold. You'd think it was near November . . . .

"Rat run over your grave?"

"That's what Alecia might say."

"My mother, too." Poper wiped his cup rim with his napkin and sipped his coffee timorously. "Have you ever been able to pin him down to when his spells really started? You know, like in childhood or after Vietnam or whatever?"

"No. But I don't think it's anything quite that easy, Poper." She smiled tolerantly. She was more and more beginning to realize why Matthew did it so often, himself. That was mostly what you had to do in life . . . tolerate the predictability of most people's thoughts. She sipped her coffee to drown a sigh. "But I first became aware of them, myself, back in . . . when was that? Sixty-nine? Yes. When he made that crazy pilgrimmage of his to the New Mexico desert looking for the birthplace of our generation. At least that was what he said . . . ." She continued to sip her coffee. "But I think it was something else."

"Oh, yes. What, then?"

"We were living in New York then, going to Columbia. That was not long before we went to Woodstock . . . ."

"You-all were at Woodstock?"

"Yeah."

"That must've been scar . . . ah . . . something?"

She nodded, ignoring Poper's slip toward his reality. "I'd've been at Altamont, too, but Matthew wouldn't let me go with him, and I guess I was afraid to try it alone. He arranged to meet me at Yellowstone because he was afraid that Altamont might turn into a real nightmare . . . ." She sipped again at her coffee then nestled the chipped cup into its saucer. One more cup of coffee before I go into the valley below. "And, it did, if you recall, become a real nightmare."

Poper nodded. "Read about it."

"Me, too, damn it. Me, too!"

"Strange though, you know?"

"What?"

"Matthew's prediction."

"Maybe. Maybe not. He always seems to be able to predict things. Why I can remember him telling me—that same year I think it was, after he'd come back from that damned desert—that Capital City would have twice as many movie theaters in seventy-six as it had in sixty-nine." She paused.

Poper's mouth was partly opened as he awaited her next words.

"And just figure it out for yourself. Here we sit in seventy-five, and there are twelve theaters. In sixty-nine there were six. And what's so amazing about it all is that in sixty-nine, two of the six theaters were about to close down and he knew it. Everyone around him saw movies going under the avalanche of television. "But," she grinned, "not my Matthew. No sir. He saw more movies. And, as usual, he was right."

"Very strange . . . . You know, we were just talking about him being so damned right about things all the time just before you came in."

"Anyway, maybe it all gives more credibility to his theory that the secret of humanity is in birth and not in the search for the father crap we're always being fed in books and literature classes."

"I don't understand . . . ."

"Well, he's been alone in his beliefs before and been proved to be right. Why not with this new theory of his?"

Poper de javeau shrugged. Without realizing it, he glanced at Matthew's seat to make sure he wasn't sitting in it.

"Part of his theory proof is the notion that Ulysses isn't really based on the theme of the search for the father after all, rather on the theme of birth. He uses the Oxen of the Sun episode where Mrs. Purefoy is giving birth and Stephen and Buck Mulligan and the boys are raising hell in the waiting room as his point of departure . . . ." She frowned. "I think . . . ."

"So, what does he say about it? I've never heard this one before, and I'm his office mate. I thought that I heard them all . . . first."

"Well, let's see. I'm not too familiar with Ulysses . . . ." She touched her pouty lips with fingers warm from the coffee cup. "It's got something to do with the Oxen of the Sun giving birth to the psyches of Stephen and Bloom . . . of man . . . ."

"Does this new theory have anything to do with his growing obsession with that damned dissertation of his on the vaginal symbols of literature?"

"I think it's all tied together somewhere in that computer of his he calls a brain . . . everything from the milk white sea in *Moby Dick* to the Houston Astrodome to interstellar space . . . ." She paused, fumbling with her cup, not looking at Poper but at the tabletop. "And, it's all linked up, somehow, with his search for his best friend who he thought had been killed in Vietnam. I think that's why he went into that desert all those years ago . . . ."

"Well, Emmy Lou. I guess we'll never know that for sure, huh?"

"No, probably not."

"But, you can still reconcile him with Jason. It's important that you do. Believe me, I know what it's like to not have a father." He sipped nervously and without caution at his coffee, seeming to forget the dirty cracks in the cup and the germs lurking there.

"I hope I can, Poper. I surely hope so."

Emmy Lou sat in their aqua-over-white VW van's chair-like seat. The van had replaced the

Travel-All that first winter back in Capital City when what was left of the heater had finally gone on them, and Matthew had become convinced that the old International was irreparable. So, they traded it for three hundred dollars difference on the VW van, money which Matthew had earned by writing advertising campaigns for two local real estate firms. He had always been good that way. Crazy as he was and impossible as the "material" world seemed to be for him at times, he could always raise sums of money in a hurry when they really had to have it. He could create and write ad campaigns, build houses, or deal dope with the best of them when he had a mind to. But he never seemed to have his mind to any of it for very long. Nothing seemed to hold his mercurial mind except the teaching and the writing.

As she glanced into the side mirror, Emmy Lou realized the road was clear. She turned on the ignition, pushed in the clutch and turned the steering wheel slightly to the left as the van began rolling into the street from its parking place in front of the West Side Presbyterian church. They used to have dances in there on Friday nights after they played Capital City in football or basketball.

She never could understand why they didn't have dances after baseball games too. Poor Matthew'd been in more than one tussle because of her being part black, though she mostly passed unless people knew her background. Not many folks knew the facts even now . . . that she was the Mayor's maid's niece who lived with them as part of the family because her mother had deserted her when she was born a bastard.

As the van gathered momentum on the downhill toward Hillsboro, she popped the clutch with the VW in first. It sputtered, caught. She revved the engine as she applied the brakes at the red light and shoved in the clutch. Matthew had promised her he'd fix the damned thing if he could ever figure out what was wrong. She felt it was just that the battery was low, maybe one of the cells was dying . . . like Jason . . . or dead. Matthew was avoiding his father as much as he was avoiding fixing the van.

"If I didn't love the crazy fucker so much, then I'd leave him for the cruelty he shows to Jason, damn it!" She felt her fist hitting the steering wheel. I know he's ornery, bullheaded . . . just like Matthew is. I know he's a destroyer . . . just like Matthew says. I know he's

Matthew's father . . . whether Matthew admits to it or not. He does want . . . no, need . . . his son's forgiveness and understanding. To see that poor old man wasting away in front of my eyes . . . . "Makes me weep . . . ." She turned right with the green light, running through the gears as she steered the van along Hillsboro Street which started at the Capitol in the center of the city planned for a site near Isaac Hunter's Tavern and ran west past the State Fair Grounds where it became two lanes for the last eight winding miles to Roanoke Park.

"I ought to leave anyway, the way he's been acting lately . . . ." Brooding like Camus' Marceau, not wanting to do anything but get high and stay for days in those damned forests behind the trailer. He's built some kind of lean-to near the pond where he keeps his fishing lines and such. Often he brings home bass for the freezer . . . and that's not bad. We like fish. All that protein and iodine. It's his other camp . . . miles deep into the forests . . .further than I've ever been in, I guess, because even I can't find it . . . the one he refers to as "Deep Camp" . . . that is when he refers to it at all . . . .

That's where he keeps his Montagnard cross bow. I know he practices with it when he's away, though he never says so. Denies it if I ask him directly. But I can tell. He used to bring home rabbits and squirrels sometimes, implying he had trapped them. But those holes in their necks weren't from trap claws.

They were bolt wounds. She knew that much! It was sort of like when cat began bringing home the game it was learning to catch and leaving it on the front porch for our approval. Then, one day, about a year ago, Matthew stopped bringing home game. He became even more secretive about his time in the forests. The only places he spent more time were the tower or the Amphitheater Gardens.

Emmy Lou let up on the gas and tapped the brakes while down-shifting to third as the van ran up a little too close on the rear of a battered fifty-six Chevy pick-up. As she hit the gas, passing the pick-up in the eastbound lane when the way was clear, she saw a shotgun on the rifle rack hung across the rear window of the truck. Matthew'd be furious if he saw that. He hates guns as much as I do. It's an affront. That's what it is. I thought Matthew hated all weapons . . . but he damned sure seems to have developed a kind of love affair with that frigging Montagnard crossbow of his. I don't see the difference myself between that and a gun . . . . Both are idiot winds . . . .

It must be really hard on him, though, being on such good behavior for all this time . . . four years . . .going on five now . . . . It takes a lot of energy out of a person to be good . . . at least as good as he's capable of . . . . After all, it could be that he was going through male menopause . . . at thirty-one? Not likely. Or? Another woman? One of his students, maybe? Those girls worshipped him. They'd do anything for him. Absolutely anything. She saw it in their eyes . . . and, so would the boys.

But, no. My only real competition is the same as it's always been . . . his wild thoughts, his rampant imagination, his all-consuming intellect that sometimes seems to siphon knowledge indiscriminately like tomato suckers. This Kent State thing today really set him off though. More than usual. Wow. Then, again, it set me off too! World's really gone to hell since Richard became king; now even after he's been run off his throne like a farmer from his outhouse by a swarm of hungry horse-flies, his legacy lays on the land like a killer frost. What was it Dylan said? What's wrong is right, and what's right is wrong . . . . Something like that.

"Wonder if there's anything more on the Kent State thing?" Emmy Lou flipped on the radio which was always tuned to WDBS. The closing bars of "Dark Side of the Moon" nearly startled her. Then the announcer's voice rumbled through the tinny speaker dangling below the dash by its wires. Matthew was supposed to fix that too . . . .

"Jason Parkrow, Mayor of Roanoke Park, said this morning in a statement released by his press secretary from his home where the Mayor is recuperating from a slight illness that (and I quote): 'The Kent State decision was only right and just. Political leaders, educators, and military personnel should not be held accountable financially for doing what was deemed necessary and proper under stressful circumstances . . . such as those which prevailed in 1970 on the university campuses in Ohio and the rest of America.' The Mayor's statement went on to say that it 'would be disastrous to the American way of life if damages were ever awarded under such circumstances by any American court!'"

Emmy Lou kicked the floorboard with her left foot as she flipped off the radio in disgust. "I'll bet Matthew already knew this . . . at Mac's . . . ." How the hell does Jason expect me to ever persuade Matthew to talk with him if he keeps running off at the press release with such drivel as that. "Damn!" Why can't the old goat keep his mouth shut? He's a politician, after all . . . . She had to chuckle. "Well, Jason, if ever there were any lingering hopes of a reconciliation, I'm afraid you and your press secretary have just fucked them . . . royally!"

A blue Cadillac darted in front of the van from an unmarked dirt-and-gravel road by the fair grounds. Emmy Lou shoved the clutched in, downshifted, and hit the brakes hard, but even, like a pro driver. Tires squalled beneath her. The beehive mannequin behind the wheel of that spit polished, new Caddy shot a look at her over a chinchilla-wrapped shoulder that, if looks could kill, Emmy Lou would've been dead.

"Christ! You'd think that I was the one who pulled out in front of you . . . bitch!" Emmy Lou felt her high cheeks rushing with blood. Moisture blurred her vision, though, so she fought the tears. "Damn tears. They come so quickly . . . ." Guess she owns the road because she can afford a Cadillac gas-guzzler. Right? Wrong! Emmy Lou punched the accelerator to the floor and ran back through the gears . . . a safe distance beyond Beehive Betty. You ought to be driving a Ford, lady. A Gerald one. That's a sister? Emmy Lou spat out the crack in the door window.

"Shit!" A little trucking music, if you please, to calm my shaking body. She again flipped on the radio and began to hum and sing with George Harrison.

> *Don't need a love in, don't need a bedpan,*
> *you don't need a horoscope or a microscope*
> *to see the mess that you're in . . . .*

As the tune took her over, she smiled and bounced up and down on the cushioned seat in rhythm with the music.

> *If you open up your heart, then you will*
> *know what I mean.*

We've been kept down so long,
Someone's thinking that we're all green.
While the Pope owns fifty-one percent of
General Motors,
The stock exchange is the only thing
that's qualified to quote us . . . .

Aprospogo. Mayor Jason Parkrow was stenciled in black on the silver mailbox. The red flag was still up. Beside it, the gravel driveway gleamed like hominy in the sun now breaking through cumulous clouds overhead. Like Matthew, she could remember when this was nearly all forests, when the highway was only a dirt path going only to the power plant two miles west—a steel gray tower, with heavy black cables sliding from it over the tops of pines, maples, and oaks toward the small settlements dotting the forests. But for years now the woods had been vanishing and the road had become a two-lane blacktop stretching to Chapel Hill.

"At least," she smirked as she geared down three times before turning into the driveway, "they didn't force interstate Forty through here. They fucked up somebody else's land instead. And, as Matthew says, it wasn't because his father didn't try to get the damned thing run through Roanoke Park." Because Jason did. Emmy Lou remembered that much herself. Old Jason lobbied his ass off to get an exit ramp at Roanoke Park when all else had failed. He had not been successful, so it was his very next election when he had relied so heavily on Matthew's war hero status to get himself re-elected in spite of that failure . . . though only by a couple of hundred votes. Not what you would call a mandate, that's for sure . . . . But, somehow, he'd held on all these years . . . .

The Parkrow home sprawled in a natural meadow in the maples about two hundred yards from the highway. The cinnamon Continental which had, over the years, become Jason Parkrow's trademark since he'd first been elected mayor was parked in front of the newest addition to the house, a two-car garage. He was still at home, then. Well, sure he is. That's what the radio news reports said. Against her will, Emmy Lou side-glanced out the window toward the next house a few hundred yards away. It had been built on top of the place they called the hole. Matthew's never seen this garage or that house over the hole. He doesn't know that the maple grove is all that's left. Never could get up the courage to tell him that Jason had filled in the hole and cut all the rest of the trees down around it and built a house on it and sold it. Matthew'd have killed him with his crossbow probably . . . well, in his nightmares anyway. I don't really think he'd actually kill his father . . . not physically at least . . . .

As she turned off the engine and jerked up the emergency brake, she wasn't all that sure. She was sure that she had not turned around in the driveway before cutting off the engine. So, she'd just have to jump the damned thing in reverse. A little more tricky, but she'd seen Matthew do it many times. No problem. No one yet peeping out of the kitchen windows covered with bright pink-and-blue flowered curtains. No one yet at the door. There seemed to be no one at home, but she knew they were both inside. They had to be. Maybe they hadn't heard her drive up. She fumbled in her purse, finally extracting a bent joint and some of Mac's matches. She lit the joint after straightening it with careful fingers, inhaled deeply, and held the smoke in her lungs for a long time. It rushed to her brain. "All right!" A few hits and I'll be able to play at this peacemaker shit once again." She held the joint between her flushed lips, stretching in her patched jeans and threadbare work shirt, both spattered with old paints. She picked at dried clots on her thighs, remembering . . . .

Jason: I'll buy you whatever you want, Emmy Lou, honey. Matthew can't buy you what you want. He can't even buy you dinner.

Emmy Lou: The first thing I do in new clothes, Jason, is paint.

He gawked at her as if she had said that she'd eaten fried shit cakes for breakfast or something.

Jason: In new clothes? The new clothes I buy you?

She nodded.

Jesus, why do I give a damn about all this shit anyway. Must be my sign. Today it said in the paper that Aquarius was to be more diplomatic and tactful in family affairs. Hell, I thought they were talking about those stupid reruns with Sebastian Cabot and company on channel five. It's on a par with their news coverage and editorial policies. She sucked a deep drag off the joint, then snuffed it in the ashtray as she picked up her plain leather pocketbook, handcrafted by a North Carolina mountain woman out of Blowing Rock. Matthew'd given it to her for her birthday last year. He had bought it for her. He could buy things, just not the things Jason would want him to buy. She shoved the van door open. It squeaked and rattled as she dropped to the cement and slammed it shut. There. They should know that I'm here now. The Aquarian peacemaker . . . or is that pacemaker?

Through the middle of the three kitchen windows a black face peered between barely parted curtains into the cool August morning. Alecia waved, smiled a toothless smile showing her purple gums. She'd long since lost all vanity, though she used to be quite a looker. Not smiling, Emmy Lou waved back as she shuffled through the open garage door toward the kitchen entrance. The door was opening before she hit the first of three brick steps to the entrance. When she entered, Alecia hugged her as though she'd been in Alaska for years rather than just having had coffee and sweet rolls with her a couple of hours earlier.

"Lordy, chile. Am Ah glad to see ya. Am ah ever glad . . . . The Mayor's getting on worse, chile . . . worser and worser . . . ."

Emmy Lou pushed out of Alecia's smothering embrace. "I don't know if you'll be so glad to see me when I tell you what I've come to tell you."

"Lordy, chile. Ah'm always glad to see ya." She reached for Emmy Lou's hands, but Emmy Lou kept backing away from her. "What is it, chile?"

"Where's Jason?"

"In the back, lying down for a spell, chile. He had a real bad attack just a few minutes ago. This sickness is near 'bout to get him, ya know?"

"I know." Emmy Lou drooped her head into her hands.

"And dem news folks won't leave de poor man alone." She wagged her pepper and salt head, tears welling in her dark eyes.

"I know." She patted Alecia's arm. "I know it's hard on you, Alecia. That's why I really hated to come back here this morning."

"Hate to come by and see Alecia? What's wrong wid you, girl?"

Emmy Lou turned her face away from the fears of the only woman she had ever known as mother. She couldn't look her in the eyes and tell her what she had to tell her.

"Matthew said . . . . Alecia, he believes that the only thing he has that his father can't take away from him is his ability to not forgive him. He said no . . . ." "Den, Master Matthew's good as kilt dah mayor . . . same as if he done pointed a gun at his haid and pulled dah trigger hisself . . . ."

"Alecia! You don't have any right to say that! Jason's as much to blame as Matthew . . . if not more. Haven't you heard the news this morning? What the Mayor said, knowing how his son . . . and I . . . feel?"

This time, it was Alecia who turned her eyes away from the tears of the young woman standing in front of her, the only one she had ever known as daughter.

"Come on, Alecia? Be real. If Matthew's pulling the trigger, then Jason's driving him to it. Shit! He just manufactured and loaded the goddamned gun. That's all!"

In his fifth floor corner cubicle of The Tower, Matthew adjusted recently acquired Ben

Franklin style reading glasses that he had just cleaned using his flannel shirt sleeve. "One of the penalties of encroaching age," he chuckled at the piles of books and papers cluttering his desk as he struggled with making the glasses stay up on the bridge of his nose. Each time he bent over to look at his work, the glasses slid down his nose and tugged at his hair. Finally, his ponytail fell in wild black curls over farming-hardened shoulders as it tumbled from an overly stretched violet braided elastic band.

Possibly, that was the reason his generation wasn't supposed to have trusted anyone over thirty. Citizens over thirty often didn't see well without assistance, he chuckled. However, he had to admit, there was nothing wrong with the view out of the two windows that converged in his office at a ninety-degree angle—the northeast corner of the tower. In fact, it provided him with a virtual panorama along Hillsboro Street in the direction of downtown and the Capitol. Against the distant gray-and-rose late morning horizon, he could just make out it's dome above the Capitol Park trees. That was the center of *his* city. Would it hold up against stately plump Buck's bowl of shaving cream and straight razor?

DESHIL HOLLES EMAUS.

Let's go south to Holles Street. First words of episode fourteen of *Ulysses*. Mocks the Fratres Arvales. Sung by twelve Roman priests . . . the Arval Brethren . . . in honor of plenty and fertility. Matthew scribbled notes on the yellow legal pad in front of him.

DESHIL HOLLES EMAUS.

The Tower sat atop a sprawling library and media complex which was somewhat like a cathedral, itself, to a plenty of fertility. It was just a matter of how selective one wished to be regarding fertility. Was a lot of Dewey-decimaled garbage more desirable than a few gems? Or, did the few gems, perhaps, only crystallize as a result of all that card catalog crap?

DESHIL HOLLES EMAUS.

Ah, yes. Just the sort of thing that should be occupying his time when he had so little of it left to complete his dissertation. No matter how often he stared at it, the desk calendar beside his note pad still read the same as in his regular office: August 28, 1975, the first day of fall classes. Only a few more days of reprieve before he'd be back to grading papers and counseling students again. The pad he scribbled on was nearly the same dull blond color as the table that served as his desk in his classroom, in everyone's classrooms.

Hoopsa, boyaboy, hoopsa cries the midwife. Then on to Tacitus and Sallust. Aelfric's Anglo-Saxon alliteration: *Before born babe bliss had. Within womb won he worship.* Wolfe. Sterne.

Melville, too, explored the womb from beginning to end. From chaos to chaos via any arbitrary kind of order. Ishmael's symbolic shipwreck is literal. Whereas the psyches of Bloom and Stephen break up in the ultimate shipwreck of language.

Matthew slipped his tattered Bobbs-Merrill edition of *Moby Dick* from beneath his opened and dog-eared *Ulysses*. Scrawled in the margins, his life tattooed the dark-edged pages in academic code. Notes and comments through two undergraduate readings in the middle sixties, one reading while awaiting trial in Washington, one time two years ago when he had taken a graduate course in Melville, and again, now, for his dissertation. Each time it was new.

"Call me Ishmael." Matthew flipped the pages through to the end where Ishmael clings to Queequeg's coffin as their ship, the Pequod, is sucked up in the vortex of creamy whiteness that is Melville's sea.

> *And I only am escaped to tell thee* . . . . *It was the devious cruising Rachel, that in her retracing search after her missing children, only found another orphan.*

Fearing not that he would become his enemy, Matthew became absorbed in his scrawling on the page. Some of these ideas had been playing around in his mind for weeks . . . only as whispered gibberish. Even on paper, he wasn't sure what he had, where he was going. He only knew, for sure, that he was going to get that Ph.D. He was going to become a professor at the University by the end of this academic year. If the dissertation didn't work out exactly along the lines he expected, then he would take it along the lines that worked out. And, then, he and Emmy Lou would get married. Matthew jerked his head up from his writing when he sensed someone behind him.

"Matthew?"

That single word from that one voice froze his spine. Yet, he still was able, somehow, to mark his place and finish his notes before leaning back in the wooden swivel chair with leather cushions, then, turning in the direction of the face with that voice. He gawked at the figure in the cubicle doorway. Rubbed his eyes. Looked again. "Yes?" He jerked his reading glasses off. Of course. That was it. He couldn't see anything at any distance with them on. "What may I do . . . ." His voice cracked. "My God!" His body trembled as he struggled to get out of his chair, nearly fainting as he stood. "My God. I can't believe it." Lazarus. "Ward! Ward Crampton!"

"I've looked everywhere for you, today, man. You're a hard one to track down." Ward Crampton reached out with open arms. The unkempt man lunged toward him, tears disappearing in his beard. "I seemed to keep on just missing you . . . ."

They embraced. He never would've recognized Matthew by his looks. The long hair . . . the beard . . . . They made him look so much different than he remembered. But, Matthew felt the same. He always had . . . since he was a child. Warm. Trembling. Unsure. Like his Doberman Lazlo was when . . . .

Yes. That night had been the longest one of his entire life. Even longer than nights in the VC Field Hospital when he didn't know if he'd ever even walk again. What truly made that particular night seemingly interminable was the inevitability of his decision. Linda bedded him down for the night in the corner of that gutted building in the alleys of Agadir. He knew that he had no choice. Or, at least, the choices available to him had created a situation where he realistically had *no* choice. What was it she had said to him that day? "You'll be Lazarus or you'll be dead"? Well, he hadn't done all the things he had done to survive only to die, then, in the deserts of Morocco. Not for something that was a freaky accident.

By the next morning, there was only one condition he felt he could reasonably demand in order to somehow save a little of his shattered face. Lazlo had to be allowed to go to the States with him. Linda would have to rescue his Doberman from the beach hotel where they had abandoned him.

Linda had grinned. "I'll take care of it personally, honey."

Matthew heaved in Ward's lean arms in the doorway of his cubicle. "I . . . I looked all over for you, too, man . . . for years after Nam . . . . Christ! I thought that I'd killed you, man!" Suddenly, he pulled back from this gaunt man in the doorway whose flesh, somehow, still seemed cool from the grave. His eyes. They were the same slate slits, a little more washed out maybe, but the same. His face. It retained its baby-like expressions. But, the lines down his cheeks had begun to harden.

"Jesus! I searched all over America for you, Ward. Even after I knew you must've really died in that crash, I kept on looking . . . . Atlanta, Woodstock, New York, Chicago, Altamont, even Alamogordo . . . ."

How could Ward wreck this trembling young man with the bearded face and the head full of flowing curls? What pain he had put him through already. Look at him. He almost collapsed as he retreated into his chair in relief that he isn't my murderer after all. How would he feel, I wonder, if he knew why I was back from my self-dug grave.

His old friend, Matthew. Ward averted his eyes, sliding his vision around the cubicle. Its walls were bare except for a calendar hanging just above Matthew's desk. The passing days had been marked off in blue magic marker just like a short-timer's calendar. His eyes gravitated to the windows. "Nice view of the city you've got here, man."

Matthew could not respond. He could only stare at the resurrection standing in front of him, his words short-circuited somewhere between his brain and his esophagus.

"Shit, you can see the capitol from here. I'll bet that's a great view at night when the dome's all lit up, huh?" Ward was not sure he could do this thing he had to do. But, he also was not sure he had any choice. "Only the best for the best TA and Ph.D. candidate, right?"

Hell, he knew what it was like to be the best. He could still hear the sounds of the jungles near Cambodia as if they surrounded him now. His mantel as the best. Torches circled them in the kerosene-soaked night. "But, Colonel Ting, I can't fight Lieutenant Jesse. He was my bunk mate at the hospital. He's . . . he's an American. He . . . he is my friend."

And, that was pretty much the way it was now, as well. If he didn't succeed in sabotaging his childhood friend, it would be back to Agadir and murder charges. There was no doubt, whatsoever, in heaven or in hell, that he would be convicted. Even Linda would testify to having bought guns and drugs from him and Rainier. She would say that Ranier approached him on Oasis Road that day to talk about some kind of deal or another. She'd swear that, during a heated disagreement, Ward Crampton, alias Spiderman, pulled a dagger from under his cloak and stabbed Rainier. He then forced her to run with him in Rainier's half-track which he stole. She and old Bow-Tie had it all figured out just in case they ever needed to throw him back to the lions. He was sure of that.

Ward's jaw muscles rippled. "I'm really sorry, Matthew." He forced his eyes toward Matthew's quivering face. "I know it must've been hell for you, man." He chewed his lower lip. In spite of himself, tears swelled in his eyes for the first time since Lieutenant Jesse's neck snapped in his hands. Yet, the tears could not fall. "I was able to escape, but I just couldn't face coming back like this." He slammed his fist into his dead right knee. "My major league career, gone. My life, gone. What was I going to do? I couldn't just . . . ."

DESHIL HOLLES EMAUS.

Matthew half-smirked. His eyes released their hold on Ward's flesh. Something was not right. It was not unlike the feelings he had experienced when he first met Crayon at the Democratic Convention demonstration in Chicago. When he reached out for Ward in his mind, in his feelings, Ward wasn't there. "Sure, Ward. My wounds were only in the brain. I guess I could face coming home like that a lot easier than you could come back with a bum knee." It was as if this man standing before him was just another nugget of fool's gold. A zombie of the Ward Crampton he had known.

Matthew stumbled up from his chair.

DESHIL HOLLES EMAUS.

"At least you could've let me know that you were alive, for Christ's sake!" His hands dangled at his sides like a gun fighter's. Where's my pistol?

"I'm truly sorry, Matthew . . . really, truly sorry . . . ."

Don't take your gun to town, Emmy Lou had begged and begged. So, he'd put his idea guns away like the gun fighter hangs up his forty-fours for the woman he loves . . . that is, if he lives long enough to find her in the first place.

DESHIL . . . .

In his mind, his fingers clutched for the pistol now hanging from an Emmy Lou wall.

HOLLES . . . .

"You'll have to come out to dinner this evening, Matthew. You and Emmy Lou. You can meet my wife, and my dog . . . and you and I can talk about old times . . . ."

EMAUS.

* * * * *

"Alecia was pretty damned upset, Matthew."

"She had no right to be."

"Well, whether she had a right to be upset or not, she was. And, now, she'll blame it all on you if Jason dies. That's all I know."

"Just because I wouldn't be the man who came to dinner, huh?" He slurped his semi-hot coffee from a white mug with commercial dishwasher cracks shot through it. "So fucking what? I don't give a shit who Alecia blames for what. She belongs to Jason. I don't!"

"You can be so unforgiving sometimes, Matthew." Her head dropped into her hands to hide her tears. "And so fucking cruel."

"Now, you two young folks better quit that quarreling," Ms. Mac scolded as she approached with their luncheon order. "That kinda mischief comes to nothing but no good, you know?" With her entrance came the reassertion of the smells of burgers and barbeque and the country style steak smothered in gravy "special," the clatter of silver ware against plates and tables, and the murmured dissonance of lunch time conversations about particle physics, this year's football schedule and bowl possibilities, Gautier's poetry, automobile break-ins on campus, the economics of freezing oil prices, and the availability of yoga classes near campus all packed into the crowded diner.

"It's okay, Ms. Mac. Just one of those on-going disagreements that all couples have. Nothing to be concerned about." Matthew could not remember a time when Ms. Mac gave off such an aura of disapproval in his direction. That was usually reserved for Poper.

"Watch your face, now, honey. This special is real hot."

Emmy Lou lifted her face from her hands and sat back in her chair so that Ms. Mac could set her plate on the table in front of her. She wiped her eyes on the sleeves of her blue work shirt. "Thanks,

Ms. Mac."

She sort of shoved Matthew's special in front of him with a disapproving grunt. "More coffee?"

"Thanks, Ms. Mac. Yes, please."

"Be right back . . . ."

As she turned to fetch the coffee pitcher, she shot a look at Matthew as if to say, 'don't you make that girl cry again while I'm gone.' Almost by reflex, he nodded reassuringly to her that he understood and began to wolf down the fork-tender round steak, green beans, and creamed potatoes and gravy as if he were on a time clock.

Emmy Lou still played with her food. Matthew mumbled through mouthfuls of Ms. Mac's thick, flaky biscuits which she had served them despite the fact that the special didn't offer biscuits, only white or wheat bread. But, Ms. Mac knew that they both dearly loved her home made buttermilk biscuits.

"Jesus. After all that searching . . . all over this fucking country . . . and he just shows up in the Tower . . . ." He continued to sop up the remaining gravy on his plate with another biscuit.

"What are you babbling about?

"Ward."

"Ward?" Her face contorted. "Matthew, I thought you'd put that ghost to rest a long time ago . . . . Ward's dead!"

"No."

"Yes, Matthew!" Tears blinded her eyes. "Please don't do this again."

"But, Madame Bovary. Listen to me, goddamn it! Ward **is** back!"

"Wwwhat?"

"He's back from the grave, Madame Bovary. As alive as you or me. Or so he seems. He just showed up at my Tower office about an hour ago. "

"What are you saying?"

"You heard me."

"Yes, but I don't believe what I'm hearing. You're telling me that Ward Crampton—our Ward Crampton—the Ward Crampton you almost gave up this relationship to try and find—is alive and right here on campus?"

"By Jove, I think she's got it!" Matthew mocked in an awful

imitation of a *My Fair Lady* English accent. "He's working on his M.A., and he'll be a TA. Teaches two Freshman comp classes."

"You seem to be taking this pretty well."

"I'm not taking it at all. That's the only thing saving me right now. I'm anesthesized on a table. I'm not taking it at all!"

"Jesus, Matthew. Speak of the devil. Look, on the TV!"

The head-and-shoulders shot of TV5 reporter Ida Stone filled the 19" screen perched on a corner shelf about eight feet above the floor. "MIA Ward Crampton was welcomed home yesterday by Roanoke Park Mayor Jason Parkrow who made one of his few public appearances in the last several months due to a persistent but undiagnosed illness.

"He presented Mr. Crampton with a key to the city . . . ." Video footage of Jason Parkrow presenting an over-sized key to the city of Roanoke Park on the steps of Roanoke Park City Hall replaced Ida on the screen. " . . . . The city where Ward Crampton grew up and played All-American baseball.

A photograph of Ward in his State University baseball uniform flashed on the screen. "He inked a deal with the Chicago Cubs after his first team All-American senior season. Young Ward Crampton was being heralded as the next Ernie Banks. He seemed guaranteed of a bright future in professional baseball.

"But, suddenly . . . ."

Helicopter gun ships flew across the screen firing into dense jungles beneath them. Rockets exploded. Small arms fire cracked from the cover of the canopies.

"The Vietnam war got in the way of his budding baseball career. His country called, and Ward Crampton answered that call. But, a VC rocket exploded the helicopter he was riding in over the Iron Triangle. Because his right kneecap was mostly torn away from his knee, he was not able to avoid capture. And he knew, very well, that once his leg healed, the ten or fifteen percent loss in range of motion in that right knee was definitely enough to keep him out of the major leagues. It didn't, however, prevent him from escaping from his captors and hiding out from the communists as best he could for several years. Just a few short months ago, he was finally able to make his way to Morocco where he pleaded with the U.S. State Department to help him get home."

The announcer's head-and-shoulders shot returned to the screen. "After a great deal of red tape, Ward Crampton was repatriated nearly seven years after he was captured. Unfortunately, he arrived home too late for his father, Henderson Crampton . . . the last of the old style country doctors in these parts. Ward and his new bride flew into the Capital City-Durham Airport just hours before his father's funeral. They were unaware, until their arrival, that his father had passed away."

Video footage of Ward hugging his wife in front of a West Capital City house flicked across the screen.

"Now, he and his wife, Linda, will be living in this modest, historically restored home in West Capital City near the State University where Ward is working on his Masters degree in literature and teaching Freshman composition."

"Linda?" Matthew's jaw dropped involuntarily. He covered it quickly with his hands. The woman in Ward's arms turned toward the camera almost as if she had heard him.

"Jesus Christ!" he muttered. "The 'sexy wife' Poper was telling me about at breakfast—right here at this very table . . . . That was Linda Tallefero."

"Are you babbling again, Matthew?"

"No. Ah . . . no. I was just remembering aloud that Ward invited us over to his modest, historically restored home in West Capital City for dinner this evening . . . to talk about the old days and meet his new wife and his dog."

"Linda, this is Matthew Parkrow, my oldest and dearest friend from childhood."

"Matthew. It's a real pleasure to meet you, finally. I've heard so much about you."

"We're colleagues, now, in the English Department."

"My lord, Ward does go on about you all and your exploits before the war and all. . . ."

Molly heeled at Matthew's left side. Her pink tongue drooped between bright canines. As she hassled, drops of moisture dribbled from the end of her tongue onto the thick grass. Her eyes sparkled with a sense of adventure. She seemed to smile.

"Especially that wonderful grand slam home run you hit to win the high school baseball state championship."

"Linda." Matthew quickly shook her hand almost without touching her skin and definitely without nibbling at her bait.

"And, this is Emmy Lou Black, Matthew's . . . ah . . . our . . . ah . . . friend." Ward cleared his throat. "Also from childhood."

"Emma." Linda barely nodded at the woman she hardly looked at as she spoke.

"Emmy—with a 'y'—Mrs. Crampton. Emmy Lou."

Ward couldn't help but notice that there was no handshake between the women. In fact, if anything, this last of the Magnolia drenched Dog Days—already unseasonably cool—suddenly became very frosty.

"And . . . . Ward? Linda? Allow me to introduce our dog, Molly. Shake, Molly." Molly looked up at Matthew as if to ask "Do I really have to?".

Ward bent over in front of her, his hand extended. "Well, hello there, Molly."

Linda remained aloof, glancing behind her toward the house.

Molly lifted her right paw.

Ward grasped the paw for a few moments, shaking it up and down. "Hel-lo, Molly. Well, hel-lo, Molly."

She dropped her paw back to the grass, again heeling at Matthew's side.

Cicadas chirruped in the monstrous magnolias, elms, and oaks that cluttered the small yard surrounding a stone and brick two-story early American house built around 1897 by one of the first professors at the State University. Most of the weather-knurled and time-crusted trees were here long before the Edwin Stuart Millere house, recently restored under state and federal Historical Preservation grants.

Emmy Lou looked at Ward as if she still couldn't believe what she was seeing. "Ward . . . ." She opened her arms to him. "Oh, Ward. We all thought you were dead, honey!" She sobbed against his chest. "It's like you've come back from the grave . . . ."

Ward held her close, like the sister she had been. Her earth smell almost erased his mission for a moment as he caressed her tangled curls. "Yes." He grinned over Emmy Lou's shoulder at Linda. "Like Lazarus."

Linda glared at him.

"We're so glad to have you back where you belong."

"Thanks, Emmy Lou. You just don't know how much that means to me, honey . . . especially coming from you." He pulled back from her a little so that he could look at her face. Tear stained and tangled, she was still one of the most striking women he'd ever known . . . even more now than he had remembered. Aging had refined her features. "Why don't you come along with me, Emmy Lou, and help me with the Margaritas?"

"Sure, Ward."

Ward nearly pulled her arm out of its socket as he pulled her along behind him toward the front porch. She flashed a look over her shoulder in the direction of Matthew and Linda. There was something about that Linda Crampton, something bordering on the sinister. She couldn't quite put her finger on it yet.

Matthew nodded almost unnoticeably to her as Ward whisked her off toward the most prestigious rental house adjacent to the State University campus.

"Okay, Ms. Crampton. What the fuck are you doing here?"

"Why," she smirked, "nothing special, Matthew honey. I'm just going whither my husband goest. You know?" She lit an Egyptian cigarette from the pack she pulled from a pocket in her high-collar gingham dress.

"Yeah. Sure. And, out of all the men in the fucking world, you just happen to end up marrying my closest childhood friend whom you knew I thought I'd killed? Sure, babe! And, I'm President of the John fucking Birch Society. right?"

"Why, Matthew. I'm surprised that you'd try to impugn some kind of sneaky motives to my being here."

"Jesus, Linda! You talk like a professor's wife already."

She stepped close to him, pouting. "It's not like you didn't have your chance, honey." Her pouting lips grimaced. "More than one, as a matter of fact."

"Look, Linda. I wasn't ready to get married in those days, and I'm still not married in these days." He stepped back from her. "So, I guess you came out for the better this way, didn't you?"

"Yes." The smile which burst across her ruby lips was barely containable. "I guess so. But." Again, she stepped close to him, almost touching his body with hers. "But. Sometimes, you know, in the privacy of darkness just before sleep." She reached up and touched his beard with her finger tips. Molly yipped.

"Don't." Matthew stepped away again. This time he put his hands out between them.

Her head drooped. She could not look him in the eye like this. "I'm sorry, Matthew. I'm not here to cause any trouble between you and your Emmy Lou Black."

"Then," he mumbled, lifting her face up so that he could look into her eyes, "why **are** you here?"

"Why, indeed," she chuckled. "I told you before, Matthew. Ward got this assistantship here at his old university." She dervished in small circles away from him. Her gingham dress swirled above her knees in a huge rippling cloth circle. Molly barked and nipped at her feet.

"And, after all, Ward **is** my husband." Linda whirled around the front yard, dodging the exposed roots of oak after elm after magnolia.

She pirouetted in front of him. Once again, she pressed against him, now sweating profusely. The dampness matted the bodice of her dress against her breasts. Her nipples—large, thick, and dark, as he remembered—bulged like knots in the gingham cloth.

"So."

Pirouette.

"Here."

Pirouette.

"We."

Pirouette.
"Are."

"I guess," Emmy Lou began. She felt sure that her pouting grin was about as charming as Ms. Scarlet O'Crampton's. "You might say that Matthew and I are like a couple of Billy Pilgrims . . . ." She glanced in Matthew's direction.

"You know, the protagonist in Vonnegut's *Slaughter-house Five*."

Lazlo hunkered under Linda's legs, whimpering at Molly. She sat on her haunches between Emmy Lou and Matthew. Lazlo had been in a lather ever since Molly had crossed the front door threshold. Her female scent quickly permeated the house as she sniffed from room to room characteristically exploring her new territory. He persistently explored Molly's wagging tail.

"We just seem to continually get stuck in the sixties, you know?" Matthew continued, squeezing Emmy Lou's hand. On the pale gray quilted rug covering most of the lustrous oak-pegged floor of the Millere house living room, they sat leaning against the silver and gray brocade sofa which sprawled the length of the picture window in seven modules. Each was three feet wide. Outside, the lawn rambled down to a narrow, West Capital City street lined with sycamores and more magnolias.

Ward's father had left him the family home in Roanoke Park as well as their vacation cottage on the beach near Fort Lauderdale. But, as soon as Henderson's will had been probated, instead of moving in, Ward had sold the family home to a local real estate developer. Some guy they had gone to high school with, according to Ward. Matthew couldn't recall him, but Ward, obviously, could.

No one knew why he sold so quickly or why to a developer who planned to bulldoze the house and outbuildings and holly stands to create a shopping center. Ward had not offered any explanation. Certainly, none was required. And, perhaps even among past friends, none was needed. This zombie who called himself Ward Crampton was clearly not the person he had grown up with, not the friend he had searched for all over America. That Ward Crampton had promised years before that he would never give up the Henderson home and its surrounding acres of pines, oaks, and several thick stands of holly . . . some of the few natural holly stands still left in Roanoke Park. This Ward Crampton had sold the place before his father's grave had settled.

"Some more of this Lebanese blond?" Ward did not wait for an answer. He finished filling the bronze hash pipe. This was the smoking of the peace pipe, and it was his responsibility to make sure everyone got stoned enough to be peaceful . . . if that was possible with this assemblage. At the least, he had to keep Linda in control. Matthew sure seemed in control on his own. He showed absolutely no sign of recognition or surprise when he was introduced to Linda.

"It's top quality shit, to which I'm sure your heads can already attest." Ward knew that he had to play this thing out little by little. Let Matthew take the bait of renewed friendship. Don't force him . . . not yet, anyway. Not unless you have to . . . . There was plenty of time to be subtle about this business. If only he could convince Linda of that . . . . She wanted this so badly that he feared she might get antsy and go for the jugular too soon. That would definitely blow the whole charade and send him directly to a Moroccan jail. Do not pass go. Do not collect two hundred dollars. Telling that damned story at dinner about how they had captured Ranier's half-track and left him in the desert was already a little more risk than was really appropriate at this stage . . . or necessary . . . especially when it was his neck at risk . . . not hers. She, of course, ended the story with a sly smirk twisting her candy lips.

"Yes, Matthew. Please have some more. We can get plenty more where that came from, can't we, Ward?" Linda glanced out of the corners of her eyes toward them but focusing on Emmy Lou's paint-spattered jeans. "You, too, Emma Lee."

"Emmy Lou, Linda," Ward corrected in hisses before Matthew could get the words onto his tongue.

How many times was this jerk female impersonator going to pull this name game crap on her?

"Oh, you mean like . . . ." She drew in a deep breath and began to sing: "Lou, Lou, skip to my Lou . . . . Skip to my Lou, my darlin'?" She batted her eyelashes at Matthew . . . the coy southern belle, demurring.

"Here, Emmy Lou." Ward stoked the pipe and passed it to her. Smoke curled around her copper face in the stagnant air of the historically correct nineteenth century American living room.

Emmy Lou's lips trembled with her resistance to the impulse to destroy this woman she hardly even knew. This was not like her at all. Linda Crampton seemed, however, to bring out the worst in her.

After handing her the pipe, Ward kicked Linda in the shins with a nod and a smirk. Turning toward Matthew as he settled onto the gray quilted rug, his legs folded somewhat awkwardly in a half-lotus. His lips transformed into a smile. "We have this incredible connection straight from Morocco." This ought to just slay Linda. "Remember the guy Linda told the story about at dinner? Ranier?"

Matthew nodded. "He's your man in Morocco. Right?"

Ward shrugged. "You got me, Matthew . . . ." His cheek began to twitch. Cool. Be cool, goddamn it! "Well, he was . . . ." He shrugged again, more exaggeratedly than the first time. "Until we got out of there. But, if you want it, I'll be glad to help you get some . . . or whatever you might need . . . you know?"

"We really appreciate that, Ward . . . Linda." His eyes slipped in the direction of Emmy Lou tapping Molly's mouth to see if she could grab her fingers before she pulled away. Molly almost always won this game with her. "The dope around this part of the universe is pretty average . . . and hard to find sometimes even at that."

"That's true, Ward. Nothing like The City, that's for sure. Cheap and killer."

"That's New York, alright."

"When were you ever in New York, Ward?" Linda pulled Lazlo's ears back. "Stop your fucking whimpering, you impotent piece of shit!" she whispered into them as if she were crooning him to sleep.

"In your dreams, Linda. In your dreams only, my darling . . . ."

"Speaking of dreams, Mr. Crampton." She leaned up from the dog's ears to Ward's. "That bitch is upsetting our Lazlo," she whimpered just loud enough for the others to hear. Lazlo also whimpered. "See what I mean?" He writhed beneath her hard touch as she pulled his ears back again and rubbed his neck with her other hand. "Do something, goddamn it!"

"What," he whispered behind his right hand, "do you want me to do for Christ's sake?" He did not want Matthew and Emmy Lou to hear this bull shit.

"Make them put her outside," she snarled. Lazlo whimpered

again, seemingly in agreement with her suggestion.

He shook his head . . . twice.

Linda struggled to her feet and swayed in the direction of the kitchen. She seemed to break some kind of spell with her movements . . . . "Coffee anyone?" . . . . with her words. Lazlo yipped and whined as he followed his mistress beyond Molly.

"Yes, thanks." Matthew glanced at Emmy Lou. She nodded. "Make that two, Linda . . . ."

"Ward?" She was working hard at ignoring Lazlo until, suddenly, he rolled over on his back yowling and spewing cum into the hem of her gingham dress.

"Huh? Oh, yes, please."

"Goddamn it, Ward! That does it!." She turned on Matthew, spewing her words at him. "You see what your dog has done. Get that bitch out of my house . . . now!"

Matthew drew in a complete breath for control. Linda was really pushing the envelope now. He patted Emmy Lou's thigh when he became aware that she was trembling. "It's okay, Madame Bovary. It's okay . . . ." He slapped his thigh twice. Molly retreated to his side. "Heel, Molly. You're going outside before you get blamed for Ward shooting off too." Molly's tail nearly wagged off of her body at the sound of the word outside. She leaped after Matthew as he shuffled in the direction of the kitchen door.

"Why don't you get out our Light Year Two Thousand game, Ward, while the coffee's making?" Linda followed her words out from the kitchen back into the living room where they all sat once again sans Molly. "It's like a seventies version of 'Winkie Dink and You.' Don't you think so, honey?"

"Something like that. Instead of drawing bridges for Winkie Dink to cross over raging rivers, you blow the fucking bridges up!"

"You shoot airplanes and helicopters out of the sky."

"You bomb air fields."

"You can even choose between regular bombs and napalm."

"And . . . . You can annihilate entire populations with nerve gas!"

"What?" Matthew's head swam in hashish whirl pools. Familiar ghouls gnawed at the edges of his brain once again. He knew that he had to watch himself. Getting ripped in the company of intimate strangers was not among the most astute things he had ever done. Sure, he had known them both before . . . . In another life, so it seemed. But, that was then. This was now. And, now, they were strangers, pure and simple, not yet to be trusted.

"Are you alright, Matthew?"

Emmy Lou's cool hands caressed his arms. He nodded.

Ward was, suddenly, on his feet as well. He nearly trotted across the rug toward the darkening hallway. "I'll get the game. You can see for yourself. Meanwhile, be thinking about that hash thing. I've still got a helluva pipeline in from Morocco. Right, Linda?"

Linda did not answer. She had slipped, once again, into the kitchen, unnoticed among the words and phrases.

"Anyway, maybe we can work something out, you know?" His words echoed in a flat sort of way out of the shadows of the hall. "This game is neat as shit, man! You can also play ping pong, hockey, squash, or tennis."

"The game!" he barked as he emerged from the hallway, a huge pastel red box clutched in his arms. The name was brushstroked in pastel green: Light Year 2000: A Television Game for All Ages.

In three giant steps, Ward reached where they sat, crosslegged, on the rug, waiting for their coffee. He set the box carefully on the rug between them. "Take this baggie. There's probably a quarter in there. I've got plenty, believe me. If you guys really like it after you've smoked it for awhile, then let me know. So, the next time I go to El Paso, you could even ride along if you wanted to. It'd be a real hoot, man . . . ! You. Me. And, my main man, Don Amerika . . . ."

Matthew nodded. He was unable to speak. His brain raced through memories . . . clogged with questions. What was going down here? First, Ward shows up deus ex machina with Linda Tallefero in tow. Then, it turns out his dope connection from Morocco to El Paso just happens to be a guy named Don Amerika . . . ?

"Are you sure you're okay, Matthew?"

"Yes, Madame Bovary. I'm sure."

"Anyway, this game, man, is something else."

"All you do is jack the system into the TV."

Linda set the pewter coffee set beside the game box while Ward walked to the other end of the room and rolled the television toward them over the lumpy rug.

"Close enough, Linda?"

She nodded and seated herself in a position so that she would be between Ward and Matthew and as far away as possible from Emmy Lou Black.

Ward rattled his way into the box, extracting the control panel and AC jack from their cardboard nests. He plugged the jack into the back of the TV and connected the panel to it. When he turned on the set, a dotted white line split the screen vertically. Two very short lines appeared, one on each side of the divided line. They somewhat resembled paddles or rackets.

Matthew relit the pipe which was still half full of sweet ocher hash. He took a small hit sucking it deep into his lungs before he passed the pipe to Emmy Lou. He shrugged. She took a hit, shrugged, and passed the pipe to Linda without looking at her. Linda wiped the mouth piece on her gingham sleeve hem before she sucked on it.

Ward, still rummaging in the cardboard box, finally pulled out a rifle-like plastic shooter with a telescopic sight and a cord attached to the butt plate. "You can shoot stationary or moving targets with this baby." He held the plastic gun aloft with his left hand. "It's a lot of fun, you know?"

"Guns are stupid."

Emmy Lou nodded.

Linda poured the coffee.

"What do you mean by stupid?"

"I wouldn't touch one of the damned things with your hands, much less my own." Matthew leaped to his feet. "There's a better way to demonstrate! I'll show you."

Matthew bolted for the kitchen and the side door leading to the garage where their van was parked facing down hill in the direction of the highway, where Molly had been exiled.

Emmy Lou heard Matthew's voice from the garage. "Come on Molly. Let's go for a ride, girl." She heard the exiled Molly yap. The van door open and slam shut. She could hear it roll, catch, sputter, and roar off down the driveway toward the street and Ebenezer Church Road more than seven miles away, leaving her stunned and stranded on the living room floor of the historically restored and preserved Millere house.

The time she was alone with the Cramptons seemed like hours to her, though it was only thirty or forty minutes. The three of them took turns playing ping-pong and tennis and avoided discussing Matthew's sudden exit. Even Emmy Lou wasn't entirely sure what he was up to this time, but she'd bet her bottom dollar that it had something to do with that damned cross bow of his.

* * * * *

"Okay, Ward." Matthew stumbled through the kitchen door, forty-three minutes later, shaking his cross bow above his head as he fell into the living room. "Get one of your real guns and we'll hit the woods . . . do this thing for real." He was breathless, sweating in the sudden change from fifteen degrees outside to sixty-five in the living room. His eyes sparkled. "I'll show you guns aren't worth a flying fuck!"

"Jesus, Matthew!" Ward looked to Emmy Lou.

She nodded. "There'll be no peace until you do."

"Well, if you really want to, Matthew?"

" Ohhhh, but my souffle will fall!"

"Just give me a minute to get my gun. Okay?"

Matthew's glittering eyes gave no sign of anything. "Take all the time you need."

Ward shuffled, once again, across the quilted gray rug to the dark hallway which led to his den where he kept his considerably shrunken arsenal. He shook his head, muttering to himself as he entered the darkness of the hall. These weren't the actions of a gun merchant and dope smuggler and murderer.

Linda sat silent, not knowing what to say, how to react. This wasn't anywhere in their scenario alternatives. And, what's more, her tour de force dinner would be spoiled. She chuckled to herself. But, for a change, Ward Crampton alias Spiderman, Sheik of Morocco, was going to have to deal with a situation all by his lonesome. That, alone, would be worth this unpredictable detour.

Tops of pines, oaks, maples, and an occasional sycamore soaked sanguine in the sun setting in the woods behind the Millere house and its neighbors . . . a twenty square block hammock in the midst of the spreading city, kept whole. As a part of the historical preservation grant used by the university to restore the house. A brown hawk hovered above. Spotting a silver squirrel scampering across crackling needles and leaves, its cheeks bulging with acorns, the hawk tucked its broad wings and dove for the trees toward its unsuspecting prey like a spot shot from the sun.

Click clack. Shotgun hammers cocked.

Twang. A bamboo shaft sizzled through the crisp evening. The hawk shrieked as the arrow thudded into its side and nose-dived into the loam of the forest floor. The silver squirrel, startled by the sound of the hawk's body hitting the limbs of a towering oak tree nearby, scurried up a lone mulberry tree which was twisted and stunted beneath taller trees though it was heavy with late-ripening berries.

Footsteps muffled in the brittle carpet of leaves and pine needles, moving toward the spot where the hawk twitched one final time.

Matthew began to smirk as they neared the felled hawk. If only he could cry like he used to, die like he used to . . . a little with the death of each other living thing. If only . . . . But it was no use. That was gone. "See?" He turned his head, speaking over his shoulder.

Ward followed him, slowed by his stiff leg. It had been giving him more trouble since he'd been back in this humid climate. "See what?"

Matthew could not look directly into the hawk's face. "See . . . ah . . . ." Weren't its eyes gouged out like one of Estevan's sacrifices? "See . . . how . . . ah . . . quiet it is lying there?"

"Yeah, sure." He could see the laughter hidden deep in Matthew's eyes. He could see it in his old friend's smirk. "See how quiet the hawk is. Yeah, right!" He shook his head, still not quite sure that he believed what he had seen. His twelve gauge dangled over his left forearm. It was still cocked but unfired. "Uncanny's what I see, Matthew. Goddamned fucking uncanny!"

"I told you, man." Matthew stroked the well-oiled cross bow snuggled under his right arm. He stole a quick look. No. The hawk's eyes were there, wide and glaring in the midst of startling death. "Guns are obsolete. This little baby is not only silent but obviously deadly."

Ward nodded. He could see that now . . . .

"No better defense, man. No better . . . ."

"Defense? Defense against whom? Against what?" Could he have sensed something? Ward uncocked the shot gun with his thumb, easing the hammer back into place. No. But it was strange that he hadn't blinked an eye lash at being introduced to Linda as his wife. Certainly he remembered her. Certainly she had told the truth about knowing Matthew. And, Matthew and Linda did stay behind when he and Emmy Lou had gone inside to fix their drinks.

"Against . . . ." He paused, shuddering in a sudden breeze breaking through the trees. He could hear it coming toward them through the limbs and leaves as he stooped and scooped the hawk up from the ground.

"Against . . . ." The jet soared past sunset over the desert in his memory. Ember-eyed Estevan. His bolt had pierced completely through the hawk's body. Thank God, Matthew sighed. It still had its eyes.

"Against them!"

"And, just who the hell is 'them,' Matthew?"

"The civilizers . . . the idiots who want to destroy all this in the name of progress . . . ." He kicked up rotted leaves with the toe of his boots.

Ward shook his head. "Come on, Matthew. Make sense, man. You can't really believe that kind of mental masterbation."

"Why not?" His eyes glowed like camp fire coals as he extracted the bolt from the still-warm hawk's feathered body. "When, with my very own eyes, I witnessed my own father poison the Christmas snow? Masterbation—mental or otherwise—pales in comparison!"

"Because . . . because you're a part of that out there just as much as me or Linda or your father, Mayor Jason Parkrow or, even, Emmy Lou . . . or anybody else for that matter." He grunted a sigh.

"Did you know that I was a grown man, Ward . . . in the middle of a fucking war . . . before I discovered that just because something is rotten doesn't mean that it is intrinsically bad?" He cackled. "Did you know that?"

"You're no different than any of us, you know?"

Matthew wheeled on his heel, flinging the hawk to the loamy forest floor. Leave it for the crows . . . and the ants . . . . "You're wrong about me, Ward, you know? Very, very wrong." He stalked toward Ward's residence, wiping the split bamboo bolt clean of the warm thick blood with a handkerchief he had brought along for just that purpose. He stuffed the blood-stained cotton back into his jeans before returning the bolt to the leather quiver slung over his shoulder. That was how he'd left old Estevan in the desert, wasn't it? For the buzzards and the condors? If there were any condors still left alive.

"They're out to get us, man!" he screamed over his shoulder at Ward.

Ward breached his twelve guage Mossberg—a present from his late father twenty Christmases ago—as he limped along the path yards behind Matthew, retracing their steps toward the house that Millere built. His Mother had used it to blow her brains out in their front yard when she was notified that he was missing in action and presumed dead in Vietnam. It still held two loads of birdshot . . . unfired. He'd not been able to get off either barrel before Matthew's cross bow shaft was already whizzing toward the hawk. Poor, crazy fucker. He doesn't know how right he really is.

Extracting the two shells, he dropped them into the pocket of his red-yellow-and-black plaid hunting jacket. The woods were silent again except for their footsteps breaking fallen twigs and crushing leaves and pine needles. The soft soil stank of dead things. Or does he?

Suddenly, Matthew froze in front of him, cocking his head to listen. Ward's ears perked. Was that a scream coming from the house?

Matthew shot as straight and as fast as one of his bolts for the house, sprinting through the woods, his cross bow held in his right hand. Ward followed, a little more awkward with his stiff leg and under the weight of his shotgun.

When Ward, winded, fell through the garage door into the kitchen, he had been hearing Linda's screams of terror for a few hundred yards. Linda, now, cowered beside the refrigerator which spewed ice circles from the freezer door, still hissing. "Nigger slut! Nigger slut!"

Across the kitchen, Matthew struggled with Emmy Lou's arms which he had pinned to the cabinets above the sink. Her left hand still clutched a knife so tightly that her knuckles and finger tips were white.

"Nigger slut! Nig . . . ger sss . . .lut bassss . . .tard!"

Each time Linda hissed, Matthew had to fight to restrain Emmy Lou. "Ward!"

"Yeah . . . ah . . . what the hell's going on here?"

"Quick. Get this knife out of Emmy Lou's hand before I decide to let her loose."

"Christ!" Ward raced to Matthew's side. "You wouldn't?" Emmy Lou's fingers were like vice grips on the wooden handle as he wrenched the butcher knife from her grasp.

"I was sure tempted!" Matthew released her arms but hugged her around the chest as she tried to lunge at Linda. "Quiet, Madame Bovary."

She snarled.

"Quiet."

She quivered.

"I guess," he tried to joke, "she must've gotten stuck in the sixties again." Emmy Lou nearly dove under his bear hug. "She probably thinks that she's Tony Perkins. You know, in 'Psycho' . . or something?"

Linda, who by now had been reduced like Lazlo to a lump of whimpers, huddled beneath a continuing shower of ice circles.

Matthew held Emmy Lou fast. "Come on, Madame Bovary." He turned on Ward who stood in the center of the asphalt tile kitchen floor between them and Linda. All he wanted, right now, was to get Emmy Lou the fuck out of this restored modest home in West Capital City. "Let me take you home."

"A story may be a whaling adventure like *Moby Dick*, but that doesn't mean what the story might have to say to the reader—to you—is limited to the eighteen hundreds and whaling. A story might speak to us from any time and place. Any questions? Comments?"

Matthew scoured the faces of his students for any signs of being unsure . . . incredulous . . . lost . . . . Everyone seemed, at least, to be putting on a good front about understanding this summation of what he had been discussing with them for most of the class hour.

"Okay, everybody. Please arrange your desks back into the lines like you found them. You know the drill by now. And, please, pass up your outlines . . . the ones you marked up in your groups earlier in class. I'll go over them this weekend. Then, on Monday, we'll finalize them. On Wednesday, you write in class from your outlines."

Desks scraped. Voices whispered, giggled, grumbled. "From your group work, it seems like everyone is getting this outline stuff. But, are there any questions?"

Desks were properly rowed. His students stood by their desks, books in hand, waiting. "Okay. Hearing none . . . . Class dismissed! Have a great weekend!"

In almost perfect unison, most of the students bolted for the door. "Mr. Parkrow . . . ."

"Yes, Kathleen?"

She shoved a fistful of soiled and crumpled outlines across the front table as she passed. "Have a nice weekend grading outlines," she joked. "We'll all be thinking about you when we're cheering on Ron in the Red and White game." She clicked her tongue as she sashayed in a very exaggerated manner toward the door. "Poor Mr. Parkrow."

"Tell Ron to score one for me since he couldn't find the time for class today . . . ."

"Oh, I almost forgot, Mr. Parkrow. His outline's on the top of the pile. Our group decided that we'd go ahead and critique his too." She faced him again as if expecting his question.

"Even with him not in class?"

She nodded.

"Sort of *in absentia*?"

"I guess." She started to turn and leap through the doorway into the weekend which dangled its dazzling possibilities like ripe fruit or a cold six-pack. But, she stopped herself in mid-turn. "That was okay, wasn't it? I mean, you did say that the group should make its own decisions about stuff like that. Right?"

"It's fine, Kathleen. It's not like Ron's a marginal student or anything like that anyway."

"Thanks, Mr. Parkrow." She turned and vaulted the threshold scuffed and gouged by nearly a hundred years of students. "All kidding aside, have a great weekend." She glanced down just to make sure that she was outside of the class room. "Matthew."

Before he could respond, she vanished in a wisp of weekend magic. Matthew wrapped a rubber band around the outlines and stuffed them into his pack that sat upon the generations of shellac that peeled away at the corners of the blond table. He could not help but notice that most of the papers were well marked-up. Usually, that was the results of good group work.

"Matthew. Hey, man."

That voice. Even though it no longer surprised him, its hollow resonance still sent chills up and down his spine. Matthew looked up from his open pack. He just wasn't used to it yet. He didn't know if he ever would be. "Hey, Ward. What's happening, man?"

Ward entered the room that had been Matthew's room for the past four years, a stack of books wrapped in his gangly arms. He stopped in front of the table and deposited his books with a sigh. "Jesus, so many new books at once. I've got Introductory Literature I in here this hour."

"Lit I?" Matthew struggled with his impulses. After all, Ward was new. He didn't know the department protocol. "But, I thought you had two comp classes?"

"Yeah." He beamed. "I did. But, Mr. Scythe offered me this class?"

"When did they add a Lit I class?"

"Just this morning. It was a last-minute expansion class because of over-enrollment . . . or something like that." He grinned without reservation. "Isn't that just great?"

"Yeah. Sure." Why did Ward get the new class? Usually, Ward would have been given one of his composition classes, and he would have been reassigned to the new lit class. "That's great." But, with Scythe calling the shots, he didn't really have to ask why, now did he?

"You've got a Lit I class, too, don't you, Matthew?"

"Yes." And, I was supposed to have first rights to any openings.

"Maybe . . . ah . . . ."

"Right after lunch . . . ."

"If you don't mind . . . ."

"In this very room . . . ."

"You could . . . ah . . . well, you know . . . give me a little advice on how best to handle this kind of course." Ward shot his best I-really-need-your-help grin across the flaking table between them. "I mean, it ain't composition, for Christ's sake!" He paused, waiting for a response that did not seem to be forthcoming. "Aw, come on, Matthew. It'll be just like old times, man. We'll be working together again."

"Well." Matthew smirked in return. "Okay. But, only on one condition." He paused, awaiting a response from Ward before he could proceed.

"What condition, for Christ's sake?"

"You tell me whether my grand slam was really fair or foul." He grinned, himself, without reservation. "Truth. No lie." Matthew sensed a quiver in the upper left side of his grin. For a few moments, his upper lip seemed to pulse and twitch out of control.

"What the fuck, man. What makes you think that I know?"

"You were standing by our dugout, remember?"

"Yeah. So?

"So, our dugout was along the first base side of the field. You had a perfect view of the right field line."

"God fucking damn, Matthew! Don't you ever let anything rest for Christ's sake?" Ward turned his back to Matthew to keep from shouting. "Don't you?" he hissed.

"No. I usually don't, Ward." Matthew grabbed the zombie's right shoulder. "No." He spun Ward around to face him again. "I . . . don't . . . give . . . up . . . easily!"

"Okay! All fucking right, Matthew!" Ward suddenly became aware that he was shouting loud enough to attract the attention of every TA in Three Ten, despite his efforts not to. Ward inhaled several very deep breaths, releasing each one slowly until he felt an inner calm taking control of, and lowering, his voice volume.

"You want me to tell you that the fucking home run was foul. Okay. Yes. Your historic grand slam home run was a foul ball! How the goddamned umps missed that call is beyond me even to this day, man." He shrugged. "But, they did."

"Why didn't you say anything to me then, Ward?"

"Because, if you'd had any corroboration at all, you would have ruined our scholarship chances and any big league opportunities I might have had. And, what the fuck did it matter, anyway? You gave everybody the story-book ending they were looking for, Matthew. Why should I take that away from them . . . or you?"

"Perhaps . . . and I don't mean to be overbearing or unduly puritanical about this . . . but, just perhaps, because their story-book ending was based on a foul ball, based on a lie."

"Listen, man, the reality of the situation was that you clobbered a fucking grand slam to win the state championship in the greatest high school baseball game probably ever played in this fucking state. And, the umps saw a fair ball. That's what they saw. So, who am I to question their call. Or you, for that matter?"

"I don't know about you, Ward. In fact, I guess I really don't know you at all anymore. There've been too many years and too many nightmares between us. But, I do know about one thing. It's me that it was happening to. It's me who has lived with the lie. That's who I am to question the call of the umps. That's who I am."

"So, you've questioned, and I've answered. Now, tell me, Matthew, friend of my childhood, has the reality changed as a result of your inquiry into the truth . . . and my response? Will the reality ever change for that moment? Or will it endure as the indelible, defining truth of that time and space?" He pushed his chest against Matthew's. "Tell me, goddamn it! Tell me! Now! You arrogant, self-righteous fuck! Will it change anything or not, goddamn you?" Ward had his fingers around Matthew's throat before he could control the spew of hatred that seemed to explode from inside of him like a volcano.

Matthew's face drained of blood. His brain began to starve for oxygen. Ward's fingers tightened deeper into his throat. He had, obviously, lost control. Matthew feared that his life might truly be in danger in this moment. Just as he was summoning his remaining strength to knee Ward in the balls, Ward released his death-like grip on his throat as suddenly as he had grabbed him.

"Jesus, Ward," he rasped, massaging his neck as he forced the words out through painful vocal chords. "Cool . . . out . . . man. Cool . . . fucking . . . out."

"Cool out, yourself, man!" He turned his back again on Matthew. "You need to quit looking for things that you got no business looking for. It could get you in some real trouble, man."

"Look, Ward. I've been in real trouble before, my friend. Real trouble doesn't scare me."

"I'm really sorry to hear that, Matthew. Believe me it should. It sure as hell scares me."

"No, Ward. You know what really scares me, man?"

"No, what?"

Matthew stuffed the last of his books into his pack and cinched it shut. "You, man. You scare me." He snatched the pack from the blond, flaking table that still separated them.

"Well." Ward began to shuffle his books around on the table between them. "That's a start."

Part Three

BE AT ONE WITH THE DUST OF THE EARTH

Tao Te Ching

Stalling Bow-Tie became more problematic with every day that passed. She understood his impatience all too well. After all, he smelled gunpowder and blood or, at least, the stench of torched reputations and lives laid waste. Vamp dialed the antique white-with-imitation-gold-trim instrument of Mother Bell that always resided on the front leaf of the cherry wood early American roll top desk in the study of their modest historically restored home.

More than three months had passed since that encounter from the absurd with Matthew and Emmy Lou. Her very life threatened right here in her own fucking house. Yet, Ward, had still not come up with any real plan for destroying their target.

The telephone at the other end of the connection rang three times. She depressed the receiver into the fools-gold cradle, then picked it up again, placing it to her ear.

Vamp knew that it was no longer possible to leave it up to Lazarus. His way, whatever it was, was way too slow for Bow-Tie . . . and for her . . . .

There was a dial tone. She dialed again . . . .

The phone was picked up before the first ring was completed. "Hello?"

"Vamp here . . . ."

"Bow-Tie here . . . ."

"I'm having to take things into my own hands, Bow-Tie. Lazarus just isn't living up to the promise of his resurrection."

"Do what has to be done, Vamp. The target must be hit properly by the end of the spring semester."

"I understand, Bow-Tie."

"Very good, Vamp. Just make sure that Lazarus doesn't contaminate the target. That is crucial!"

"Yes, Bow-Tie. I'll take care of everything and . . . ."

"Everybody. Right?"

"Every man is reducible to his dick in my mouth," Linda assured Bow-Tie. "Even you, my most trusted and revered savior and mentor." She brushed her ever so slightly parted lips close to the telephone receiver as if it were Bow-Tie's actual lips. "Even you."

"I'm sure of that, my number one." He coughed. "Keep me informed in the usual manner. I'm counting on you, Vamp. We're all counting on you!"

"No problem, Bow-Tie. Next communication one week from

today at 6:30 p.m. This same number."

"Good luck, Vamp."

"Thanks, Bow-Tie. Goodbye."

"Goodbye."

* * * * *

Linda slipped Ward's Faculty Parking Card into the card reader slot. The parking validation ticket slipping from a slot below the card reader showed that it was still Columbus Day. 9:06 p.m. Ward and Matthew wouldn't return from the MLA Convention in El Paso until late Sunday night or early Monday morning. The red-and-white gate arm lifted.

The entire long weekend remained as the loom upon which she would weave her fatal web. She extracted the card, then steered her British Racing Green square-back MG roadster into the English Faculty parking lot. She recalled teasing Bow-Tie that his gift must be a 007 car.

"No," he assured her. "The only thing this car'll do, my dear Vamp, is go fast as all blazes!"

One car and one truck remained. The truck, she assumed, belonged to the janitor.

"Yes," he had almost hissed into the receiver, "Of course I remember you. How could anyone ever forget you?"

"That's so sweet, Mr. Travis. Nobody could ever forget your kindnesses to my husband either . . . . And, of course, to me . . . ."

"What can I help you with, Ms. Crampton?"

"I need to get into English tonight, Mr. Travis, and I don't have a key. Ward, my husband, he left me his parking card but not his building keys . . . . And . . . and he just called this evening and told me he needed some things from his office. He's at the MLA convention, you know?"

"No, ma'm. I didn't know that." He had paused a moment as if thinking the problem through. "Where you comin' from, Mrs. Crampton?"

"Just a few blocks away. Maybe, ten minutes at the most."

I was supposed to be leavin' about now, the time you'll be gettin' here," he had told her over the telephone earlier. "But I tell you what."

"What, Mr. Travis?"

"I'll just leave that basement door—the one right off the parkin' lot that all the TA's uses— ajar for you."

"Yes . . . ."

"Then, you can let yourself in if I have to leave before you get here. How's that for service, Mrs. Crampton?"

"Oh, that's just marvelous, Mr. Travis. Just marvelous! Now, I won't be bothering anybody in three-ten, will I, Mr. Travis?"

"Oh, no ma'm. Just Mr. Dryden left in there, and he won't mind a'tall."

You're such a dear, Mr. Travis. Thank you . . . ."

Vamp, not Ms. Crampton, was her persona as she entered English from the dark rear basement door at eleven minutes past nine. True to his word, Mr. Travis had wedged a wooden doorstop between the metal door and the metal sill so that she could enter without a key. But, if that was Travis's truck, where was he? She'd have thought that he'd have been waiting to . . . catch a glimpse of her thighs as she walked up the stairs. But, not in this light . . . or lack of it. Next time she saw him, she'd have to show him a little tit or something. Maybe let him drool on her a little.

She could barely see the stairwell in the nearly total darkness. That overhead light always seemed to be out even though everyone knew that this was the door most TA's used in their late-night comings and goings between English Building and The Tower. The lights that helped her see surrounded the parking lot a few hundred feet behind her. Maybe, that was where Travis was, right now. Locating a working light bulb, cursing that he missed his chance to look up her dress from under the stairwell.

As she entered the door to three-ten, she could hear a typewriter clacking away near the far end of the very rectangular room which held eighteen TA's. Must be Poper, she concluded. Travis had told her over the telephone that Poper was the only one left in the building besides himself. She unbuttoned her tangerine silk shirt blouse all the way to the waist of her pastel blue mini-skirt. As she wiggled her torso, she was pleased with how her body came out of the blouse. Not too much. Just enough. Button one button about half way down to make it look like . . . well, more like . . . an accident, she schemed.

While she strolled passed the first of the TA cubicles, she buttoned that middle button. "That's it," she murmured. She opened the door. Stepped inside the room. She flipped the night latch. The room was dull green in the overhead lights to her left and pitch black to her right. She shut the door. "Hello . . . . Anyone here . . . ?"

"Well . . . yes. Ah . . . who . . . ah . . . is it?"

"It's Linda . . . Linda Crampton . . . ."

"Oh . . . ah . . . ."

"Is that you, Poper, honey?"

"Oh . . . yes, come on back."

His voice bounced off the metal dividers that broke the large room into some twenty cubicles. "Okay." She sauntered down the aisle between rows of cubicles until she came to the cubicle Poper shared with Matthew. She wanted it in his chair. Matthew's chair. As she entered, Poper started as if he had been stuck by a pin in his ass. Then, his jaws went slack. His eyes bugged out of his head. She was making a favorable impression, then. Good. "Hel-lo," her voice crooned nearly an octave lower than normal, "Poper, honey." She slouched into Matthew's chair still warm from his body."

"He . . . hello yourself . . . ah . . . Miss Linda." His voice strained at about an octave higher than normal and not purposely.

Her skirt rode up her thighs so far that Poper was not left with any doubt that she had no panties on. "Ward's off reliving his youth or something in El Paso with Matthew at that frigging MLA conference. Why aren't you there?"

"Oh," he blushed, "I'm no good at those kinds of things."

"Poper, honey." She leaned forward, allowing her nipples to show from under the blouse. "I've got this itch . . . here." She guided his hands to her breasts. "And here." She touched his hands to her vagina. Poper's mouth was so dehydrated that when he tried to kiss her inner thigh his lips stuck to her skin.

"Here, let me."

Poper trembled naked in his swivel chair while Linda licked and bit his inner thighs and his testicles and crooned her bargain to him. "Anything you want me to do and as much of it as you want tonight, Poper, honey. But, you must help me . . . . You're the only one with the power to do this Poper, honey. I'm counting on you . . . ." She touched the head of his penis with the wet hot tip of her tongue.

"Oh, anything . . . . Anything . . . . Anything . . . ."

"Get Matthew Parkrow off of the faculty." Her voice suddenly seemed to sizzle as bubbles frothed at the edges of her lips. "I want him disgraced . . . drummed out of the University the same way that traitor was drummed out of the Army for being a deserter!

"I don't care how . . . ." She sucked his penis deep into her mouth for just a few moments, then spit it out as he shuddered. "And 'What for?' is none of your fucking business. Got that?"

"Okay!" He grabbed her head with his hands and forced her face back onto his genitals. "Okay!" He felt her close, hot, wet taking him up . . . . "Just don't stop!"

"Just don't you worry, Poper, honey." She grinned up at him between his knees. "Just don't you worry . . . ."

The soft jaundice lights from the mounds of flowers overflowing the Magus Funeral

Parlor's special home viewing display ricocheted off Mayor Jason Parkrow's bronze casket like a mine blast. Matthew shielded his eyes from the brilliance of the explosion. The last time he had been in this house Jason had not been home for Christmas Eve. That had been seven years ago. Now, here was yet another Christmas Eve with Jason absent. Oh, sure, his physical body was actually present. But that was all that was left . . . the husk . . . dressed out in his favorite blue serge suit.

Matthew recalled the red telephone receiver palpitating in his hand as if it were about to explode when he picked it up.

"Hello?"

"Matthew?"

"Yes . . . ?"

"Ah . . . Jill. Jill Jackson. Ah . . . I'm Jason's . . . was your father's . . . press secretary."

"Oh, yes . . . Jill."

"I'm so sorry, Matthew, but I must inform you that the Mayor passed quietly just a few minutes ago in the arms of your best friend Ward Crampton."

Jesus, who was she trying to kid? Jason Parkrow didn't do anything quietly. Not even die. Alas, last laugher. You died about as well as you knew me. Hell . . . . You didn't even die when you should've, back before the meadow lark's last beating wing struggled against your aldrin snow. You bastard! How like a piece out of Don Amerika's wax museum you seem to be now as you repose in your flag-draped casket. Why did you go and die on me? It was my duty as a son to draw faster . . . to steal more bases. . . to earn more degrees . . . to experience more shit . . . . But you weren't supposed to take it personal. It was simply natural . . . . All that aldrin. So many different things known by the same name.

And, Ward did mean something to him. Matthew had not quite figured that out yet, but he was sure that it was a long way from friend . . . much less best friend.

"Even in death, Jason, you are unforgiveable."

"What did you say, Matthew?"

Ward's voice startled him once again. Matthew had not realized that he was actually speaking aloud. "I said I still can't forgive the old bastard, even now, dead as he is"

"That was what kept the old man alive, you know . . . waiting for your forgiveness before he drifted off to his own version of the great beyond . . . ."

"If that were really true, Ward, then he'd still be alive, now wouldn't he?"

"What do you mean?"

"Well, he isn't still alive is he?" Matthew reached inside the open casket. Ward grabbed his shoulders from behind attempting to hold him back, from what he didn't know. Matthew began shaking his father's corpse . . . . "Is he?" he shrieked. "Is he . . . ?"

"Jesus, Matthew. He was your father!"

"And why would you be the one then? He died in your arms. What were you even doing here at my father's house at all, Ward?"

"He . . . he was once . . . once like a father to me, too, Matthew."

"Jason Parkrow was never like anyone's father to anyone . . . except possibly to Emmy Lou . . . ." That was a puzzle in itself. "He was an asshole politician of the lowest order . . . willing to sell his land and his soul and anyone else's he could grab in order to gain a vote or two or a little taste of that magic thing called power . . . ."

Ward hesitated. "That may be, but . . . ." What was he doing? Was he going to tell Matthew? Hell, he already knew that Jason died in his arms, right? He might as well know the rest . . . or at least a well-edited version of the rest.

"He deserved to die unforgiven by his only son, Matthew, whose birthright he betrayed for the key to the Mayor's Office."

"Maybe . . . maybe you're right . . . but . . . ."

"But what?"

"But . . . ." Ward finally succeeded in prying Matthew's fingers from Jason's suit lapels. He held Matthew's hands firmly in his and inhaled very deeply. "But . . . I forgave him for you . . . ."

Matthew gaped at his childhood friend, incredulity spread across his face like the shadow of a cloud over the sun. Once he seemed to grasp the full import of his words, he wrenched his hands free of Ward's grasp. "You what?" he screamed. "You did what?" Matthew's fingers clenched at his jeans in an attempt to keep his hands from flying straight at Ward Crampton's throat.

"He was delusional, Matthew. For a few moments just before the end he thought I was you . . . or he wanted to think that I was you.

He begged my forgiveness, so I forgave him, Matthew."

"You what?"

"I forgave Jason in your stead"

"You had no right!"

"Maybe not, but it's done, and there's nothing you or I or anyone else can do about it now." Ward pivoted away from the glistening coffin and began to walk away. Suddenly, he turned back to face his old friend who was obviously and perhaps understandably furious and confused. "Look, the old man died at peace with himself and the world because he thought you had forgiven him. Yet, you didn't have to forgive him at all. He got his peaceful death, and you kept your integrity." He shrugged. "What's the harm in that?"

"Plenty's the harm, Ward! Plenty's the harm!"

"You mean you would've denied Jason even a peaceful passing?"

"Yessss . . . ." Matthew snarled. "That's exactly what I did or at least I thought I did. He didn't deserve to die peacefully, goddamn it! He deserved to die the way he made others live . . . in torment." Matthew turned back to his father's corpse encased in the glistening casket. "It was a fucking foul ball, Jason," he whispered loudly. "You hear me in there?" He leaned close to his father's right ear. The flesh was cold to the touch of his lips. "It was a foul ball . . . ."

The ringing telephone aroused him from a sleepless stupor. He had actually dozed off for a few minutes. He breast stroked through the death dreaming air toward the jangle jingle. Spring semester was half over. His Florida tan had faded. The Air-conditioned Gypsy seethed with gas from the extinguished pilot light on the kitchen stove. He grasped the receiver in both hands almost falling off the bed. "'Lo?"

"Matthew?"

He coughed, tried to clear his thickening throat of the acrid air. Instead, the sick thick air permeated every taste bud and pore. "Yeah." Suddenly he recognized the smell of the trace element in the gas.

"Matthew. Honey. I need you."

"Hold on. I'll be right back." He dropped the receiver to the side table, leaped from the bed and bolted down the three-foot-wide hall for the kitchen bouncing from one wall to the other. He flung open the front door. As a late night wind whipped across the porch, it sucked the gas through the opening into the starry night. They were blurred, the stars, like Van Gogh saw them. He took a deep breath of the fresh wind, then shot to the stove. He could tell which pilot was that pilot by looking through the air holes in the covers. The left one was burning. The right one was dark. He turned off the gas feed.

Emmy Lou's voice sounded like a recorded doll's voice. After months of waiting, the call comes at three A.M. while I'm under attack from the natural gas system, he marveled. He scooped up the receiver. "Madame Bovary? Sorry."

"Yes, Matthew. What happened? Are you okay?"

He could hear the strain in her voice. "Yes. It's just that damned pilot. It went out again. I smelled it when the phone woke me up." He shook his head. "Guess it's lucky you called." He would continue to tell himself that the pilot just went out by itself like it had done dozens of times before over the past five years.

"I guess it is! My god! That pilot's truly dangerous." She heard the quivering in her own voice and slowly brought it under control. "Matthew. It's Molly. You know, I bred her?"

"Well no I didn't. Is she okay?"

"Well she's about to whelp. Please, can you come?"

"I'll be there as soon as I can."

"Oh, thank you." She went limp, almost dropping the phone.

"See you soon. Don't let her whelp without my help." He forced a chuckle.

"I'll try." She did not even attempt to match his forced chuckle or even to skewer his awful attempt at humor as she likely would have before. "Bye."

"Bye."

Goodbye was what she had written to him months ago. He had not heard from her since he woke up late on the morning after Jason's funeral and found the note she had left along with the copy of Jason's will with a single paragraph heavily circled.

> *And let it be known to all concerned with this will that Emmy Lou Black, who for all these years has been known as the niece of Alecia Black, is my daughter by Alecia Black and is to be considered as much a legal part of my family as my legitimate son Matthew.*

He had tried frantically to get in touch with her. She dropped out of school. She hid behind Alecia at Jason's house where she lived with Molly. He was convinced there was more to it. He just didn't yet know what that "more to it" was. He had actually been willing to go back into that house to find out, but he was always met with the shades in the house pulled shut against the world and Alecia's front door mantra: "Emmy Lou don't *never* want to see you again no more, Master Matthew. She's too ashamed."

He grew up with Emmy Lou. He had *lived with* her. Loved her. Shared nearly all with her. She was a very tough woman, independent minded, not shackled by stereotypical thinking. There had to be something more to this.

He had promised her he would come thinking it was *she* who needed him. Jason's house loomed off to his right through the few pines still standing in what was left of the yard he used to know. So he had come back to this house again. Maybe the answers were stashed behind the lightning rods or sealed inside those storm windows and tightly pulled shades. He steered the van up the steep cement driveway parking beside an apple red Volkswagen bug. Must be Emmy Lou's. He snuffed the joint he'd smoked on the way in the brimming over ashtray in the dash. The house looked like a chalk drawing on a blackboard in the four A.M. darkness.

Alecia answered the door as she had each of the many times he had shown up here at all hours of the day and night, trying to get by her to Emmy Lou to assure her Jason's revelation did not matter. He didn't care that they were half related, that they were somehow brother and sister. They always had been anyway. They had talked it out many times, their feelings about being so much like brother and sister they felt like they were committing incest when they made love. They had gotten past all that once. Why not now? Why does it make a difference when it is as physical as it is emotional? He wanted to take her in his arms and tell her how he loved her and always would and no other woman could ever take her place. He would have to become celibate if she would not come back to him. He was falling into little pieces without his glue, Emmy Lou. She would expect a little humor from him, too.

"Master Matthew, you just don' never give up, does you?" Alecia shook her head. "Come on in." She opened the door wide into the living room. The frescos on the walls were intensely alive. The colors vibrated like Emmy Lou's special pigment, pig's blood red. Matthew stepped over the metal threshold. Had she somehow found blue and green and yellow pig's blood? "Where's Madame Bovary . . . ah, Emmy Lou?" Alecia closed the door behind him. It swooshed shut over the threshold like a safe or a mausoleum sealing. He peered about the lightless room. Only the kitchen light off to the left illuminated the paintings on the walls. Jason on the wall facing you as you enter the front door, smiling in a Panama suit leaning against the front fender of his 1975 Mark IV. Alecia as she was in Emmy Lou's early memories, shapely with a protruding butt and large breasts. Her dark face was almost blue in the dim light. Her teeth, which she no longer had, shimmered like pearls between thick almost saucer-like lips parted in a laugh which she also no longer had. She was to his right, to Jason's left. On Jason's right, Emmy Lou, naked and as copper beautiful as when he first moved in with her in New York except for her face which was half white and half copper, her full lips gnarled like an old oak root, her green eyes wild with sparks of red shooting from them like fire. In her left hand she held a voodoo doll of Jason, her fingers dug deep into the straw of his chest. The straw bled. In her right hand she held bloody genitals.

Oh Christ almighty. "Where is she, Alecia? She called for me."

ALECIA:
(gliding between the front wall which was draped on both sides of the door with sheets and Matthew as he turned, approached the sheets)

"Master Matthew. Thar's something you gotta know."

MATTHEW:
(attempting to sidestep the old maid and yank down the sheets): What? Why are you preventing me from getting to this front wall? It should be of me . . . ."

ALECIA:
(putting up her bleached palms to stop him)

"It's not finished, Master Matthew. Emmy Lou says nobody sees it til it's done . . . specially not you!"

EMMY LOU:
(entering the room from the bright kitchen with a pewter tea service, the pot steaming, on a pewter tray with the Wedgewood cups and saucers)

"Not yet, Matthew. It's not completed."

(She beamed in spite of herself as he turned to her voice.)

MATTHEW:
"If you say so, Madame Bovary. If you say so. I could never deny your smile anything."
 (He reached for the tray)
"Or your tears. Here, allow me."

EMMY LOU:
(handing Matthew the tray and gliding to the sofa which sat in front of Jason's wing-tip-shod feet)

"Over here on the coffee table. Guess it ought to be tea table . . . for this morning anyway. We still have some time before Molly's ready."

MATTHEW:
(following her to the couch and placing the pewter tea service on the mahogany table)

"Okay."

ALECIA:
(also following Emmy Lou, then Matthew, to the couch and plopping down in the middle between Emmy Lou and where Matthew would now have to sit)

"I'll serve."

MATTHEW:
(slouching onto the end cushion of the couch, frowning at Alecia)

"Don't you always?

ALECIA:
(pouring tea into the cups and passing them to, first, Emmy Lou and, then, Matthew, taking for herself only after she served them)

"Now more'n ever, Master Matthew because, now, finally, I's gonna tell you de truth about this whole mess."

EMMY LOU:
(almost dropping her cup and saucer, it clattered on the table)

"No, Alecia, you can't do that."

ALECIA:
"Can't not . . . ."

(She wagged her streaked gray hair twisted into a kinky ball on the top of her head.)

"Can't not, Emmy Lou."

MATTHEW:
"What do you mean, the truth? What truth?

(His mind flashed on eyeless pictures, on pictures of eyes, of eyeless ghouls gnawing at his innards. Old Estevan told him the truth once a long time ago and it ended up costing him what was left of his life.)

"Hell!"

(He'd said almost those same words to Estevan that early morning on the desert when hawks became jets in the fracturing sky.)

ALECIA:
"Well, it all started when Emmy Lou was just done being born and I brought her back here to live."

EMMY LOU:
"No, don't . . . please . . . ."
(She trembled.)

ALECIA:
(her face stern, turned away from the pleading Emma Lou toward the expectant Matthew)

" I took her to a palm reader over in Roanoke Park. Sister Sosostris was her name. She told me, while Emmy Lou suckled at my nipple, that the baby was smart and artistic . . . that she was, indeed, a prog-i-dy . . . ."
EMMY LOU:

(still shaking)

"Pro-di-gy!"

ALECIA:

(continuing as if she had never been interrupted, also sipping her tea) "But, Sister warned me that a terrible thing loomed in Emmy Lou's future."

(Alecia set down her cup and saucer and stood up from the couch. Shaking her finger in the air and imitating the old palm reader, she continued.)

"Take care, Sister whispered, that your baby does not marry her brother."

(She slumped back onto the couch.)

EMMY LOU:

(her head buried in her hands, sobbing.)

"So, I can't, don't you see, do anything else than what I'm doing— painting the record of our lives in our cave."

MATTHEW:

(wagging his head, his mouth agape)

"No. I don't see. I don't!"

ALECIA:

"You mean, you *won't*. Sister knew all about me and your father. She knew that Emmy Lou was a bastard . . . yes, I'll say it. A bastard baby . . . ."

(She too broke into tears running down her craggy black cheeks.)

"She wasn't no quack, no fake. She was a clair . . . clair . . . ."

(She glanced back at Emmy Lou once again for help.)

EMMY LOU:

(her head still in her hands but aware of the silence after the word was left dangling)

"Clairvoyant . . . ."

ALECIA:
(nodding as she turned back to face Matthew)

"Yeah, clair-voy-ant. She knew for real, Mas . . . ah . . . Matthew!"

(Her old yellowed eyes lay in her broad creased forehead like lumps of old dung, welling with old tears.)

MATTHEW:
(irritated, remembering Madame Sosostris)

"That's just old wives tales, superstition, junk fed us to keep us down, coincidence . . . ."

(He began frothing at the edges of his mouth.)

"Emmy Lou? You know better . . . ."

Emmy Lou hunched on the couch, her taffy hair flowing over her shoulders, arms and hands hiding her face still buried in her bluejean lap. She did not answer, only sniffled trying to control her sobbing. Here sits the broken genius . . . the prodigy. But where was his Madame Bovary? Had she, too, fled in the face of her curse? That woman who had helped him, unwittingly, to face his own curse. Didn't she realize how kindred they really were? That he had his own special curse. That all people had their own special curses. The one he had embraced by chance (or was it?) near Alamogorda was his alone as this prophecy-come-true was her's. He murders his father. Emmy Lou marries her brother. They produce . . . Fat Boy and Little Man.

Emmy Lou bolted upright, wiping her eyes with the paint-spattered sleeves of her blue workshirt. "We'd better get to Molly." She started for the kitchen.

Matthew followed her into the brightness of the kitchen that forced recollections of his father's casket. He could hear Molly's whimpers in the garage. Once in the garage he realized there was only room for one car. Emmy Lou's new bug. She told him that they had offered her two of them for Jason's custom-designed Continental. Beyond, where the other half of the garage used to be was a brick wall and a top-and-bottom opening door. Set into the bottom door was a two-way dog door. He frowned at her.

"I used the money those car people insisted on giving me, after I told them I didn't need or want two cars, to build a real nice kennel area for Molly and the puppies." She was quick to notice the disapproval in his scowling face. "But, Matthew, she loves it out here. It's private, away from the noise of the house. She can go in and out as she pleases. and I've had another doggie-door installed in . . . . Look at the kitchen door behind you."

Matthew turned. There was another two-way door for Molly to go in and out of the house as well. Matthew flushed. Should've known she wouldn't shut the damn dog out. "I'm sorry, Madame Bovary." He pivoted back toward her, reaching out to touch her shoulder. She shrank from him. His fingers trembled. He jerked his hands back to his sides. "I'm so sorry." He sucked in a deep breath. "It seems I'm always apologizing to you for something or other." Matthew walked past her still crouched figure and opened the top and bottom bolts on the kennel door. He pulled open the two doors and stepped inside.

The room's aroma was not a new smell at all but more like the mown hay and pine straw which was strewn over the indoor-outdoor carpet. Molly's head snapped up when she heard his steps. She yelped hello, tried to get up but she was too far along with the first puppy. Her back thighs quivered. "Hello, Molly . . . sweet girl." He tiptoed to where she lay on a pallet of old blankets in the far corner of the room. Kneeling beside a parsons table next to the pallet, he patted her shivering head. "It's been a long time, girl." On the table were all the necessities for the whelping. Hot water, a sponge, alcohol, thread and scissors in case she needed help with cleaning away the sack or severing the cord; a pile of clean towels. Under the table newspapers were stacked about eight inches high. "We'd better get newspapers down fast Emmy Lou. Emmy Lou?" He snatched up a handful of papers and began to spread them in layers over the blankets, gently moving Molly as necessary. "Come on, Emmy Lou!" He heard her reluctant footsteps on the straw. *Hey Jude don't make it bad, take a sad song and make it better, remember to let her into your heart, then you can start to make it better . . . .* Under his breath he sang the song as he worked.

"If you want, I'll lift her. It'll make putting the paper down easier." She knelt beside him, stroking Molly's back thighs and talking to her in soothing tones. "It's okay, girl. Everything's gonna work out fine."

"Okay." She shook as she helped him with the newspapers.

She still seemed to smell of that last campfire all those years ago, all smoky and warm.

"I feel so sorry for her now." She gently lifted Molly's head, then her rear as Matthew slid paper under her. I even feel a little guilty about mating her, you know?"

He paused as the last layer of paper was completed. "When was that?"

"Not long after Jason died."

He started to touch her hair as it fell all bright and smooth over her right shoulder. But he stopped his reflex action in time, stood up. She never knew he tried. He clenched his teeth, cleared his throat. "Okay. Then let's have nothing but good positive vibes from here on. For our sakes and for Molly's, and for the puppies that are coming into this mess of a world. All right?" Thank god they're not children . . . .

Emmy Lou nodded under her shining hair, Her hands still shook as she stroked Molly's muzzle while she lay on her left side breathing rapidly after a labor pain, then slowing as she began to rest.

"Get ready, Matthew, I think the first one's on its way. . . ."

Matthew dropped to his knees beside them. Hoopsa pup pup . . . Hoopsa pup pup . . . . He and Emmy Lou watched Molly resting, her eyes closed. She breathed as if she were asleep. Then the ripples along her stomach as one fetus began to turn. The ripples flowed along her hips. Her vaginal opening shuddered. They could hear sucking sounds as the first puppy prepared for entry. Molly pulled to her feet, her tail drooped toward the newspepers as if she were about to deficate. She turned and struggled to reach toward her rearend with her muzzle as a fetus plopped in its sack into the world, dangling from her vagina by its afterbirth and umbelical cord. Molly tore the sack from the head of the puppy so she could get at it and began to clean away the mucus around its nose and mouth with her tongue. Clear the passage way. She continued cleaning the sack away and massaging the little black-and-white body with her tongue. As she chewed through the cord, she also jerked at the afterbirth half in her and half out and, pulling it free, she gobbled it up, almost choking before Matthew could take it from her. He dampened a sponge in the still warm water and began to massage the puppy's squirming body. Emmy Lou's eyes were brilliant.

"Why doesn't it yip or something?"

"Soon. Don't rush it." Matthew turned the four inches of puppy which looked like a carbon copy of Molly over onto its back. "Him."

Emmy Lou giggled. "Wow!"

On its back the puppy boy began to squeak and yip, finding the sounds better than the silence of the womb he had endured for sixty-three days.

"Wow is right. Man! Shit! Birth! Goddamn!" He shook his head in wonder. "Christ, this is fucking incredible . . . . Here." He handed her the sponge. "Touch him."

She massaged the puppy as it squirmed back over onto its spread-eagle legs swimming in place on the newspaper and moaning with pleasure. "God . . . ." She grinned and carressed the puppy's delicate head with one finger.

"Yes." Matthew grinned also. "Backwards."

"You and your compulsion to see irony in everything . . . ."

"Joke," he chuckled putting his bloody palms out in front of his face. "No fight . . . ."

"Okay." She smiled again, still stroking the puppy as Molly laid down and whined for the puppy. He began to blindly grope his way toward his mother's sounds. "But it's another one of those damn traits you acquired from hanging out with that Stephen Dedalus character." She snorted.

"That's what you get when you're the son of an Icarus with broken wings." Matthew, too, guffawed. Molly whimpered. Ripples began in the lower stomach still swollen with puppies to be born, Slowly they worked their way to her spine and down, across her thighs.

By nine-thirty the sun was high enough over the house to shower through the windows in the front wall of the kennel only a few feet from where they still huddled around Molly's miracles. Two puppies still squirmed under her tongue. The last to be born. Sun streamed into the straw on the floor. Where the light touched it directly, the straw seemed to burn. Ten black-and-white puppies nursed at her teats. Her milk had come down early because of the special vitamins Emmy Lou had been giving her. Matthew had checked by squeezing her nipples. Milk dribbled from all twelve teats.

Matthew's eyes were popped open like he'd done a couple of L.A. turnarounds. Sleep. What the hell. Sleep's only the organizer. Do that as you go along and you don't really need sleep. His eyes found it difficult to cover over the pity he felt for her as he turned to her from the patches of blazing straw. She kneeled in her jeans and paint-spattered work shirt, now cradling the two newest puppy girls in her lap like Our Lady of Madonna. No. Mixed memory. Get your tapes straight. Lady Madonna. Our Lady of the Harbor. Lennon and McCartney. Cohen. Like Gleason said in the *Rolling Stone*, our real poets are our songwriters. Never before in American popular music had the poets written the songs or the songwriters written the poems. One, two, maybe even three (if we're lucky) times in a century a generation comes along that, because of circumstances they are subjected to, revolutionizes the country. We've all read it in those catastrophies called public school history books. 1776. 1861. The nineteen thirties. The sixties. We are one of those specially destined generations. We are the force of natural revolution in the only country in the world that recognizes that force officially in its founding documents. Thanks Thomas. Strange. From her lap to poets to politics and back to her lap. "You know we haven't even said hello yet . . . ." He grinned, finally able to mask the pity as she glanced up from the only saddlebacks in the litter. "So, then, how are you, Madame Bovary?" Suddenly he realized he had decided to use the water pot as an ashtray. They didn't need the water any longer. Everything, indeed, *had* worked out fine. "What are those paintings all about? Why wouldn't you talk to me, see me all this time?"

"Shsssh! Shsssh!" She rolled her head in circles holding her ears with her hands. "Noooooooo . . . ."

"But . . . ." Words collided in his throat constricted in amazement, fear, at her instantaneous transformation. She sat calm, smiling, again caressing the puppies.

"But?" She giggled nervously. "But let's talk about you. I hear things. Even though I'm inside this house most of the time, I hear things."

For a flash she seemed to be distracted by the layers of smoldering straw surrounding her like their many past campfires on cold nights. Her eyes seemed to wander off into the morning toward the cloud the sun's rays were filtering through. Suddenly she was back.

"I'm sure. I'm sure you do hear things, Madame Bovary. There's lots of talk . . . always has been. You know that."

"Yes. but this is different talk. The words of the night when I'm alone in my room or in here with Molly . . . still alone. This is talk about Florida, about how Ward and Linda and Poper, yes even poor squirrel Poper, have conned you into taking up this cause of student's rights."

Matthew struggled with whether to nod or shake his head. "Ah . . . . I must admit I don't have a very clear memory of Florida, Madame Bovary . . . or much else since Ward reappeared and you disappeared. It's like I've been pulling a Rip Van Winkle for the past several months . . . ."

Again her spirit seemed to become disembodied. He remembered that sparkling Budweiser sign in the Holabird Inn. Donaldson. Klopps. *When in the course of human events* . . . . Her lips moved like a puppet's but her larynx made no sounds.

"Linda's the one, you know," her hollow voice pronounced. "She's the one who placed the copy of Jasons will in the mailbox. She put her palms up between them, her head off to one side so he couldn't force her to look into his eyes as if she were staving off a werewolf or vampire with a cross. "Don't ask me how I know. You won't listen . . . you won't believe me anyway. It is part of my curse, you know. Of course you know. You're a student of literature. You must know about Cassandra." Again, as suddenly, her eyes took on life's glint. She was with him. "Why, Matthew? Why take it all upon yourself? This students' rights issue may ruin you."

Matthew's lips pulled thin and tight as a half-hitch. How could she know about Florida? Get away. Rest. That's what everyone said he needed after Jason's death. After the funeral, Ward and Linda invited him to go with them to Florida, to Henderson Crampton's vacation home. Ward had not sold that.

"Do you realize what you're risking?"

"I think so." He lit a Winston, his first cigarette since Molly had begun delivery. "But it has to be done by somebody." He shrugged. "Guess it might as well be me," he chuckled. "After all, I am the walrus."

"Even when you *know* you'll end up alone?' She completely ignored his attempt at humor. She couldn't believe he was allowing himself to be so naive. Her eyes glared at him.

"Alone?" He wagged his head. "No. Not all alone."

"Oh, really? Who, may I ask, can you count on?" She lowered her head, again staring at the luminous straw scattered over the floor. "You weren't even able to count on me . . . ."

His words caught in his throat like slivers of glass. "But, Madame Bovary . . . ." Tears forced their way into his eyes. He turned away. *And any time you feel the pain, hey Jude refrain, don't carry the world up on your shoulders . . . .*

Emmy Lou stood, brushing straws of fire from her jeans and shirt. The two newest puppies went straight for Molly's teats when she placed them near the mother, squirming and squealing in the midst of their eight brothers and sisters. "People," she mumbled, "are just like that." She pointed to the pushing, shoving puppies grappling for a teat. "They don't care about you, man . . . or me." She began wandering toward the door. "I'll get us some breakfast. Alecia sleeps late these days. She's old. I hardly sleep at all. Do you?"

Her bright hair glimmered in the sunlight still pouring through the front windows. He knew now what it was . . . what Alecia had really been trying to tell him. But she, herself, believed all this mumbo jumbo too much to be a clear messenger. It had to come by seeing Emmy Lou like this. She was his no longer, if she ever had been his, or him, hers. She turned in the doorway. His face froze at the sight of her face divided between sunlight and shadow with the same gnarled oak snarl from her self-portrait.

"In the end, Matthew, not one will stand with you . . . ." Her head jerked away from the room brimming with the odors of recent birth and straw that seemed to burn without being consumed. Amidst squeaking hinges and banging wooden doors, Emmy Lou vanished into the Ides of March morning.

Café Sloth had been a steel cutting plant in a previous iteration. The steel beams and girders that formed the frame of the building still remained exposed so that the space seemed to exist within the internal confines of a gigantic fossil or the disintegrating skeleton of an outhouse sprawled on its side near the Alamogordo observation blockhouse. Kathleen Jurgenson and Ron Dawson sauntered through the bowels of the fossil as if they owned it. "Professor Parkrow," they shouted in unison over the crowd's voice.

He motioned to them to join him. "Matthew here. We're not in class."

"Well, Matthew," Kathleen hurled at him as he ordered a round. "Dee Dee Spinoza, you know, the student body president told us she wants to talk with you after your reading." Kathleen brushed her taffy hair back over her left shoulder leaving her right side exposed to the stabbing strobe lights from the stage like the electronic chords of *Purple Haze* suddenly exploding from Hendrix's guitar as the music geared up for the night.

He was nearly lonely enough . . . desperate enough . . . . Her earlobe seemed to throb with the anticipation of his touch. It would be so easy. She was so close. His hand seemed to begin moving without his being aware of it. Then he realized and stopped it immediately and focused the hand on the beer just plopped down in front of him by the waitress instead of Kathleen's naked earlobe

"I know Dee Dee really well," Ron chimed in. "She wouldn't waste your time, Matthew. It must be really important."

"Yeah, we think she wants you to speak at the rally tomorrow."

"Okay, you two." He raised his Coors bottle. "From my private smuggled stock." They raised theirs and clicked together and drank. "We'll get together with Dee Dee at the end of our night of poetry and music and beer."

The music abruptly stopped and the club manager, Chris Nestor, tapped the mike to make sure it was live. It popped loudly from the stage speakers. "Welcome folks to Café Sloth and to our special feature each night . . . our poetry readings by some of the most promising talent of our times. Tonight's very special guest is Matthew Parkrow, Associate Professor of English and Creative Writing at State University. He's a man who really needs no introduction. On campus just ask a student. Here at the café, just ask the person next to you. So, without further ado, Matthew Parkrow!"

"Matthew! Matthew! Matthew!" the packed crowd cheered.

"Guess you're up," Ron goaded.

"Yes, I guess that's me they're calling for." He mocked a sigh of resignation as he scooped up his sheaf of poems and threaded his way between tables toward the stage. For an instant, he flashed on Altamont when he was struggling through the crowd trying to get to the stage to help with the wounded.

As he picked his way through the building's steel bowels and his own memories, Poper came up behind him and walked with him to the stage as he spoke. "Sorry, I could only stop by for a minute. I really cannot stay. Really. I'm sure I probably know most of the poems you will read tonight. Anyway. I just wanted to come by and show my support, you know, for this event and for the students and the poetry."

"Thanks, Poper." Matthew clapped him on the shoulder. "I'm touched." He leaped the few inches to the stage. "Good evening, everyone!"

"Good evening, Matthew!"

Under the red waning moon, the Capital City Outdoor Theater slumbered in the early morning ground fog rising from the rushing stream below. Because the gardens were so serene a barrier against the city, Matthew often referred to the stream as *Lethe*. The stream of forgetfulness meandered and infused the surrounding gardens. Moss flourished in the sunken mortar joints between the stones of the amphitheater, itself a structure that had co-existed for decades with fecund but artfully pruned and tended gardens strewn along the wandering banks of the wide, shallow brook fed by the same spring head twenty miles west that made the pond in the woods near his deep camp gush up from underneath the earth.

The amphitheater's recently sandblasted pre-cast concrete shell which defined this stage glared out in the night like a wide beacon to Matthew as he picked his way along a path he practically had memorized from the many trips he had made here over the past five years to meditate under the mantra of the stream. He still found it odd that he would come here, in the midst of the West Capital end of town only a few blocks from the church where he used to go to dances after their high school football and basketball games to find his own special Don Juan spot for meditation. And, he really needed that spot now. He had gone and done it for sure. Dee Dee Spinoza did not want to discuss the philosophy of her namesake. She did want him to be the keynote speaker at their rally. And, he stepped into a huge pile of it by telling her it was an honor to be asked and he would let her know in the morning.

Crickets rubbed their legs together. Their high pitched, minor key songs charged the air. Bull frogs bellowed up ahead by the stream. The perfume of magnolias clung to every sound and every movement. Was that a nightingale? Or just the croaking of tree toads? He anticipated the lone snowy owl hoot and screech. He knew the owl lurked in the park somewhere. On moonlit nights it prowled the gardens for mice or other small creatures venturing into the moon drenched darkness.

"HOOOT . . . . HOOOT . . . . EEEEEEEEH!

His breath lodged under his Adam's apple. Blood stuck in his ventricals. His heart seemed to fail just for a moment as his vision blurred and the garden path disappeared into the desert of the amphitheater's top row. Owl's eyes flared out at him from thick deep shadows of the single pecan tree in the gardens. Its branches, heavy with spring leaves, canopied the path above the amphitheater's ninth circle. Branches uncharacteristically in need of pruning shoved across the path. Those green eyes surrounding saucer-like yellow pupils seemed to block Matthew's way.

"HOOOT . . . . HOOOT . . . . EEEEEEEEH!"

He hesitated, medusaed by those owl eyes. They were a lot alike, him and the owl. They were the only ones of their kind left alive in this place, relegated to singing their startling songs under the darkness of night . . . and chasing their prey under the light of the moon. The owl held forth here in his garden domain. Matthew taught in his classroom, researched in his tower and read poetry in Cafe Sloth. It was here, in the owl's garden, that he felt a kind of peace like when he would catch a fast ball with the sweet spot of his bat and drive it deep . . . going, going, gone . . . . And, those days were, indeed, gone . . . gone forever, yet he could still remember those singularities of perfection. So, it was here, in the owl's garden, under the owl's relentless stare that he would achieve some kind of calm, some kind of peace with himself for what he had done and for what he was about to do.

"HOOOT . . . . HOOOT . . . . EEEFEFEEH!"

Everything Emmy Lou had predicted was actually happening. Once he had let it be known that he was taking a very personal and active interest in the growing students' rights movement on campus, he found that he was becoming gradually more and more isolated from the faculty and even the other graduate students. Somehow they didn't seem to see themselves as students. They saw themselves as part time faculty who still had some classes and other requirements to complete before they could become full time.

Actually, he was surprised at Poper's visit earlier and his continued loyalty. He knew that Poper must feel the same way as most of the others. Yet he even told Matthew that Scythe had already approached him about moving to another office "if he no longer wished to continue sharing the same office with that rabble rouser, Parkrow."

According to Poper, he had told Scythe that he enjoyed sharing office space with Matthew . . . a lie he would not normally tell . . . even under threat of death.

And, he still had his students. They were not deserting him.

Hundreds planned to attend his previously scheduled teach-in on students' rights this morning in support of the student rally . . . before he had agreed to speak . . . just hours from now. He would facilitate the discussion on students' rights in University policy making. At noon, he would address the rally in the Brickyard as the keynote speaker. Or would he? What would he . . . .

"HOOOT . . . . HOOOT . . . . EEEEEEEEH!"

". . . . Do?"

In order to avoid the overhanging branches of the pecan tree and the owl lurking among them, Matthew was forced to turn inward, down to the next level of seats in the amphitheater. The luminescent concrete shell still held the dark faceless face with atomic eyes somewhere inside its cave-like stage. The mouth of the gargouille moved in Trouffeau-like light and shadows.

FEMALE

[Enters stage left, crossing to upper stage right as she speaks]:

"I've been told to avoid you like the plague. Did you know that?"
[She glances over her left shouder toward off-stage left.]

"Come on! Don't dilly, Dally."

MALE

[Enters stage left, crossing to center stage where he plops down with a thud as if he will never move again]:

"This is not dallying, Dilly. This is simply stopping."

FEMALE

[Noticeably irritated]:

"No stopping is simple."

MALE

[Equally irritated]:

"It's capable!"

FEMALE:

"What's capable?"

MALE:

"Stopping"

FEMALE:

"You mean, possible?"

MALE:

"No, I mean capable.

FEMALE:

"Use it in a sentence, please.

MALE:

"Capable. Stopping is capable of being simple." [He pauses, then spells out the word letter by letter almost as if he is being forced by some kind of conditioning to do so] "C . . . A . . . P . . . A . . . B . . . L . . . E . . . . Capable!"

"Matthew?" the glowing dragon's mouth hurled his name toward him as he paused on row eight to watch the actors on the stage.

It was the female's voice. "Yes. Is that you, Kathleen?"

"Yes, sir . . . ."

"And Ron, Matthew. . . ah . . . Mr. Parkrow."

"What in the world are you two doing here at this time of the morning?

"Well, we thought that since . . . ."

"Since this scene we're performing at the rally later this morning takes place at dawn . . . ah . . . ."

"We'd . . . ah . . . ." Kathleen interrupted. "We'd like to rehearse it under real-life conditions, you know."

"Oh, really?"

"Well, not really"

"Then what, really?"

"We thought you'd be coming here to contemplate what's going to happen today . . . ."

"And we just wanted to be here for you, Matthew . . . Mr. Parkrow."

"That's really the what of it, sir."

"Mr. Dryden's here to. He's backstage."

"Carrot? He just stopped by Café Sloth before my reading too."

Kathleen smiled. "Yes sir." She didn't understand his being here either. Never thought Mr. Dryden had the balls to stand up for anything or anyone including himself. Maybe she had been wrong.

"Tell him that I'll come down soon, but first I need some time to myself over by the stream."

The musty odor of moss crushing beneath his shoes as he squatted along the bank of the bubbling *Lethe* overwhelmed him for a moment. There was a storm brewing. He could feel it gathering around him like a mack or a serape, a soliloquy or a colloquy, a birthing or a deathing, an unearthing or a resurrecting, a shrouding or a crowding. There was a storm gathering against him just as Emmy Lou had predicted. What was he to do?

"What am I to do?" His words fell softly onto the gurgling surface of the stream swollen by two days of heavy rains like withering fern branches. "What am I to do?" Of course he had to laugh. He had let himself in for the whole frigging mess. So, whatever he was to do was up to him and him alone . . . and was probably already out of his hands anyway.

It was a time to sit still . . . .

"Quick Artie! Pan Those Students carrying the black coffin! Zoom in on the leader!"

Artie released the trigger. Swinging the camera one hundred and eighty degrees from an impromptu skateboard contest developing to the left of the library steps where the microphones stood beside a rostrum and the leaders of the students began to fill the stone benches that fronted the brick walls on both sides. They separated the first level from the second level of brick steps. Artie's every move was cued by Ida's voice. She had a "nose for news" like some people had "green thumbs." Getting the shot, however, now that was news of a different angle!

"Now!"

He triggered the color porto-pack, focused the lens, then panned the procession, finally zooming in on the leader's skeleton mask and matching suit he must have saved from Halloween thinking he was Guy Fawkes or somebody.

"Okay. Now pan the entire area quickly . . . and hold on the empty areas of the brickyard."

Artie obeyed the voice in his ear. "What next, Ida?"

"Wrap it, Artie!"

"Wrap it?"

"Yes!"

Artie stared at his watch. Eleven fifty-five. "But . . . the rally doesn't even start for five minutes, Ida?" His eyes squinted toward her in the bright mid-day sun.

"We got what we came for, Artie. Nothing here but a sparse gathering of a few whacky students racing skateboards and wearing Halloween costumes."

Artie pointed off in the distance where, behind the glare of sunlight off glass buildings, students swarmed toward the brickyard. "Look!" Still not multitudes like when he used to cover the biggies in the sixties but . . . . "Lots of kids still coming." He cocked his head like a chipmonk. Well, Ida, what do you think of that? Huh? "Now I don't have much of a news nose, but that's news, ain't it Ida? Speakers, cheers, boos . . . . TV audiences love mobs, don't they?" He squirmed in his out-of-place gray suit. If you worked cameras in the field for TV 5, then you wore a gray suit. That was the way it was.

"You got plenty of footage of the brickyard with no students around? Right?"

Artie nodded.

"You got the skate boarders and the coffin parade, right?"

Artie nodded again even though he was pretty sure that Ida couldn't see him nodding at this distance given the glare of the sun. He could see where this was going.

"Good! That's all we need to nip this thing right in the knickers." She paused as if reflecting. "That's most definitely a wrap, Art."

He didn't even bother to nod this time. He simply began packing up his gear for the long trek back to the news van where Ida awaited him.

Ward and Poper huddled behind the giant oak tree between English and Round Hall that had become known as "Matthew's oak" beause he often taught his classes under its branches. Hidden but still in view of the library steps. A crowd was gathering. Not as rowdy as we were, though, "do you think Poper?"

"Huh?" Poper jerked his head toward Ward's voice. What do you mean, do I Think . . . make that a small t. Did Pope think? Or Dryden? John, of course. He wrote about cities. To hear Matthew talk nobody ever wrote about cities before that bunch of French buffoons. He says that Dylan's their heir but nobody's listening. Stupid peasant. Garbage for a brain. Scares hell out of you though, when he looks right into you . . . and there's nothing you can do about it.

"The crowd's not as noisy as we used to be, do you think?"

"Oh . . . ." He hung his head. He had misunderstood the question.

Poor Poper, shivering in his powdered skin for fear of Matthew finding out he's helping us and of me finding out that the reason he's helping us is because lovely, lilting Linda has suddenly become a raving expert on Eighteenth Century lit and her absolutely most hated writer is Laurence Sterne. And she has probably carried him over the spermfalls of ecstasy like only that scheming vamp can, each goose bump raised on your skin premeditated. Poor whispering little mouse. The gall of the fool! He's hardly worth the trouble.

The way Ward was shaking his head, the sadness in his gray eyes, his position of standing over him looking down all made Poper feel lke he was in his own coffin and Ward was viewing him. "Don't know if they're more noisy or not." He glanced around him at the open ground shaded by other scattered trees, mostly oaks. "But there was a noon class cut strike planned for today. That might account for the late crowd arrival." Poper didn't want to admit that he had never experienced a rally or protest before. He felt so exposed here. His only protection at all had been that Matthew believed they all were supporting him. But that shield would be battered to smithereens by the time this rally was over. Matthew would soon know that he was responsible for getting that drop/add change considered and passed by the faculty senate. He could easily deduce from that and a few other hints that he was helping Linda, too, on the dope frame. Matthew would soon know it all. They had to get him really good . . . . Poper leered up at Ward's now scowling face. Or he'd come after them . . . for sure.

"You sure you planted the shit at his trailer?"

"Exactly where the warrant says." Poper struggled to not whimper.

Ward's face retracted, turned back toward the library steps aross the expansive brick courtyard. "You better not've fucked anything up, boy." Ward snarled at his milky face. "Bow-Tie'll have your ass . . . then mine, and I really wouldn't like that one fucking little bit. And I'll bet you that Linda will like it even less than me . . . ."

Poper pouted, his head turned away from his tormentor. "I did my part. Don't you worry, Ward Crampton, I did my part."

"I did my part," Ward mocked. "I did my part . . . ."

"There's been some talk around, mostly among those FM rock reporters." Stella hitched the macramé belt which clung to her jump suit where it sloped into her hips. "The story is that some professors are holding students over until twelve-fifteen, forcing them to either miss the rally or walk out on the professors' classes. Ingenious intimidation tactics, don't you think?"

Jay Kramer chuckled, oggled the mint green silkiness below his favorite female reporter's belt where she shimmered. "Gonzo politics . . . in spades." He grinned. "Or should I say, in black orchids." Jay tipped the hat he'd never bought and twirled the mustache he'd never grown. "Just so happens I'm an expert on that very subject, my dear . . . ."

"Fascinating. All that poise and quarterback confidence."

"Yeah, long as I'm in the armchair, not in the pocket." He

nudged the creamy softness of her side with his elbow.

"Ha . . . ha . . . ha . . . ." she giggled. Well, it beat etchings all to hell. Nobody in their right mind would say anymore, "Come on up and see my etchings." Nowadays is different. It's Gonzo politics or you don't score with the really hip chicks. Stella purred. "Maybe we could get together afterwards for a little rough and tumble Gonzo politics . . . huh?"

"Gon . . . zo.

"Okay. Gon . . . zo." She licked her Elke Sommer lips. "Maybe we'll get a good article out of it too."

"City Editor's orders were to play it down." Jay encircled her sinewy waist with his once All-American quarterback arms. The polyester of her jump suit was cool against his arms. "So I don't know about the big article, but . . . we can take a shot at it."

Stella felt him squeeze her, heard him guffaw. She might even get the article through this time, with this particular version of Jay Kramer, hot shit reporter. At least he should be a marathoner. His muscles still have their tone. Could be worse. "Oh, yeah, Jay baby, well, I'm real good at that taking a shot thing . . . yes I am . . . real good." She brushed his crotch with hers as she eased away from his embrace, blowing him a kiss as she drifted toward the library stairs. "See you after its over. Okay?"

"Okay." Out of the corner of his eye Jay caught a glimpse of Ida and Artie carrying their gear toward their TV5 Mobile van. He waved until they had to acknowledge him. Then he dodged his way through the crowd now beginning to swell the brickyard, finally cornering them as they got into their van. "I see the TV people are wrapping it before the rally even begins, huh?"

Artie nodded and continued arranging his gear in the back of the van. Ida lit a Virginia Slims menthol and inhaled. "We do what we're told . . . just like you do, Mr. Kramer." She exhaled a stream of smoke in Jay's face. He coughed. "No different, Mr. Kramer."

"At least we're going to cover the rally, not cover it up!"

"Oh, we're not covering it up, Mr. Kramer. Are we Artie?" Artie nodded, not looking up. "You can bet your sweet ass on that!"

"Really, Ida." Jay mocked being bludgeoned. "There's no need for all that violence, now is there?"

Artie nodded again behind Ida's back.

The mikes on stage squealed, hummed, fell silent. The crowd began to tighten toward the library steps. "Testing . . . one . . . two . . . testing . . . ." The Student Union President flashed a copper smile, then moved off to the left speaker bank. "Thanks, Steve, for the patch into the mikes." It was a radio voice. Yes. Without looking behind, he answered. "WDBS's our friend, Jethro. Any time."

Instead of picking and strumming and singing protest songs, the demonstrators milled around the brickyard while a pock-faced boy stood on the stone steps of the library now being used as the stage for their rally, creating whistling, crashing sounds like interstellar combat on a portable synthesizer.

And here I go again, flinging myself headlong into the arms of my enemy. Just like Jason said I would. Once I step onto that stage, everything I have worked for over these past five years will evaporate like the morning moisture on my garden . . . what's left of it. My teaching career at State will be over. My teaching career anywhere will likely be over. Scythe will see to that.

Is it worth these stakes, especially knowing that you're going to lose no matter what? Can these students possibly know or understand what you'll be sacrificing for their little drop/add policy revolt? It certainly doesn't stack up to "The whole world's watching" now does it? Or does it?

That was the inevitable wall against which all inquiry ultimately crashed and burned. Who valued what? Probably if we examined my pending actions as close to the wall as possible without crashing and burning, then we might actually discover that students fighting the administration over arbitrary and capricious academic policies and exercises of power is exactly where "The whole world's watching" began.

"You'll be completely alone, Matthew!" her gnarled face of light and shadow screamed inside his skull. "You can't even count on me!"

"Matthew?" Her voice cracked trying to overcome the electronic crashes echoing off of Round Hall. "Dee Dee Spinoza," she nearly screamed as she extended her hand. "We met at Café Sloth."

"Yes, I remember. You're why I'm here."

"Yes. It was a pleasure meeting you. We've all heard so much about your classes." She grinned. "Kathleen believes you can part the seas and walk on water." She paused, still grinning. "Well, can you?"

"No . . . ."

"Well, thank you so much for coming and doing our keynote today anyway. You are truly so well thought of around here . . . ."

Matthew stroked his beard, looked off to one side toward Round Hall. The students were beginning to gather in clumps around the brickyard. "Thanks. That's nice to hear."

"Since you're the keynote speaker, you will come fifth." She smiled. "Symbolic and all that, huh?"

He nodded. He was to be the completion of the pentangle? "Well, it's a fine day for it." Matthew nodded again as Dee Dee Spinoza agreed.

"Thank you, again," she chirped, shaking his hand again and bustling off across the stage toward a clump of students near the microphones.

Matthew sat on the edge of one of the stone benches, pulled a stack of note cards from his flannel shirt pocket and began shuffling them like he'd learned in Reno back in seventy when he and Emmy Lou had fled New York, ultimately for Denver. Later, Denver for here. And, where is she now? In that dead man's house—that moldering miserable man posing as his father—painting murals on his walls for posterity's sake. Suddenly he was aware of jeers at the fringes of the crowd solidifying in the brickyard. He looked up. The television van was pulling out of the parking lot beside the library as the first speaker was being introduced by Dee Dee Spinoza as their very own non-voting representative on the Faculty Senate, Eddie Sawyer. There was a smattering of applause for Eddie. Lots of looking around. They were ill at ease. They did not know what to do.

Hell, we used to be coached. Couldn't leave anything spontaneous to chance. Is that Emmy Lou hiding behind that post under Round? Wish she were up here with me. She knows. He touched his other shirt pocket, feeling the folded envelope inside. But I have her note at least . . . in remembrance of things which flowed from future to present to past like a baseball from Tinkers to Evers to Chance. And chance made fools of us. Who'er those men with her? Look like SBI or something. Can't be sure from here. The hood on her jacket fell back to her shoulders as wind swirled through the brickvard and under Round. No . . . . Not her at all unless she dyed her hair black.

"I'll congratulate him after it's over," Linda whispered to the stout young man who was leaning against one of the concrete pillars that held Round Hall fifteen feet above its reinforced concrete base. "That way you'll know the right person to take down. After that, it's up to you and your partners."

"Check."

"Be sure to let him go on a PR bond though. That's important . . . very important! Ah . . . he's always showed in court in the past and we don't really want him in jail. He might still lead us to his contacts." Linda pulled her trenchcoat tighter in a sudden imagined breeze.

"Check." The agent checked the inside pocket of his suit jacket. The baggie was still there. All soft and powdery white documented as taken from Matthew Parkrow's trailer during a warrant search of his premises. "Possession of cocaine'll take care of that freak for a good while . . . ." He smiled, showing her the top of the baggie inside his jacket. "Just in case we can't make the other charges stick."

Linda's face flushed carnelian in the shadows of Round Hall. Poper had actually done his job. She wasn't sure if five blowjobs and seven fucks with Poper Dryden were worth one little bag of cocaine planted in the kitchen cabinets under the sugar in Matthew's brown Jugtown sugar canister. But she'd take it. "Good. We want his credibility shot to hell, his teaching career destroyed. We want him ruined as a functioning human being . . . ."

"Check." The agent tried to smile but couldn't, readjusted his jacket and glanced toward the library steps where the speakers were sitting in front of the small lumps of people on the stage-like steps. He couldn't look at Mrs. Crampton. His stomach couldn't take that diabolical smile pasted across her face anymore. And, he'd learned long ago in his fifteen years with the SBI that you don't cross the feds . . . . "Whatever you federal types want is what we've been ordered to do, ma'm."

"Be cool," a stringy-haired freshman whispered to the girl in front of him who was just lighting up a joint. "Plain clothes cops off to your left.

She turned around. Her dimpled cheeks filled with smoke looked like a blow fish. She stared at the freshman, her bright brown eyes saucered.

"Over there." He nodded over his left shoulder. "Under Round . . . something's going down."

She offered him the joint, being careful to keep it low and in front of him and those clustered near them. Her cheeks relaxed as she exhaled. "Thanks, man. Have a toke . . . ."

"Sure." He smiled. "Appreciate it."

Bluegrass Bob spit out the side of his mouth. "Man, I'm telling you there's government agents all over this brickyard!" He leaned over to Jethro's ear to whisper. "Listen Jethro. Those tv jerks are gone. This could be really big . . . a radio scoop for a change."

"Shit, Bob, I can smell an agent." He sniffed the air in all directions. "Nothing . . . not even a local yokel fuzz."

Bluegrass Bob shrugged his shoulders. "All I know is what I'm gettin' from the students."

"But use your common horse sense. This dinky rally is not *that* important. Just a few students with nothing better to do."

"Well, it's not like the old days, that's for sure." Bob heaved. "There used to be agents *everywhere* back then . . . weren't there, Jethro?"

"Back then? That was only a couple of years ago . . . ."

"Hell, maybe it's somebody that's here at the rally who they're after?"

"Maybe one of the speakers?"

"What's this about agents?" Jay Kramer's cherub face poked between them. His teeth fairly glowed as he turned his head first toward Jethro's poker face and then toward Bob. He held his gaze on Bob's twitching green eyes. "What about it Bluegrass Bob?"

". . . . That because of the dramatic increase in drops over the past two years, the drop period be decreased from nine weeks to two weeks with an additional two-week period in which the student will be able to drop a course with a *W* withdrawal notation on his or her permanent record." Eddie Sawyer hesitated. He wanted this to sink in good. "That's the basic resolution as it was passed unanimously by the Faculty Senate." He cleared his throat, waiting for a few jeers to subside. "Now, we must remember a couple of things, here. First, the resolution passed by the Faculty Senate was one concerning *students*. Second, no student representation went into the making of this resolution." He was interrupted by increasing stamping and boos. "The one student who was allowed to be at the meeting— me—didn't have a vote . . . and, what's more, wasn't allowed to even participate in discussions concerning the resolution." Eddie slammed his fist down on the rostrum. "Something's gotta be done about this kinda shit! As he stomped off to his seat, students cheered.

The still-growing crowd responded sounding noisy but not committed, yet for a second the front rows began to slowly flow together as they raised their hands above their heads and clapped like they would've at a concert which particularly pleased them. Strange, the strong connection between a political rally and an artistic concert. Both basic expressions of the culture. Yes. Both have performers. Yes. And. Yes. Audiences. A bridge as pure and strong as the one between Jimi's *Star-Spangled Banner* and *Purple Haze* at Woodstock. "You don't have to stick around, we're just jamming," he mumbled that morning before the dawn, after the rains had drenched them. Tomorrow, they would be hungry. Today, they would celebrate . . . . What? Nationhood? Does anybody remember when it happened? Certainly not today? No, today is Jefferson's birthday. Yes. I know him. Touched his mind once doing LSD. It made me cry, I remember, and that became the first time I couldn't seem to stop. That movie about Van Gough made it worse when the Amsterdam children threw stones at the poor, crazy fucker. I couldn't watch television after that . . . for months. Even missed the World Series . . . . The A's beat the Reds in seven.

Scythe made Nixon's mistake at the Watergate Hotel on June 17. Breaking into your opponents headquarters? Now, that was a haughty naughty. Happens everywhere all the time. How many times has Scythe been through my students' papers? Must've been at it again last night. They were in order Tuesday when I left the office. And, anyone looking through them would think they were in chaos unless they knew what my red numbers mean. Simplest of systems to catch meddling. Just consecutively number each paper for all students as they are randomly placed in the file box. Matthew chuckled behind his right hand as if he were coughing or clearing his throat. He had suspected that of Scythe for years now. That was why he had initiated his special filing system. Then, last year, he received an anonymous tip that seemed to confirm his suspicions. According to the tip, Scythe had been seen snooping around his cubicle on numerous occasions when the tipper was coming in late to grade papers. Just this morning he had found a typed note on his desk outlining what another source had seen only in the last few days. Scythe pretended to be heading for the closet in the back—the room where all the old papers were stored. The note assured me that he was about to step into my cubicle before he heard someone else in the room. I'd swear the note was typed on Poper's typewriter. Now, a note from his typewriter is pretty much confirming that it *is* Scythe who has been rifling through my students' papers off and on for the last five years. His filing system scheme had triggered the fact that someone had done so several times a year for the entire time he had been a Ph.D. candidate. And, really, was there anyone else he so offended?

". . . . Five times in a row Teacher of the Year . . . Matthew Parkrow!" Dee Dee Spinoza's words interrupted his thoughts. He should have been thinking about the speech. She turned from the microphone and motioned toward him with her right hand. Matthew stood from his perch on the stone bench, stretched a little from the toes and shoulders, hitched up his jeans and shuffled across the stage to the podium. As the quiescent crowd became aware of him, *they* burst into rifle shots of applause, one building upon the other like echoes in a canyon.

The brickyard's reverberating like the old days. They're responding as we'd all hoped. 'Somebody who can walk down them steps and lead the whole bunch down the street to the Capital.' That's what Steve with the copper smile had demanded above all else at the meeting with Dee Dee. 'And a lot of the students know him either by being in his classes or hearing him read at Café Sloth or just dropping by his office or his table in Mac's. He's always willing to talk to the students about anything. He's almost a legend. Let's ask him.' Matthew accepted reluctantly, knowing somehow his career was on the line but feeling the need of these students above that. The applause turned into yells and screams and stamping on the brickyard.

What to do? They want something . . . . And, I don't have a guitar to burn . . . .

Suddenly Matthew raised his clenched right fist, shaking it at the sun as he grasped the podium with his left hand. In the first row he was sure he saw himself. Suddenly the Reporter's sadness swept over him all the way from the Chicago streets of sixty-nine. "Happy birthday Thomas Jefferson . . . ." His head drooped. "We sure could use you here today!" He toyed with his note cards and smiled as the cheers crescendoed and died voice by voice. As he cleared his throat, his legs quivered. Nervous? Jesus. Well, the whole world may not be watching this time but that's still a lot of people. Man, it's just like a class, only a good deal larger. Cleansing breath.

"I'm supposed to make a speech to you which will drive home the message of this rally today and of the protest of over five thousand petition signatures in only three days against the proposed drop-add policy changes.

"Being both a student and a member of the faculty you might well understand my concern for self-determination in both roles. Self-determination is not merely a right of a student or a teacher or a citizen that can be arbitrarily given or taken away by the reigning authorities. As citizens we are not born to be forced. We breathe after our own fashion, and gathering here today damn sure proves our concern for our birthright: to be self-determining human beings with power over the decisions that govern our lives in this country, this state, at this university! That's what this . . . ." He swept his arms around and up to indicate them all ". . . . is all about today . . . the right to self-determination!"

Matthew glanced over the crowd packing closer toward the brick stairs as he spoke. The sun glistened off their heads like off bullrushes in a marsh as they shouted and swayed in rhythm. Matthew raised both fists above his head. They cheered, then fell silent as his fists opened into outstretched fingers.

"Education without representation is as valid a rallying cry against an overzealous Parent syndrome as taxation without representation was when this nation . . . ." They were shrieking. ". . . . when this nation heaved in the early pains of its birth.

"But, you can't talk about education by quoting student drop

344

statistics!"

"No!" the crowd responded tentatively.

"You can't talk about education while supporting policies that cavalierly ignore learning as the basic premise of this (or any) university!"

"No!" The response grew louder.

"You can't talk about education when you support policies that are based on a worn out mold cast from threadbare attitudes!"

"No!"

"They say, 'We had to do things this way, so you have to do the same.' It's this attitude which has forced young people into the streets for centuries in the name of freedom as it forced us to do in the sixties. It's this attitude which is responsible for thousands of GI's who died in the rice paddies and rainforests of Vietnam or were crippled physically or mentally for life . . . ." His voice cracked. He paused, inhaled. Exhale. Inhale, slow. Exhale, slow.

"Now I know it seems a long way from wars to drop policies being forced on students . . . on us at this university. But we've seen it all before, this chip, chip, chipping away at our mountain of freedom.

"And," he continued, pointing his finger toward the administration building off to his left behind a stand of hardwood trees where Ward and Poper huddled in the protection of his oak and a row of glass-and-steel-and-brick buildings. "And, it's the most delicate of problems. You know why? No? Well let me tell you. It's because they tell us these things are being done for our own good . . . just like what they said about the Speaker Ban Law back in sixty-four that prohibited speakers of one particular ideology from speaking on-campus at state universities. What's more important is that such things are being done without our consent!" Matthew altered his tone to sound more jibing in his delivery. His legs stopped quivering. He smiled. "That attitude is contagious. Its last known manifestation has been isolated in San Clemente."

The crowd laughed, cheered, whistled. They were having a damned good time, now.

"To prevent another such epidemic of overzealous parent syndrome, both teachers and students must be alert to abuses of power no matter how slight or well-intentioned they may be; for apathy is a vacuum. Vacuums will be filled, and apathy's space will surely be filled by manipulators of power—both well meaning . . . ." He paused. ". . . . And otherwise'" Matthew felt the crowd's voice lifting him up.

"Because we are students, does that require us to forfeit our natural freedom?"

"No!" The crowd tentatively responded.

"Are we going to demand a voice in decisions affecting our lives?

"Yes!" Their voice was suddenly loud and demanding.

"Are we going to let ourselves be denied our right to self-determination?"

"Hell no!"

"There are those who would demean this gathering. They say it's much ado about nothing. After all it's only a drop/add rule, for god's sake.

"Well, I was at Columbia University in May and June of 1968 when we shut them down."

Cheers.

"And, do you know why the students took over that university?" He paused. Of course they didn't. The media didn't cover that one very well either even in New York City. "Because the President of the university tried to unilaterally shove a new rule down our throats. A rule that the students had no say in whatsoever! Does that sound familiar?"

"Yes! Hell, yes!"

"Don't EVER let others tell you that something that is important to you is not important! You have a right to determine that for yourself!"

"So, let us commit ourselves here, today, to these words by Henry David Thoreau who went to jail as a symbol of his resistance: 'it matters not how small the beginning may seem to be: what is once well-done is done forever.' Thank you." Matthew slumped from the rostrum, his head spinning on the vibrations of cheers and applause leaping from the brickyard as he shuffled across the stage again being careful of the wires and again taking his seat on the stone bench. The weight he'd felt the crowd lifting from him while he clung to the podium was heavier now than ever . . . oh, the sudden weariness. He feared the pressure would crush his sternum and spatter the blood from his lungs onto these bricks . . . .

"Well," he mumbled into his beard as the faculty senate representative attempted to present their side of the issue amidst hecklers and whistlers and shouters now gathered in force in the front rows hugging the steps. "Well, I guess I've gone and stepped in a pile of it, now . . . with both feet."

When Poper rushed up the library steps to meet him as he left the stage and hugged him, saying, "Great speech, Matthew!" he sensed that he was in the grips of something more than his office mate's arms. More even than he had imagined. More real. More immediate. Men on each side. One behind. Another replacing Poper in front who slipped to the edge of this new maelstrom of people and fell, trembling, into Linda's arms. Matthew felt surrounded. Matthew was surrounded.

"Matthew Parkrow?" The agent shoved his fists into his jacket pockets as he sauntered up to Matthew, a smirk on his ruddy lips, a gleam in his steelie eyes. He stopped only inches from Matthew.

Matthew's eyes met his as he stopped. What the fuck's going down here? The agent's eyes shifted to the pebbly asphalt of the steps. He shook. Real agents don't shake, do they? Matthew drew back until he felt the bulk of the man behind him pressing him forward again.

"Are you Matthew Parkrow of Route 7, Box 224, Capital City, North Carolina?"

Matthew shrugged his shoulders, forced a laugh. "You got me . . . ."

"This is no laughing matter, Mr. Parkrow." The agent wiped his nose on his jacket, sniffed. "Damned spring colds . . . ."

"Professor Parkrow to you, sir."

The agent sniggered. "Not for long, good buddy. Not for long. You see we have two warrants for your arrest, Mr. Parkrow."

"What?"

"Come with us please, quietly, or we'll have to cuff you in front of all these people you were just speaking to . . . ."

"For what?"

"You have the right to remain silent. If you relinquish that right, anything you say may be used against you in a court of law."

"Huh?"

"You have the right to an attorney. If you cannot afford one, one will be provided for you."

"What the fuck?" He feinted bolting between the agent and his partner to the left, but the ones behind and to his right grabbed him very forceably before he could move more than his knees in the direction of that hole. He shrugged the two men off of his right side. "Could I see your warrants . . . and some ID? You didn't show me any ID's, now did you gentlemen, so I don't even know if you are really law enforcement."

"That's it!" The agent in front stepped back, pulled a police special from his right pocket, keeping it close to his chest so it remained mostly hidden from the dwindling crowd. "Don't fucking move, Parkrow!" The agent suddenly pressed the cold nose of the .38 against Matthew's third eye. "Cuff him, Smiley." His lips twitched in a sardonic grin. "Make them tight. We don't want this guy trying to run on us again. We might just have to shoot the fucker."

"Hands behind your back . . . ."

"Aw, come on. Jesus . . . . Give me a break here, agents or whatever you are. How can I not move and put my hands behind my back simultaneously?"

"Shut up!" Click. "You really are one big smart ass, aren't you?" The hammer seemed to cock all by itself.

A different click and he felt the cool metal of the cuffs surrounding his right wrist. "I've got rights, man. I've got a right to see the warrants . . . and your IDs."

"Give me your left arm, boy, before I break it . . . ."

Click. He felt the metal around his left wrist. Click.

"You're under arrest for trafficking in a controlled substance—to wit, cocaine—and . . . ."

A different voice snarled at him. "Move it mother fucker!" Hands shoved him from behind. He stumbled. Maybe he should just fall to the ground and refuse to move like they used to in the old days when the cops tried to arrest them. Instead, he allowed them to shove him through the dispersing crowd unaware of what was happening in their midst. He wanted to cry out for help. Do it! Do it!

"And for the murder of . . . ."

Murder. My god what murder?

"Hey, Smiley, is he all right?"

"Yeah, he's just making gurgling noises in his throat . . . you know, like we used to make when we drank RCs when we were kids."

" . . . . one Estevan de Niza in the White Sands desert on or about July 13, 1969."

"Hey guys! Jay Kramer, Capital City News." Jay flashed his press credentials. "What's going on here, gentlemen?" Without a word or even so much as a ripple in the fabric of movement and time two agents converged on Jay. The two tackle-size agents shoved Jay Kramer through the crowd toward their campus instant operations center under Round Hall.

Matthew was trying desperately to keep his focus, but Jay Kramer being spirited away without a word was making things look pretty damned scary.

"There ain't no statute of limitations on murder, boy."

So, Estevan's curse had finally passed to him. Emmy Lou's prophecy was being played out right here, right now, before his own eyes. But, he thought he was beginning to see why . . . why a lot of things. Why Ward wasn't at the open forum class this morning and none of the other eleven instructors he had promised. Why Poper was skulking around in the hallway spying from the shadows while the forum was in progress. Why Linda now smirked as she walked beside him through the emptying brickyard toward the parking lot. The same smirk she had on her lips in Florida.

But, I'm cool. They won't find anything at the trailer . . . the old Gypsy's clean. Any personal stash is buried at one of my two camps. No, fool! That's part of her smirk. Linda hit him with it once more over her left shoulder as she peeled off from the group surrounding Matthew and sauntered toward the towering oak. Lounging beneath it were Poper who he thought warned him about Scythe, and, of course, his good buddy, Ward, who watched out for Jason until he died. Ressurrected Ward, the Lazurus of his generation come back as a zombie to infect what's left of the human species with more of that vacuum virus . . . apathy. Standing over them, his eyes shaded by his pudgy hands overlapping at his forehead, a nearly bald man wearing a red-white-and-blue madras Bow-Tie stared in their direction.

"You were his office mate, weren't you?" Bow-Tie mumbled in the direction of Poper.

"Oh, no . . . ah . . . I mean . . . ."

The car door slammed almost hitting Matthew's head.

"Do you understand your rights as I have stated them to you?"

Matthew hunched in the back seat of an SBI car, his wrists cuffed behind him, in Capital City, North Carolina, in the United States of Arnerica . . . land of the free and home of the brave . . . . Let freedom ring . . . . He could not help but smile and wag his shaggy head as the agents piled into the car and the one next to it . . . and the one next to that one. Damn, there'd been seven agents and three cars involved in his bust.

"Could I have a cigarette?"

The three agents gaped at each other. They had no instructions on how to respond to such a request.

Matthew first felt weary long before his most recent time in jail. When he was just back from Vietnam he could not sleep. No matter what, he could not sleep. He was twenty-four and a rock. An island. But, no man is an island? Yet, no man could still not sleep. A neutrino. A quark. There was little in this world that he combined with without great difficulty and often grave consequences. He did not combine well with the Army. Despite his decorations, they had also tried him. He had, at times, fantasized that he might be from another planet, for when he looked around he saw other-worldly ghouls. He didn't want to be Michael Smith. He didn't want to cry. He didn't want to be Richard Nixon. He didn't want to lie. He had already been a soldier even though he didn't want to fight. He didn't want to shoot them down but he was nobody's sacrifice. He didn't want to be the last farmer. He didn't want to die. Alas, he still could not lose himself in that beatific lack of consciousness he longingly referred to as sleep.

His jailers told him it was his imagination. Sleeplessness and weariness were old folks infirmities, they had all assured him. And, the weariness did seem to lift off him quickly enough like morning fog off the Blue Ridge mountains when he found himself on the society side of the jail bars once again. You're a rock. You're an island. The sand of him swept through his mind. Yet, he still could not sleep.

He huddled in a yolk of sunlight, his body occupying the space located at the west end of the conference room in English. The windows to the east blazed like *shook foil* in the morning sun coming up past the Bell Tower. Between the windows and himself was a long, blond table, thick with generations of shellac. At the far end, one brown leather-cushioned easy chair with armrests. Matthew chewed at the thumbnail of his left hand as he panned his eyes down the line of three chairs on the left and three on the right, the same as the first chair but without armrests.

> *Hello darkness, my old friend*
> *I've come to talk with you again*
> *Because a vision softly creeping*
> *Left its seeds while I was sleeping*
> *And the vision that was planted in my brain*
> *Still remains*
> *Within the sound of silence*

Just last night he finally escaped that cell. Over two weeks behind those city bars . . . there had been times . . . . Even freedom did not give him sleep. Only another morning of more newspaper crap. "Long hair's a relic," the neighborhood barber was quoted as saying in The Huge Disturbance (a newspaper as local as the barber). The barber continued: "I cut more hair now than Carter's got little brown pills. They look like rabbit pellets you know.

"Them young boys's comin' back to their senses, that's all."

That was when I knew I had to proceed on the assumption I have held for some years now, since I came out of that desert, that ninety-nine percent . . . ile of what we know is made up, and the other one percent . . . I'll bet . . . is best left up to bald barbers, nearsighted newspapers, tunnelvision and scalloped scholars like myself. Walking on eggshields I think it's called when you know what you're doing. Fools walking in where Eugenes fear to tread, if you don't. Crack the blasted hearts made of stone that never break because the only love they have to give will be the love they take on Blueberry Hill under Fats Domino's piano. She came in through the bathroom window, flushed herself into my heart. Emmy Lou.

He had not seen her or talked to her since the morning Molly had dropped her puppies. She had saved his life that morning with her phone call, though he guessed she never knew that. She had also told him how it would all end . . . just like this . . . if he had only listened. Oh, he had listened. It was heeding the words he heard that he didn't do.

He still did not know how she found out he was in jail. All the officer told him was that a Ms. Emmy Lou Black had posted his bail and he was free to go . . . . And, by the way, the officer had told him, "there is an envelope from Ms. Black waiting for you at the Officer of the Day's desk when you check out of this place." He had smiled as Matthew collected his personal belongings from the jailer. "Believe it or not, Mr. Parkrow, some of us here—many of us here—are veterans too and we're all real sorry about all this mess that's happening to you."

Matthew had shrugged.

"It seems we had no choice . . . ."

Matthew had nodded.

"It was either do our jobs here or lose our jobs." He had hung his head slightly.

"I know." He had reached out and touched the jailer's shoulders. "I understand, and thank you."

How could he smile now, in this conference room awaiting a hearing that would very likely end his career as a teacher? Only an insane person smiles at the prospect of his own death, don't you know? Only a lunatic acts as his own Judas goat. Emmy Lou always said I could, that I was possessed in that way. "You can be the leader and the led, the living and the dead, Matthew. And, she's right. I am a rock. I am an island. And, I still cannot sleep.

In the theater of his mind, her hair fell like light down her bronze shoulders as she bent over the gas stove. Her nose quivered in the aromas of applesauce cooking. She was the same as the poneytailed beauty who until last quarter had dabbed and stroked at the canvas on this easel. Her voice was muffled by the bubbling apples. "Doing any work, Matthew? Need to keep at it, you know. All this other stuff . . . . Me. Molly. Your students." She shrugged around her. "It's all part time . . . ."

In restless dreams I walked alone
Narrow streets of cobblestone
'Neath the halo of a street lamp
I turned my collar to the cold and damp
When my eyes were stabbed by the flash of a neon light
That split the night
And touched the sound of silence

His left shoulder twitched as he shifted from his right to his left buttocks in the space of a metal swivel chair with two of its three rollers missing and the arms . . . he had to just about hold them in place with his own . . . situated in the west end of the conference room nearest the door in the *Venus de Milo* chair. Jesus. Let's get this thing done . . . .

The inevitable movement of things forced Matthew to come out of his thoughts and back into the room with its bookshelf-lined green walls and to smirk as members of the Ad Hoc Committee on Faculty

Discipline filed past where he sat slumped in his cast-off swivel chair. After six of the seven chairs were filled, the department chairman entered briskly, adjusting whitegold glass frames with his right hand while he cuddled his Riverside Edition against his pale blue suit coat with his left. As he passed from behind Matthew into his right eye's peripheral vision, the Chairman stopped, his gray eyes fixed on him. Matthew twitched under the weight of compassion in the man's eyes. He hadn't expected that. The Chairman wagged his peppering head. "Such a waste . . . ."

"What was that, Mr. Chairman?"

"Oh, nothing, Wally. How's your Hawthorne book going?" He squeezed Wally Poindexter's boney shoulder and grinned. "Be ready soon, I'm sure." As Wally nodded, the chairman turned toward another familiar voice.

"See you brought your own Bible, Charles."

"Why yes, Edgar." Charles Chairman's tight lips loosened into a smile and quickly tightened again. "I find it far more convenient than having to hunt for one when you need it." He hurried to the opposite end of the table. As he slid into his chair, he reverently eased his Riverside Shakespeare onto the oak table directly in front of him.

"Mr. Chairman?"

"Mr. Scythe?"

Scythe fidgeted in his chair at the Chairman's right. "Shall I read the charges?" He waved the thick file marked Matthew Parkrow in the air. All of the committee members clapped until Charles Chairman stared them down, looking under his glasses at each one in turn.

"First things first, Mr. Scythe." Charles fetched a miniature gavel from his inside coat pocket and tapped the table top. "This hearing by the Ad Hoc Committee on Faculty Discipline is now in session." He nodded at Scythe.

"Mr. Scythe."

"Mr. Chairman, first a point of order, if you please. You forgot the second part of the committee's name: 'and on Student Discipline Where The Two Overlap Resulting From the Student Uprising of April 13, 1975 at the State University.'"

"Duly noted for the record, Mr. Scythe." Charles Chairman's forehead furrowed deeply as a slow scowl spread over his previously neutral face.

Scythe plopped the folder onto the table, opened it and extracted some legal-size typed pages. Before he began, he reached into his cashmere jacket pocket for his reading glasses. "Mr. Chairman. The Ad Hoc Committee on Faculty Discipline and on Student Discipline Where The Two Overlap Resulting From the Student Uprising of April 13, 1975 at the State University has evidence to support the following charges under the authority of the Campus Disruption Code, paragraph four, subparagraph A, items three and twelve against Matthew Parkrow, Assistant Professor and Department of English Ph.D. candidate, to wit . . . ."

"Reporters!" The panting voice behind Matthew belonged to a security guard. He'd been there all the time, just invisible until needed. Also, waiting. Outside the door, in the hall. Matthew turned his head toward the voice. The guard's face was red, his jowls puffing, as he struggled to get his breath. "Swarms of 'em!"

"Shut that door! Now! Lock the room from the inside!"

As the guard slammed the door, Wally loped from his seat at the blond table nearest to Matthew to the door where he began fumbling with the knob.

"Pssst. Wally."

"Huh?"

"The little brass button on your left . . . ."

Wally looked back at the door knob, pointed a finger at the protruding button.

Matthew nodded. Wally pushed in the button and loped back to his seat. "Okay, Mr. Chairman. It's locked."

"Good. Now, proceed, Mr. Scythe."

"Sir?" Scythe's face screwed into a relief map of wrinkles. "Do I have to repeat the beginning?"

"No." Charles jerked his glasses off of his nose and began to clean them with a freshly laundered handkerchief his wife put in his left trouser pocket each morning.

"We just want to make sure this is done properly, Mr. Chairman." Scythe lowered his head though never taking his eyes off the Chairman's eyes.

"Oh, I *understand*, Mr. Scythe." Charles winked, a somewhat smirk on his thin lips. "Believe me, I *understand*."

"Yes. Ah, the charges then." Scythe shuffled the papers in his trembling fingers. "I . . . ah . . . here we are." He cleared his throat. Adjusting his hornrims, he cleared his throat again. "To wit: 1) in violation of item three of the Campus Disruption Code, Matthew Parkrow did willfully use classroom facilities and schedule teaching time for political and propagandistic purposes; and 2) in violation of item twelve of the Campus Disruption Code, he did willfully incite both students and faculty to riot." Scythe could no longer keep his mouth in check. "And we, the Ad Hoc Committee, can prove these charges, Mr. Chairmen, beyond any reasonable doubt." His fallow lips stretched across his nicotine-stained teeth in a hideous grin.

"No doubt, Mr. Scythe, but this is not a criminal proceeding or even a court of law." Charles slid his gaze from Beau Scythe to Matthew Parkrow. "It is simply an administrative hearing."

"And the final charge: in violation of Section I of the Code of Conduct for Faculty and the laws of the state, he did willfully and with full knowledge participate in the use of controlled substances with his students . . . ."

"Now, that's a little too much for an administrative hearing isn't it, Mr. Scythe?"

Matthew shifted in his rickety chair again, peering down the table into the morning sunlight cascading through the east wall windows above and behind the Chairman's shoulders.

Scythe's body language seemed almost defiant of the Chairman's words.

"Regardless, this body will not consider charge three. That is now a police matter under investigation and is significantly out of this committee's jurisdiction. Beyond that, Mr. Scythe, if I may interject here that my understanding is that nearly every student on the State University campus is willing to testify that, to their knowledge, Mr. Parkrow never used or sanctioned the use of any drugs around them."

Matthew had answered the phone last night when it rang and rang for, it seemed, hours. The robot voice at the other end told him to report to the conference room at eight-thirty in the morning for a hearing on his case. What case? The phone began ringing again just around dawn interrupting his sleeplessness. After the fifth call, he smashed the message machine against the wall and ripped out the cord. He was convinced for just a moment that he had somehow inherited Jason's phone. Garbage cans rattled like bones of his old International Travel-all come back to haunt him. The same man dumped egg shells, milk cartons, vienna sausage cans . . . all touched by other hands he had also never seen. He stumbled from bed, located a joint on the night table built into the wall at the foot of the bed and lit it. He remembered Captain America saying it was a nice way to start off the day. Along the way we lost it . . . a green and yellow basketcase forever and ever . . . A is for the apple that contains us; M is for the many who entertain us; E is for everyone who explains us; N is for no one who refrains from us . . . . Whirring pressed last night's egg plant casserole into the beer cans from after the casserole. They were already collecting down the road when he walked to his mail box for his morning paper at sunrise.

"Mr. Parkrow?"

"Yes?"

"How do you plead to these charges?" He watched as the weight of the question slumped the young man's shoulders toward the table. Next, his head will droop, Charles worried.

Matthew shook his head, put his hands up against the blinding light. "I will enter no plea."

"You must plead, Matthew."

> *And in the naked light I saw*
> *Ten thousand people, maybe more*
> *People talking without speaking*
> *People hearing without listening*
> *People writing songs that voices never share*
> *And no one dared*
> *Disturb the sound of silence*

"No. If I plead, then I sanction this hearing." Matthew felt his body quivering inside, muscles tightening in his back, his stomach, his neck . . . . "I refuse to participate in [he shrugged his shoulders while he indicated the room with his upturned hand] this!"

"Hurmph!" Scythe pounded his powdery fist on the table. "You've got a lot of gaul, boy!"

Matthew's lips curled like a cornered dog's. "I don't recognize *you!*" He leaped to his feet, overturning the swivel chair that clattered to the floor, and brandished his arm in Scythe's direction. ". . . . Or your committee . . . or your right to even have a hearing at all!" Matthew reached behind him and snatched the chair upright, slumping into it again. "As far as I am concerned, for the purposes of entering a plea, you don't exist . . . ."

"Matthew . . . ." Charles's voice quivered as he readjusted his glasses, then stroked his blue chin with piano-player fingers. "My boy, all you have to do to stop this entire proceeding is to say you were misguided . . . ah, that you misunderstood the motivations and goals behind the uprising. After you were arrested, thousands of our students rioted and destroyed university property . . . ." He wheezed. The young man's body hunched in that gray chair winced as though he had struck him with a whip. "Withdraw your support for these radical actions . . . ." He wheezed again, then stroked first his chin then his *Riverside*. "Then you could stay on here." He glanced around the table at the pasty faces. "Agreed." He nodded. One by one they reluctantly returned his nod. All but Scythe. The best he could do was force a small sardonic smile.

Matthew's mind raced. He could hear Jason's prediction that he'd screw up teaching, too, running like a tape on fast forward in his head. He could feel his teeth beginning to grind against each other. His mouth was drying fast. His fingers clung to what was left of the arms of the *de Milo* chair. "But I wasn't . . . ." He wagged his head. "I wasn't . . . ."

"Just say it," Wally whispered behind his right hand as he leaned across the corner of the table toward Matthew. "You don't have to mean it. Just say it."

"Lie?" Matthew mouthed without a sound.

"Yes. Anything . . . ." Then you can sleep.

"So, he's obviously guilty, Mr. Chairman!"

"Scythe's right!" the chorus seated around the blond table chanted in response.

"Mr. Chairman, if he will not plead, then he must be guilty."

"Scythe's right!" the chorus seated around the blond table again chanted in response.

"But, Mr. Scythe, it more logically follows that if he will not plead, he is, indeed, doing what he claims to be doing . . . ." He let his sentence trail off as he drummed his fingers on his *Shakespeare*. "Which is, of course, to deny our authority . . . ."

"Right, Mr. Chairman!" Scythe and the chorus responded.

"That makes him defiant, possibly even arrogant . . . ."

"Right, Mr. Chairman!" Scythe and the chorus again responded.

"But his actions do not necessarily rise to the level of guilt for any particular infraction."

He nodded at the members of the Ad Hoc Committee, his eyes finally glued to Matthew's figure, dark and sullen, slumped in that old chair. "Well two can play at that game." He smacked his palm on the table top. "We don't have to recognize his right to not recognize our right to hold this disciplinary hearing."

Scythe scratched his head. "Sir?"

"Give me that old time inquisition. It's good enough for me," Charles muttered sarcastically almost under his breath. "Proceed with the Committee's case, Mr. Scythe. We'll just hold this hearing with the defendant *in absentia.*"

> *"Fools", said I, "You do not know*
> *Silence like a cancer grows*
> *Hear my words that I might teach you*
> *Take my arms that I might reach you"*
> *But my words, like silent raindrops fell*
> *And echoed*
> *In the wells of silence*

Like Dante! Matthew snatched at the life boat of companionship no matter how sarcastically cast. The poet had been convicted in Florence in 1302 of being a bad leader because he refused to cowtow to those in power. They tried him *in absentia.* If it was good enough for Dante then I guess it's good enough for me. Give me that old time inquisition, give me that old time inquisition, give me that old time inquisition, it's good enough for me.

Scythe moaned as if the doom of Sisyphus had been doled out to him with no justice. "Yes, Mr. Chairman."

Charles Chairman looked down the table toward Matthew, clucking his tongue against his teeth. "Wally, would you please have the guard bring in the first witness?"

"Su . . . sure, Mr. Chairman." Wally bolted for the door, fumbled with the knob and the lock again. Through a crack, he whispered to the guard. "Bring in the first witness."

As the first witness entered the room, Matthew could hear the voices of angry reporters in the hall, pressing against the door like the smell of musk that pressed against his nostrils as the witness passed close behind him. Thought about her and that last night in Fort Lauderdale all morning morning's mignon. Remember that night and the *Tennessee Waltz* and the last day on the beach. "I went to sleep in the sun, today," Linda's mouth had chewed like a parrot's beak as she slipped the halter straps from her crimson shoulders. The pink cotton slipped down the still firm curves of her breasts almost showing her nipples as she leaned over the table for a light from Matthew's matches. When she exhaled the smoke her lips persed toward his and she ran her carnelian fingernails across the material where her nipples buldged. Poper and Ward were jabbering behind her back about some new work on Pope.

"You say," she whispered in a cloud of smoke, "you need a typewriter, honey?" She licked her lips. "Think I got an ancient upright hidden away in the den from when I fantasied myself as the reincarnation of Virginia Woolf or something.

"Really?" To look at her looking like right out of Albee. Never would've dreamed it. Her hair glistened like Biscayne Bay in the moonlight showering the Florida Room of the Crampton's vacation home as he felt her nails on his flesh.

"Let's go see, what'cha say?"

Linda. She grinned, now, as Wally escorted her to the other end of the table where Scythe was setting up a folding chair which was to serve as the witness chair. Charles slid his *Riverside* across the table . . . . He'd known she was going for the couch in the den, not for any typewriter, upright or otherwise. He needed and she was more than willing, that was obvious from the time they had entered the living room from the sliding glass doors connecting to the Florida Room. The pink halter was already clutched in her left hand. "God, Matthew, it's been so long . . . almost seven years. Do you still have the serape I gave you?"

"Place your hand here." The Chairman guided Linda's hand to the soft leather cover. His wife had the volume re-bound for him last

Christmas. The original hardback cover was so worn . . . . "Do you swear that the testimony you are about to give is the whole truth."

So help you Shakespeare. Christ, I can't believe he's actually using that book instead of a Bible . . . or nothing. Matthew's head drooped further between already bent shoulders.

"I do." Linda crossed her silky legs under the lace smock she wore. You could hear the sound of nylon sliding across nylon. The lace weave was close enough that you couldn't really see through the dress, but her dark tan shimmered in the morning sun through every small opening. Her glazed eyes latched onto Matthew's drawn face and stared at him zombie-like throughout her testimony.

"Just begin at the beginning, Mrs. Crampton." Scythe touched her arm as he cooed and appeared not to notice that she recoiled from his touch. "We all know how painful this must be since Mr. Parkrow was supposedly your husband's very best friend. Just tell us in your own words . . . ."

"Thank you, Mr. Scythe." Her voice was muffled, broke for a moment. "My husband was his friend. Not me. For some reason he disliked me. So it was Ward, my husband, who had most of the contact with him until his father died on Christmas day. Matthew seemed very upset by his father's death . . . almost over-reacting, you know?"

Scythe nodded, smiled.

"Ward felt a kind of responsibility to both the dead Mayor who had been like a father to him since his return from captivity in North Vietnam and to the Mayor's son and his best friend, Matthew Parkrow. So, out of kindness, he invited Mr. Parkrow to visit with us in Florida for the remainder of the holidays."

"That's when you saw firsthand what kind of radical Matthew Parkrow was . . . is?"

"Mr Scythe!'

"I'll rephrase the question, Mr. Chairman." He blushed under the webbing in his cheeks. "What did you learn about Matthew Parkrow while he visited with you and your husband in Florida?"

"Well, it wasn't until the day before we were ready to leave Florida and come back for the spring semester that I noticed anything out of the ordinary. We'd been to Cape Kennedy . . . ."

"When you say 'we', to whom are you referring?"

"Myself, my husband Ward, our dear friend and Mr. Parkrow's office mate Poper Dryden as well as Mr. Parkrow."

"Continue, please, Mrs. Crampton."

"Well, Mr. Parkrow starts kicking up a fuss as soon as we get back to our home in Fort Lauderdale. We're on the beach, you know. He wants a typewriter. 'Our Cape Kennedy conversations have inspired me!' he says. You see, he claims to be a writer, though I've never seen anything of his published anywhere."

"Mr. Scythe?"

"Sir?"

"Do we have to have these continual slurs of Matthew's . . . ah, Mr. Parkrow's character?"

Scythe seethed. "But, Mr. Chairman! That's what this hearing is all about, isn't it? To determine if this man's character is in tact?"

"Mr. Scythe?" Charles fumbled with his glasses. Jerking them from his face, he began cleaning them with his handkerchief, attempting to force control. "Mr. Scythe," he whispered.

"Mr Chairman?"

"Let's at least have a little less polemic from you and your witness and a little more positive proof . . . if that's not asking too much?"

"Yes sir."

Couldn't beat her out of my mind this morning. Her and Florida. That's the key. The key of C on that typewriter she found for him kept sticking as she continued to plead with him to help her and Ward with their newly adopted cause of student's rights. "You're their natural leader," she kept repeating as she would bring him shuddering home again and again until his resistance was destroyed. "The students'll trust you." He knew that. The ones who knew him already did. "And it is absolutely necessary to do something . . . something spectacular . . . to bring attention to the apathy of this decade . . . right? And because he said yes, finally gave in to yes, he stood this morning pressing legs of trousers to his only suit under the steam jets of the electric iron to appear before this august Augustian body. Kkkkkwathump coffee perked behind. Soles bruised a little from his bare feet on the concrete floor of the jail cell, so he stood curly toed, ironing in the kitchen on the table full of books and papers stacked precisely according to rules of anarchy and necessity.

The suit had been scattered in three closets. The pants, Harpo large. They were in the linen closet. Coat, in the Groucho tradition, hung in the closet in the bedroom by the bathroom. South end of the Air-conditioned Gypsy. Tie? 0h Chico! In the storage closet tied around a few paperbacks. Just push this button. Whoosh. Four years of wrinkles and moth shit, fini by the steamjet iron. Resurrected for today's inquisition. Napoleon in rags to his Waterloo. Eliot to his Pound? Slides off the edge. No. Pound of flesh or Pound of religion. His knees have trouble bending. It's damned hard to kneel. Biological. Must be something in the cartilage, tendons. Calcium deposits, knees stuffed stiff as plaster. God, no! They'll mine him with more headlines.

RELIC RANTS, RABBLE ROUSES

". . . . And he was very persistent in trying to persuade us to become involved in 'this radical movement of his. Some latent SDSism, I suppose," she sneered.

"Mrs. Crampton! Please stick to your recitation of facts, if you please."

"Surely, your Grace . . . ah . . . Mr. Chairman." Her nylons sizzled as she uncrossed and re-crossed her legs very deliberately.

"Of course, we all resisted his entreaties."

"All?"

"Yes, Mr. Scythe. All."

"And who comprises 'all', Mrs. Crampton?"

"Myself, of course, and my husband, Ward, and our dear friend, Poper Dryden."

"And you all three refused to help him?"

"Well, not exactly . . . ."

"Well," Scythe persisted. "What, then, do you mean?"

"We sort of went along . . . just a little . . . you know?" She shifted in her chair so that her black hair caught more of the sunlight making it sparkle like amethyst. "Just so we could do what we've done . . . help bring the radical bas . . . ." Her voice broke. She fumbled in the small yellow leather purse she clutched in her lap for a handkerchief, and as she sobbed into it she tried to continue. "The radical communist . . . he deserves what's coming to him . . . ."

"That's enough, for now, Mrs. Crampton." Charles patted her arm. "We only need the facts, not your opinions. Thank you. Or your tears. You may go."

As she shuffled past him, Matthew was sure he saw her wink. What an actress she was . . . and not a word about what they were really up to . . . not a word about the bust she obviously helped engineer, the cocaine Poper planted in the Gypsy. If he didn't know CHAOS was out of business, he would swear that was who they were all working for . . . .

It all gets jumbled. Present becomes past with other pasts. Future, present. New thought is the future which soon is realized in the present and, all too soon, enshrined in the past. From the past we learn planning; in the present we act upon the plans and simultaneously plan for the future which is what we are planning for. Thus, we have the past yielding sensation which results in reaction which is thought in the continuing present and action in the present, both of which lead to results which make the future the present and the present part of the past . . . . Anthropomorphization of thought. This room with its pipe and cigar clouds and empty testimony spilling blue through the sunlight.

Travis, one of the custodians in English, was swearing that Matthew had been in room three ten many a night with students. That was, of course, true. Scythe pounced like a cat at the information. "You saw this?"

"Yep."

"Could you hear what they said?"

"Well, most of the time they was whispering . . . ."

"Yes. Go on . . . ."

"But once I heard him talking about how taking over the school was the students' only chance . . . and he said something about the old guard . . . meaning all of us . . . ." He motioned around the table. "But, I couldn't make all that out."

"Anything more you can remember, Mr. Travis?"

Travis's bald head glowed in the sunlight as he raised his wrinkled face to look down the table at Matthew. "I don't mean to cause no trouble for that boy. He's always been right nice to me and all." He dropped his gaze from Matthew's cold eyes back into his own lap. "But I'm swore to tell the truth."

"Go ahead, Mr. Travis . . . you must!"

"Well . . . ah . . . this one other time I remember real good. He was in his cubicle with some of his regular night visitors . . . some of them students came by almost all the time. I was cleaning up the next cubicle and they hadn't heard me come in they was talking so wild."

"When was this?"

"Last Tuesday night, just before y . . . ."

"And what was he talking about then?" Scythe interrupted.

"I heard him telling them students that nobody had any right telling them what to do . . . ."

"That's fine, Mr. Travis. Thank you." He turned toward Matthew's scowling face as he began helping Travis from the chair.

He was finally getting to the commie. "Any questions, Mister *in absentia*?" He smirked. "If not, Mr. Travis, you may step down." He guided Travis around the chair and aimed him for the door.

"Wally. Next witness."

"Another witness?"

"Yes, Mr. chairman. We have several more to call to complete the Ad Hoc Committee's airtight case against the defendant." Scythe fidgeted with the lapel of his panama suit. "The next several witnesses are . . . ah . . . literary experts from outside the department . . . ."

"To what possible purpose, Mr. Scythe?"

"To testify to Mr. Parkrow's misguided literary theses and heresies and the danger of these to our students . . . to us."

Charles's forehead sunk into his hands. "I think we can rule that as unnecessary evidence."

"But . . . ."

"Don't 'but' me, Scythe. Do you have others whose testimony is directly related to charges one and two or not?

"One other, sir."

"Then bring this witness on . . . continue!" Charles Chairman nearly shrieked, flourishing his arms as he spoke. "Continue, unless Mr. Parkrow is willing now to reconsider our earlier offer?"

Even this phenomenon can be analyzed with the anthropomorphization of thought yield equation. $T > A$, when T is time continuing (past, present, future) and A is

Anthropomorphization of thought, that is, the results in the equation: $S > R > t > a > A$, where S equals sensation, P equals reaction, t equals thought and a equals action . . . .

"Mr. Parkrow? Are you still with us?" Charles's face was a mask of slate surrounded by sunlight behind him. "Matthew?"

"Oh . . . *in absentia* . . . ." Axiom. That no thing can be known exactly accounts for the infinite variations of any single thing. Thus given phenomena, such as fear or NASA or the proverbial elephant, can be described in as many ways as there are beings to describe them and there are words to use in such a description. *So* anything is limited by the words and their combinations legitimate for purposes of that particular thing or phenomenon and by the number of cognizant beings experiencing that particular thing or phenomenon. He knew what his explanation was of this particular phenomenon that was currently taking place in the English building conference room.

"Do you, now, wish to recant your stand and remain here, on this faculty . . . ?"

And, he was sure that Charles Chairman and Scythe and Wally Poindexter and everyone else in the room had his or her own explanation. "*In absentia.*" Thus the preciseness of the yield equation is directly proportionate to the number of knowns. Conversely, the ambiguity of the equation increases proportionately to the number of unknowns. So, given one or more of the variables, the yield equation can proportionately be used to analyze any given phenomenon within the limitations of what is known and what is not known . . . .

Words were running across his lips without sounds attached. Stop that muttering. A part of him wanted to take them all off the hook . . . explain to them . . . that he was just struggling to speak. They already think you're looney. Now, they will also think you have finally dropped off to sleep and are in the midst of some dream.

"In light of the situation . . . ." Scythe motioned toward Matthew's rocking body, dazed in the *Venus de Milo* swivel chair. He seemed to be muttering to himself. Scythe wagged his head. Then, as if suddenly awakened, he barkered: "Mr. Chairman. Members of the committee . . . . our star witness!" His arms flourished like the Chairman's had earlier but toward the door.

Wally, bring in Ward Cramptom. Yes, Mr. Chairman, Ward Crampton, the young baseball All American who was presumed dead in Vietnam but who miraculously survived in spite of nearly fatal leg wounds that ruined his chances at a professional baseball career. He has come back to his home university to make a new start. He was doing well until his supposed oldest and closest friend from childhood, Matthew Parkrow, began to cause him to fear for his very job, for the welfare of his lovely wife who testified earlier, and for this university." His eyes glowed. "Mr. Parkrow's revolutionary sympathies and activities began to reflect on him as well . . . by association, if you will." The door opened a crack as Wally peeked into the hall. The reporters and spectators jeered and shoved toward the crack just as Ward slipped through. "Ward Crampton," Wally muttered more to himself than to anyone in the room. Even Matthew turned in the direction of the conference room door as it opened. Matthew thought he caught a glimpse of Poper's carrot top in the door glass as the door was shoved shut. Ward glanced around the room. Charles, Scythe, Leach, Edgar Jones. Wally Poindexter, the faculty Whippet, beside him now flipping the door lock. They all stood. Finally his eyes fastened onto the back of Matthew's bowed head. His black curls glistened in the sunlight from the window behind the Chairman as if they were oiled. Matthew, poor Matthew. I had no choice. No alternatives. He is just a pawn about to become a king with absolutely no idea what that means.

> *And the people bowed and prayed*
> *To the neon god they made*
> *And the sign flashed out its warning*
> *In the words that it was forming*
> *And the sign said, "The words of the prophets*
> *are written on the subway walls*
> *And tenement halls"*
> *And whispered in the sounds of silence*

Those in attendance began to applaud as Ward paused at Matthew's side. "I'm so sorry, Matthew . . . ." His whisper was hoarse and constricted and nearly inaudible through the applause. He reached out with his left hand to touch his old friend's shoulder.

Matthew cringed from his touch as if his hand were a cattle prod. "You don't understand, Matthew. You don't understand . . . ."

Once Ward was seated, Scythe moved in for the kill. "For the Record, please tell us your name and address . . . ."

"My name is Ward Crampton, and I live in the Millere House."

"And, what do you do, Mr. Crampton?"

"Do?"

"Yes, Mr. Crampton. What is your job?"

"Oh," Ward chuckled. "I'm a teaching assistant in the English Department and a candidate for the Master of Arts in English."

"And, I am given to understand that you have a rather unusual specialty that you are persuing. Is that correct?"

"Well, yes, I imagine so. I guess you could call it that . . . ."

"And, what is that unusual literary specialty, Mr. Crampton?"

"Well, ah . . . I'm sort of concentrating on sports and sports-related American literature. You know, like Ring Lardner or Bernard Malamud's *The Natural* or Ernest Hemingway's *Old Man and the Sea* . . . ."

"You might say that your literary specialty combines your life-long interests in both literature and sports . . . primarily baseball?"

"You could say that, sure . . . ."

Scythe stood and leaned over the layers of shellac covering the blond conference table in Ward's direction. "Would you say, Mr. Crampton, that you were more or less forced back into the academic world when your helicopter was shot down in Vietnam . . . leaving you with a stiffened left leg and depriving you of an otherwise sure fire major league baseball career?"

Ward sat rigidly in the witness chair. His gray eyes tore at Scythe's watery brown ones. How should he answer this one? "In a sense . . . I guess. Realistically, if I hadn't been wounded and held as a POW, I probably would be playing ball for Chicago right now. But, life . . . ." He broke off to stifle a chuckle. He attempted to make it look as if he had choked on something, but he didn't think he had actually fooled anyone. "Life has a way of dealing you the cards it wants to." He shrugged and pretended to choke again. "Then, I guess you have to play them the best you can . . . ."

"Where's all this going, Scythe?"

"To the credibility of the witness, Mr. Chairman. Here sits a wounded war hero who has had to make great personal sacrifice for his country . . . an honorable, believable witness . . . a colleague, Mr. Chairman."

"All right, Mr. Scythe, we all accept that what Mr. Crampton has to say should be given sufficient weight. Now, proceed with the relevant testimony, if you please."

Scythe attempted to clear his throat and swallow at the same time which created something between a belch and a word. "Yes . . . ." The sound echoed across the room and back seeming to bounce off of the heads of the spectators. "Mr. Chairman . . . ."

"Continue, then . . . ."

The others around the glistening conference table nodded in a chorus of mumbles and balding heads.

"And, you are married to Linda Crampton who testified earlier?"

"Well, not exactly . . . ."

Scythe's face sagged noticeably. "Wha . . . what do you mean, Mr. Crampton, by 'not exactly?'"

"Well, this is going to take awhile . . . ."

Forty-five minutes later, Scythe snickered, "That's a pretty far-fetched story, Mr. Crampton. Do you really expect any of us to believe this James Bond kind of stuff?"

"Mr. Scythe, you spent an interminable amount of time convincing us that Mr. Crampton was to be believed, yet now you want us to *not* believe him?"

"Mr. Chairman, I have corroborating witnesses . . . ."

"Who, Mr. Crampton?" Scythe demanded. "Who?"

There was a rustle of people on the back row as Linda began to squirm her way passed a group of the philosophy faculty, aiming for the door an escape from what she knew would be coming given Ward's denial of their marriage and description of them as federal agents.

"Ah . . . Mrs. Crampton, my dear 'wife', Linda. You should stay." Ward grinned. "In fact, darling, it is imperative that you stay. Please take your seat. After all you do play the lead role in this charade . . . this masquerade perpetuated through fear and coercion manipulated by none other than my own 'wife'. This play was scripted to bring down and destroy my old childhood friend,

Matthew Parkrow because he was allegedly a danger to society. As it turns out the motivations were far more petty . . . simply severe jealousy and the resulting hatred toward Matthew because he had once had the audacity to spurn her affections . . . ."

"Tell the truth, Ward!" Linda leaped to her feet so strongly that she nearly knocked over the chair in front of her occupied by a portly woman in a white laboratory smock. "Tell them the real truth, the whole truth husband dearest."

"That is the real truth, the whole truth as I know it, Linda." His slate eyes began to actually twinkle. "Why don't you come on back up here and tell us all here what your version of the truth really is?" He paused, staring directly into her eyes as if she were only inches, rather than twenty feet, away. Linda huffed and dropped back into her chair.

"Mr. Chairman, if this body is really interested in the truth and not just in an easy lynching, then I believe I can shed considerably more light on the real truth here. Since it is obvious that Matthew . . . ah . . . Mr. Parkrow has absented himself from participation in these proceedings, then the only point of view you are hearing is the one of a man obsessed with his own version of Matthew Parkrow's destruction . . . a man who is so bent on hurting Matthew in every way he can that he even assigned me, a brand new TA, to teach a new Lit I class last fall instead of Matthew who, by every right within the normal pecking order in this department, should have had instead of me . . . ."

"Mr. Crampton . . . ? Ward?"

"Yes, Mr. Chairman?"

"You've certainly hit a nerve here. I don't want . . . no one at this table, I hope, wants . . . to persecute Mr. Parkrow. We've offered him every opportunity to renounce his ways and remain here with us in English . . . ."

"But, Mr. Chairman, don't you see? I can demonstrate to you . . . to all of you . . . that Matthew Parkrow has nothing to renounce!"

"Well, it's highly irregular . . . but . . . this is an irregular sort of situation anyway, is it not?"

"Yes, Mr. Chairman, it certainly is."

"I protest! I protest! I protest!"

"Protest all you wish, Mr. Scythe. This panel is not a tool for anyone's personal vendetta. So, please just sit down and shut up!"

Scythe slouched into his seat mumbling, "Well, I never . . . I just never . . . ."

"Proceed Mr. Crampton."

"First, Mr. Chairman, I would like to recall Mr. Travis."

"Is Mr. Travis still present?"

"Yes, sir, Mr. Chairman," Travis responded with a mumble as he shuffled from the back row.

"Please take a seat, Mr. Travis."

He seated himself in the witness chair.

"And, remember that you are still under oath . . . ."

"Yes, sir."

"Now, Mr. Travis. You testified earlier, however I don't know what you said because I was not present at the time. So, we'll just start off from scratch together. Okay?"

"Okay . . . I mean, yes sir . . . ."

"Okay is just fine, Mr. Travis . . . just fine." Ward glanced at Linda still seated in the back row looking more and more like a trapped animal. "Do you remember what happened on Columbus Day this past October, Mr. Travis? Specifically, what happened with regard to Mrs. Linda Crampton that night here in the English building?"

"Ah . . . well . . . ."

"It's okay, Mr. Travis. We all want to hear the truth. Even me . . . especially me."

"But it's your wife, Mr. Crampton."

"I know, but this is much more important, Mr. Travis. So, please tell us what happened that night last October . . . Columbus Day."

"Well, sir, Mrs. Crampton had called me up about getting into English but she didn't have no key. She said she needed to get something for you, Mr. Crampton. Said you was at that MLA Convention or something like that."

Ward grinned but nodded.

"Anyways, I left the basement door adjar for her 'cause I was leaving. But there was a bulb out at the basement entrance, so I went looking for a new bulb."

"Than what happened?"

"Well, sir, I replaced the light bulb. Then I made one final swing through the building before I left 'cause I had left that door open. No telling who else might've come in besides Mrs. Crampton.

"So, when I checked in on three-ten, I saw something that just turned my stomach, Mr. Crampton. And, that's what I've been hidin' all this time . . . ."

"Please go on, Mr. Travis. Tell us what made you sick."

Travis's basset hound eyes looked at him so pitifully he almost wanted to cry. "Ya'll sure, Mr. Crampton? Here, in front of all these people?"

"Yes, Mr. Travis, I'm sure." Ward smiled. "Especially in front of all these people."

"Well then, it wasn't a pretty sight." He hung his head and spoke down into his chest. "She was down on her knees . . . ."

"By 'she', you mean Linda Crampton?"

"Yes, sir."

"Go ahead . . . ."

"She was on her knees in front of this Mr. Dryden."

"That's Mr. Poper Dryden, Matthew Parkrow's office mate?"

"Yes, sir."

"Continue . . . ."

"She had her skirt up around her waist and her blouse unbuttoned and she was . . . she was . . . was . . . ."

"Yes, Mr. Travis. 'She was' what?"

"She was . . . what you call it?"

"Performing oral sex."

"Ah . . . yes, sir." His face seemed, for a moment, to burst into a surge of red flushes. He was almost in tears. "I'm sorry, Mr. Crampton . . . ."

"It's okay, Mr. Travis. You may step down now. Thank you."

"But . . . ." Scythe leaped to his feet, toppling his chair onto the carpet.

"But what, Mr. Scythe?"

"I want to cross examine the witness, Mr. Chairman. Yes. Cross examine the witness."

The Chairman stared him back into his seat which had been righted by Wally Poindexter as he spoke. "Not today, Mr. Scythe. Not to . . . day, sir. Continue, Mr. Crampton."

"I call, as my next witness, Mr. Poper Dryden."

"Mr. Dryden please take the stand."

Poper reluctantly raised his head which he had buried in his hands during Travis's testimony. "Yes, Mr. Chairman," he muttered as he stood and sort of wobbled toward the witness chair.

After several minutes of testimony, Poper began to blubber. "B . . . b . . . but . . . you knew about all of this all along, didn't you?" His lips curled back from his nicotine-stained, yet otherwise perfect, teeth. "Didn't you?" he snarled, lifting his head up for the first time to look Ward in the eye. "Didn't you?"

"Yes." Ward nodded. "I knew all along . . . ."

"Yet, you did nothing . . . said nothing . . .?"

"I couldn't . . . ." He hesitated, glancing over his shoulder toward the rear of the room. In the aisle seat next to the door sat his excuse. "Until now . . . ."

Poper sat upright finally. "Is that all?"

"Oh . . . yes, Mr. Dryden. That is all." Ward sucked in a deep breath. "And, thank you for being truthful with us, Mr. Dryden about what actually happened in Florida as well as in English." Poper stood. As he walked by Matthew's chair, Matthew raised his head and caught his eyes glancing down at him. Matthew reached out and touched his right hand as he passed. Poper nearly smiled but kept on walking toward his rear row seat next to Ward's excuse.

"For my final witness, Mr. Chairman, I'd like to call Mr. Ranier ibn Al-shaikh."

Linda had reduced herself to a size four ball in her seat and could not see what was going on. She could only hear. With those words, her size four ball exploded with memory.

"Mrs. Crampton?"

"Yes?" The voice in the telephone had been somehow familiar."

"Linda Tallefero Crampton?"

"Who is this? How did you track me to this number in English?"

"You don't be recognizing my voice . . . my accent?"

"You do sound familiar to me . . . but I just can't . . . ."

"Agadir, my dear . . . ."

"Oh shit! Ranier?"

"You still be owing me something Mrs. Crampton. Do you be remembering your promise and your confirmation of that promise when you be returning for the dog?"

"That was a long time ago, Ranier." She lit a cigarette and inhaled deeply. "So quit beating around the mosque, Ranier. Just tell me what the hell you want."

"You, Linda. Just like you be promising. I am coming to collect . . . or . . . ."

"Or?"

"Yes, that's right. Or . . . ."

"Or fucking what?"

"Just be taking my word for it, Ms. Linda. You wouldn't be liking it . . . not one little bit."

"Would you please take the stand, Mr. Al-shaikh?"

Ranier stood from his end seat, just five chairs away from Linda. His eyes caught her's, wild and without focus. He nodded in acknowledgment and smiled, then proceeded to the witness chair.

* * * * *

Slightly more than half an hour after the committee retired to the ante room to discuss what they had heard from Ranier ibn Al-shaikh, they returned. Once they were all seated, the Chairman raised himself shakily from his overstuffed chair at the head of the glowing blond conference table. Once he steadied himself he began to speak very slowly and deliberately and almost inaudibly.

"Matthew Parkrow. This Board of Inquiry finds that, even though you were obviously led, possibly even tricked, into this activity, you *did* ultimately act irresponsibly on your own. We love you like a son but we cannot take any chances whatsoever with our own responsibilities to our students. You have demonstrated no willingness to cooperate with this Board of Inquiry, and that leaves us with really no choice in this matter. You are hereby relieved of your assistant professorship responsibilities and privileges and dismissed as a Ph.D. candidate. A formal letter stating the findings of this committee and its unanimous decision shall be entered into your permanent record, and a copy will be provided to you via the United States mail service."

Matthew stood after the Chairman completed his pronouncement. "I have done nothing wrong . . ." he muttered. As he turned to leave the room, he stumbled. He had not realized the toll of two weeks in the city jail. Strong arms suddenly supported him and helped him walk down the aisle toward the double doors at the rear of the room. He did not have to look to know who those arms belonged to. For the first time, he sensed Ward Crampton at his side just like they used to sense each other in the infield.

* * * * *

"Did you see what happened here, ma'm?"

"I'm not entirely sure, officer."

"What do you mean, you're not entirely sure? I don't understand, ma'm. Either you saw what happened or you didn't. Which is it, ma'm?"

"Well, I mean, yes, I saw something, but I'm not sure . . . . I mean, I don't believe what I saw."

"Well, ma'm, I can understand. It was a horrific incident. You must be quite upset just seeing this here hit-and-run and the victim being torn apart it appears. But, you'd be doing a good thing if you could just tell us anything that would help in apprehending this killer. Just tell us what you think you saw. We would really appreciate it."

The witness looked on either side of the teenaged police officer, then behind him, searching for the other person since he kept referring to "we" and "us." She decided to ask even though it seemed silly. After all, if she could see what she saw, then perhaps she could not see something as well. "Is there someone with you, officer?"

"Ma'm?"

"You know. You keep saying 'tell us' and 'we would really appreciate your help.'"

"Oh . . . ." He blushed in the twilight. "Ah . . . no, ma'm. It's just police lingo . . . ah . . . ma'm"

"Really?"

"Really, ma'm. Just a twist of phrase, ma'm." He grinned, but only for the moment before he realized the indecorousness of what he was doing. Then, his official business poker face reasserted itself.

"You mean a *turn* of phrase, I believe, officer?"

"Oh, yes, ma'm. That's it. Just a turn of phrase, ma'm."

Her recollection was nearly in tact now. Yet, the more clearly she remembered the events that had just transpired the more sure she was that what she thought she had seen had to be impossible.

"Ma'm?"

"Yes . . . ."

"If you don't mind? The accident? You know, what you saw?"

"Oh, yes. Well that poor woman . . . ."

"You mean the woman who was hit?"

"Yes. The woman who was hit was crossing from English to this side of the street on the red light and the walk sign. She hadn't taken more than a few steps into the crosswalk when some kind of truck or something squalled into a right hand turn aiming right at her. The vehicle struck her directly with its front end, knocking her to the pavement." She closed her eyes against the image of that poor woman's body . . . . "And then . . . and then . . . ."

"Yes . . . . And then?"

"The vehicle drove right over top of her, dragging her body all the way to where you found her when you arrived. Once the body broke loose in pieces from underneath, the vehicle sped away."

"What did the vehicle look like? What kind of truck was it? Did you get a license number?"

"It did not seem to have a license plate and it looked like nothing I had ever seen on the streets before . . . only in the movies . . . ."

"I don't understand, ma'm."

"I don't understand myself, young man . . . ah . . . officer."

"Ma'm?"

"It was one of those Nazi things. Not a tank but smaller . . . . Sort of like a truck?"

"Oh, sure. A half-track . . . ." He stared at her closely to see if she was for real. "You couldn't have seen a half-track on the streets, ma'm."

"That's what I keep telling myself, officer, yet every time I remember the accident that's what I see . . . the same contraption hits her . . . and drags her . . . ."

"A Nazi half-track, ma'm?"

"Yes, as crazy as it seems, officer, that's what I actually saw."

"A Nazi half-track, ma'm?"

"Yes, a Nazi half-track."

Wake Up!

This is the end
Beautiful friend
This is the end
My only friend, the end
Of our elaborate plans, the end
Of everything that stands, the end
No safety or surprise, the end
I'll never look into your eyes . . . again
Can you picture what will be
So limitless and free
Desperately in need . . . of some . . . stranger's
hand
In a . . . desperate land . . . .

from *The End*, Jim Morrison
& The Doors in concert

From the pocked asphalt parking lot, the Seaboard terminal seemed abandoned.

"Drive," he had said.

"Where?" the other had asked.

And he had answered, "The train station."

And, Ward, the other, had done so.

And, here they were, facing a weathered brick Seaboard passenger terminal from another age.

Matthew stepped out of the Buick Skylark onto the nearly shimmering tar-like surface. Eruptions of asphalt peppered the parking lot like a primordial meteor shower had hit the place. He glanced about. No evidence as yet of life in any form. The more he stared the more nothing moved. It was as if he was seeing through eyes that showed nothing and saw nothing . . . Jason's dead eyes.

He scuffed the steaming asphalt with the toe of his right Converse running shoe. "I ask you to take me to the train station, Ward, and this is where you let me off? Not one car in the parking lot. Not even a single taxi waiting for a fare. Can this be the right place?"

"This is the only place left, Matthew."

Tufts of rye grass struggled through the growing cracks in the asphalt toward the blazing sunlight. The first and only signs of life.

"This place?"

A line of six bleached-out burgundy Pullmans on the southbound spur . . . strung out like the chitterlings of some gargantuan hog. He shook his head and scooped up the overnight grip Ward tossed gingerly into the tar pit with him. As he approached the groaning building, Matthew heard Ward slam shut the Skylark door. But, he did not look back. The engine revved, then quickly began to move beyond his aural sensory capabilities. But he would never look back on this scene and see himself glancing over his shoulder to see if Ward was still watching him. He knew with some empirical certainty that he was not. Also, he did not want to turn to stone or into a pillar of salt depending on the story.

Matthew's eyes darted left to right and left again, left to right and left as he navigated the broken asphalt traps that erupted every few feet.

"Will all this put an end to Chaos . . . finally?" he had asked just before opening the Skylark door.

"Of course not, Matthew. Linda harbors this insane notion about the immortal perpetuation of Chaos. She'll never let it go."

"No. You're right, Ward. Not ever."

"So, even after all this, you're still a bail jumper . . . ."

Matthew had nodded.

"Maybe I can help fix that."

Matthew had nodded.

"And a fugitive from Chaos . . . ."

Matthew had nodded again and, this time, smiled thinly.

"I'm sorry Matthew, but I can't help you with that one." He had wagged his head. "I'm afraid you'll be looking over your shoulder for a long time to come, man . . . ."

"I know . . . ." Matthew had nodded. "Someone else told me that once."

The thin smile collapsed into a black hole that was his mouth. Without realizing it, he was weaving back and forth across the parking lot, his canvas grip under his arm like an M16. Damn. "Stop this, you fool!" He had not been on a train since he and Ward left for Holabird. That was sixty-six . . . what seemed like a lifetime or two ago. That time they departed together. This time he was on his own.

Ten years after . . . . Both products of their fathers so the two Hardy Boys were told.

"Who is this character Crayon?"

"A guy I met a long time ago . . . your absolute physical twin."

"And why would he make bail for you out of the clear blue?"

"I chased him half way across this country thinking that he somehow might be you. We ended up marching together and getting arrested during the Democratic Convention in Chicago, and we witnessed the end together at Altamont. Anyway, it seems that he read about the demonstration and my arrest and shit in the *Voice*. I guess it's still his newspaper of choice. So he tracked down Jason's number and, of course, he got Emmy Lou on the line instead. Emmy Lou said he immediately offered to help."

"Well, he's going to lose his ten thousand in bail if you get on that train. You know that, don't you?"

"Yeah, I know and so does Crayon. In fact, he told Emmy Lou to make sure that I ran. He, it seems, doesn't care about or need the money. It seems that he and his girl Nina finally got married and moved to Manhattan to open their own business—H. I. I. Hippies

Investments Incorporated. I guess they both just have a natural talent for investing. Now, they have more money than god. But, they still don't trust the so-called establishment and its justice system. So, guess I'll be staying with them for a while. They've got this huge loft . . . ." Matthew had cut himself off.

"Ah, that's great, Matthew. Don't worry, Chaos will not find out anything from me. I just wish this could have all ended differently. I wish we could have ended differently . . . ."

Matthew had shrugged. "Thanks for trying . . . and for the ride."

He drives away. I remain.

The asphalt seemed to burn right through his running shoes in the unseasonable heat. It felt like August. But our mothers? We Hardy Boys were more their products than our fathers' weren't we? Are babies the only fruit of thy womb . . . ?

He had long since closed the Skylark door. The driver had long since driven the car away. "Emmy Lou . . . Emmy Lou . . . Emmy Lou . . . ." Still, here he stood, his head slumped into his hands. The glaring sun made his eyes ache. Rubbing his bleary eyes dry with his right fist, he continued to pick his way through the asphalt eruptions toward the terminal entrance, his left hand now clutching the bag that held what remained of his possessions.

He began very slowly, very gradually to extract the slender smile from its black hole. The last time you were in a train station—this same exact one to be precise—you had your worldly possessions in your Army issue duffle bag. This time you're reduced to an overnight canvas grip. At least there's been *some* progress.

The iron doors at the terminal entrance each had four wire-mesh glass windows in the top half. The right door's hinges sounded like startled crows as Matthew pulled it open and entered the terminal. The squeaking of his running shoes on the polished tile floor echoed off the whitewashed plaster walls like their voices did off of the walls of the Caves of Darkness and Light in Malaysia. Beyond the rows of pew-like benches that stretched across the middle of the room, Matthew thought he saw a light behind the Dispatcher's window. He squinted through the sunlight pouring through the front windows. Yes. And the window was only half-closed. He skirted the maze of benches, walking closer to the walls.

As he passed twin marble fountains set into the wall, cotton mouth attacked him. One fountain was black marble. One was white. The time was that's how they were used, too . . . better believe that shit, boy! Things change. See. You just got no patience. Now, everybody can drink out of the same fountain except when they can't. He leaned over the nearest one, slurping the cool water as his right hand attempted to adjust the knob on the black marble fountain so the spout would not shoot water up his nose or dribble down his beard.

Despite his best efforts, as he pulled away from the fountain, he had to wipe his beard dry with his right flannel sleeve before he shuffled on toward the dull light behind the Dispatcher's half-open and half-closed window. The chirps of his rubber soles ricocheted off the whitewashed plaster walls. Involuntarily he started to hit the floor with his arms protecting his head. "Jesus!" Ducked at the sound of my own shoes walking. "Jesus!" At least I didn't actually get down on the floor, just almost. He had to laugh at that.

"Have a snort, young fella?" The drunk seemed to appear from among the curved, polished benches just to the left of the Dispatcher's window.

"What?" Matthew jerked toward the crackling voice. "What did you say?" That tattered coat. A Goodwill special when he had the money once in Denver . . . or was it Kansas City . . . or Phoenix perhaps?

"Some of this . . . ." He sloshed around a half-empty bottle of Richards still partly covered by wet tatters of a brown paper bag. "Look like you could use it. Good for what ails you, you know."

Matthew watched his shaking hand reach out for the bottle. "No . . . ." He jerked his hand away from the hideous whiskered face that, shaded from the sunlight streaming through windows behind it, seemed to have no eyes. "No . . . . No . . . ."

"S'okay . . . ." He slid down the pew in front of him into a heap on the floor cuddling the bottle of Ripple like a baby and clutching a grimy polishing rag, his words muffled in the folds of his moth-eaten overcoat. "More for me . . . ."

Matthew bolted for the half-open window. "Hello! Anybody here?" He stuck his head under the wooden window frame. "Anybody?"

"Hold your horsepower . . . just hold your horsepower . . ." An old voice incanted from the other side of the wall.

Behind the window was a cubbyhole room about five feet square with a small metal desk just under the window. A row of rusting file cabinets covered the back wall. In the center, a naked light bulb with a green felt shade over it drooped from the ceiling. Behind him, the wino groaned in after-exertion induced slumber. The pull string dangled below the light causing a stretching and bloating snake-like shadow to wriggle over the polished cement floor. The door to the right opened, and a hunched, bald prune of a man shuffled in. A green eyeshade that matched the color of the shade covering the light bulb covered his forehead. His ashen chin jerked up and back with every stiff step.

"Can't get a minute's peace around this danged place . . . . First it's Richards over there wanting to polish the benches again. He's just back from Phoenix, you know . . . ."

"No . . . ."

He seemed startled for as long as it took him to pick up his thought. "And now it's *you* . . . ." He sighed and stared up at Matthew's face still stuck under the window. The old man's eyes were nearly invisible under the shade he adjusted as he stepped closer to this shaggy intruder who dared to poke his head under *his* window . . . . "So whatcha want?"

"Ah . . . ." Matthew abruptly extracted his head from beneath the window guillotine. "A one-way ticket on the Silver Meteor to . . . ah . . . ."

"Baltimore . . . ?"

"No . . . ah . . . ." Why would he say Baltimore? Could he be the same old man who sold him and Ward their tickets to Fort Holabird all those years ago? "No . . . ah . . . Manhattan . . . ah . . . New York City . . . ." He reached for his wallet. "This is the right place, isn't it?"

"Yeah . . . yeah." The Dispatcher's withered hands seemed to be all purple veins as they began the old ritual of piecing the ticket together, stapling, stamping. "It's the *only* place."

"You sure that kind of ticket's good on the Silver Meteor?"

The Dispatcher scowled. "Think just 'cause it ain't printed out nice and fancy by some danged machine it ain't no good, do ya?" His forehead furrowed like a plowed field. "That'll be forty-three sixty eight . . . ."

Stupid. He might as well have said it aloud. He clearly implied it with that smirky scowl and his dangling sentence. And, he's probably very exactly precisely correct. I have been in the garden a long time. Yes. Fallow now as Scythe's lips, unplowed plot strangled in jimson, rag weed, milk weed, rabbit tobacco, blackberry . . . nothing on that ticket like the garden I am leaving . . . . Matthew shoved two twenties and a five across the counter and under the still half-opened window. His fingers followed the pen knife slashes and the coin gouges in the smutty oak, reading its history with his fingers as he waited for the Dispatcher's hands to make change . . . and present him with his ticket. His fingertips found the letters m p and w c scraped into the surface with the tip of a key. He could not remember for sure but he thought the key was to the Crampton vacation home in Florida.

"Your ticket . . . ." His chin jerked back. Light flashed under his shade. "Your change . . . ." The skin around his yellowing eyes was indefinable like unset putty.

"Thanks." Matthew stuffed the change into his front jeans pocket as he turned away. "Oh, I forgot . . . ."

"Yes." The Dispatcher had not moved. "Your bags . . . ?" He shoved the window all the way up. The wood in the frame creaked with the movement; it echoed like bats.

"I just have this one." Matthew lifted his grip onto the counter as he turned back toward the Dispatcher who was already stamping a baggage check, tearing off the stub and handing it to Matthew almost in a single motion.

"Sure you wouldn't rather take this on the train with you?" He hesitated before snapping the tag onto the bag's handle. "You can, you know."

"No . . . ." Matthew shrugged. "Ah . . . I lose things . . . you know."

The Dispatcher's fingers snapped the check card through the thick elastic thread attached to it. "No . . . ." As he tossed the bag toward the door, the check fluttered from the bag's handle like a banner or a flag.

"What time?"

"You got . . . let me see." He turned to face the back wall where the filing cabinets stood. "Dangnabit! I keep forgetting that clock broke years ago. The train officials took it down years ago, but if you look real close you can still see the circle it left." He turned back to the window, glancing at the battery-powered Timex on his left wrist. "Grandkids gave me this watch last Christmas. 'It takes a licking and keeps on ticking,' you know. It was a good Christmas."

"I'm sure it was better than mine . . . . The time?"

"Oh, yes." He peered under his eyeshade at the still new looking watch face. "You got exactly sixty-seven minutes 'til the Silver Meteor arrives."

"Thanks."

The Dispatcher nodded and turned away. "There's fresh towels in the men's room and hot water, too, for long as it lasts. Richards and the others around here get to it pretty early . . . ."

"You're a kind man." Matthew smiled. He touched his lips with the tips of his fingers tracing what the smile looked like, then skipped off through a row in the benches to the bathrooms on the front side of the terminal, his sneakers chirping all the way.

The men's room door hinges screeched like more startled crows. "The Dispatcher's set me up," Matthew muttered as he huddled in the stall furthest from the door. He snuffed the roach he'd been smoking and ate it when he heard voices and sounds suddenly surrounding him. "Damn!"

"More Richards, Ripple?"

"More Ripple, Richards?"

He sighed. Thank god. It's just that wino and a buddy. What does that mean? The Dispatcher didn't betray me? Shit, these two must smell the grass.

"Hey, it smells like that hippie's in here too, Ripple. You in here, good buddy? Have a drink now, won't'cha?"

"Goes good with what it is you're smoking . . . ."

The other's voice . . . Ripple . . . was twangy. Must be from the hills. So sit here on your version of the shore with the arid plain surrounding you or . . . . Matthew squirmed on the plastic seat listening to the water hum through the pipes when one of the winos flushed a urinal. The chain of functions lacks something. Sensation yields reaction yields thought. Thought yields action yields results—

the anthropomorphization of thought. The yield equation has missing links, unaccounted for phenomena to account for. How are we to bridge the gap between sensation and thought or between thought and results. Can it be further mended? Amended? *Entelechy*. No use at all?

Suddenly he found himself bursting through the stall door quite out of control and bowing before the staggering Richards and Ripple. The pair nearly fell over backwards. "May I present to you, Matthew Parkrow's Traveling Medicine Show . . . ." With the flick of his wrists he produced one joint for each of them which he had stuck under the sleeves of his jacket before he had made his entrance. "Great dope, man. Even better than wine . . . . You will know your *Entelechy*." They each took a joint, looked at it in unison, rolled it around between their fingers. "And, it is guaranteed to blow your mind."

"*Entelechy*. Minds me of something you catch like a cold or bad hygiene," began Ripple. His voice screeched like an out-of-tune violin. "Minds me of the times when we've had to roll our own when things was tough."

"Yeah . . . like now."

They shucked around on the floor, chuckling and smelling their joints. Together they nodded. Lit up. Ripple first, then Richards. "Sit right down, gentlemen . . . right here." Matthew motioned toward the rear wall. "That's it."

They groaned as they attempted to settle in.

"When you take in the smoke, suck it deep into your lungs and hold it as long as you can before you let it out . . . ."

"Oh . . . yeah . . . feel that, Richards? In your . . . ."

"Yeah . . . a kinda tingling in your brain?"

"Yeahhhhh . . . ." Ripple slumped closer to the cement floor. "Didn't think I had one left." His white hair and stubbled face almost disappeared inside his new overcoat. It was almost actually new. Only been worn by one other guy . . . some rich fella that died in Phoenix, right there on the street. Him and Richards stripped the old gent before anybody came around the park where they were sleeping one off when the old gent walked by and fell dead almost at their feet. Flipped for the overcoat. Poor Richards will need a new one come winter . . . maybe some other rich old guy with a good overcoat would drop dead for him.

"Wow, man, I'm shivering . . . cold!"

Ripple took a slug of Richards's Richards and handed the bottle to him. "Here, have a hit of this . . . warm you right up." He winked as Richards took the bottle and downed a long gulp.

"Ahh . . . ." Richards shook a little as he sighed and smacked his lips. "Mel . . . low . . . right?"

They both nodded as they sucked on their joints and chased each hit with a short slug of wine while slowly they slid down the tile walls almost as if they were gradually melting into puddles of dirty cloth on the cement floor. Like poor, squirming Poper. You'd've thought I was going to eat him alive yesterday when I ran into him in the office. Scythe had given me two hours to "vacate the premises." I told him I thought that was a real estate term, and he was just getting his technical jargon a little confused. He had smiled and repeated, "Two hours, in whatever jargon you choose." When Poper saw me coming down the aisle between the line of cubicles he turned chalky.

"Poper, it's okay, man. You did what was right . . . for you."

"No sweat?"

"No, a Blimpee." Nothing changes easy. Nothung changes.

"Lunch, then." Poper slipped through the doorway of their cubicle as Matthew approached. His eyes. Like a startled deer, ready to bolt but frozen. "Yeah, lunch. A few papers to grade first . . . ." A few papers to grade? Who the hell are you kidding, boy? You got the sack. Yellow Doris and nowhere to go. Where's my homespun. Cubicle. I won't even be here when the tower strikes twelve and plays the alma mater. He entered the cubicle as Poper streaked for the door of room three-ten. Desk cluttered like my head. *Lighthouse*. Flux. *Ulysses*. Union. *Dialogues*. Exclusion. *Poetics*. Dusty, empty like my brain. *Deus ex machina* a letter amongst the ruins of literature. Strong hand writes my name. Cares how it looks. Stationery. Who do I know would have stationery? Christ. Padded chairs. He slumped into the soft swivel chair behind his desk. That's one of the ways they get you. I liked the fucking softness of the chairs. Letter's been opened. He glanced at the envelope again. Wrong room number.

Dear Matthew,

I want to thank you personally for the wonderful speech. I know you've been hit hard as a result, but I truly believe that your speech has been instrumental in turning the tide in our favor. So for all of us, the students of State University, I want to thank you for your courage and your sacrifice.

Respectfully,
Dee Dee Spinoza

Hey, you, get outta my sunshine. It has rained on my garden. The sun is shining through thick pine tops. This morning on Air-Conditioned Gypsy's porch. Clack clackclack clack clackclack. Matter, form. Matters form into *The Affects of Sodium Pentothal on Banquo's Ghost*. Still, there will be no Emmy Lou. She smothers in the clutches of Jason's ghost while she paints grotesques in the best southern tradition on the walls of his house for posterity . . . . Maybe, Renee, you walk away from me because I'm eager to be confirmed, even by a letter from Dee Dee Spinoza. He glanced again at the puddles of cloth slumped under the sinks in the railroad station bathroom. Must act before they walk away too through the doorway of unconsciousness.

"Rise and shine . . . !" Matthew leaped to his feet spreading his arms above his head. One last step for mankind. "Gentlemen!" He sighed. "The Matthew Parkrow Traveling Medicine Show is proud to present direct from out of nowhere the one and only 'Revolutionary Circus' featuring the barked-out ring master whose glib oratory has astounded and confounded millions in its day . . . played by truly yours, yours truly." He swept to the floor with his most cavalier bow as Richards and Ripple both bumped their heads on the sink traps above them. They rubbed their heads and clapped twice. Did they also know this was his last performance? "You ask about . . . about the . . . ah . . . ah . . . American Dream?"

They shook their heads as if choreographed.

"Well, I'll tell you about it anyway. Doctor Thompson traced it to a burned down diner on a vacant lot in Las Vegas." Matthew shook his finger at them huddled in their overcoats, their eyes beginning to close.

"The road to get there is freedom. The key to the burned out diner is liberty. Years ago my friend and I, we scratched our initials into the Dispatch counter with it." His fist pounded his palm. "Self-determination for every man and every woman regardless of age or inclination."

Matthew stopped when he heard the snoring. "Ripple! Richards! Don't go to sleep now!" Out of frustration, he kicked their feet until they struggled up the wall a bit and opened their eyes. "That's better!"

"What?"

"Huh?"

Matthew giggled behind his hand, almost losing control as he watched the two old men continuing to nod off and sliding further down the wall.

Beads of spittle flecked his lips. "For the first time, let's begin to actualize our collective potential to be participatory individuals from birth. These United States cannot survive without a total rededication to the principle upon which it was founded: single mindedness of purpose for collective survival and individual freedom." Union. Flux. The poles. "Only when all individuals are free will the compound, the nation, be free. When the nation is free, it is unassailable!"

Sleep. Sleep. Snore. Snore your asses off. I envy you that, but sleep is highly overrated. He pivoted on his rubberized heel and stomped across the cement bathroom floor to the exit. "You don't care in the least, do you, that self-determination is the anthropomorphization of thought?"

The bathroom door swooshed shut behind him. His shoes squeaked once again across the gleaming tile floor of the terminal as he navigated his way toward the double doors with tin covering the bottom halves, dented and scarred from baggage carts repeatedly banging them open to the passenger platform.

He could hear the Silver Meteor moaning in the distance, closing quickly on the station. The Dispatcher scurried from behind his window, his gimpy legs stumbling across the tiles with Matthew's grip dangling in his right hand. He banged one door with the leading edge of the bag and wedged between the doors onto the platform just as the Silver Meteor screeched to a stop.

Matthew wept amidst the sounds of the Silver Meteor's click clacking wheels gaining speed as it pulled out from the station. Although he dangled precariously from the single step below the swaying platform between passenger cars, he still shook his right fist at the two silhouettes waving at him from the bathroom window. His left arm began to relax on the protective hand railing almost unconsciously as the parking lot's hundreds of asphalt eruptions slipped by. Emmy Lou's note in the mailbox had also been contained in a plain white envelope. No name. No address. No return address. No postage.

> Matthew—
> Here's some more cash. It's yours anyway. If you need more just let me or Alecia know. Crayon promised he would make you disappear, for if you do not, you will surely perish.
> Emmy Lou

One hundred hundred dollar bills tied together with a thin red ribbon had dropped into his lap from the envelope. The rye grass clumping between the eruptions in the parking lot seemed to burn in the sunlight like his crossbow in the last fire . . . last night . . . at his last camp. He had burned everything, even his journals and his copies of *Ulysses* and *Moby Dick*. If Emmy Lou was right and the object of all this was to destroy him, then he dared not leave any trace. All that remained was his grip and the few clothes he stowed in it. And, of course, the memories of others.

The drone of steel on steel crescendoed beneath him. His body swayed. Nothing he could do about those. Perhaps he was the remaining trace.

"The dream is over!"

He let go of what was left.

# # # # #

"The dream is over!" No! His muscles instantly flexed backward trying to lift his body back onto the car platform. He didn't mean to let go . . . . He didn't! He heard his own shrieks above the screaming steel wheels of the Silver Meteor as if they were the product of some other voice. Too late . . . . The rail bed rushed up toward him . . . . He visualized himself hitting the gravel face down while all around him seemed to be in super slow motion. He had made a terrible mistake . . . a momentary lapse . . . of . . . .

Hands dug into his shoulders like tongs into blocks of ice. They felt like Crayon's hands at Altamont. They felt like Ward's hands at the end of the hearing. Saved again! Now I'm not only a saved interstate fugitive but I'm a *careless* saved interstate fugitive.

"That was a close call, son. You'll have to step inside now and find a seat in one of the cars. It's just too dangerous out here when she's moving . . . the train, I mean."

Matthew turned. The Conductor's face seemed to be split between light and dark like Emmy Lou's face in her self-portrait. He shook his head trying to clear his vision.

"You see, you just about got yourself killed, son."

Matthew could barely hear the Conductor's ragged voice slashing at the rasping steel with the wind rushing past his ears as the Silver Meteor gathered northbound momentum. He finally focused the Conductor's face. He allowed the Conductor to help him into the car in front of them. He spotted a window seat half-way up the aisle and continually excused himself to the young woman on the aisle as he stumbled through her legs, his baggage check and ticket still crumpled in his fist. He shoved them into his denim jacket pocket just before flopping into the seat by the window so he would not lose them too. Okay, so he had, again it seemed, survived in spite of himself.

So . . . . It would be back to Manhattan. Crayon and Nina would get him safely underground until the heat abated. But, he would be back, just like the problems that had not been resolved. The sixties was not merely history. It was not instant nostalgia. It was a time bomb waiting to explode once again upon the consciousness of a future generation. The name may change. The look might be different. The station in life may have altered. So, blame it on the

Conductor, if you must, but Matthew Parkrow would be back.

The hair of the young woman beside him had the color and fragrance of Sourwood honeycomb, something he knew he would not very soon smell again. She was struggling to continue reading a paperback copy of *Franny and Zooey* with a Columbia bookstore sticker on the back. He smiled at her somewhat automatically.

"Columbia?" He motioned toward the sticker on the book.

She nodded.

The train whistle wailed . . . . Emmy . . . Lou . . . .

"I went there myself . . . way back in the sixties." The Silver Meteor hurtled beyond the city limits. Em . . . my . . . Lo . . . u . . . .

She closed *Franny and Zooey.* "A teacher . . . ?"

He managed a genuine grin this time. "I was once. Now I'm just a Schrödinger's cat without a box."

She smiled. "Which are you? Alive or dead?"

He grasped her extended earth warm hand. "I'm Matthew."

She squeezed his hand. "Hi Matthew. I'm Rachel."

This is the end, my friend. The End.

The Author

Timothy Brannan is a Viet-Nam veteran novelist, poet, composer, and painter born in Raleigh, North Carolina. He holds a Bachelor of Arts in English and Philosophy and a Master of Arts in Literature and Writing from North Carolina State University. Both as an undergraduate and a graduate student he was mentored by the late Dr. Guy Owen (*Ballad of the Flim-Flam Man, Journey for Joedel, The White Stallion and Other Poems*). With Guy's help, he submitted the first pioneering creative writing Master's thesis ever accepted at North Carolina State University nearly thirty years before the university established an official writing program. Timothy later earned an Ed.S. from Appalachian State University and a Juris Doctor from Florida State University.

Much of THE END is rooted in Timothy's personal experiences in fighting what he has often referred to as the two wars of the sixties: The Vietnam war and the counterculture war.

CONTACT INFORMATION

You may contact Timothy Brannan or the Publisher at
info@geminipublish.com.